David Bergman is a leading gay scholar and critic, an editor, and a prize-winning poet. A professor of English at Towson University, he is the author of *Gaiety Transfigured: Gay Self-Representation in American Literature,* and the editor of *Camp Grounds: Style and Homosexuality* and *The Violet Quill Reader.* Bergman has published poetry in many of the leading literary journals, including *The Paris Review, The New Criterion,* and *The New Republic.* He has been the editor of the *Men on Men* books since 1992. He lives in Baltimore, Maryland.

Karl Woelz is a contributing writer for *The Harvard Gay & Lesbian Review.* His work has appeared in the *Lambda Book Report, Best American Gay Fiction 2,* and *Men on Men 6.*

MEN
ON
MEN
2000

BEST NEW GAY FICTION
FOR THE MILLENNIUM

Edited and with an Introduction by
David Bergman and Karl Woelz

A PLUME BOOK

PLUME
Published by the Penguin Group
Penguin Putnam Inc., 375 Hudson Street, New York, New York 10014, U.S.A.
Penguin Books Ltd, 27 Wrights Lane, London W8 5TZ, England
Penguin Books Australia Ltd, Ringwood, Victoria, Australia
Penguin Books Canada Ltd, 10 Alcorn Avenue, Toronto, Ontario, Canada M4V 3B2
Penguin Books (N.Z.) Ltd, 182–190 Wairau Road, Auckland 10, New Zealand

Penguin Books Ltd, Registered Offices:
Harmondsworth, Middlesex, England

First published by Plume, a member of Penguin Putnam Inc.

First Printing, January, 2000
10 9 8 7 6 5 4 3 2 1

Permissions for the stories can be found on pages 321–322.

LIBRARY OF CONGRESS CATALOGING-IN-PUBLICATION DATA:
Men on men 2000 : best new gay fiction for the millennium / edited with an introduction
by David Bergman & Karl Woelz.
   p. cm.
   ISBN 0-452-28082-6
   1. Gay men—Fiction.   2. Gay men's writings, American.   3. American fiction—20th
century.   I. Bergman, David,   II. Woelz, Karl.
b PS648.H57 M49 2000
813'.01089206642'09045—dc21   99–045321

Printed in the United States of America
Set in Bembo
Designed by Julian Hamer

PUBLISHER'S NOTE
These are works of fiction. Names, characters, places, and incidents either are the products of the authors'
imagination or are used fictitiously, and any resemblance to actual persons, living or dead, business
establishments, events, or locales is entirely coincidental.

CONTENTS

INTRODUCTION

Y2K—which sounds like an order for lubricant—is here, and with it the obligation both to reflect on what has happened and to project into the future. In its own peculiar way, Y2K does oil the wheels of memory and smooth our way into the future.

This is the eighth volume of Men on Men, the longest running series in gay literature. Begun under the editorship of George Stambolian, it soon became what one critic called "the Old Testament of gay writing," a nearly canonical text. The first volume includes a remarkable collection of writers—Andrew Holleran, Ethan Mordden, and Robert Glück. In 1986, when the first volume appeared, Dennis Cooper, a contributor, had published only one novel and Kevin Killian, another contributor, none at all. AIDS had only begun to shrink the ranks of gay men. But now, sixteen years later a third of the authors in that first volume have died of AIDS, including Sam D'Allesandro, Robert Ferro, John Fox, Michael Grumley and Richard Umans. George Stambolian himself succumbed to the disease as he feverishly put the finishing touches on volume four. But AIDS has not completely broken the continuity between these first volumes and the present one. We are delighted to welcome back Edmund White, one of the original contributors, to the pages of Men on Men. His "Venice Story" is in part about the changes that have been wrought upon his generation of gay men who were brought together first in joyful celebration of their desires and later as witnesses to their untimely death. Edmund White is not the only Men on Men veteran, as David Groff, Richard McCann, and David Vernon also make reappearances here.

We want to underscore this continuity. So much in gay life seems to be a search for new trends, new faces, the next big craze. Indeed, it is this search for change, variety and difference that has made gay culture so exciting, innovative and challenging. Men on Men takes enormous pride in the numbers of young and unknown writers who have appeared in its pages and gone on to make important contributions, and a large portion of *Men on Men 2000* will introduce readers to such exciting new authors as William Lane Clark, Bill Gordon, J. G. Hayes, Michael Villane, and Patrick Ryan. But in this process of constantly reinventing ourselves—a process that virtually every gay man has to go through—we sometimes lose sight of what we already possess, what we already are becoming, the changes already on their way. Such writers as Edmund White, Bruce Morrow, Brian Bouldrey, and Jim Grimsley—writers who have already established themselves as important voices—do not stand still. They, too, are changing, evolving, starting over, and it's important that we don't lose sight of their development in our rush toward novelty.

But for all the continuity in Men on Men through eight editions, there have been important changes. We are glad to announce that for the first time Men on Men will be jointly edited. The reason is practical, as the work became too much for one person to do alone. Although the flesh was willing, the spirit was weak. Younger, fresher hands (and eyes) were needed to go through the manuscripts. What has amazed us is how much we have agreed with each other. As the pool of manuscripts was winnowed down, we found ourselves disagreeing about only a story or two. The experience has proven again what we have known all along: for the most part, good work rises to the surface, but there is a portion of the best work that is so individual, so challenging, and often so disturbing that there will be little agreement about its worth. But for that very reason these are the stories that Men on Men must make room for if it is to remain a vital source to reveal the range, the power, and the pleasure of contemporary gay fiction. We would be very surprised if any reader liked *all* of these stories—neither one of us would have chosen *all* of these stories—but we think that it would be a very narrow sensibility that would not find most of the works of fiction finely crafted, forcefully expressed, and sharply imagined.

We've introduced another change. In the last few editions of Men on Men, the stories have been arranged in the alphabetical order of the authors' last names. This provided a fairly random method that had the advantages of being reasonably clear, of avoiding pigeonholing stories in silly categories, and of highlighting the arbitrariness of any table of contents. And as long as Men on Men was edited by someone whose name began with *B,* this arrangement seemed fair, but as soon as Bergman was joined by Woelz, who had found himself repeated at the end of many lines and lists because of the spelling of his name, the tyrannies of alphabetization became apparent. We have, consequently, devised a different method that is equally clear, equally arbitrary, and, we hope, somewhat fairer, listing the stories in alphabetical order of the titles. We were pleased by the way that this method brought out new and interesting combinations while preserving the diversity and individuality of the stories.

Since the mid-eighties, when *Men on Men* first appeared, gay men have faced many changes—a new public visibility, a recognition of our political and economic importance, changes in employment, the establishment of gay marriages (in Europe). But much of gay life has remained the same, and in a very real sense AIDS has made sex more problematical. Despite efforts to change the way gay young people come to view themselves, they still find coming out, like breaking up, hard to do. Just when we thought we had read every variation on the coming out story, we have been sent some new and exciting ways of depicting it. We were struck by two different directions coming out stories are taking. The first direction was exploring how class and ethnicity affect young people. Working class kids have always had a particularly rough time of it, and Kelly Mc-Quain's "Erasing Sonny," Bill Gordon's "Home" and J. G. Hayes's "Regular Flattop" explore how difficult it is for kids growing up in ethnic neighborhoods, where solidarity is the best defense against marginalization, to deal with a sexuality that would cut them off from their families and friends. McQuain and Hayes find in tattoos, signs written on the boys' bodies, indications of the difference that has marked them for life. Alexander Chee's "Gold" depicts coming out for a person of mixed race. The other direction is how popular culture affects the way young people come out. In "Scarecrow," Tom House's Alan thinks of his attraction to other boys in terms of heterosexual romance—the courtly love of Lancelot or the tragic love of *Romeo and Juliet,* which he's reading for school. In "Boulevard," Jim Grimsley's Newell views desire through the perspective of pornography and tabloid news items. Bruce Morrow moves in both directions. "Ciccone Youths 1990" places his defiant black drag queen in historical perspective as if the RuPaul Moment (or the Madonna Moment) is now history, requiring African-American teenagers to find new strategies and alignments for coming out.

Morrow's "Ciccone Youths 1990" is also a story about AIDS, and we have found it interesting that just as the death rates for AIDS have dropped, gay writers have—after a period of avoiding the topic—begun to reexplore what has happened and is happening to them. We don't think this is a mistake. The first wave of AIDS writing grew out of an immediate crisis, a period when that pain needed to be put on the table. But after that first wave there was a pressing need to assert that our lives were not just about death and dying. As W. H. Auden reminds us in "Musée des Beaux Arts," his poem written at the beginning of World War II, suffering must be allowed to assume its "human position," which is to say, that it happens while "someone else is eating or opening a window or just walking dully along." This lull in mortality has provided us with an opportunity to reflect on the immensity that has befallen us. We cannot remember a story since Allen Barnett's "The *Times* as It Knows Us" that has plumbed the grief of AIDS so deeply as Richard McCann's "Universe, Concealed," nor has placed that loss in such a rich religious context. Jeff Kuhr's "We're All Chicken Here" shows again how humor can reveal the humanity of people with AIDS as well as seriousness can. Brian Bouldrey's "Holy Spirit Bank" places AIDS in an international perspective. Len Ingenito-DeSio's "A Really Weird Thing Happened Recently" returns to a central emotional and moral problem of gay life in the Age of AIDS: how two people of discordant HIV status handle entering into a relationship. The difference between those who are HIV positive and those who are not is perhaps as big a divide as between homo- and heterosexual, or male and female, in David Vernon's haunting story, "Arrival." And just as important as these stories in which AIDS is in the foreground of the narratives are those in which it appears as the defining context. The events of Patrick Ryan's "Second Island," as well as those of Michael Villane's "the color or rain," cannot be properly viewed except against the underlying—if understated—pain of AIDS, and in David Groff's "The Third Person," there is a fourth character who plays havoc on relationships, the seductive urgency of AIDS that alienates the affection of a physician from his lover.

We expected to get many stories about coming out and AIDS, but we were surprised by the number of very fine stories that dealt with gay men as fathers. William Lane Clark's "Quiet Game," Jim Provenzano's "Quality Time," Craig T. McWhorter's "Silent Protest," and David Tuller's "Sperm-and-Egg Tango." It is strange that it has taken so long for these issues to be addressed because so many gay men are also fathers, but sometimes it takes a while for the imagination to catch up with reality. What is particularly interesting is the way these stories explore the problematic role of the non-biological parents (or David Tuller's tale, the problems of being a sperm donor), an issue which lesbian writers have for many years explored with moving results.

As we slide into Y2K, what is striking is not that the new millennium brings a rupture to gay culture—history will, we believe, find that our historical divide began in 1981, when reports of a new disease of unknown origin first made the papers—but, rather, it brings a persistence of the issues around which gay life has moved for nearly the last twenty years. And there is something more that has persisted, the willingness of men to use the resources of language not only to witness the truths of their existence but also to challenge us to imagine more fully the terms in which we wish to live. Now at the dawn of the new millennium, *Men on Men* renews its commitment to the pleasure and challenges of gay fiction, and to the vitality and power of literature in our lives.

ARRIVAL

David Vernon

X. Joe tells Shelly something she already knows.

"They're not going to let you take that into the line," Joe says.

"It'll be our secret," Shelly says, putting the frozen banana inside her jacket.

Joe starts to tell Shelly something but stops himself. Not here. Not today, he decides. He watches Shelly maneuver the plastic-wrapped, frozen banana inside her coat until there is no hint of it at all. Joe thinks it would be wonderful if all secrets came chocolate-coated, covered with peanuts, and could be hidden under a thick, black, vinyl jacket.

Joe and Shelly pass the boy overseeing the entranceway, and Shelly retrieves the dessert on a stick and takes a bite. "See, nothing to it," she says.

IX. Joe and Shelly catch up.

They're at Disneyland, two thirty-year-olds, in line for the ride, Space Mountain. They follow a winding course up a concrete ramp that leads them to an area of rope switchbacks. From where they stand in the slow-moving line they can see the white dome that covers the ride. (Angry meringue, Joe called it in the eighth grade.) He used to appreciate the design, in a loopy sort of way. Today, Joe thinks the dome is a bit severe. Too "Night on Bald Mountain" for his taste.

An overcast February sky diminishes the dazzle of the park

today. Several yards away on the Tomorrowland Stage, a band plays an uninspired cover of Prince's "1999".

"My apartment in Brooklyn is amazing. It was just restored a year ago. No one can afford to live in Manhattan these days. I can't believe I've been there for two years and you haven't visited yet. Both of us in New York, we'd have an amazing time," Joe insists.

"I've been promoted to assistant buyer," Shelly says, talking about her job at a department store. "And I ran into Miss Zorn. Sophomore English. Can you believe she's still alive? She looked like she was a hundred even back then!"

"There are no single men in New York," Joe says. "Somehow, all of a sudden, relationships are 'in.' Last year it was Furbys, this year it's monogamy. Who knew?"

"Do you remember when we came here on the class trip? You, me, Gilbert Kruus, we almost got caught smoking out on Tom Sawyer's Island. Well, I read that Gilbert Kruus died last year of liver cancer. Do you remember him?"

"Was that the year I picked up that reindeer? I mean, the guy who dressed like a reindeer in the Disneyland Christmas parade? I think it was. That's awful about Gilbert. I think I remember him."

"I've been seeing a guy from work. He's really something. I think it could be serious," Shelly says.

VIII. What Joe and Shelly aren't saying to each other.

Joe: You must have lost twenty pounds. And your look. After all these years you finally retired that hippie, Topanga Canyon thing. Going for Ann Taylor casual. Why does my absence seem to have a revitalizing effect on the world? You seem so different. So preoccupied. I used to be able to tell you anything. Why can't I talk to you anymore?

Shelly: Why wear a "Nobody Knows I'm Gay" T-shirt to Disneyland? Isn't that overkill? You always want people to know we're not a couple. And going on and on about this party and that exhibit! Your renovated apartment in Brooklyn that you can barely afford! God, how tedious. Is this really the person who used to be the center of my universe? You don't even look like the Joe that escaped to New York two years ago. You seem so defeated! What happened to my best friend with the off-balance sense of humor? (The Joe that, after seeing the movie *Koyaanisqatsi—Life Out of Balance*, whispered that he wanted to make a movie about his life called *Boyaanisqatsi—Boy Problems Out of Balance*, full of men traveling too fast in every direction, creating magnificent orange and magenta blurs in the sky to the deafening beat of Philip Glass music.) What about the Joe who used to wander hotel lobbies with me and crash convention parties? (At an undertaker's convention once, Joe stuck a label on his jacket that read "Hello, My Name Was." What the hell happened to that Joe?)

Shelly thinks about how Joe has made her laugh, really laugh, how they'd grown up together and become family. Instantly she starts to feel tender again about her best friend.

He seems scared, Shelly thinks. Maybe not scared, he looks . . .

Shelly thinks she's placed it, then quickly discards the thought from her mind.

VII. The line is a metaphor.

Shelly thinks the line to Space Mountain is like her life: endless waiting, but through patience and perseverance, she makes it to the front. Finally, Shelly, the girl no one would talk to in high school, is in front.

Joe thinks the line is like life, organized, overwhelming, and depressingly tidy. Play by the rules. All those rules. Wait your turn. Give a hoot—don't pollute. Be kind, rewind. Do unto others . . . followed by two minutes and forty-five seconds of pleasure, then it's over. What did it all really add up to?

VI. "Space stations ready."

"That's what I love about this ride," Shelly says. "Those little touches that make you believe you're actually going on a journey."

The line has moved inside a mock space station. A disembodied voice speaks from a hidden sound system. The lights are dim. They've been on this ride a hundred times over the years. But Joe's instinct is to turn and leave. It's a journey he's not sure he wants to take.

"Command control. Rockets waiting," a stern male voice announces from a speaker.

"Roger," a female voice counters.

"Who's this guy you're seeing?" Joe asks.

Shelly's features turn on. She's been waiting for this all day. Too often she's been on the other side of that question, a dull, demeaning place to be. But now her dance card, as her grandparents used to say, is filling up. *Don't worry, Shelly. You're a pretty girl. Such a pretty face. One day the fellas will come to their senses.* Then your dance card will be full. "His name is Ralph Lazzaro. He's so . . ." She stretches out her arms to indicate that there are no words to describe Ralph. In truth there are words. Considerate. Older. Divorced. Chubby. An intellectual Adonis. What there are no words for, though, is how he's helped turn her life around. With his encouragement. With his passion for her. "He reminds me of you," Shelly says, "except he likes girls, thank God." The line turns a corner. "And you? How's Kevin?"

Joe steals a breath. His chest is tight. "Over. Says he needs space."

Joe had met Kevin Lebow the week before moving to New York. One month, and several late-night phone calls later, Kevin showed up at Joe's apartment.

Kevin was a personal fitness trainer and through several referrals got a few clients and soon after, a job at David Barton's gym. Without much incidence or discussion, Joe and Kevin were a couple.

Joe couldn't help but wonder about this tremendous event, finding the love of his life at this late stage of the game. He could finally consider all the vapid L.A. Chads, the faux-Mediterranean Marcos, the up-and-coming TV soap opera Jaasons, and any boy for that matter who surgically altered his name, as just target practice for the real thing. Kevin was exciting to be around (everything about New York, and about Joe, thrilled him), and Kevin was also beautiful. Who needed to take two subways into Manhattan to go to museums when you could just stare at Kevin, standing naked on the hardwood floor, peering out the window.

But it was Kevin's kindness that really got to him. When Joe asked him how he felt about dating someone who was HIV positive, Kevin responded that they were two guys in love, in the greatest city in the world. How could that not last forever? And Kevin would clip articles out of newspapers about the progress in AIDS research and medications. On the number 2 train to Manhattan one night Kevin showed him an article he'd found where the Centers for Disease Control announced that AIDS-related deaths had dropped to number fourteen on the list of the nation's top killers. "It's like the billboard chart," Kevin told him. "You're not number one with a bullet anymore, sweetie. You're number fourteen and on your way down. You're a has-been. Your Bananarama. You're Sheena Easton, babe."

Then, in the winter there was an alarming drop in Joe's T-cells. A change in medication. Another change in medication. A hospital visit. The shingles. Another hospital stay.

Kevin found a sublet in SoHo. He said he wasn't moving out. It would just be closer to work. But a week after his move, Kevin stopped returning Joe's phone calls. Finally, in the middle of the night, Joe took the subway into Manhattan and rang Kevin's doorbell until he answered.

"The notion of illness is very confusing for me," Kevin told Joe. "I'm trying to work through this."

"We can do that together," Joe said. Kevin was sitting on his bed, beautifully naked. When Kevin covered his lower body with the bedsheet, Joe knew his answer.

"You were supposed to be getting better," Kevin said, starting to cry. When he'd finished, he looked up at Joe with his fractured face. "I'm beginning to think it's the media's fault. The media lies," he whispered hoarsely.

"I'll talk to them about it," Joe answered. He started to leave.

"I know I'm being terrible," Kevin said, "but I've never had anyone die on me before."

Those last words are what stayed with Joe on the ride home. He had never considered the possibility that he was dying. Joe had no conception of death. The idea of it was either too clichéd, like the ending of some Mare Winningham Lifetime TV movie, or too profound, like the scores of books he'd noticed on the subject; books with titles like, *Death: The Final Stage of Growth, Dialogue with Death,* and *Dignified Departure.* (Where was *The Complete Idiot's Guide to Death* when you needed it? Joe wondered.)

By the time he reached his apartment that night he was furious with Kevin. Making excuses for his own fear and inadequacy. Joe didn't even want to dignify Kevin's accusation by dwelling on it. He cleaned out his bank account and took this trip home to Los Angeles.

"I'm sorry it didn't work out between the two of you," Shelly told Joe, as the line turned a corner. Shelly had never met Kevin, but imagined that he was perfectly nice like all the others. She didn't know if it was just homosexual men in general, or just Joe, but there seemed to be some problems about commitment. Joe never could find anyone who he thought was good enough for him. She wondered if Joe had broken Kevin's heart.

Joe and Shelly pass a sign warning visitors that they must be in good health to ride Space Mountain. They both glance at the sign as they inch past it. Shelly catches Joe's eyes.

"You know you're old," she says, "when you actually start read-ing these signs." This makes both of them laugh.

Joe imagines how great it would be if every person came with a warning sign. How different things might have been if Kevin had come with one.

WARNING!
THIS IS A HIGH-MAINTENANCE PERSON!
HE WILL TAKE YOU THROUGH A MAZE OF DIZZYING HIGHS AND PITCH-BOTTOM LOWS! HE WILL NAVIGATE YOU THROUGH THE TWISTS AND TURNS OF COMMITMENT, BUT WHEN YOU ACTUALLY NEED HIM, HE'LL DROP TWENTY STORIES OUT OF YOUR LIFE! WE'RE SORRY BUT EXPECTANT BOYFRIENDS SHOULD NOT RIDE.

V. The happiest place on earth.

It's true. No place is happier than Disneyland. Coming here, Shelly thinks, is like visiting an old friend. Visiting Donald and Minnie. Friends. And walking through the park today she sees couples holding hands, pushing strollers. And the babies! Fresh-eyed wonders! For the first time Shelly can imagine herself having these things.

V. The happy-EST place on earth.

Joe was certain he heard right. The woman driving the tram from the parking lot reminded them to take note of where they were parked. Of course Shelly had already done this. They parked in "Thumper 5." As the tram pulled up to the gate the woman's amplified voice welcomed everyone to *the happy-EST place on earth.* Emphasis on the "EST." This really opened Joe's eyes. EST. He's looking at Disneyland with a new set of eyes today, seeing things he's never noticed before. This cult. This conspiracy. Sinister, smiling teenaged employees. What are they so goddamned happy about? What secret do they know? People dragging around wheelchairs like it was a day at Lourdes. Be Young Again, Come To Disneyland! The Happy Denial conspiracy. Everything's great. Life's a plum. The future, a peach. No crime or sickness here. Even Uncle Walt was on ice somewhere waiting. Joe had already visited his old friends today, Combivir and Nelsinavir. Best friends, Joe thinks, that will turn their backs on him like all the other medications before them. Already today Joe vomited in the bathroom on Main Street and had the shits in Critter Country. It's not even noon yet.

IV. "We have to find Doc."

"I beg your pardon," Joe says. He couldn't have heard Shelly right. The Space Mountain line inches forward at a funeral's pace. The blue tint burns Joe's eyes. And the nausea is churning like a mad teacup. "A doctor?"

"Doc. The last of the seven dwarfs. For the photograph." Shelly's long-standing project of taking pictures of Joe with each of the seven Disney dwarfs is nearing completion. When the two of them first met, Joe revealed his childhood fear of these characters. ("Freakish trolls," as Joe called them.) "When za project ist finished," Shelly has promised in her best Doctor Ruth imitation, "you vill be fearless." She has snapshots from over the years of Joe with all of the freakish trolls, except Doc.

"Launch control ready."

Shelly looks at Joe, the dear, and sees he is sweating. He's fine, she tells herself. He'd given her quite the scare years ago when he tested positive. But then came the medicines. The protease cocktail. Life making good on the promise that Joe and Shelly would grow old together. Shelly stares at her friend's face until she finds an arrangement of his features that she can recognize. That's it. There we go. Joe is doing great.

III. "How many in your party?"

Joe and Shelly sit in the front row of their milky-white rocket ship. A bar descends, strapping them in place. It's too tight. Joe can barely breathe. He looks up at the blond boy who is in charge of launching the ride. Eighteen. Unconcerned. He reminds Joe of someone. Who? Someone he and Shelly went to school with? Someone he's fucked? The boy checks the seatbelts. But Joe can't take his eyes off of him. Then it hits Joe. This boy looks like him. When Joe was nineteen. When Joe was unconcerned. Undamaged.

"Space Station ready for lift-off."

Shelly grabs onto Joe's knee out of excitement. Punctuation. Then she sees Joe staring at the young employee. She hates when Joe flirts. Why can't he just be with her?

The ride is about to start when Joe turns to Shelly, passes a shy, half-crescent smile, and says, "I don't want to do this."

The rocket jerks forward.

II. Space. Particles. Matter.

With a loud thundercrack the rocket shoots through darkness. Joe clings to the safety bar as the rocket makes several jagged turns. He can't see the tracks. Only the phantom shadows of other rockets whisking by. Joe braces his grip on the handlebar, his body is slammed one side to the next. Shelly grabs hold of his damp hand. He can't see her but he sees the glow of her skin. Glowing like a prophecy. The rocket dips and plunges downward. There are sounds. Gales of laughter. Screams. A falsetto shriek careening by. Hints of color. Ruby. Magenta. Joe wonders if this is what it might be like being dead. Particles. Matter. Gas. A part of space. Nothing but motion. No connections. No tracks.

Down

The ship zooms into a furious spiral. The wind whips Joe's face. He can't get out of this darkness, can't penetrate the motion. Shelly is screaming. Joe wants to scream too but there is no sound. He has no sounds. They're lost inside of him.

Down

Matters and particles, Joe thinks. This is where the future has delivered him. He knows the future.

The ship sails out of its curve and blasts into a tunnel with bright blue flashing lights. It sizzles to a stop.

I. Arrival.

"Exit to your left," one of the employees yells at the arriving space ship.

Shelly grabs Joe's damp hand and leads him out of the ship. They walk through a long tunnel with posters of planets lining the wall. People rush to the exit.

Soon, Shelly thinks, they'll be spilling out into Tomorrowland. They haven't eaten lunch yet. Shelly wants to get home early, though. She promised Ralph she'd try. When should she broach this with Joe? She wants to spend time with Joe, but she has her own life, too. Joe walks as far down the silver hall as he can manage, then pauses. The trembling has overtaken his body. He has to stop. He slides to the floor and sits.

Shelly is two steps ahead before she notices that Joe is not beside her. She turns and sees him sitting on the carpet, arms hugging his legs. He is framed by a poster of the planet Pluto behind him. He's sobbing. She wants to put her arms around him, but this vision of him is hypnotic. She can only stare, as do passersby. It almost doesn't even look like Joe. The man on the floor is older. Stitched together by grief. The man on the floor looks sick. Shelly breaks her gaze and sits down next to Joe and puts her arm around him. He starts to speak. His voice is hoarse. She doesn't want Joe to speak. She covers his mouth with the palm of her hand. But he does speak. And what he says, in a voice she barely recognizes, is something that Shelly already knows.

BOULEVARD

Jim Grimsley

On Monday morning they changed the movies in the quarter movie booths. There were fifteen booths at the back on the men's side, in a dark room behind the curtains, and each of the booths had a door, but in fact if you walked behind the booths you could easily go from one to the other, and Mac and Newell changed the movies that way, before the store opened. Some of the films were still doing pretty well, so Mac said those could stay, especially the one with the carpenter and the guy on the back of the truck, and the one about the two guys on the couch, entitled *The Biggest He Ever Had*. So far Newell had not watched any of the movies beginning to end, but that morning he became curious, and he noticed, as they moved from the men's section to the other one, that most of the movies were about men being with men, and there were only a few booths showing movies that had women in them. He had never noticed this outside the curtains. Newell knelt at the side of each of the movie players, removed three bolts, and opened the hinged back cover, and Mac held the new movie while Newell unthreaded the old loop from the projector, closed it in its case, then took the new one and threaded it through the rollers with exactly enough slack to please Mac, who supervised, pointing and directing without even bending to look at the machine.

"We got to get some of these new machines," Mac said, watching Newell struggle with one of the projectors, "I keep telling Philip."

"Who's Philip?"

"The owner," Mac said, hitching up his pants and taking a long drag on his cigarette, and shambled to the front of the store with the exhale swirling around his head.

Newell watched one of the new movies before the store opened, a short subject in which a man dressed like a lumberjack caught another man looking at him in the woods, and then came up to him and grabbed him, and then the frame stopped for Newell to drop in another quarter, and then the lumberjack pulled the other man, who looked a little shabby, like a tramp, pulled him down onto a log, and they straddled the log facing each other, the shabby man staring at the arrogant lumberjack, and then the lumberjack took the belt out of his hands and looped it around the other man's neck and pulled him violently forward and then the movie stopped and the screen went dark and Newell fumbled for another quarter and quickly dropped it and the image blurred and came to focus, the lumberjack unbuttoning his red flannel shirt with his belt around the shabby man's neck, pulling him forward, and the man raising his hands, helpless, to run them inside the red flannel shirt along the lumberjack's body, and glimpses of the body, the layer of hard muscle cut with shadow, the two men pressing against each other, then the whirring sound, the light dying in the screen, while Newell held the next quarter ready and slid it into the slot. The scene changed when the screen lit again, and the lumberjack was naked to the waist and the shabby man was running his hands up and down the lumberjack man's crotch, up and down, and Newell knew he had seen pictures of this in the magazines but this, the moving image, even this one as blurry and out of focus as it was, this one showed him something. The shabby man pressed his pale fingers against the denim, fumbling for the zipper and opening it, scene changing, the lumberjack jerking forward with the belt, bringing down the shabby man to where the man could taste him, and then the screen went dark and was fed and came on again and now the first man was rocking his hips into the shabby man's face, they were both straddling the log and moving as easily with each other as though the shaggy bark of the tree were a comfortable cushion, two bodies moving together, scenes cut jaggedly into one another, and suddenly both men were kneeling on the ground, with the lumberjack behind the shabby man, with all their clothes thrown onto the grass and the lumberjack spitting into his palm, and then the screen went dark again, then the lumberjack was fucking the shabby man, and Newell made a short, sharp laugh, only a moment or so, at the sight, but at the same time he felt a tingling in the tip of his tongue and around the rim of his lips. He caught the salty, peppery smell of the booth as the first man leaned over the other one, and his body was one long thumping motion driving in and out of the shabby man, they were coiled together on top of their clothes with the log in the background, the lumberjack saying words that caused him to sneer, as if he were being cruel, or trying to present that he was being cruel, and after the screen went dark and Newell slipped the last coin in the slot, the last loop revealed the lumberjack collapsing over the shabby one and then some footage that embarrassed Newell of the two cocks shooting stuff and dripping stuff and then the film was over and Newell went back to the cash register in a daze.

Mac greeted him by saying, very simply, "I'll fire you if I catch you looking at them movies all day."

"Yes sir," Newell answered, and his eyes focused on the cash register as he took a deep breath, inhaling the scent of last night's dose of carpet cleaner.

But he had never seen anything like that movie before, and all day he was seeing it in his head, the man unbuttoning his red flannel shirt and wrapping his belt around the shabby man's neck, pulling him forward so viciously, accusing him of something with these gestures, and the shabby man so willing to let this happen, to run his hands over the bare skin, the broad shoulders, images that would rise up in Newell's head so vividly he might have been standing in the booth with the next quarter in his hand. A few customers came in and bought magazines, some of them with women on them and some not, and as usual the men buying the magazines laid their money on the counter and looked down or away or up, while Newell slid the bright-colored magazines into a bag and felt, himself, embarrassed as much as anyone, because he was sure everyone could tell he was thinking about this movie, about these two men and what he had seen them do to each other. For it had become as vivid to him as if it had happened inside the little box with the screen on top of it, happened only this morning at the moment when he started to watch. It gave him something to day-dream about, while he was making change.

The evening and nights were busy, especially in the movie booths, and Newell heard murmurings and gurglings and whispered voices from that direction, and he realized he had heard this noise before but had not been aware of what it was. When the store closed, he balanced out the cash drawer in front of Mac, and it counted out to the penny as usual, but today Mac had mostly left him alone to run the cash register, and so the old man was particularly pleased with himself for having hired Newell. "I knew you was a kid with a brain. Most kids don't have a goddamn lick of sense."

"I know." Newell sighed.

Mac was counting the stacks of quarters from the movie machines, with the change boxes stacked beside him. "That movie you was watching made a lot of money today. People must like it."

Newell shrugged. "It seemed like it was all right to me."

"Maybe you have an eye for this stuff. What do you think?"

"Maybe I do."

Mac handed him a roll of quarters and said, "Go back there and look at the rest of them."

"I ain't watching the ones with the women in them."

"Well, shit, I already knew that."

"All right," Newell said, and turned and headed to the movie booths, while Mac leaned his chair back on two legs, his pants hiked up past the top of his socks and his bald white legs shining in the light.

By the time Newell came out again, Sophia had arrived and started to clean. He had seen her before, an older woman with a big-boned body, cheeks sunken, mouth mostly toothless, given to wearing wigs and old party dresses while she cleaned the store. She sometimes spoke softly to Mac but ignored Newell, and tonight he hardly saw her as she emptied the waste cans and sprayed the front of the display case with glass cleaner. He had stopped after four of the movies, as much as Mac's roll of quarters would pay for, and he had seen things he never thought of seeing before. Two of the movies were very bad, featuring thin, pale, unattractive people fumbling with each other and stripping off their clothes, when Newell would have preferred they keep them on; and he watched these two movies dutifully. But the third movie was about a carpenter with a very hairy torso, a short man with black hair and a mustache and a solid, thick, carved body, bronze skin, brown eyes, who met a younger, taller man at his worksite and took the young man back to his truck and allowed the younger man to begin to touch him. They took off their clothes. The nakedness of the younger man was beautiful, lanky and lean, and the nakedness of the carpenter was astonishing, he had a very large penis and it dangled loosely and seductively along his rounded thigh, jiggling when he walked, and he ran his hands along it. The gesture struck Newell, the display of the length of it, and the movie went on but Newell stayed stuck there, at that moment, until he noticed what they were doing on screen now, that the carpenter was grabbing the younger kid pretty roughly and making him straddle the ladder that hung down from the back of the truck, and then straddling the ladder behind him, and this all reminded Newell of the other movie, the tree trunk and the two men facing each other across it, and the carpenter pushed himself inside the lanky fellow, who made a face for the camera like something strange was happening inside him, and they moved together like that on the ladder, and everything seemed to go fine for them. He watched that one all the way to the end and then decided to watch one more before he headed home.

The next movie was called *Night Crawler,* according to the sign on the door, and a picture above the words, torn out of one of the magazines, showed a man in shadow, back to the camera, hat pulled low over his eyes, a room of indeterminate size and shape, and the movie began exactly in that way, with the camera panning the room full of phantoms, then lingering on the bare back of the man, the curve of his deltoid, and then the man turned around and there was Rod the Rock, facing the camera, and Newell's breath left him and his heart began to thud against his ribs. He was grateful for the pause when he needed to put in another quarter because he could stand there, hardly able to believe it, before the image appeared, lagged, shook, steadied itself and became Rod the Rock again. He was playing with himself, exactly the way he had done in the pictures, and he was looking at the camera while he did, and he was big and getting bigger, and then he was looking through the camera into the center of Newell, and moving in perfect time, and Newell got hard in his pants and pressed himself against the movie machine, and Rod the Rock drew him closer, posing that body, showing it this way and that in the light, and running his hand up and down, the limberness of it, the slick motion up and down, and the self-satisfied look on Rod's face, the certainty that the sight of him was pleasing to Newell. Quarter after quarter he watched until he hadn't any more quarters, and he stood there with the whole tape, which he had seen through nearly twice before the money ran out, contained in his mind. But he refused to touch himself in the movie booth, which seemed dirty to him, in some way. He waited till his excitement died down and headed to the cash register intending to ask for more quarters, until he saw the look on Mac's face, the expectancy.

"What did you think?" Mac asked, "which ones did you watch?"

So Newell told him that the first two movies had ugly people in them and that nobody would want to watch them, and then he said the carpenter movie was pretty good, and then he said, "But I really like *Night Crawler*. That's the really good one."

Mac chuckled and said, "That one's been playing for six months and it's steady money every week. People like that guy or something. I don't know what it is."

Sophia had begun cleaning the store, running the vacuum along the carpet between the racks of magazines, wearing her favorite black wig, or at least the one that Mac claimed was her favorite, a big twisty high-combed number that made her look like a country music queen; she had wrapped a rag partway around her head, as she did sometimes to indicate she was on duty. She wore a white polyester one-piece pantsuit with flared bottoms and attractive white sandals, flats. Mac caught Newell staring at her, so Newell asked, "How old is she?"

"I don't know." Raising his voice over the vacuum, he asked, "How old are you, Miss Sophia?"

She flicked her hair back casually, wrinkled her nose and went on with the vacuuming. Mac laughed and Newell, embarrassed, said good night to Mac and nodded to Sophia on his way out. He was struck by the strong, harsh bones of her face and the pale fuzz on her chin. Her nose, thick and bulbous, shaded thin lips. Because of the hairdo, which was falling as much as it was rising, Newell could not see her ears, but the lobes hung down thick and fleshy, and long earrings hung down from the lobes and tangled in the hair; and while she could have been a woman with any of those features, Newell gaped at her in recognition, and then she bent over and he saw her cleavage, real as far as the eye could see, and he was confused again. So he left the bookstore with Sophia in his head, instead of Rod the Rock—Sophia with the body of an old woman and the face of an old man—and while he was walking away he could not remember whether he had said good-bye to her.

But later he remembered the movies again, when he was soaking in a tub of hot water, lying there with the lights out and only the streetlight spilling in. He carried the movies with him while he let the tub drain, dried himself, cleaned the tub, and tidied the room, all in the dark. He made his way across the room to the bed, which he had already turned back. The feel of a quarter in his fingertips and the smell of the booth, a strange blend of spices, vivid as he closed his eyes, so tired he was sliding into sleep, and the motion of the carpenter's body as he swung the ladder down from the truck, as he jerked down the boy's shorts and made him naked, as he mounted the ladder behind him, separate images, motion that repeated itself, while in a room somewhere, maybe a room in the empty warehouses along the waterfront, Rod the Rock waited alone, his back to the door. He had taken off most of his clothes in the heat and he was just standing there, and Newell was outside in the corridor, he could hear Rod the Rock breathing, maybe smell the smoke of his cigarette, and later his mouth would taste like a cigarette, if Newell could only get into the room. He was tired, though, and sleep dragged him down into itself in spite of the movies, but he carried with him the shadow of bodies moving, the knowledge that it was all about motion. In his dreams he would see motion, rarely a face, only the parts of the body moving, all night, and he waked with a throbbing erection in the morning and carried himself quickly to the bathroom. He felt as though he had hardly slept at all.

For weeks it rained, a stretch of wet weather that the local people appeared to be accustomed to, coming every year around this time, late July and all through August. People shook out their umbrellas and spread them overhead with a tired look, and everyone wore raincoats even in the heat. Newell kept his umbrella standing in a big tomato can by the door and emptied the can every day, the water sickly brown. He worked from morning till late at night, never questioning the hours, and soon he had grown accustomed to the low-ceilinged rooms, the plywood shelving, the old plaster walls painted a dull orange. What he did not know, what concerned him, was the name of the place, but even when he asked, Mac only grunted and stubbed out his latest cigarette in the mound of dead butts in front of him. He had seen Mac open the checkbook once, when he was writing a check to the man who kept the Coke machine stocked, but the checks said only A&R Distributing, nothing about the bookstore at all. By then he had learned that Mac didn't like to get particular where the business was concerned, and so he never asked what A&R Distributing was.

At the entrance to the booths, Newell fashioned an attractive display featuring photos and titles of all the movies. One morning, watching the usual game of men choosing a movie, he noted that two of the men eyed each other and moved into the movie booth section together. He wished he could guess which movie they were going to see together and figured it would be the one about the housepainter who comes in through the window and pulls down his white bib overalls to reveal a very large paintbrush, and the man who lives in the room fondles the painter and later so does his boyfriend, who comes back to the bedroom wearing a suit, and Newell had an instinct that the two men would choose this movie, and suddenly all the rumblings and mutterings from the movie section took on a new meaning.

The power of it awed him, that here was a thing, in these magazines and in these movies, that would draw so many people, furtively, and yet compel them in such a way. To go into the booths together. To do the same things in the booths as they were watching on the screen. To move from booth to booth, partner to partner.

Once Mac, who had ears for a different sound, walked to the curtain at the entrance and said, "I don't hear no quarters falling into no machines in there. I hear plenty else. You keep them quarters turning them movies, you hear?"

Back at the cash register he advised Newell, "You got to get so you can hear every coin drop in the slot. Else they'll stay back there and fuck all day and we won't make a dime."

The pay gave him a charge, every week, the same extravagant stack of bills in cash, the same white envelope with the amount written in cash, and Newell pocketed it and kept it in his room in his wallet that his Uncle Jarman had given him, and he paid his bills out of it and had a lot left over, more than he had ever imagined. So he had a phone put in his room and bought new shirts and colognes and a gold chain like the one he had seen and then some nice leather shoes and then a shirt made out of linen. The linen shirt, a soft lavender color with full sleeves and a narrow collar, felt so extravagant to Newell that he hung it in his closet and felt terrified at the prospect of wearing it, as though people would be staring at him and whispering, and so a couple of times he put it on, and then felt self-conscious and took it off and hung it up again.

One day while he was counting the rolls of quarters in the safe below the cash register, a customer's shadow fell across him and he looked up at the face of Henry Carlton, pale and round, a five-dollar bill thrust forward in his stubby, hairy fingers. "Hey," Newell said as he straightened up, "you want some change, I guess."

"I didn't know you worked here."

"I been working here since June. I never seen you in here before."

"I haven't been in here lately."

"You want the whole thing in quarters?"

Henry nodded and Newell counted them out. Henry started to speak, then ducked his head and turned away, and Newell said, "Look at that one about the artist model and the artist. Everybody is looking at that one."

"Thanks," Henry said, and slipped through the curtains. Some other people were already in the booths and more people went in while Henry was there, and Newell was steadily counting out quarters. People were buying magazines, too, and Newell was recommending the new Rod and Rock magazine *Chain of Desire* to a lot of people. They were asking about the movie but Mac never knew what would be available. Traffic in the bookstore remained brisk in spite of the rain outside that had been falling for such a long time, and Newell had forgotten about Henry when he appeared again and asked Newell what time he got off, and so Newell agreed to meet him at the Corral. When he did, he asked, "Well, did you like the movie?"

When Henry smiled his face relaxed and he became suddenly very pleasant. "It was all right. There was this man in the booth watching that movie you told me about, and I went in there with him, and honey, we had us a time." He spoke quietly and matter-of-factly, and rolled his eyes a little as if to show what a good time it had been, and it reminded Newell of the way Henry had walked off into the shadows in the warehouses that night after they went dancing.

"But what did you do?"

"You mean exactly?" Henry giggled. The music in the room had suddenly got soft, and Henry leaned close and told him, in detail, and Newell sat there and tried to picture it. He made Henry repeat certain parts and explain. Who had remembered to bring lubrication, for example. How did they have room for so much in those little booths?

"The only problem is remembering to put in the goddamn quarter," Henry said, and arranged a series of matches on the bar counter in the shape of the letter *N*, and set fire to them, a flash of sulfur and flame. The letter burned into the polished wood of the countertop, where many other people had also burned their initials. The bartender, bobbing back and forth to the beat, came over to inspect the handiwork and asked who that was for. Henry pointed to Newell, and the bartender said, "Welcome to the brotherhood," dancing away again.

So then Newell went out often, with Henry, which proved to be better than going by himself. Each time they went out, Newell felt something stirring in himself, most acutely when he happened across the man who resembled Rod the Rock, but at other times as well; he tasted the feeling and let it go, tasted it and let it go, again and again, while Henry hung out in the bathrooms and sucked dick or handled it or ogled it in the stalls half the night. Newell joined him one night, finally, and watched Henry go down on a man in a business suit, a pallid fellow with a bald spot and a surgically repaired lip, and Newell hardly got a look at his penis, though he had a pretty good view of Henry's head bobbing up and down. Later he watched a shirtless cowboy with a nice tan but a soft abdomen and slack shoulders open his zipper as though to show off, and then another fellow, in a pair of very short cutoff blue jeans, wool socks, and hiking boots, joined the first fellow and they stood in front of the urinal working their hands along themselves in a way that Newell had always been taught was nasty, to be done only in private and furtively. Here two men were standing in front of Newell in regular clothes in a bathroom and grinning at each other and then trading hand jobs and smiling through the whole thing, and Henry finishing his work on the balding fellow and giving the eye to a flaccid redhead with white-blue eyes and a smattering of freckles across his cheeks and tiny nose. Newell could hear Henry slurping in a most enthusiastic way, though the sound left Newell a little queasy. Henry was there for the night but Newell took a break after a while, getting air on the balcony upstairs, where a perfect stranger offered him a puff on one of the funny cigarettes. He held the smoke in his lungs till his ears were ringing, and when he let it out someone was shoving a bottle of poppers under his nose and his head began to swim in circles.

Staggering down to the bathroom, he had the impression that someone had recently been touching him along the hips, sliding hands along his hips, and it occurred to him that this might have happened on the balcony, the bearded man might have been squeezing Newell's hips with those ham-sized hands of his, and with the rushing and roaring in his head Newell could hardly be sure, but he thought somebody had recently been touching him, only a moment ago in fact, and Newell had felt uncomfortable, or maybe uncertain as to where he was, and he had pushed away from the man and started for the stairs and forgot what had happened and then remembered it again, halfway down the stairs heading to look for Henry.

Every time he went out with Henry he felt himself being pushed a little further, and after a while he wondered how long it would be before he let someone back him into one of those stalls in the bathroom, before he let somebody get down on his knees in front of him, or else got down on his own knees, and looked up at some stranger's face as Henry so often did, licking his tongue around his lips to moisten them before reaching to unzip the stranger's jeans. But so far Newell only stood and watched. So far that was all he wanted to do.

Or did he want more? Or did he know what this wanting was? This sheen of wanting that rippled across Henry's face in the bathroom at the Corral, this hollow place to fill with something inside? And maybe this was why he traveled with Henry, as much as anything could be, that his hunger remained so palpable? Newell followed him and watched him and learned.

When Henry came to the bookstore during the day, he would stay in the booths for a long time and then come out and tell Newell exactly what he had done, and with whom, and often enough Newell could match Henry's description with someone for whom he had made change. Henry liked to do almost everything you could do with another man, including things he called rimming and going around the world, which had to do with sticking his tongue into someone's butthole, and he described it graphically for Newell one afternoon while Mac was upstairs with the girls.

"But doesn't it stink?"

Henry rolled his eyes. "That smell is heaven on earth, honey. You don't know what you're talking about."

"You're making this up. Nobody would do that."

"I'm not making anything up." Henry always spoke mildly, regardless of what he was describing or the effect the description had on Newell. "It's fun. You'll see. You'll end up with your tongue up somebody's asshole one of these days. We all do."

"Do you brush your teeth afterward or something?"

"Don't be stupid."

"I mean it. It sounds so gross. I would have to brush my teeth a hundred times."

Henry shook his head and shivered. "You'll find out."

He stood there with his mild white face like a moon and his pale, lumpy body leaning against the booth where the tallest of the dildoes stood, and he looked Newell up and down for a moment, as though he wanted to talk about something else, then thought better of it and instead said good afternoon.

One night they were wandering in the warehouses again, and Henry wanted Newell to stay and watch him, at least, this time. They wandered for a long time through the shadows and at first it seemed there were not so many men, and then they came to the maze, a place where low walls and partitions had been built, nearer the street than the river, but with the upper floors torn up and the whole setting open to the night sky, the haze of streetlight and the faint shimmering of one or two bright stars. The sky so different from Pastel, walking at night in the field near the trailer park, made him homesick for the first time that he could remember. A place where he could see the stars, where the sky was black. Henry coughed, patted Newell on the back, handed him a cigarette. They wandered into the narrowing space. Newell moved in a haze again, and followed Henry and saw other men sliding past them. Henry rounded a bend of the maze and Newell followed into a space where a man was already waiting, standing there, thick at the hips and soft-waisted, slope-shouldered, with jowls and thinning hair, the kind of man Henry went crazy for, and so Henry moved toward him and they started to touch each other, and Henry looked back to make sure Newell was standing there, and Newell grinned and felt the pleasant rush of the drug through his head, and Henry looked back at him as the man in front of him was unzipping his pants and reaching inside, and Newell stood there and watched for a while, till Henry forgot about him, and then wandered farther, doubling back and taking another turn, another turn, a long narrow strip and then a room where something was happening and he stood in the shadow as a witness.

In the space stood the white-faced man dressed all in black, a black suit and black sweater, catching the little light there was and shimmering, and with him was Rod the Rock, the man Newell thought of as Rod the Rock, especially now as he stood in the fall of streetlight, in a place where he was framed against the open dock and the Jefferson Bridge ablaze with light, his skin gleaming and bare, someone else in front of him, someone dripping wet and pushing back his hair as though he had climbed out of the river only a moment ago. Running his hand up and down Rod the Rock's chest, hair sliding between his fingers, and then the man with no face slumping against one of the support posts, leaning there while the two men in front of him twined round each other, Rod the Rock reaching for the man, scooping his body close. Other people stopped to watch, but Newell stayed hidden in the shadows, while the man devoured Rod the Rock, mouth to mouth, taking control of him as if with a poison or a drug, Rod slumping against the hard blonde and letting himself be backed against a wall, and then slapped, sharply, across the face, and then slapped again, and then kissed, and more of this for a long time, until they disappeared into a corner of the room that looked like a shadow. Newell waited for them to appear again but they never did.

He dreamed that night that he had seen the man rising out of the river dripping with water, walking toward the shadows of the warehouses, walking into the shadows and vanishing, and then seeing it again, the man rising out of the river, climbing up the side of the dock like a spider, crossing the twilit space, empty now, where ships once loaded and unloaded. In the morning he felt vaguely queasy, and was glad to go to work and do the usual things. He changed the movie display and put out different pictures of the new Bruno movie. People would think it was a different movie and see it again. The night before, the shadows moving through it, had left a haze on him, but hardly any more than that.

He picked up the newspaper that Mac had already read and leafed through it, reading about a prayer vigil in hope for world ecology on the square, and then about a party given by newlywed Louisa Huntington-McIvey, a pleasant luncheon to honor the governor's wife on her birthday, at the stately Huntington home on

Chalmette Avenue, and a few pages further, a picture of Rod the
Rock, or of the man Newell had come to call Rod the Rock in
his mind, only the caption under the picture read Herman
Lebeaux, and the story was about his murder, that he had been
found dead in a house on Chocowinity Street, the cause of death
and motive unknown. Newell folded the paper and laid it down.
His heart was racing and he wondered if he would dare to read the
article again. In his mind he was seeing the blond man backing
Rod—backing Herman Lebeaux, as it turned out—against a wall,
slapping him sharply, slapping him again, and Herman's face
thrown into shadow so that his expression could not be read at all.

It was as though he had seen the crime himself, as though he
had watched as casually as the man with no face, and when he did
pick up the newspaper and read the tiny article again, including the
cryptic phrase that police were investigating the murder scene, his
hands were trembling and he felt as though he was going to be
sick. He stared at the picture, the same face that he had seen in the
bars, the same strong jaw and muscular neck, the same short-
cropped hair, but wearing a shirt and tie. Maybe it wasn't the same
man after all? But no, Newell recognized the face, he had stared at
it often enough. So he was distracted by the thought of this crime
all day, and that evening for the first time his cash register came up
thirty-nine cents short, and Mac blinked at him in surprise, and
said, "You feeling all right?"

"Yes sir. I don't know what happened."

"Thirty-nine cents ain't no big deal, but you always come out to
the penny. And you been acting funny since I got downstairs."

After work, with the streetlights coming on and the streets filling with people, and the late October wind bringing a sharp chill,
he walked down Chocowinity Street till he came to the address
noted in the newspaper, an apartment house with the same orna-
mental ironwork on the balconies, the same closed shutters on the
windows facing the streets, the same locked gate leading to a private courtyard, as most of the other houses on the street. Only the
street number identified the house as the scene of the crime re-
ported in the newspaper. Newell walked home, but when he
climbed the stairs and faced his own doorway he could not bear to

go inside, so he climbed down to the street again and visited Miss Kimbro instead.

He had come to find her every bit as odd as time passed, in terms of the richness of her oddities, as she had seemed when he first met her. The bookstore, for one thing, puzzled him, because he knew from his own job that a bookstore needed to make money, even one like Miss Kimbro's, and he hardly ever saw customers inside her store, and hardly ever saw Miss Kimbro doing any of the work that he himself did in the course of his own job, like unpacking boxes of magazines and pricing them and checking inventory and re-stocking the shelves. Today she was standing behind her counter with the big orange cat beside her, and she was reading an old novel with yellowed pages. She offered him a cup of tea without saying a word or putting down the novel, which she carried one-handed to the china teapot. The tea was like most of the tea she served him, hot, with milk and sugar in it, so that it tasted rich and creamy, and he liked it but was still becoming accustomed to the idea of tea that was hot when you drank it. She had already added the milk and sugar, handing him the cup while she kept reading the book. He stood there and presently picked up a book himself, James Joyce, and he read several words of the first page but they didn't seem to be in the right order, and he read them again and they still seemed that way, and so he put the book down and sipped his tea.

"That's a hard book," she said.

"I guess it is."

"How's your job going?" She kept the book raised in front of her face so that he could not see her lips move.

"Fine. I like it."

"You must make plenty money, working the hours like you do. You get that phone in your room?"

"Yes ma'am." He knew she was watching him, so finally he pulled out the scrap of paper from his shirt, the newspaper article that he had cut out and folded carefully and put there. "Did you see this?"

"In the paper? I don't read the paper, it's a bunch of mess." She picked up the clipping and read it and looked at him. "What about it—did you know him?"

"No ma'am. I saw him, I mean. I saw him a few times."

Something gentled in her expression and she lay down the book. "It bothers you?"

"Yes ma'am." What bothered him was what he had seen at the riverfront, but he preferred to let that go.

"He was a handsome man," she said, inspecting the picture again. "Name doesn't fit him, I'd never pick him for a Herman."

So they discussed the murder and other murders for a while, and she recounted that the night of the nun murders she had hardly been able to sleep, for the heat, she had thought, though it really hadn't been that hot, and she kept waking up in the night with a feeling like she were strangling. "Sure enough the next morning those nuns were dead, and the police still haven't solved that one."

"You think they ever will?"

She shook her head with a serious air. "There's murder around here that nobody ever finds out about."

Upstairs he hid the clipping inside that first issue of *Brute Hombre,* which was now merely an elder in his sizable collection of magazines. He sat down and waited, sure enough, and in a few minutes it began to rain, and rained all night.

He lay in bed that night, unable to sleep or even to close his eyes for fear of something moving in the room when he could not see. Something moving against the lids of his eyes, bodies moving, not the ones on the riverfront but the bodies from the movies, men behind men, men over men, men twined around each other, shooting wads of stuff into each other's face, and something about the sex gripped him, and he was curious about the movies he had avoided so far, the one that was supposed to have fist-fucking in it, and the one where the men were dressed in leather and doing things to each other, judging from the pictures he had permitted himself to inspect, that were hard to understand. Binding each other and hoisting each other up in harnesses, in disturbing costumes. These images surged through him while he lay exhausted in the bed, twisting himself in the sheets and once or twice standing to look out the window, at the crowds passing on Boulevard late into the night.

Toward morning, though still in the dark, Newell dressed and went for a walk. He headed to the river, but not to Auerole Square: he walked to the riverfront where he had seen Herman Lebeaux vanish. Entering the warehouses, his heart thudding, he forced himself forward through the echoing spaces. A few shadows flitted here and there, and he shrank from them all but still walked forward, his breath coming harder. He was afraid for a time he would not be able to find the place without Henry, but finally he neared the edge of the maze. He stopped there and listened. Silence inside. He stepped forward gingerly. All the spaces were empty. He crept to the place where he had stood when he saw Herman Lebeaux disappear.

When he turned around he thought he saw someone, a pale shadow sliding out of the corner of his eye, and his heart thudded and he backed out of the space, backed way from the maze and then, unable to breathe, stumbled forward till he came to an open bay and rushed into the air. The unused dock stretched up and down the river, not a soul in sight. Overhead, the sky had begun to lighten. He walked toward the square and the church, the towers visible against low clouds, and finally gathered his nerve and cut through the dark warehouses to the street behind.

He lay in bed in his clothes, waiting for the sun to come up. When it finally rose, he bathed, shaved, and drank a cup of instant coffee loaded with nondairy creamer. He sat dull-headed on the edge of the bed, feeling at last that he could sleep, now that it was too late.

Newell scanned the paper and found nothing at all about Herman Lebeaux, and nothing further the next day, and the next he read another short notice that Herman Lebeaux's family from Plaquemines Parish had come to claim his body and that the investigation into his death was continuing. He was described as a homosexual drifter and would-be film star, and Newell's heart jumped. He wondered for a moment if Herman really was or had been Rod the Rock. In a final cryptic sentence, the paper stated that his body had been found hanging in the basement of the apartment building on Chocowinity Street but that he was not known to have lived in an apartment there. The day following, nothing appeared, and the next day, nothing again.

The money he was earning worried him even as he spent it. He bought new sheets and pillowcases and towels, a down comforter and a big electric heater, he bought curtains for the windows and then bought paint and painted the room a soft, bright yellow. He bought new clothes, many pieces of which he was embarrassed to wear, the shoes too fine for his feet, the shirts too soft. He sent money orders for fifty dollars at a time to Flora and when he called, she gushed over him like he had really made something of himself. "It's just a great bookstore," he answered one Sunday afternoon when she asked him how he was making all that money selling books. "We got people in and out the doors all day and all night."

"Well, I swan."

"I tell you what, Gramma, you and Jesse ought to come down here. I can buy me a rollaway bed and you and him can sleep in my bed. You ought to."

"I'd love to get down there one of these days," Flora answered, but in a noncommittal way.

He had tea with Miss Kimbro every so often, and she sometimes took the occasion to remark on what a fine job he had done, turning that room upstairs into a showplace. "You got it looking so nice up there, I ought to throw you out and double the rent on the next fellow," she remarked, and from her expression it would have been hard to decide whether she was serious.

"I been looking at a rug," Newell said.

"No."

"Yes ma'am. I got my eye on a nice braided one down at Stearne's. You know where that is?"

She picked a bit of lint off her sweater and wrapped it tight against her. The damp December winds cut to the bone, and the puny gas heaters were hardly enough to keep a room warm. "You ever read anything else about that man?"

"What man?"

"Herman Lebeaux."

The memory flooded back, the night in the hunting ground, and Newell was startled that he had let it slip so far away. "No, I never read anything else."

"There was a little bit in the paper today. 'The police are continuing the investigation into the murder of Herman Lebeaux, but there are no leads.'" She laid the paper in his hand and he studied the article. Some murders remained unsolved and people wanted somebody to investigate why there were so many. People were worried, a commission ought to be appointed, and among the cases was the death of Mr. Lebeaux, found beaten and hanged on Chocowinity Street.

"Don't look like they're going to find any killer."

"No, it doesn't," Miss Kimbro agreed. The topic had made her moody and she was quiet for a while. When she spoke again, what she said was "You could get a nice used Oriental rug, but I wouldn't buy it at Stearne's."

So he became disturbed again, but that night, like many others, he waited in his room till nearly midnight, then dressed and went out walking. He had bought a used leather jacket at a thrift store on Beale, the leather cut the wind and the lining kept him snug, along with a pair of soft leather gloves. Odd, that the feeling of the leather would please his hands so much, a clean caress. He roamed the bars most often without Henry now, and he often felt as though he were on the verge of something. In the disco that night, a man asked him to dance, a handsome man in good-quality trousers and a starched shirt, a sweater tied around his shoulders, and Newell started to say no because he knew this man would not like him, but the song was something he liked, let me run let me run let me run, a long low moaning woman's voice, and a beat that coursed through him, so he let the man lead him onto the floor and soon he was moving among the others, thankful for the music. When the song changed, the man kept dancing, and they stayed on the floor till late, the floor crowded by then, bodies pulsing against one another. Newell could feel it in himself, the change that was coming, that he was nearly ready now, that something would happen soon. So he kept dancing that night, till the beat was one long wave passing through his bones. When the man finally got tired he tried to lead Newell to the bar but Newell got his jacket instead and headed outside, and he never saw that man again.

He had become used to the territory by now, though parts of it made him nervous. To reach the hunting ground, he had to walk through streets that were altogether empty at night, where the buildings were mostly deserted. Some of the streets were pitch dark, the lights broken or shot out; one night he had seen a car stop underneath one of the high lamps and aim something upward and fire, a couple of shots to find the range and then the light went dark, just like that, as the car sped away. He walked with his hands in his pockets staring resolutely ahead, and when he reached Elyseum he allowed himself to trot across the street.

He had explored the abandoned riverfront a long way in the dark, and some of it he had visited by day, so that he knew it better now. The entrance he liked best was the one marked "13" on the wide, broad doors of the loading dock, because you could get to the big open rooms from there, and the places where men fucked within sight of the river, almost out in the open; but you could turn another way and find a labyrinth of what had once been offices, not the place where he had watched Herman Lebeaux vanish but another place like it, and men congregated in the smaller spaces here. He headed there tonight, and by now it no longer surprised him to find men, even in the December cold, because that was part of the attraction, after all, to be here under all weather, all circumstances, all hours of the day and night. He found the spot he usually liked, hidden in the back of one of the rooms, and he waited till somebody brought somebody else into the room, he could see only the shadow of the bodies, a single mass, but he could hear them, he could hear the two men admiring each other, showing themselves to each other, and he could hear their hands on each others' clothes, he could hear them kissing, he could hear everything that happened after that. He could hear how the desire changed the sound of their voices, so that they began by speaking in deliberate whispers and ended with sounds that could not be made into words at all. Sounds that hardly seemed human, and yet he had learned that nearly anybody could make them, given the chance.

He was falling toward that place in himself, he could feel his descent. The process was compounded by the movies he watched at the bookstore, the dreams he made up to stimulate himself in the dark. Now that he was used to the bookstore he could feel the furtiveness of the customers, their awe as they entered, their perusing of the magazines as if they simply happened to be glancing in that direction, and then the hand, drawn downward, slowly, to touch one of the covers, to turn the magazine to learn whether the photographs on the back promised more. A certain look on the face indicated whether the man would buy or not; a certain slackness came to the jaw and a keenness to the eye. The grip of the hand on the magazine would change. Men chose their movies with the same silence, the same fixedness, and Newell could feel them, late into the night sometimes, drifting from booth to booth the same way bodies drifted back and forth in the warehouses along the riverfront.

But he had never gone back to the booths. He had stopped buying magazines for himself. He felt himself drifting nearer and nearer a place in himself that would open out like a flower and cause the rest of him to be transformed, but the pictures and the movies were no longer what he wanted.

He had begun to want something, and he had begun to fear what it might be. In his bed at night he had begun to crave a thing beside him, with him, not quite a person but a force, something that could at once protect him and consume him, and though it made no sense this was what he felt. He had the image of himself devoured within a great darkness that wrapped around him like the strongest arms.

When he studied Mac he wondered what the old man was like when he climbed the stairs, when Dixie or Starla or one of the other girls met him and took him into a room for a long, careful massage. He wondered what sounds Mac made, what his body looked like, moving with the flow of pleasure through his nerves. By now, Newell had seen enough pictures, enough movies, so that he could imagine almost anything, even Mac's white, soft body, his thin legs and flat ass.

"This business will make you think about fucking all the time," Mac said one day, "to where you can't even stand it, to where you don't even want to think about a naked woman," but that same day he crept up the back steps to the massage rooms and disappeared for an hour and a half.

Miss Kimbro said to Newell one Sunday, during tea, while he was licking a buttery biscuit crumb off the tip of his finger, "You do know that I like women, don't you?"

"You like them?"

"Oh yes. I like them very much." She had flushed a bit and seemed suddenly younger.

"Well, I did see you with a woman in here, once."

"Oh, you're telling a fib."

"You had her shoved against the back wall, and you had your hands all over her. This nice-looking woman."

She blinked, then shrugged.

"Did you always like women?"

"Oh, yes. Even when I had a husband. He was a very nice man, for a man, but he couldn't do anything about me."

A customer called her away and he sat with his teacup cradled in his palms, the warm china along his skin. He liked that he could smell her when she walked away, a hint of sweat with a sweetness to it, her flowery deodorant dissolving into the air. He wondered what it would be like to be a woman and to kiss her. He wondered what it would be like to desire her, but he could hardly imagine such a state.

Upstairs, alone, he spoke to himself in a quiet voice, and even though he was alone the words unsettled him: "I like men. Did you know I like men?" He said them aloud a couple of times and sat on the new chair he had bought, beside the window, where he could watch the street below.

He dressed carefully, imitating styles he had seen on the streets and in the bars. He wore a tight white T-shirt with straps, tight jeans and a flannel shirt. He inspected himself in the mirror and thought he had nice shoulders, nice arms. He combed his hair the way his barber Chris had taught him. He touched behind his ears with the cologne that smelled like clover when it's cut, and he stuffed some bills in his pocket and locked his door. He thought he was good-looking, he carried that with him down the steps, and he ought to know by now.

He avoided places where he would have found Henry, visiting a couple of bars he had never seen before, then spent the late part of the evening in a bar called Blacksmith's, on Telemachus Place. Men had been coming up to him tonight and talking to him, he had been talking to them, he felt easy about it, and he wondered what the change was about, though he had his suspicions. In Blacksmith's he had been sitting alone for a while when a man approached him and started talking to him, and something about the moment made Newell aware of the man in a particular way, as though taking his scent. This man had a strong face with a heavy shadow of beard, and his hair was mixed black and gray, cut close to his head. He had a thick body, wide round shoulders, the backs of his hands hairy and brown from sun, firm veins standing out. He was as old as Jesse, Flora's boyfriend, or maybe a few years younger than that, but his body was hard and lean, and he eased next to Newell at the bar to speak to him in deep whispers, drawing closer as he spoke. What stuff he said! "You're about the prettiest thing in this bar. You got the prettiest mouth. Do you know how pretty you are? I come into town looking for something just like you. Can't believe there's a handsome thing like you sitting in here all by yourself. Can't believe you don't belong to one of these men in here, can't believe somebody doesn't already own you body and soul. I'd be the one to take care of you if I lived around here. You know that, don't you? You feel that about me. But I'm trapped. You know what I mean. I'm trapped in a life I can't escape. I have a wife and kids and my wife suspects that this is what I really am, I mean this, here, this man in front of you, thinking about what a beautiful thing you are, and my wife suspects this, and I've had to hide it from her for all these years. It makes me crazy to want you like this, in front of all these men. Don't you want to come with me? I want to take you somewhere. Don't you have somewhere we can go? I can get us a room. I want to be with you. This is crazy, the way this feels. Do you want another drink?" They drank another drink and another and Newell stopped drinking after that, and listened, kept the man close, felt himself wanting to get up from the stool to go with the man, while the night deepened and the bar filled with men. His name was Jerry Thibodeaux and he was an offshoreman home for a few days. His wife wanted him to stay home and kiss her ass but he had to go out. His wife probably knew exactly where he was but he had no choice, he had to find out if there was somebody waiting, and now he knew. By now he was pressed close against Newell and when he talked he sometimes leaned in so that his lips brushed against Newell's ear. The sensation was transfixing, worse than any alcohol, and when Newell laid his hands on Jerry's chest, Jerry sagged against him and sighed and Newell felt a force binding them, and when he moved his hands Jerry's eyes glazed, the power of it, all that power flowing in Newell's hands.

He had come to the point, and now he moved. They would not go anywhere, they would stay here, and he fixed on this immediately and knew it was the right choice, though he was only choosing by instinct. He unbuttoned Jerry's flannel shirt and slid his hands inside to ease it open, and it was like a movie as he moved, one of the good ones, his hands easing open the shirt, the tight shot of the hard brown body, the corded stomach, the thick, hairy chest, and then Jerry gripping him hard at the back and Newell relaxing, like it was being filmed and he knew what to do. He knew it really was a movie now because a space was clearing around them at the bar, as Newell opened Jerry's shirt and reached his hands in Jerry's pants; the movie was about the hard, lean older man and his need for the tender, choice young one in front of him, and Newell saw the scenes in his head, everything coming together, the man's ginger kisses and then Newell descending along his body, sliding down his pants, taking his soft tender tongue of meat inside, kissing it till it grew and everybody was watching, and in the middle of the action Newell saw himself as though he were one of the people standing and watching, and he was amazed to see how much he had learned on the job at the bookstore, because he copied the blow job perfectly. Jerry was sagging back against the bar with his hips going up and down, that tension so perfect, so urgent, the cock rigid in Newell's mouth, Newell moving on it, now slow now fast, people watching and some of them starting to grope each other but most simply rapt at the live action. Only when Newell had to swallow the stuff, or try to, did he falter, choking some and pulling back, then drying his mouth afterward with a napkin the bartender handed him, with Jerry pulling himself back together while some other men moved affectionately close to him and ran their hands along his body. The bartender brought Newell a drink on the house. Newell washed away the peppery taste in his mouth, still smelling the man's crotch, indescribably warm and yeasty. He sipped the drink but felt his head clear, completely sober.

They would talk about the kid who gave the blow job at the bar last night, did you see that? They were still staring at him to see what he would do next.

Jerry was surrounded by his own admirers now, and Newell walked away without saying good-bye, without responding to anybody, neither to the man who groped him fore and aft nor the man who tried to stick his tongue in Newell's mouth. He pushed them away and carried his drink to the door. He walked outside, rubbing a hard spot of dried semen from the corner of his mouth, sipping the liquor and walking to the river walk, where he listened to the ship's horns till nearly morning.

"CICCONE YOUTHS 1990"

Bruce Morrow

1.

"Come on, y'all. We got to make it before the video comes on," Evilean said as they passed throngs of tourists tramping through Times Square. An imposing, six-feet tall figure, she wore a cute little red and white gingham schoolgirl dress with white knee-high socks and size sixteen silver combat boots she'd spray-painted herself. "I want you girls to practice. And you do need practice."

"We need? You talking about what we need?" Josephine shouted, and looked to EmmaJean, who kept running out in the street, pretending to hitch a ride, and then to Carl, who always trailed behind so he could keep an eye on everything, and then back to Evilean. "You need an athletic bra, bouncing around like that." Josephine didn't take anything from anybody even though she always appeared very demure and elegant like her namesake.

"Mine's paid for. Real, honey. I'm lactating, baby," Evilean said, hoisting her ample bosom up to her face. Like many a bargain shopper, Evilean had made sure she'd gotten her money's worth. "And you?"

Giving a good Naomi jiggle, EmmaJean interrupted, "Hush your mouth, Evilean, before your mother reach out the sky and

Quotations are from the following: Milan Kundera, The Book of Laughter and Forgetting, *1980; Madonna/Shep Pettibone, Vogue, 1990; and Brian Keith Jackson, "Three Fairy Sisters."*

slap you sane. You hear me, gal? What time is it now? We'll make it, won't we?"

Josephine loudly sucked her teeth. "Least my mother's dead. Yours just left you for dead."

"That's why we gots to stick together. Nobody likes us, everybody hates us. Now, would somebody tell me what time it is?" EmmaJean put her hands on her hips and asked again impatiently.

"You can't read that clock up there, can you?" said Josephine. "Central Park Temp., 64 degrees F, 8:06 P.M. Can't you read? Up there. Fool."

"Oh. Why's there a clock up on top of that building?" Emma-Jean liked playing the stupid role; she thought it made her more innocent and, therefore, more desirable—simple, not simple-minded.

"Don't be so stupid, EmmaJean," said Evilean, still holding her breast in her hands. "So people can't make excuses for being late. That's why the one on top of that other building got a different time."

Carl sucked his teeth, then gestured, with much exaggeration, up to the clock. "There's no excuse for us missing the Madonna video. Don't just stand there, let's get to it."

They danced their way up Broadway, turning heads as they went along. They were *passing*—at least sometimes.

"How does that line go?" asked Josephine.

"What line?" asked Evilean.

"What does She say before all the star stuff? 'Look around, everywhere you turn is heartache, it's everywhere that you go. You've tried everything you can to escape the pain of life that you know.' I know pain. I think I really do."

"Bouncing breast!" Evilean announced loudly. "Now that's pain."

"Well," said Josephine, "you shouldn't have gone for that grandmotherly, Barbara Bush look."

Carl, who sometimes went by the name Miss Terry—but most of the time didn't because he thought it took too long for people to get it—ignored Evilean doting on herself and looked at Josephine for a long time. There was something there, something to Josephine's interpretation of Madonna's song, something about people just out and out denying pain, Carl thought. Like when Evilean's brother saw her working the piers and he came over, spit in her face, ripped her Donna Karan cashmere sweater dress off, and stabbed her right in her left tittie, silicon pouring everywhere, and Evilean telling her brother, "Butchie, Butchie, I'm going to buy you a Mr. Softee if you good, Butchie. I'm going to get you a Mr. Softee ice cream cone. What flavor you want? Half and half?"

Carl became so taken by the idea of pain and denial, so involved in Madonna's words playing over and over again in her head, that without realizing it, she began dancing in half-time, quarter-time. The four girls had nearly come to a halt in front of a busy seafood restaurant on Broadway.

"You mean we should loosen some attitudes around here?" Evilean asked.

"Yeah, girl," Josephine answered with a flip of her wrist.

The four girls looked at one another, captured by their own daring. And the corners of their mouths started twitching—to the beat of "Lucky Star." Then suddenly they all let out short, shrill, breathy sounds, very difficult to describe as singing. Just listen to a few of Her old—pre–voice lesson—records for examples.

2.

Somehow these four drag queens (and their idol, Madonna) have captured my imagination and I've overlaid their story on all the stories that I tell nowadays. That's how my mind's been working: like my blankets, layered and layered upon me to keep me warm. Stuck here in this bed, a prisoner in my own home, I get chilled so easily that when I'm reading the paper, I spread it out over me too. When I first read about a gang of girls going around randomly sticking women with needles on the Upper West Side of Manhattan, giggling as they ran away—without even thinking about it, those girls became *my* girls, my comforter. I couldn't stop thinking about them. I even gave them names, Evilean, EmmaJean, Josephine, and Carl.

It was all in the papers. *The New York Times, Post,* the *Daily News.* Such a sinister act. It probably even made *USA Today,* if you can imagine that. I immediately thought the worst: that those girls were using infected needles and randomly exposing their innocent victims to HIV—or some other horrible creature. Premeditated murder. What an unimaginable act. Or, at least, no one would believe a story like that if it was made up. It's too horrible, too sickeningly evil. But true. Imagine the fear that was planted in each and every woman pricked by one of those needles. It's a fear that will never ever leave them, a horror that may lie dormant for months, and for years after repeatedly being tested for every disease known to man, only to awaken, one day, with a nagging cough that just won't go away. Or fatigue that's paralyzing. Or a fever that won't let you sleep at night, get the rest that you really need. Nightmares. Chills. Sweat-soaked sheets. A new skin mole that just wasn't there the other day.

See, I don't live in *that* fear anymore. Chills and wet sheets, yes. A weight problem, no. Dry skin and gingivitis, yes. Nappy hair, no more. Not after my third really scary bout. I now have what my momma would call good hair, fine, straight hair, as soft as a baby's before it turns nappy. Momma always did talk about how my hair didn't turn until I was four and a half, and then it drew up as tight as a prostitute's hand over a five-dollar bill. She talks like that. Momma would love my hair now if she could see it. But she won't. See, she would never visit a sick person's home. It don't have to be AIDS. It could be malignant cancer, chronic heart ailments, strep throat, pinkeye, or just plain old old age. My momma does not visit the sick and the shut-in—that's where her Christianity ends. And she wouldn't dare visit me. Nor I her.

See, I don't get out much nowadays. Most of my meals are delivered and I'm desperately trying to see if I can get some home-care in here. A little sweeping and dusting. A little shopping for necessities. Most days I spend in bed, propped up with about seven pillows, reading anything I can get my hands on. And writing. During the high-rolling eighties, friends used to visit me; but now they either don't come around or they've passed away. A lot have passed away. Used to be all my frightened friends would pay me regular visits and we'd talk about the old days, all the stories about the piers when they were still covered and you could go there any time of the day or night and travel from floor to floor to floor, and have all you could ever imagine. They came for the stories, those long, winding tales; but mostly they stopped by because they were afraid, scared of being tested, scared of the virus, scared they would die a long and agonizing death without friends or family or health insurance. Scared the hospitals wouldn't take them. And scared of life with no sex. Can you imagine that?

These friends, whom I loved and still love dearly, came up with the bright idea that I should write down the sex stories I told all the time so they could take the stories home and read them in solitude—relieving some of their built-up frustrations—but I turned them down. I wasn't ready then to turn my life into pornography and I wasn't ready to write, either. It would have been too exhausting—not for me, of course, but for them.

After my fears of the virus went away (I couldn't play ignorant forever), the anxiety was replaced by anger. Anger at the Moral Majority wanting to starve me out, cut off all of my means of support, force me to capitulate and make public confessions of my sins; anger at William F. Buckley suggesting I brand myself (tattoos weren't good enough) so all would know; church leaders telling me how it was all predicted at least three times in the Holy Bible. But before I could go off on all these motherfuckers, I hid (it wasn't difficult)—when I lost the little job I had, lost the insurance I had, lost the friends I thought I had.

Friends soon became a damn scarcity. Except one, a young man by the name of D., who generously offered me his insurance. (Everything has since come out into the open; but I'm still reluctant to reveal his identity.) Shy, delicate, *and* intelligent, and with the milkiest of blue eyes, D. was employed at a corporation with good coverage, dental, medical, emergency, everything, but which was filled with powerful homophobes who immediately fired discovered gays. But because my friend was good at his job—indispensable—the company decided to make him an exception. And D. in turn passed on his good fortune to me.

During those years of being uninsured I was able to make all the necessary visits I needed to the doctor. If Ronald Reagan could be president, then I might as well try to get over, too. I was one of the first in my ever-shrinking group of friends to test HIV positive, and I was the first to get fired from a job—with the minimum of health coverage in the first place—which the "Majority" had declared high risk for infection to the general population: I was a hair stylist, a hair cutter, a hairdresser; these very Christian men didn't want their vulnerable (docile) wives gossiping to the likes of me or exchanging any of those bodily fluids while I teased their hair. You know: a gouge of the comb, a slip of the scissors, a pick of a perm scab.

When D., shy, delicate, *and* intelligent, asked me if I wanted to go to a doctor of my choice for all the visits I desired—for free!—I kissed him right on the lips. The first and only. I asked him to get me all the right forms with all the right policy numbers and sign them, and to give me the name of a doctor who would take payment directly from the insurance company. That seemed to give me and him extra protection—I wouldn't have to forge D.'s signature, and I wouldn't have to cough up the money up front.

Which is how under someone else's name I came to get medical care.

The doctor didn't have a good bedside manner (he never warmed his stethoscope or his stubby fingers) but he did get me on an early experimental AZT/ddI study. Soon enough, though, I started getting sicker from the medicine than from the disease—dizziness, low blood pressure, nausea, more diarrhea—and I was dropped from the study. Of course this also disqualified me from any other experimental studies because those were the rules of the clinical protocols: no experimental crossover. But I was still happy, comforted to know I would be taken in at the nearest hospital, which happens to be very private.

On one of his frequent visits D. announced that his boss had given a large donation to Advertisers for AIDS Research. I had never been happier for a fad to arrive. (I'm not sure those ribbons were around yet or not. But trends do come and trends do go.)

"He was a little ashamed to tell me," giggled D. "He certainly wouldn't want it to get around that he believed in helping immoral queers. He just couldn't help himself."

"Fine, fine," I said. I giggled a bit, too. I knew this man. Well, I used to know his son very well—too well—but that's enough said about that.

"He wants complete anonymity," D. said with mock seriousness. "All I'm supposed to do is be the spokesperson for the company. He says he's donating one hundred thousand dollars!"

"Well, that's a start," I said. "What took him so long?"

D. claimed his boss had improved. He yelled less. He didn't try to squash people under his brown suede Gucci loafers anymore. He had begun to have qualms about his conservatism, the old booming Reagan/Bush years that stripped the country bare. It became known around the office that he did indeed have a son and his son was a mediocre ballet dancer—as if that meant something. We can't all be Nureyev. D's boss made as much as he could of the speck of kindness left in him; and staring out into that mesmerizing maze that we call midtown Manhattan, the city between two rivers, his eyes would show signs of a light sedative and an inbred sadness—the sadness of a man who has come to realize that this skyline, with all of its granite and glass and glory, held nothing but suffering for him.

3.

Evilean, EmmaJean, Josephine, and Carl are tossing attitude every which way as they make their way up Broadway. Past—and passing!—movie theaters with new neon marquees, card tables set up on the sidewalk with magazines and used books and bootleg cassette tapes laid out. "Check it out. Check it out, baby. Fellas? Hey?" Past and passing throngs of people, young people, old people, white people, black people, Latino people—people-of-color people. "Fucking *maricones.*" They make their way past grown men, mostly drunk old men, sleeping on the new wood benches in the recently renovated Broadway median. "Baby, those real?" Taxis fly by still-yellow lights, past ultracultural Lincoln Center, where lines of big black limos deposit frail pale patrons who walk in pairs of two, arm in arm, never looking to the side, as if in a sociocultural trance, their eyes trained only on the well-lighted three-tiered water fountain and the enormous, well-hung (but way ugly) Chagall in the opera house. But the lights of Broadway are calling

Evilean and EmmaJean, Josephine and Carl. Tower Records. Discount Clothes. New York Style. The Gap. The Twenty-Four-Hour Bagel Shop. "Spare change? Spare change?" "I'll take a dollar, too." "I just need some money so I can get me some of what I need." A store window sign reads, GOING OUT FOR more BUSINESS. Your business! Cheap Persian rugs stretch across the sidewalk. "For sale, ladies. Everything's for sale." She's for sale. He's for sale. That fine specimen over there is available at the right price. Some people simply shriek as our friends go by. Some people hurry into stores with fear in their eyes and credit cards in hand, ready to Visa any discounted designer product they can find.

No one sees the gleam of metal, thin as a pin, silver, in Evilean's hand as she and her posse make their way uptown. They giggle loudly.

"She will just love it," says Josephine of their plans. They have grand plans for the night. Big plans. "Just wait," she assured her friends before letting out a shrill, breathy sound. Carl, Evilean and EmmaJean agree and respond the same.

They're having a good time.

4.

I read a lot—a lot of books, a lot of newspapers, and tons of magazines. Passes the time away. I came across this picture, in one of those weekly newsmagazines, of a row of uniformed men wearing orange rubber gloves. There they are looking in the direction of a group of people wearing T-shirts and jeans, business suits and ties, holding placards and marching in a circle before their eyes. The picture was taken right before a clash with the police, who are guarding a federal office, a homeless shelter, City Hall, or the convention center, where a scientific conference is taking place. The protestors have taken over an entire city avenue by taking two steps in place and one step forward, lifting first one leg and then the other, all to a simple chant: "Fight back. Fight AIDS."

Protest is magic. It reminds us that we can do something since *we are* these United States. Our blessed Madonna (that is, Evilean's, EmmaJean's, Josephine's, and Carl's idol, Madonna), had also cut this picture out of the magazine and would stare at it and dream. She, too, longed to protest in the streets. All her life she had looked for a group of people she could take over the streets with. First she looked for them in the Catholic Church (her father was a religious fanatic), then in New York City, with dance (Martha Graham) and music ("I'm Burning Up for Your Love" and "Like A Virgin"). She moved on to movies (*Desperately Seeking Susan, Who's That Girl*), and to concerts (The Blond Ambition Tour). She took on causes, like preserving the Brazilian rain forest ("Don't Bungle the Jungle"), Amnesty International, and racism ("Like A Prayer"). She appeared in the theater as a pawn of big Hollywood powermongers and became the pawn of big Broadway profiteers (*Speed the Plough*). Finally, she returned to the streets ("Vogue"), hoping she could at least become one with her fans—which meant she always forced them to think and say exactly what she thought and said, and together they formed a single body and a single soul, a single ring and a single protest to keep others from taking her number one position on the charts.

Her four most devoted fans were in their neighborhood record store poring over the lyrics of Madonna's "Vogue." Carl was reading aloud: "Ladies with an attitude, fellows that were in the mood. Don't just stand there, let's get to it. Strike a pose, there's nothing to it. Vogue."

They didn't say anything to each other for a while. They let the words sink into their heads, the music rise in their minds, the beat take over their bodies. Before you knew it they were bending their arms around their heads so they looked like living, modern-day Egyptian hieroglyphics, but not much like runway models direct from Paris.

"That's right, y'all," said Evilean, giving everyone a happy look. The four girls looked into one another's eyes, then the corners of their mouths began twitching with satisfaction, and finally they let out short, breathy sounds in the upper reaches of their vocal registers. And then another one of those sounds and another.

Meanwhile, Madonna roamed the streets of the city between the rivers utterly alone. Suddenly she raised her head as if sensing a rhythmic riff on the crest of a dusty breeze. A fragrance from the subway perhaps? She stopped, and in the depths of her soul heard the scream of a void yearning to be filled. She felt that somewhere nearby a protest of angry people was gathering, perhaps somewhere not far off a group of people was holding placards and chanting for human rights. . . .

She stood there for a while, looking around nervously. Then the secret beat suddenly disappeared (Evilean and EmmaJean, Josephine and Carl suddenly stopped voguing; their faces fell at the thought of a night without a party), and Madonna, restless and on edge, made her way home through the cool streets of the city between two rivers.

5.

I was in a protest once. It was in the spring of not-too-long ago and our new mayor had just decided to admit homeless PWAs (not quite POWs) to general population homeless shelters. During the election he had said it was too dangerous for persons living with AIDS, sick people, or people highly susceptible to disease to be placed in filthy shelters, and PWAs should be given single rooms to live in, with easy access to health care. So, like the simpleton that I am, I voted for him. Didn't even give it a second thought. I usually don't vote, but since I've been cooped up in this house I've had time to read the newspapers every day—too much time to think, if you ask me. It was definitely time to turn over a new leaf. So I mailed in my absentee ballot.

But things—attitudes—didn't change much when our new mayor set up his new office in the basement in (of all places) City Hall.

I got up to protest at 6:30 A.M. and took the train downtown, took the first open position in the protest ring, and marched and chanted for the memory of our mayor to return. We were circled by police who outnumbered us two to one. But that did not muffle our angry shouts: "Fight back. Fight AIDS." Finally, the mayor agreed to meet with us, and we left with smiles on our faces. But not for long. Not much changed. There were more pictures published of the mayor meeting with the protestors than of the actual protest.

Nowadays I'm too sick and too . . . too incontinent (that's probably not the right word) for public appearances, too weak to try
and raise a ruckus. Lord knows my momma would run away with
a hanky over her mouth and nose if she saw me like this. She can't
stand sickness. Wouldn't come near me even when I was little and
had a common cold. She'd make the soup, warm it up, but I'd have
to serve myself. I'd like to go protest at her apartment right now
and make a scene. That'd get her attention. She'd never speak to me
again. But I'm too tired for all that. I lose my breath now and again.
And that gets scary because you know the air's there, it's all over,
everywhere, but you can't get it in your lungs.

6. (On Two Different Diseases)

I'm not going to "bash" her. Her head fills the cover of this magazine. I'm not going to read her for all she's worth, with a snap of
the fingers and a roll of the eyes. A four-page feature article with
more pictures inside. How can I blame her? She, too, is seroposi-
tive. She, too, will die sooner than expected, sooner than other persons of her class, race, gender. I know her. She and I go way back.
Way back. I know all about her: where she lives, where she went
to school, what organizations she belongs to (very charitable society organizations), where her ancestors are from and how they got
here and why. Her hair could use some help, though. Look at it.
Flyaways. And she's on the cover of a nationally distributed magazine. Now if I'd done her hair, I would have given it a finishing
spritz. Photo shoots can be rough, especially if you've got an un-
photogenic subject. The rich-but-not-famous used to be my trade.
Before a grand cotillion, an opening, a big date. I was a novelty in
the world of coiffeur: a black man doing hair on Madison Avenue.
Well, I was the best kept secret around, with housecalls every Friday and Saturday afternoon. And when I handed them the mirror
after the final spray, their heads were mine from then on. But
would you look at this child on the cover of a magazine with flyaways. She's a novelty, too. And that's why she's there and I'm here.
I can't be mad at her. I don't want to rip up this rag, cancel my sub-
scription with a letter to the editor, telling him this woman in no

way represents the majority of people with AIDS. I'm sure the editor already knows this. I wouldn't want to be in a fucking magazine anyway, not the way I look nowadays. Too much foundation. I don't blame her, I don't blame her at all.

7.

Not too long ago, on one of my better days, a young man I didn't know came to see me. Without saying a word, he handed me an envelope. I tore it open and read this letter:

My dearest,
There's a rotten smell in the air and it's not coming from the Blond Ambi-
tion Tour. We're not burning up for love, either. An overloaded garbage barge
is circling Manhattan and all of the city between two rivers stinks. Espe-
cially Madison Avenue. It's as if we've been touched for the very first time.
I'm afraid our FREE garbage pickup service has come to an END. We've
been found out and I'm putting on a hoodie to try to save myself. Don't
worry, I've got you covered—with Snoopy and Linus's old blanket. It's just
like a prayer. We should thank our lucky stars if we get out of this intact.
                                                                        Always,
                                                                        D.

D. had tried to encode the letter so that only I could understand it, and I still didn't get everything he wrote. In fact, all I understood was that now, a year after the fact, my health insurance was coming to an end.

At that time I had a two-room flat in Washington Heights on Fort Washington Avenue—a very historic district in the city but most recently noted for its easy access to illegal substances and the bridge back to Jersey. Looking out of my windows I could see the highest point on the island of Manhattan, the place where old George lost old New York to the redcoats. I took refuge in that thought, in knowing just because you lose a few battles it doesn't necessarily mean you're going to lose the war.

The young man—who could have been one of D.'s lovers; he certainly was good-looking enough, seal-brown skin, a thin but muscular body; D. always had a taste for beautiful black men—

looked around cautiously, at my smelly apartment and my foundation-caked face. He obviously suspected that I was very ill and he looked at me with some mixture of compassion and pity. He was a blessing for my sore eyes so I didn't care—pity me now, take me here and now in my old crumbly apartment and I would die a happy man. We went outside and walked awhile in silence until we reached bustling Broadway. Then he told me that D. wanted to see me. A friend of his, whom I didn't know either, was lending D. his apartment in Harlem so D. and I could talk.

So the next day I got dressed, I put a rag on my head and more foundation on my face, and I took a short subway ride to the center of Harlem. Sometimes I thought D. went too far in his trying to hang with the brothahs. Why couldn't we have met at his apartment in Chelsea? Why did he have such a thing for black men and all things noir? I tried not to think about this and everything else while on the subway, tried not to look at people trying not to look at me. Like, why had he given me his insurance? Was the fact that he did not have AIDS—was indeed not even HIV positive—enough for him to not worry about now being listed on hundreds of government documents as such a person? I tried not to find answers for questions I didn't want to answer.

In the middle of the day, the stoops of all the boarded-up apartment houses of Harlem were filled with people hanging out; they stared right at me, through me, as if I weren't there. I paid them no mind. Finally, I found the right building, walked up six flights of stairs, looked for the right apartment number, and rang the bell. The apartment was silent. I rang again, but no one answered. I went back down to the street and walked around the block for an hour, assuming D. was late and I would definitely spot him, my milky blue–eyed friend, on this crowded Harlem sidewalk, walking up from the subway station. But he didn't show. I walked back up the six flights of stairs, now completely uncomfortable, and rang the bell again. Several seconds later I heard the sound of water flushing from inside the apartment. All at once I felt as though a dull knife had been thrust into my stomach.

Deep down in my own body I felt D. was not feeling well, not well at all.

He opened the door. He was pale but smiling, and he tried to play it cool. He made some bad jokes, like, "Well, here we are, finally alone in an empty apartment." We sat down, and he told me he had recently been called in by the head of his company's personnel office. She had spent an entire day questioning him. The first two hours she asked him about a lot of unimportant things, and he felt he was handling the situation. He joked with her and asked her flippantly if they thought he was going to skip lunch for this bull. That was when she asked him, Are you black? He blushed and tried to say something about his family having roots in the South. Do you now a Paul Jackson? she asked. He said he did. Was there anything wrong with that? Nothing at all, she answered. But do you happen to know that Mr. Jackson's using your insurance to get medical treatment for AIDS? No, he didn't. So you don't know anything about it, she laughed. All the office is talking about it and you don't know a thing? He went back to his innocence for a while, but then she began shouting at him to stop lying.

He told the truth. He decided to offer Mr. Jackson the insurance because he was unable to work and didn't have any insurance. The company had started donating to AIDS research organizations, and he didn't think anyone would get upset if he let someone else use his insurance. Anyway, he was never sick and all the insurance payments were going to waste. He was right, they told him, the company was committed to giving to lots of charitable organizations but it must first go through the proper channels. D. said that he didn't think it would have been accepted and she agreed with him—now all D. had to do was sign a form canceling his insurance policy, and not worry about a thing.

He signed, and two days later he received a pink slip, effective immediately. The same day he went to a competing advertising agency, where he had friends who had long been trying to lure him over. They greeted him with open arms. But the next day when he came back to take care of the papers, the head of personnel, who liked him very much, took him aside. "How could you have done a thing like that? Do you have *it,* too? There is nothing we can do for you."

At first he was afraid to talk to me. His former employer had promised to give him a good recommendation if he didn't let it get around exactly how easy it was to share medical benefits. But when he got another quick rejection, D. decided he had to see me, tell me my insurance had ceased, my discounted medications cut off.

D. was young. He was strong. He wasn't going to let this stop him. But then I realized I had become a black marker, and I began to feel afraid of myself.

"Do you think they know about the failed AZT/ddI studies?" I asked.

"Don't worry. Studies on AIDS are so fucked up that no one will ever check to see if you were in another study."

We tried to laugh, and even though the laughter lasted no more than half a second, I took it as a small promise of salvation. I tried to keep myself in check and tried to come up with a rational plan for D. to follow in looking for work. Several times during our talk he got up and went to the bathroom. Each time he came back accompanied by the sound of water flushing and a look of embarrassed panic. That courageous queer was ashamed of his fear. That humble homo was ashamed of his insides acting up before the eyes of his friend who now seemed like a stranger. And then again I thought maybe D. was not feeling well. Not well at all. But he never let on.

8.

Fifty or so fans of Madonna met in front of what they assumed was Madonna's apartment building. No one knew for sure if She lived there. Evilean, EmmaJean, Josephine and Carl stood in front of the crowd trying to get their attention. They were wearing the latest in Madonna wear: gold lamé halter tops and oversized gray pinstriped slacks with sequined panties on top of the pants. Well, the group had correctly chosen the home of their savior, and she looked down on them with a mixture of contempt and envy; she, too, wanted to be on the streets, part of a group, but she was alone, all alone in her penthouse apartment overlooking Central Park.

"We're going to do a little thing, I hope you like it. And if You are up there, Madonna, this one's for You." Josephine's voice trembled as she counted down for the girls to get into position. "Strike a pose!" and the accompanying music started, the dance version of the hit song. Evilean and EmmaJean, Josephine and Carl flexed their muscles to the beat of the music, flicked their fingers into elegant poses, twisted their bodies into the exaggerated stances of Erté statues.

The audience had no trouble figuring out that the girls had two points to make: (Point 1) that voguing was something that anyone could do, and (Point 2) that Madonna's song was intended to capture the attitudes that we all give off and to throw the attitudes back to people who don't know the same attitudes exist within themselves. They had decided to make both points using not only the words of the song, but their bodies as well.

Their golden-sheathed pointed breasts (implants! for Evilean, falsies for EmmaJean, Josephine, and Carl) bobbed up and down as they danced and grabbed at their crotches, and the audience froze into a sort of sympathetic embarrassment. It was as if these girls had escaped from a wax museum.

The only enthusiastic response to the show came from Madonna, who answered her fans' shrill, breathy sounds with her own version.

The girls marched back and forth in front of Madonna's building like—of course—models on a runway. Then Evilean took out her needle and syringe.

One of the members of the audience was a tall boy from Queens. Several days before he had asked to join the girls in their show (everyone knew beforehand that the show was going to take place) and the girls laughed him away. "Get your own act, girl. Be original," Evilean had laughed at him. They weren't going to let some nobody in on their act. It was a matter of loyalty, friendship, for that was of the utmost importance to these four girls. They had grown up together, gone to preschool together (and discovered sex soon after), fought together, and made up plenty of times before the next day. After their mothers and brothers and fathers and sisters disowned them ("Freaks," Evilean's brother had yelled as he stabbed her new breast), left them for dead (blood and silicon spilling all over the piers, he threw his bloody knife in the river and ran away), they were the only family they had left. Sisters. Evilean, EmmaJean, Josephine, and Carl. And they were not looking to adopt.

Ever since that boy from Queens had been rebuffed, he had held his grudge, and he was glad to see them making fools of themselves.

Each girl took her turn in solo performance, mostly copying the video—already in heavy rotation—even to the point of having a flash go off whenever one of them jumped in the air. Occasionally they shined their needles and faked sticking one another. The boy from Queens realized what a shame it would be to let this kind of opportunity go by. During a short pause when EmmaJean turned the stage over to Evilean, the boy from Queens walked up to the girls and took a syringe out of EmmaJean's hand and actually stuck Evilean in the behind with it—although it didn't make it through the triple layer of material: outer sequined panties, slacks, and inner panties. Everyone gasped as he kicked the stunned Josephine in the butt, then Carl, EmmaJean, and finally Evilean, the one he disliked the most.

For a moment there was absolute silence.

Then tears started rolling down EmmaJean's cheeks and, a split second later, down the other girls'.

Then the audience broke.

The boy from Queens skipped down the street and down into the subway.

Then Madonna, who had at first been surprised and shocked, caught on: The little prank had been part of the joke, showing the attitudes for what they were, and since she could not see her darling little fans' tears (she was too high, up on her balcony, to see such fine detail), she raced down her private elevator to join her most cherished ones.

Seeing their beloved superstar right before them made the girls cry even more. They went out of control.

Madonna took her darlings' state—that is what it was, a state—for a dance, and all at once a force more powerful than her coolness would allow escaped her open mouth. She laughed so hard she cried, and her body began twitching. She swung her head back and forth like an upside-down break dancer performing for a Times Square audience of tourists. She grabbed the girls by the hands and started running away from the crowd, which was in total shock. They ran over to Broadway and then uptown toward Harlem, crying and laughing at the same time.

As they ran, people turned in horror at the sight. Evilean turned and connected glances with Madonna, and they both understood what was going to happen next. As Evilean passed a woman dressed in a floral Laura Ashley outfit, she jabbed a needle into the woman's ass. The other girls laughed, then giggled even harder. Josephine and Carl had their turn with the next designer-dressed woman they passed. The laughing became uncontrollable. They did not turn to see the horror in the faces of their shocked victims. They ran. They laughed. They giggled so hard when EmmaJean missed a jab that they did not realize their idol, probably already bored with them, had faded completely from their midst. Madonna had vanished.

9.

I hear their giggles. I hear their laughter coming in my bedroom window. Sometimes it sounds like they're right here in this bed beside me, cackling, cracking up, hiding behind the headboard, at the foot of the bed, all four of them crawling under my mattress, snickering, rocking the bed, making enough noise to raise the dead.

But I'm not ready to go. At least not yet.

"Go away. Get the fuck out of here," I shout. Yell. I wake myself up screaming.

During a brief moment of weakness today, I called my mother and left a message. Most of the time I don't. Usually I call and just hang up when the answering machine starts. Since she got the answering machine about two years ago, she never answers her phone. She always screens her calls. Can't be bothered. She's abandoned me as sure as Evilean, EmmaJean, Josephine, and Carl's families abandoned them: Evilean's mother left him for dead way before Evilean's brother stabbed her in the tittie; EmmaJean's mother's boyfriend liked EmmaJean to play dead when he fucked her; Josephine's mother is dead; and, at the age of eleven, Carl's mother sold him for a nice little sum to a dentist on 169th Street in the Bronx.

My mother, like theirs, refuses to see or hear from her dying son. It's as if I were never alive.

10.

My meeting with D. in the borrowed flat in Harlem was a turning point for me. It was then I came to grips with the idea that I had become more than a burden and could not go on living among the people I loved if I wanted no harm to come to them. The only thing left for me to do was to cut myself off physically from other people and write down the stories of my life.

But I have another reason for remembering my last meeting with D. I had always been fond of him in the most innocent, asexual way. It was as if his body was always entirely hidden behind his generosity, his modest behavior, his Yuppie taste in dress, and his exclusive association with black men. He had never offered me the slightest opportunity to imagine him as sexy. And now suddenly that knife of fear had stripped him naked. He was as open to me as a lone man in the Ramble, standing behind a bush with full leather accessories on. There we were, sitting side by side on a couch in a borrowed apartment, the gurgling of the water filling the empty toilet tank in the background, and suddenly I felt a violent desire to make love to him, to rape him. Or, to be more exact, a violent desire to have him fuck me. To throw myself on top of him and take possession of him with all his intolerably exciting contradictions, his impeccable outfits, his rebellious insides, his reason and his fear, his pride and his misery. It was contradictions like these, I felt, that made up his true essence—that treasure, that nugget of gold, that diamond I wanted buried deep within me now and forever—my ass and his penis.

But I also felt his restless eyes on me, never pausing in one place, never knowing where they were going next. And when I thought about the way he was feeling, I knew, I just knew, there was no way.

When I left the borrowed apartment that day and walked out into the crowded streets of the housing development (he stayed upstairs to relax awhile) I could think of nothing but my monumental desire to be fucked by that fine boy, my friend. Like the little fine tell-tell scars around the nipples of breasts implanted with silicon, that desire will remain with me forever.

THE COLOR OF RAIN

Michael Villane

1. Whore

He hears footsteps on the street behind him, and they bounce off the walls of the buildings around him, and he starts to get hard. He knows he could get fucked, just by the stride of those steps, how far they stay behind, the way they follow him at a certain length, pursuit without stalking. Sex is what he instinctually knows. It's like the first time he ever did dope. He lay on the futon in his room, his mouth dry, touching his nipples, and even though he usually hated to touch his own nipples (someone else always has to do it), he kept drawing circles around them and lightly flicking them while Erykah Badu was nodding off with him over his stereo speakers and he knew, he instinctually knew he would die some-day from a heroin overdose, that his whole life had waited for and then created this moment, and this was the first step to an in-evitable end.

But these footsteps make him think that maybe this guy (be-cause he knows the footsteps are male) will be the one he spends the rest of his life, his youth with, which are one and the same, be-cause he could never see himself as a forty-five-year-old anyway. And then again maybe this will be the one that kills him, like that guy who is killing all those old guys and then stuffing them in Dumpsters, but then he thinks that's completely stupid because he's not old. Or desperate. At least not desperate because he can't get a man. He can't remember the last time he didn't have someone to call. Someone to fuck. And he thinks that maybe this guy could save him from all that, and he could retire from hustling and get a real job, like temping in advertising, take a word processing course, be at work at nine, leave at five, and maybe go lift and then pick up some food on the way home from the gym and cook up something quick and talk about how the day was and then fuck before you do the dishes, do the dishes before you shower and go to bed, while his come is still on your chest and stomach and as you turn to get the next dish off the counter you can feel the come, dry and hard, feel it pulling on your skin and the hairs on your abs that have grown in again because you're not trying to pass for twenty-six anymore and be a smooth-skinned man-boy but exist as you really are, with your own real identity, not one assumed for someone whose breath and hands make you want to throw up, throw up when he touches you and shoves his tongue into your mouth and you want to scream and silently you do, you scream your head off and you wonder what that hard bump is on the top of his tongue and will one grow in your mouth because he's entered you and now maybe he'll always be there even after he's come, even after he's paid and you've left, but his bump is in you and on you and maybe growing and you wonder was it worth it, as you put the last dish from the sink in the drying rack and lean against the counter feeling sick and scared and wanting to vomit the growing lump out of you, puke it, shit it out any opening, any hole in your body, and make you normal and clean and whole again, not fertile for other people's shit.

And he leans against the cold brick wall of the building, on the damp ground as the wet footsteps come nearer, and he lets a lock of his hair fall over his eye knowing that the streetlight will catch the gold highlights, and looks up as the man passes before him, close enough to feel the breeze and the heat of a body, but keeps going and gets smaller and smaller in his field of vision and his escape turns the corner and the knot in his stomach, the lump rises up for just a moment and sweeps over him in deep, claustrophobic waves but he forces it back down as he stands up from the wall and regains his balance and continues walking, walking in the direction opposite of what could have been, walking and thinking about nothing, not missing his life anymore.

2. H

He continues on past Crowbar and down Avenue B as he heads towards Seventh, to where tonight's entertainment will be found in a ten-dollar bag of dope. Or Hope. Or something like that. It all seems the same, one direction, one path taken and he starts to feel lonely and he heads down Seventh toward Avenue C and he thinks how much he loves this neighborhood, the squatters in the burned-out buildings, salsa music blaring from boom boxes on top of car roofs, the alternating smells of garbage and fried plantains. His father said the neighborhood was about as charming as Bosnia, and he thinks that's a perfect place for someone like himself.

Four stoops down he spots who he's looking for and he gets clammy all of a sudden, a little light-headed because he's new at this, has never actually bought for himself, has always gotten it off someone else. The stories about crack-head dealers with sawed-off shotguns, higher than fucking kites, blowing people's brains out just for looking at them make him think that maybe he should wait for his friend Gregg to cop for him; but he doesn't want to wait for anyone anymore, has never really been good at waiting for anything.

As he moves toward the guy in the leather jacket and baggy jeans, tank top stuck to his smooth muscular chest, he thinks he'd like to blow him for the dope instead of pay, but figures the offer alone might get him killed and he gives him fifty dollars and leaves with five bags. It really is that easy, he thinks, going around the corner, and he gets hard for the second time in ten minutes and laughs. He really is a fucking whore: In fact, he's a whore's whore, his whole life has revolved around sex. Twenty-three years to be exact, ever since he was eight and learned how to jerk off from his thirteen-year-old Uncle Kevin. His father's little brother, he would spend every summer with them, including his father's two-week vacation, which was always spent in the same rented cottage on Cape Cod, right on the water.

They went the same time every year, last week of July to the first week of August, which meant they would spend his birthday there. He would always have his birthday party on the beach, something none of the kids in his neighborhood or at school could claim. It always made up for having a summer birthday with no party at school, and for being away from his neighborhood friends, too. It is something he can always seem to remember, the taste of black raspberry ice cream mingled slightly with the salt from the sea air.

But that year, that was the year that everything changed. Kevin whispered, coaxing him onto the top bunk, taking his hand under the sheet and making him rub his cock, the way he kept staring into his eyes as he forced his hand back and forth. His horror at liking what he was doing, especially with someone who looked like his father. It excited him, his first conscious hard-on, Kevin stroking him to his first orgasm, that convulsing roll of pleasure. He had never felt anything like that before; it raced through him, rolled over him, tore him out of that airtight suburbia, pulled him out like an undertow, an undertow that would submerge him in an ocean of shame and craving, slowly drifting further and further away. The craving would always be physical, and never again would he be able to stop thrashing around long enough to hold his head above water and breathe.

But he would spend the rest of his life looking to be rescued, and he remembers John, wonders where he is; probably getting laid, or at least out on the hunt. It's pretty early yet, and he knows John would never commit to a piece of ass this early in the game. That would be like conceding, calling the game early, admitting defeat. John admits defeat only to further the cause of his Holy Grail–like self-loathing, to tell himself that the sex doesn't matter, that no one could ever really love him anyway. Kevin, John, himself: kissing a mirror image, and fucking yourself into oblivion.

He remembers reading Steinbeck's *East of Eden* in eleventh grade, the line about Cathy, how some people are born monsters, fearing that line was written for him. Was his need to devour a need for control? Even in sex he is in control. For all his mindless debauchery, he has always set the limits, constructed all the parameters. He has never even let someone jerk him off, take control of his pleasure, not since his uncle. He sometimes thinks the man who can do that, take that, or at least negotiate the surrender will be the one he spends the rest of his life with. His knight in shining armor, his prince, able to make him come with a stroke of his hand. He almost laughs at how high he has set the goals of his life, but can't, just continues on to East 4th St.

3. Play

He enters the bar, pausing at the door for dramatic effect. He hates this; he has never been good at the bar scene, small talk, the pretension of higher cause. All he wants to do is fuck. That's all any of them are really capable of, but tell themselves that it is a relationship that they want, a partner, commitment. All he wants is dick. Really big dick. He thinks maybe he should just have it printed on a T-shirt, but figures that it probably already comes across just fine.

With contrived nonchalance he walks to the bar and waits for the bartender's attention, craving a drink. The cute little blond boy-bartender *who was raised in a really small town like him and dreamed of growing up to be a bartender in a fabulous gay bar in NYC so men could ogle him* gives him his best, most well rehearsed genuine and sincere "Hey" and takes his drink order. He tips well (better with you than against you), heads with his blue margarita on the rocks, no salt, to sit on the covered, crowded pool table, does his best Sharon Stone leg cross, and begins the task of meaningful eye contact, in search of any signs of life, something to cling to in this vast sea of bodies.

He makes eye contact with a beautiful Latino boy in a tight black T-shirt that reveals the smooth rise of his chest, like small sand dunes. Gleaming black hair and eyes, skin the color of wet sand, he can see the ripple of his abs, the cut of his back—he can't even be nineteen. The boy smiles at him, licentious intent, wholesome delivery, ready to trade the best of himself to fit into a world that will gladly consume him, body and soul. He smiles back, which makes the boy blush, almost giggle. He wants him, a want he knows the boy wouldn't understand, but someday probably will. Some cultures sacrifice virgins as offerings of appeasement; he would sacrifice this boy like that, to feed his hunger, stave off the slow swell of emptiness filling his colorless soul: a soul almost transparent, the color of rain.

At almost the same instant, out of the corner of his other eye, he can see another man, the polar opposite of the boy, cruising him. Early forties, shaved head (baldness, not fashion), goatee, built like a brick shit-house. Daddy. At the least tonight's selections require decision making, the least of his extremely small list of marketable skills. And slowly but surely they are each making their way toward him, intending to stake a claim. He loves this, he hates this: the possibility of the wrong choice, the opportunity missed, the bad decision. And when left to his own devices under the best of circumstances, he will always make the wrong decision. Sexually it is a given. He feels that he must literally choose between good and evil, an angel and the devil.

Waves of desire wash over him, he can smell it, taste it, and he becomes momentarily paralyzed by the actual panic he feels rising inside, a feeling like sexual vertigo. He has no idea what to do, he wants both, he tries to think of a way to bring them both home. He knows Daddy won't mind, in fact will probably he thrilled; but he looks at the boy and knows he needs him right now, that he could never be enough, could never satisfy him, but wants him like a fix, like a bag, and he remembers the bags in his right front pocket as they rub against his semi-hard-on, and he looks up as he feels the hand carefully touch his shoulder. The boy has won, is standing in front of him grinning and blushing, the victor of a contest he has no knowledge of entering. The boy is so close he can smell him: black raspberry ice cream and salty air, his scent like truth.

He tries to say something, anything, but he can't, he's immersed in those black eyes, all that truthfulness, has never thought truth to be beautiful; but now he can't look at him, he can't smile, he can't even breathe, and he looks over to the side to see Daddy sneering at him, almost laughing at the look on his face, amused by his paralysis. He fights against the confusion but loses his breath, as if both of them are sucking the air out of him, and it scares him, the loss of control makes him angry, and he thinks, Fuck it, fuck them all. He slams back his drink, shakes off the hand as he jumps up, and heads for the door without looking back.

4. Salvation

He pays the ten-dollar admission at the counter, waits for the click of the lock release, and heads through the turnstile. His eyes adjusting slowly to the extreme dark, he can make out bodies but not faces, and he immediately begins to search for an empty booth, setting priorities: (a) get high, (b) get fucked. Life is good. These are the skills he does possess, and they begin to make him feel at ease, make the sickness minimal and exciting.

The room is a box within a box with lots of doors. You walk around the center box with a door on either side of you, most of them occupied, some of them open to almost reveal their occupants: men in various stages and degrees of exhibition and disguise. The choice between exhibition and disguise depends upon how good-bad-looking they are, what their trip is, or maybe just momentary self-esteem. The ugly and the old generally choose the dimmest light, the darkest corner: Blanche hanging her Chinese lantern, looking for her paperboy.

He was walked this hallway time and time again, has been pawed, rebuffed, smiled at, hissed at. All of the booths seem to be had, and he thinks in order to get one of them he's going to have to get someone off. Then after they release, the rush of guilt and shame will hit them and he can assume their space. He hopes it won't be someone ugly, someone who makes him want to puke. He really wants to get high first: (a) drugs, (b) dick. He clutches at this sense of order, priorities set.

Turning the corner he sees an empty room, checks the bench to make sure it's clean, closes the black plywood door by putting his foot underneath it and lifting up with his leg in order to slide the bolt into the lock. He pulls out his color vinyl X-Men wallet and two little bags, unwraps the pink plastic and unfolds the white wax paper, carefully spilling the brownish powder on the wallet, cutting four big lines with his David Barton gym membership card. He does two of the lines, leans back against the wall, not thinking, just waiting, Zen-like. And then it starts to hit him. Heat. Power. He remembers being a kid and climbing the hill behind his house so he could stand under the power lines, feel the heat from them, hear them hum. He'd lie down so he could feel them crackle, and he can feel it now, and he knows this is it, every time he starts to get off he gets this same sensation and he is back home lying in the high grass of that hill wanting to feel the crackle, the heat, feel anything, and it's rolling in, coming on, the undertow releases him (for now), stops pulling, and he floats, free, he is free and reaching for his wallet, for another line.

He does another line and his mind is washing over him, his memory breaks free from the place where he keeps it locked away, released from the undertow, and he starts to see things, the things he shuts off like a light switch at will, but now it's okay, it's fine, and he sees his family, the big brown house built into the side of the hill with the stone retaining wall holding it up, holding him up, but it breaks free, too, and purple, blue, and reddish slate goes flying and there are the men he slept with rising through the earth, heaving their way to the top and formulating an order within the chaos of his life. There is his best friend from junior high, the one after his uncle whom he used to sleep with in the tent in his backyard, and his neighbor's nephew from Chicago, who used to like to pretend they were brothers, and the guy from his Boy Scout troop who sucked him off on the back staircase of the church basement during the Pinewood Derby; the blonde from the dorm his one year at college, the first man ever to fuck him.

They start coming faster, there are so many, but he is calm and he just watches and smiles, nods his recognition, winks, remembers his first trick, the young stockbroker who had two kids and a wife who had them followed, had him subpoenaed into their divorce proceedings with her parents staring at him while he was on the stand, but even that humiliation can't touch him—he smiles, he giggles, and they keep coming and coming and they get close but never really touch (never really did) and then he sees him, he sees that lopsided grin, he sees John and everything slows down. He brushes the base of his neck against the painted plywood wall of the booth as he strains to ignore him, tries to focus on the blur of the video screen, but can't. He abandons interruption and relinquishes to the undertow.

It seems so long since he's seen him, he knows it's only been days. Everything gets slower and slower, and John starts toward him and he starts to remember their first date. They went to a movie and he held his hand, they were soft and big like his own, and he rested his chin on his shoulder, then they went for pizza. Their first kiss was in that pizza parlor with the old Pakistani man behind the counter watching them, revolted, but he hadn't cared because this was different, this was something new. They went on dates, and they would hold hands on the street. He was thirty-one years old and he realized that he was falling in love for the first time, that he wanted to be with him every day. He would call him at work every day just to say hi, just to make sure he was still there, just to feel ordinary, normal.

They were just about the same age (John was two years younger), the same height, build, and John would tease him and say that he had better abs, but he would let him, he liked the teasing, and he would throw back how he had a better ass. It felt nice when they would talk after sex, when they would read magazines on the couch and drink cafe con leche from the Spanish bakery on the corner, and John loved the movies, too, and sleeping in on Sundays. They decided they would be mature, take it slow, maybe see other people at first. They were adult, they were being realistic, but it was getting harder to turn tricks, to sleep with other men, to divide himself in two and then form into a whole person again in front of John.

Still he's not sure when everything started to fuck up. He thinks it might have been the night that John bagged out on dinner and a movie and he got jealous, thinking that maybe John was going to hook up with someone else; looking back, it was probably the truth. He knew John slept with other men, and given his own line of work (which they had not discussed; he "temped") and his own wandering eye he wasn't really sure how to broach the subject, really wasn't equipped to stake a claim. But when he allows himself to remember he knows it was the night they were fucking and he kept wanting to say "I love you." He's still not sure why he had wanted to say it, if there was even anything about John that ever warranted it. But he wanted to say it so bad it hurt, and he couldn't. He just mouthed the words while John was kissing him; he just said them into John's mouth and let them be swallowed, barely able to breathe, unable to utter the sounds.

That night he woke up after they had passed out from fucking and sat up so fast he had almost hit his head on the ceiling. He hated John's loft bed, jokingly called the treehouse—he felt too old to be playing treehouse, and the futon was too fucking thin. It was really hot and he was trying to breathe while John slept, watching him breathe as he himself struggled for air. He was having a panic attack, he wanted to leave, he was sticky and hot, there was no air and he knew if he left he would never come back. So he backed away and sat cross-legged against the wall, watching John's body, unable to breathe, watching John breathe. His body was long and stretched over the too thin futon, his breath slow, beautifully slow. John looked like he was smiling, but he wasn't smiling; he was just peaceful, the look on his face was just peace. And he thought that in the whole month that they had been dating he'd never seen John look like that. Not even after they fucked. He wondered if he looked that way after fucking someone else. And he thought about how John would sometimes get that look on his face when he was inside him, how his face would bend in disdain, his eyes would burn, and it would be someone else, not him, he wasn't there, but someone else was and he would feel that fear, that dirtiness, and his uncle Kevin would flash for a moment, that feeling, and he didn't know if it ignited in himself or John. But it was that night he re-alized that they did not make love, they never had, they fucked, and that's all they would ever do. For the first time in his whole life he had the thought that it might not be his fault, he might not be the one to blame. And he knew if he got up he would not come back. The lack of air, the heat, John's smell, his beauty had all hit him, it had hit him and he was terrified, terrified because he knew he could leave, that John could do the same and he was scared to feel anything more than he was right now. He knew when he left he would die, even if he never had before with any other man, any other time. And even if he probably wouldn't die from all this shit he was scared—and he hated being scared. He had spent his entire life trying not to be scared anymore.

So he lay back down and smelled John, trying to find truth in his scent, finding none. He traced the line of his body from the base of his throat to his belly button, staying there, smelling him again, praying to be wrong. He remembers falling asleep on John's stomach, slowly regaining the ability to breathe.

And three nights later when John canceled again (he was tired from going out with "friends" the night before) he had called him from a pay phone by the boathouse in Central Park and told John he could not see him anymore, that it wasn't what he wanted; and even when John said that he was acting childish, why be like that, he really liked him a lot and they were just seeing each other anyway, and that he thought he was really special and really sexy and funny and would miss him blah blah blah blah blah, he couldn't hear him, he couldn't see him; he had just made eye contact with a fiercely gorgeous black guy who was headed deeper into the park.

He got off the phone (he still doesn't know how) and followed the guy up the faintly lit path into the dark, into the trees where he couldn't see but stood and waited, listening to the ground give way under the approaching feet behind him, felt the hand graze his ass as it reached around his hip for the button on his jeans. He reached behind him and felt the T-shirt, felt for skin, copying the move made on him and popping open the jeans. Turning he sees nothing, unable to make out a face but feeling lips: soft, full, wet, they were on him and he couldn't feel them, off his mouth to his chin, his throat, down to his chest, and he knows the mouth is on his cock, but it really doesn't register. He tries to focus, but he's not there, and as the tongue wraps around the head of his cock he wishes he was high, feels something in himself rise up, thinks it's the lump, but not sure what it is forces it back down, makes it go away, pushes it away, comes, and walks out of the woods alone.

5. Hope

He does not know how long he has been sitting in the booth; it feels like minutes, it seems like days. He stares at the little video

screen that holds no image but a dull, gray light, and opens another bag, thinking a small line just to keep him buzzing, a really
small line, and he does another, unable to assess how much. He
tries to stand, grabs the wall, clears his head. He feels the sticki-
ness of the floor under his feet and puts away his H, his wallet,
and knows he wants to leave with someone and opens the door,
allowing exposure.

Men walk by, and he wants them but only their bodies, he wants
to get fucked and not have to talk. A man approaches him and he
looks good, kind of blond or something, and he lets him in the
booth and guides his hands up to his nipples and tries hard not to
look fucked up and then rubs his chest, kisses his neck, realizes the
door is still open, doesn't care, stubs his hand down the man's body
to his dick, it feels small, he wants it to be big; he needs to be
fucked hard by a really big dick, and he takes the man's hands off
his chest and shakes his head no, he doesn't want to, he has to go,
please just leave, and he does.

He stand at the door, everyone looks ugly. The guy he just felt
up looks away as he walks by. He thinks he sees someone who
looks familiar. It's the guy from the bar, Daddy, and he nods to him,
but he walks by. He waits and he walks by again and comes into
the booth and closes the door behind him and locks it and says
where'd you disappear to, but he can only smile, words aren't coming out anymore, and he kisses him, he kisses Daddy on the mouth
really hard and holds on to him, feels the weight of him, and they
bounce against the wall and Daddy squeezes his nipples really hard
and smiles and he slides his hands down on Daddy's dick and it's
big and he's happy and Daddy coos in his ear that he lives right
around the corner and they are leaving, click they go through the
turnstile and out onto the street, it's late, really late he thinks, he's
talking, he's babbling something, but it's babble and that's all and he
keeps moving, they are in the hallway they are in the bedroom, he
has to go to the bathroom.

Closing the door he takes out the bag, no time to cut, he dips
the edge of his gym card into the bag, flushes the toilet as he snorts,
goes into the room, Daddy is naked, he is really big, it is kind of
like he is posing. He laughs inside his head or maybe out loud, he's

not sure, but Daddy grabs him kisses him pulls him down on the bed starts taking his clothes off, he's rough, it's nice, he can feel it and then Daddy is over him and greasing his cock, and he tells Daddy use a condom and Daddy laughs and he laughs and says no glove, no love, and Daddy laughs and says fuck you and he says no fuck you and starts to get up and Daddy punches him in the face and he can't seem to breathe, he's not scared, though, and Daddy tells him to shut the fuck up but he doesn't think he's saying anything and Daddy flips him over and calls him faggot and he remembers his uncle Kevin the summer after the first one when they had sex and he came back and he waited for him, he waited for a week and nothing happened, so one night he climbs in the bunk and touches Kevin and Kevin punches him and calls him faggot and throws him off the bed and his parents came in and started yelling what was the matter and Kevin is screaming lies about you and you are crying and the look on your mother's face as she hits you your father turns away from you, won't look at you can't see you and she keeps screaming and slapping and spits on you and then Daddy is fucking you, where are you he's going to come in you oh god your nose is bleeding and the lump rises up again, it rises up and blisters, exploding inside you and everything is pulling like water swirling and it feels quiet and peaceful and the water is there the tide is in the undertow strong from when you were on the beach at your family's house and you lay on the sand and prayed to be pulled out pull you out pull you away and it gets you away and you are filling up slowly and it's quiet, but then they dragged you out screaming made you come back screaming but now you're laughing not screaming and you can feel Daddy but can't see him, it's pulling you away and you're laughing and laughing and don't think you'll come back this time, this time you think you'll stay under where it's quiet, where no one can see me, where it's safe.

ERASING SONNY

Kelly McQuain

Friday night, as he had done for the last three weeks, Sonny Ciccarelli accompanied his sister, Maria, to her boyfriend's South Street apartment. On the long walk up from the heart of South Philly, Maria told her younger brother that she and Richie Avicolli had a passion straight out of *Titanic*. "But nothing will ever wreck us," she added, making Sonny think of their parents, who didn't like their daughter dating a much older boy, even though Maria was eighteen and would graduate from St. Maria Goretti in June. So Maria lied and told her mother she was watching videos at a girlfriend's house. Taking Sonny along helped legitimize the excuse—who, after all, would bring a kid brother on a date?

Even in late winter South Street was full of guys from down Sonny's way and blacks from the projects, cocky young men strutting around in Tommy Hilfiger knockoffs. Sonny didn't care for their mob mentality, the way tempers often erupted in fists. The girls on the strip didn't interest him either—too much hair and caked makeup. Even his own sister was sometimes hard to recognize beneath all the goo she spackled on. But Sonny liked being with her, helping out.

Maria put her key in the door to Richie's building and gave Sonny a sideways look—time for him to get lost so she and Richie could take care of each other upstairs. Sonny played it cool. He hated when Maria started suggesting places he could hang out. He mumbled something about Tower Records and Zipperhead—

stores he had no intention of entering—until Maria, satisfied, headed inside. "You can buzz me up later," Sonny called after her.

Sonny kept a mental list of reasons why Richie was cool and ran through it in his head as he shifted his weight from foot to foot, trying to keep warm on the cold street. Richie was twenty-three and wore snakeskin boots, ripped Levis, and black T-shirts that clung to his rangy build. His take-no-crap attitude was evident in every flash of his thick-knuckled fists. He had an earring and long hair like someone on MTV, and a little black *diabolico* goatee that sometimes left red marks on Maria's cheeks. Sonny wondered what it must feel like scraping your face against something as wiry as that.

Usually Sonny waited an hour before pressing Richie's buzzer, but tonight was so cold that he shaved ten minutes off his usual time. Upstairs, Maria stood behind the open wedge of Richie's door, dressed only in a black lace bra and panties. She let her brother inside the apartment, then slid the deadbolt tight.

The apartment was stifling hot, a high-pitched hum emanating from the radiator against the far wall. Richie lay stretched out shirtless on his bed, his skin slick and shiny with sweat. Sonny said hello, and Richie smiled lazily in response. Maria climbed onto the rumpled bed and curled in close to her boyfriend. Richie cupped her breasts with his arm, and Sonny noticed that his left shoulder was covered with a tattoo of Donald Duck smoking a cigar. As soon as Sonny laid eyes on it, he knew he wanted one just like it.

Maria patted the edge of the bed, told her brother to take off his coat and sit down.

The boy did, then took a slug from the bottle of Jack Daniel's Maria passed him, chasing it with a mouthful of soda from the Dr Pepper he had bought while waiting outside. Richie and Maria lit up a joint. Sonny, who didn't like to smoke, scanned the new drawings taped to the walls around the room.

Richie could draw extremely well and didn't consider it a sissy thing to do. "You're the bomb," Sonny had told him a month ago when they had first met. Back then, Richie's walls were covered with sketches of Wolverine and The Incredible Hulk, heroes whose savage muscles had been crosshatched to perfection. But Richie had ripped his work to shreds two weeks ago after returning from a comic convention in New York City where he'd shown his portfolio to editors at Marvel and DC. "My proportions are off," he had fumed. "I don't know shit about perspective." He gave up drawing superheroes altogether, bought a box of dog-eared Disney comics, and began training himself in a style that would make Uncle Walt proud. But within days, Richie's true nature corroded his good intentions, as if someone had filled his ink pens with battery acid. His kiddy cartoons degenerated into dirty drawings of Mickey Mouse and Pluto gang-banging Minnie, of a buck-toothed Goofy masturbating. He hung up the new work in place of the old. Now, taped to his walls, was a copyright lawsuit just waiting to happen.

Sonny stretched out on the foot of the bed and rolled back toward the lovebirds. Maria cradled Richie's head in her lap. Her bleach-blond hair fell in loose curls as she bent over to kiss him, blowing smoke into his mouth. The pair looked at Sonny and laughed.

The boy nodded at the tobacco-loving duck on Richie's arm. "I'm going to get a tattoo exactly like that when I turn eighteen."

Richie grinned. "Why wait?"

"Need to save money."

Richie raised his head off Maria's lap. "Go to the skin scratchers around here and you'll get robbed. Some weasel from the projects will blow your head off." He took a long draught of Jack. "I could do you right here."

Richie's offer sounded like a dare. Sonny's stomach trembled.

"You don't have the guts," Maria told him. She finished off the joint and lit a cigarette.

Richie handed her the bottle as he moved closer to Sonny. "Let's see what you got, kiddo." He pulled up the sleeve of Sonny's T-shirt and squeezed the boy's shoulder. "Shit, you ain't got muscle enough for one. You'd grow and it'd stretch like Silly Putty."

He made Sonny take his shirt off and lay chest-down on the mattress. Sonny's nose pressed against the dirty bedspread, and he breathed deep the smell of whiskey and sweat. He felt Richie's hand sliding over him, gliding across the span between his shoulder blades.

Richie drummed Sonny's skin. "On your back is where you need it."

Sonny rolled over and watched Richie pry the whiskey bottle from between Maria's legs. "But I won't be able to see it," he complained.

Richie poured some Jack into Sonny's Dr Pepper can. "Do you really need to see it to know you're cool?"

Sonny shrugged. He took a drink, barely able to taste the Dr Pepper now. While Maria went to the bathroom, Richie dug through his art supplies for a bottle of India ink and a needle. Sonny watched from the bed, admiring the play of muscles in Richie's shoulders, how Donald Duck rose and fell. By the time Maria returned, Richie had threaded the needle and sterilized it with a match.

"I take no responsibility for this," Maria said, dropping down on the bed, her eyes red and sleepy-looking. She yawned and rolled over, clutching a pillow as if it were a teddy bear.

Sonny's insides were all aflutter. He tightened his stomach muscles to cage the birds within. There was no backing out now. He excused himself and went to the bathroom, where he took a few deep breaths and splashed water on his face. Would a tattoo change the person he now saw in the mirror above the sink? Last summer, a girl he had briefly dated at the Jersey shore had told him his eyes were dreamy. Sonny leaned toward the mirror, closed his eyes, and counted to ten, then looked again. His pupils shrank at the influx of light. He had big sky blue irises, and his pupils floated in them like solar eclipses. Sonny supposed they were nice. But dreamy? He looked at his nose, round and slightly heavy like his father's, dented on one side from the time he had plowed his bike into his grandmother's Buick LeSabre. He ran his fingers over his olive skin, his cheeks rosy from the medicine his mother had bought him to fight blemishes. He turned his head from side to side to study his small ears, their insides as pink and delicate as a conch shell. How would he look with an earring like Richie's? Sonny studied his mouth and wondered how he had tasted to the girl at the shore who had kissed him. He pressed his lips against the cold surface of the mirror. Nothing. He sighed, and his breath fogged the glass. The pressure of his finger made a squeak as he wrote Richie's name. Sonny studied his reflection, blurred behind the letters. He leaned in close to kiss again, but was startled when Richie yelled to hurry up. He wiped all traces of the letters away and returned to his friend.

"Don't you need an outline to trace?" Sonny asked, sitting on the edge of the bed, wringing his T-shirt in anticipation while Richie finished cleaning his back with rubbing alcohol. Richie's long legs straddled the boy, and Sonny could feel the heat pouring off his body.

"I do my best freehand," Richie assured him, sinking the needle into Sonny's skin.

Sonny sucked in air between his teeth. He was glad Maria had fallen asleep and missed seeing him jolt at the first prick of pain. He felt as if all his nerve endings had knit together and lay beneath the spot Richie targeted with the needle. He calmed himself by picturing the ocean. For two weeks every August, Sonny's parents rented a house in Wildwood, and the whole family went down, including his grandmom Antonia. There over the years his parents had taught him and his sister to ride bikes and swim in the sea, to play pinochle on rainy days. And Sonny never felt closer to any of them than during that time away, when the family relaxed into how they were meant to be.

Sonny thought again of the girl last summer at the shore. They had written each other's names in the sand, then watched the waves lap the letters away.

But Richie dug too deep, making Sonny flinch. In the window above the radiator, Sonny cold see Richie's reflection, goatee and dark eyes blurred by the wavy heat. Sonny gritted his teeth and hoped his friend wasn't so drunk that Donald Duck would turn out wrong.

A sheen of sweat broke out upon the boy's skin. Despite the pain, he was glad to be connected to Richie this way. And after a little more whiskey, Sonny truly began to feel good at being bad. He didn't mind that Richie was taking what felt like liberties with the tattoo, stretching the image from shoulder to shoulder. Maybe

Donald Duck was lying down for his smoke. Even if it wasn't the same as Richie's, it would still be special—a gift among friends.

When Richie finally finished, he threw down the bloody needle and pinched Maria's toes so she'd wake up. Sonny glanced over his shoulder, but couldn't see anything. As Maria rose all groggy-eyed, Richie steered Sonny around so the girl could look at her brother's back. In the window, Sonny saw his sister's jaw drop like the muscle had been cut. Richie started to guffaw as Maria shook her head.

The birds of Sonny's stomach stirred once again. He ran to the bathroom. Standing with his back to the mirror, he craned his neck around, figuring that Donald Duck had been given a dribbling penis instead of a cigar. Instead, on his back, indelibly written for all time, were the two worst words you could say to somebody.

Eyes bleary and skin sore, Sonny stormed out of Richie's apartment and onto the street below. He whipped on the shirt and coat he had grabbed on the way out, then staggered down the windy strip.

He didn't get far before he heard Maria call his name. He turned to find her and Richie standing disheveled in their winter coats, hugging themselves against the cold.

Richie lowered his head as Sonny stared at him. "Dude, look at it this way—I gave you something way cooler than what you asked for. You're totally bad-ass now."

Sonny wished he had laser eyes like one of the superheroes Richie used to draw; he wanted to slice Richie in two. *I trusted you,* he wanted to say, but the words wouldn't come.

Richie dug his hands deep into his pockets. "Man, don't look at me like that. I gave you a god damn *motto.* You ought to thank me."

"He's sorry," Maria said, elbowing her boyfriend in the ribs. Richie nodded. For a long moment no one said a thing.

Finally Maria sighed and then spoke. "At least he spelled it right."

Concealing the tattoo from his parents became Sonny's obsession. All through late winter and early spring, he slipped a T-shirt on before his parents entered his room and donned a robe when leaving the shower. Of course, his school friends quickly spied the tattoo when Sonny changed clothes after gym class. Incredulous, the boys in the locker room traced their fingers over each letter as if Sonny were a dusty windshield. "Enough," he finally told them, his face burning as he shrugged them off and swore them to secrecy.

In late April, Sonny's parents almost found out. One Saturday afternoon, Sonny walked into the kitchen to find his mother giving his father a haircut. Salvatore Ciccarelli sat shirtless on a wooden stool, his pizza parlor apron draped over his shoulders, newspapers lining the floor beneath him.

Salvatore's hair had inched down the hair weave he wore, and his wife Karen was doing her best to make the natural hair taper into the synthetic blend. A few years back, Salvatore had undergone a hair replacement procedure that had given him a fake head of hair he could swim in the ocean with. Every four months Salvatore went to a special salon for an expensive haircut and tightening. In between, Karen staved off hairy encroachments. She worked as a nurse uptown at Thomas Jefferson University Hospital and was used to doing things for people.

"Hi, sport," Sonny's mother said as her boy grabbed a soda from the fridge. "Why don't you take your shirt off and let me give you a trim? I'm almost finished here."

The sight of his father's obvious rug depressed Sonny. Sometimes late at night he would catch his old man watching infomercials on scalp reduction and hair plugs, and Sonny would hurry to his room to spare them both any embarrassment.

Sonny gulped down his Dr Pepper. "Ma, I'm too old for at-home haircuts," he said as the tattoo on his back began to itch like poison ivy.

Karen did one more pass of the scissors over Salvatore's ears, then wiped off her husband with a dishtowel. "I don't want my son looking like a hippie."

"Well, I don't want you ragging on me."

Salvatore rose and approached his son. The tall man moved with a heaviness that reminded Sonny of a bear walking on hind legs. Salvatore cleared his throat and spoke, his thick South Philly accent weighing each word. "Talk to your ma like that again, and you won't be able to talk at all." He took his apron off his shoulders and shook it over a trashcan.

Karen reached over and snapped the waistband of Sonny's boxer shorts, which showed above the waist of his low-hanging jeans. "I told you not to wear your pants like that," she said. "Off with the shirt." She grabbed Sonny's shirttail and yanked it up.

Sonny jerked back, but his mother held tight. As he tried to twist free, he felt the cotton fabric creeping dangerously up his back toward his tattoo. He pushed his mother's hand away. "No." He balled his fists in his shirt and pulled it down.

Salvatore started to intervene, but Karen waved him off. The woman's Irish temper shone in her eyes. "What's the matter, my son a big man now? Honey, you ain't got anything I haven't seen before." She glanced at Salvatore, who was buttoning his shirt so he could head back to his shop. She threw her scissors in a drawer and crossed her arms. "Go ahead, pay for your own damn haircut. What do I care?" She smacked Sonny on the ass. "Now run upstairs and wash for lunch."

At the top of the staircase, Maria confronted Sonny. The smirk on her face told him she'd been eavesdropping. She leaned back against the doorjamb of her room and said, "You should have told her where to shove her scissors."

Maria's eyes were red, and the little fan on her windowsill was aimed outside. Sonny smelled a lingering trace of marijuana, and was shocked to discover that his sister had the nerve to smoke weed in the house.

Maria's eyes narrowed. "She thinks I'm still seeing Richie. You haven't said anything, have you?"

Sonny shook his head. Even though he'd stopped visiting Richie, he no longer wished any shit to befall him or Maria.

Maria's voice grew tired and sad. "One day I'm going to blow this dump. Hope that woman chokes on my dust."

Later that night, Grandmom Antonia called to say she had cleared the knickknacks off her credenza and needed two strong backs to lift up her new wide-screen TV, so Sonny walked over to his pop's pizzeria after closing time to recruit Salvatore for the job.

During the day, the Italian Market bustled with life—sidewalk vendors hawking produce from beneath canvas awnings, shopkeepers stocking windows full of imported olives and cheese, fishmongers icing down crabs whose blue pincers snapped at passersby. But at night the marketplace was quiet and scary. The canvas awnings above each shop cast sidewalk shadows the moonlight couldn't creep into. The metal Dumpsters lining the curb looked like abandoned train cars, reeking of rotten fruit and surrounded with construction equipment the city was using to dig up the street. At the parking lot at 9th and Catherine, the Anti-Graffiti Network's mural of former mayor Frank Rizzo covered an entire building side, and the dead man's jowly face loomed pale and ghostly.

Sonny hurried to his father's shop. The metal gate had already been pulled down out front, so he walked around back and slipped into the hallway by the kitchen. He heard voices up front and figured his father had a card game going. But as he walked forward, he noticed the room ahead was dark, the only illumination the faint light that spilled from the kitchen.

Sonny's eyes adjusted. He spied a shape sprawled over a table at one of the booths—too many arms and legs to be just one person. He made out his father's back. Someone's slim hands moved in circles over the fabric of the man's shirt. A woman's bare legs twisted around those of Sonny's father. Salvatore mumbled and laughed, bent over the women like he was tickling her.

But he wasn't tickling her. The woman exhaled, long and low, the sound turning into a breathy version of Salvatore's name. Sonny recognized the voice as Gina's, one of his father's waitresses. She went to school with Maria.

Sonny stepped back, bumping against a countertop and dislodging a push broom that smacked against the linoleum floor. He turned and started to run, but his feet got caught. He fell. He heard scrambled movement behind him as he pulled himself up and stumbled toward the kitchen. His chest hurt, and his legs felt wobbly, like he'd just survived a fight. Before he could reach the door, a hand clamped down on his shoulder.

Sonny turned to look at his father. Salvatore stood tall and menacing in the weak light, as spooky as the mural of Mayor Rizzo. "What you think you saw is not what you saw," Salvatore said.

"I'm not blind." The boy could feel tears wanting to rise, but he wouldn't let them.

"Gina's fella left her. She was crying." Salvatore squeezed his son's shoulder, as if the gesture could mold a lie into truth. He sighed and confessed, "Life is complicated."

In the dark behind Sonny's father, Gina sighed.

"Are we clear on this?" Salvatore asked.

Sonny nodded. Words came slowly as he told his father about his reason for dropping by. The hard cast of Salvatore's eyes softened, and Sonny knew that his father would walk alongside him the three blocks to his grandmother's house, that together the two of them would move her new TV, and that they would never again speak of this night.

Karen Ciccarelli found out about her son's tattoo one warm spring day when she decided to walk home from the hospital instead of taking the 23 bus. Sonny and some friends from the neighborhood were playing basketball in a court on 9th Street—shirts versus skins, and Sonny was a skin. A bunch of girls leaned against the chain link fence, fingers laced in the green mesh, cracking bubblegum as they gossiped. Sonny ignored them. The skins were two points behind and Sonny had just been passed the ball, only a couple of steps away from a perfect lay-up, when he heard his mother scream his name. He whirled in her direction as a shirt swiped the ball and headed back down the court.

Sonny froze at the sight of his mother. She stood in her white nurse's uniform just beyond the fence, hands on hips and a look in her eye almost as piercing as Richie's needle had been. The group of girls fell silent. Sonny's mother closed her eyes, took a deep breath, and lit a cigarette before speaking. "That had better be magic marker or you're going to be one sorry son of a bitch."

Sonny was one sorry son of a bitch. Back at the house, he sat at the kitchen table and listened to his mother berate him for his stupidity. When his father came home, the boy had to bare his skin once more and show him the shameful epitaph. Unlike Sonny's mother or the boys at school, Salvatore made no attempt to touch Sonny's tattoo. Since the night at the pizza parlor, he had become increasingly remote, like a man being pulled out to sea.

Karen called a fellow nurse to see if the tattoo could be scraped off somehow. Salvatore popped open a beer. Like his wife, he wanted to know who had done this, but Sonny refused to say. Salvatore shook his head. "I served two years in the Navy without getting so much as a single mark. Now look at you." As his wife spoke on the phone, Salvatore leaned forward to whisper, "You trying to get back at me?"

Sonny shook his head. He wished that had been the case, but he knew that nothing he could ever do would even things between them.

"Don't let your grandmom see this," Salvatore warned. "You'll break her heart."

Karen hung up the phone and sat down heavily in a chair. She looked at her boy out of the corner of her eye and lit another cigarette. "You're in luck, you stupid son of a bitch."

There was a month-long waiting list to see Dr. Rubenstein, the specialist in dermatology at the hospital where Sonny's mother worked, but by calling in a few favors, Karen Ciccarelli could squeeze her boy in two weeks early. The average price of each visit—and Mrs. Ciccarelli had been assured most patients needed more than one—was two hundred and fifty dollars a pop, an amount not covered by insurance. Upon hearing the thousand-dollar estimate, Sonny looked at his father and cracked, "There go your new hair plugs," for which the boy received a backhand across the face. It was the first time Sonny had been hit by Salvatore in years. "Knock it off," Karen Ciccarelli said before things could escalate further. "We can't afford dental work, too." She negotiated a grudging truce: Sonny would work off the debt at the pizza parlor, filling the absence created when Gina—suddenly and with no apparent explanation—had given notice.

The day of Sonny's initial consultation, the boy met his mother in the hospital lobby after school and walked with her to the doctor's office in a nearby building. Karen Ciccarelli smoked a cigarette on the way. "I hope they have to peel a skin graft off your ass," she told him. "I hope to hell it hurts."

After a brief wait, a nurse showed Sonny and his mother into a small examination room, when Dr. Rubenstein eventually joined them. The doctor was in his mid-thirties with a square jaw and a straight nose, neat dark hair gelled immaculately into place. He was clean-shaven, and though his eyes were every bit as dark as Richie's, a warm light glinted in them. He could pass for Italian if not for his giveaway name, thought Sonny.

Rubenstein wore a fancy silk tie knotted beneath his pronounced Adam's apple, and a white coat like a chemistry teacher. He wheeled a piece of equipment next to the examination table where Sonny sat, then removed the dust cover to reveal a medical laser that extended from its base on a long metal arm. Sonny thought it looked like a crude, blunt-nosed version of Luke Skywalker's light saber. He listened intently as the doctor explained how the laser beam would be matched to a light frequency selectively absorbed by the brand of ink in Sonny's tattoo. The ink would break down into small particles that Sonny's body would assimilate and flush away, leaving the tattoo lighter with each treatment until it eventually faded completely.

"No skin graft?" Sonny asked.

The doctor laughed. "Do I look like a barbarian?" His teeth were so clean that they looked like they had been hit a time or two by the laser themselves. "Now, how about showing me this graffiti that has your mother so upset?"

Sonny stood, pulled his T-shirt over his head, then laid facedown on the examination table.

Dr. Rubenstein whistled. "You get that at the state pen?"

Sonny rolled his eyes and said nothing.

"He won't tell us a thing," Karen Ciccarelli said. "For all I know, my son's become a goddamn gang-banger. Gave birth to a real rocket scientist, didn't I?"

"This isn't so bad," Rubenstein told her. The man's gloved fingers traced over the letters—more softly than anyone else's had. "Amateur jobs like this are generally close to the surface. Three visits, maybe four. We can start today if you like."

"Sooner the better," said Karen.

Dr. Rubenstein asked Sonny's mother to wait outside, then donned safety goggles, which he insisted Sonny wear as well. The tight band hurt Sonny's temples but took his mind off the procedure as the doctor cleaned the tattoo, then lifted the laser and began to work. Sonny glanced backward as the pulsing light hit his skin. "Trust me," Rubenstein said softly. He gently forced Sonny's head flat against the table, away from the light.

Sonny closed his eyes. The laser's warmth grew to burn like dry ice, even thought the doctor had applied a numbing cream to the area. Beads of laser light snapped against the boy's skin like rubber bands, and Sonny was glad his mother couldn't see the look on his face. He gave in to the pain, let it spread like wings down his back and through his body, and soon it was no longer pain at all, but an electric current blanketing him like a baby. Before he knew it, the process was over.

"That's it," Dr. Rubenstein said, giving Sonny's lower back a quick pat to indicate that he was through. The gesture stirred the air against the sweat collecting there, producing sudden goose-bumps on Sonny's bare skin.

Groggily the boy raised himself off the table, eyes heavy as if shaking off a trance. He concentrated on listening as Dr. Ruben-stein pulled off his gloves and rattled on about how the area would appear white and slightly swollen for the next twenty minutes or so, after which a scab would form in the same shade as the tattoo. Sonny should neither pick at it nor expose it to the sun, and he shouldn't be concerned if he experienced some bruising. The doc-tor gave him a manufacturer's sample of antibiotic ointment and told him to return in six weeks for another treatment.

As the tingling slowly drained from his body, Sonny became aware of the doctor's eyes on him, of the slight twitch that had de-veloped in Rubenstein's temple as he scanned Sonny's chest and face like there might be something else to hit with the laser, areas overlooked. Sonny wished there were something he could say to keep the doctor in the room, to stave off the trip home with his mother. But already the doctor was clearing his throat, shifting his eyes to the floor as he spoke. "Um, you can get dressed now."

Young love eased the brunt of Sonny's punishment. Two weeks after his first doctor's appointment and barely a week after school let out, Maria ran off with Richie to Florida, drawing her mother and father's ire all the way down I-95. Sonny found out first. One of Richie's old drawings lay on his bed, a brief note written by his sister on back: *We're off to Disneyworld! Richie's going to draw caricatures and I'm going to audition for Snow White. No more evil witch and her pizza toad. I'm free!*

Sonny's parents were on the verge of filling out a missing persons report when he told them what had happened. He said Maria had called him, thus sparing them the vitriolic content of her note.

Though not entirely forgiven, Sonny's foolishness was partially erased by his sister's worse transgression. He had Maria to thank each time he finished a shift at the pizza parlor without his father dressing him down. Entire meals passed at home without his mother once reminding him that he had all the sense of a sailor on shore leave. It became almost commonplace for Sonny's mom to rest her cigarette on the edge of her plate, reach over, and cup her boy's chin in her hand, telling him, "You're all I have left, angel."

Still, his parents canceled their shore plans for that summer. Sonny marked the passage of time by the bruise on his back, how it faded from purple to green to yellow.

Only when it came time for Sonny's second treatment did Karen Ciccarelli let it slip that she'd like to have a go at his tattoo with a bottle of bleach and a Brillo pad. He hated how she vacillated between fawning over him with affection and cutting him down with stinging remarks—but said nothing as he headed off to his appointment an hour and a half early.

Sonny was glad to be far from his father's pizza ovens as he meandered north through Center City. He liked the feel of the sun on his neck as he explored the little tucked-away neighborhoods just south of the hospital, narrow streets full of brick townhouses with freshly painted trim.

Unlike at home, where Sonny's father had just hung Old Glory in honor of the Fourth of July, the houses here—if they bothered to hang anything at all—flew bright flags with rainbow stripes. Sonny leaned against a tree and watched a man and his little foofy dog emerge through a door over which hung such a flag. The man wore a Day-Glo yellow tank top and Daisy Duke shorts that showed off his scrawny legs.

Sonny's father had told him about people like that. When former mayor Rizzo died, Sonny had gone with his dad to a public viewing at the Basilica of Saints Peter and Paul. Salvatore had pointed at the altar and told his son that was where queer protesters had thrown condoms at Cardinal Bevilacqua a few years before. Sonny could still picture the ugly curl on his father's lip.

Sonny followed the man and his dog up Camac Street, embarrassed at the mincing way the fellow coaxed his little Chihuahua to go potty. Was that what their lives were all about—protests and sex and little dogs on leashes? Sonny considered throwing a rock at him, but it was too much effort.

He left them to their business and headed toward 12th Street, past a Planned Parenthood clinic that had attracted a pro-lifer with a sign that read "Abortion Is Murder." Catty-corner from where Sonny stood was a little coffee shop sandwiched between a bookstore and a gym. As Sonny approached, he saw that the café bore another one of those rainbow flags. Louvered casement windows had been opened to let in the breeze, and a number of customers, all men, sat at little tables both indoors and out. As Sonny neared, he noticed that several men sported athletic bags and wore tank tops and Lycra shorts that appeared brand-new. They looked a lot less brutish than the bodybuilders at Rocky's Gym in South Philly, but not nearly as faggy as the man Sonny had just seen with the dog. Sonny considered going in—he had the time—but felt underdressed in his baggy cutoffs and the ratty shirt he had worn in case Dr. Rubenstein's laser drew blood.

So Sonny went into the bookstore instead, bright and colorful with big reproductions of messy paintings on the walls, rows of glossy magazines, and tables stacked with books, most of which bore images of bare male torsos. A bulletin board advertised an AIDS fund-raiser called Gay Bingo. Sonny remembered how his mother had worked for a while in her hospital's AIDS ward. More than once she had remarked, as she lit a cigarette at the end of a long day, that she found it aggravating to take care of people who hadn't bothered taking care of themselves.

A boy Maria's age, with shaved hair and a nose ring, stood behind the counter and winked when Sonny looked over at him.

Sonny Ciccarelli got out of there.

Later, up in Dr. Rubenstein's examination room, Sonny felt oddly safe. Again Rubenstein traced the words on the boy's back, erasing letter by letter Richie's crude handiwork. Sonny liked knowing what he was there for, liked the sting of the needle and the pressure of the man's fingers pulling his skin taught. The pain both numbed and aroused him. The doctor's touch was alien and rubbery, the texture of a marine mammal. Sonny thought of the beach—imagined swimming with a school of dolphins, his nerves scrambled by the pulse of their sonar.

When Dr. Rubenstein was finished, Sonny's skin bubbled up like a bad sunburn, and the doctor rubbed soothing cream over it as Sonny took off his goggles and massaged his eyes. The boy's vision sparkled as he looked at Dr. Rubenstein's face. The man's dark hair glistened with the iridescence of a crow's wing, and Sonny realized the doctor looked like a slightly shorter, much more polished version of Richie. As Rubenstein repeated the same medical advice he had given the boy the last time, Sonny again tried to think of something to say to keep the doctor in the room. He watched helplessly as Rubenstein covered up the laser and wheeled it away.

"My sister's boyfriend did this to me," Sonny blurted.

It was the first time he had told anyone, and there was an urgency in his voice that Rubenstein appeared not to know how to handle. The doctor loosened his tie and said, "Well, not much of a pal, is he?" He smiled faintly before turning to go.

On Sonny's birthday, Grandmom Antonia came to the house to cook dinner for her little *bello tesòro,* trying in vain to dispel the pall that Maria's absence had cast over the family. For years, Antonia had celebrated her grandchildren's birthdays by cooking traditional meals, at first because the old woman couldn't stomach the dishes her daughter-in-law passed off as authentic Italian, then later because it was an excuse to pass along recipes to her grandchildren. She would whisper to Sonny that there was more to his heritage than his mother's spaghetti and tomato gravy. The boy knew Antonia considered his mother an idiot in the kitchen and feared that quality might be passed along to him and his sister like a birth defect.

"Only you men appreciate my work," she said now as Sonny set a heavy pot of water on the stove to boil, then pulled up a stool and watched Antonia chop a clove of garlic. Sonny didn't have the heart to tell her that nothing she cooked compared to a good Gino's cheese steak. His grandmother had immigrated to the States in the fifties, and her tastes seemed as foreign as the Italian accent that still flavored her speech—but Sonny liked having her in the kitchen, filling the space Maria had left.

"You should be watching baseball with your *popi*," Antonia chided, scraping the pieces into a saucepan sizzling with olive oil. "This is your day."

But the Phillies hadn't excited Sonny since they lost the pennant to the Blue Jays a couple seasons ago. The last thing he wanted to do was go in and sit on the sofa next to his old man, talking about loaded bases and batting averages as if this summer had turned out like any other.

"I like it here," Sonny said to his grandmother, even though he wasn't hungry. He knew she didn't really want him to go. "What are you making?"

"Mozzarella-stuffed cabbage," Grandmom Antonia told him with a smile that showed off her gold tooth. She poked his chest with the end of a wooden spoon. "That way I please both the Italian and the Irish in your blood."

The minced garlic in the skillet turned pale gold as its aroma lifted and spread throughout the kitchen. "I wish for your sake I had ingredients to do this right," Antonia said to her grandson. "This mozzarella your mama bought?" She picked up a white clump that resembled one of Richie's art gum erasers. "It no more real mozzarella than she is Italian. Real mozzarella come from water buffalo. Much darker. This is *fior di latte*—made from cow's milk. Where I lived in Italy, we had herds of water buffalo. But not so much anymore, I think. And in this great country? Forget it." She stirred the garlic one last time with her spoon. "But we Ciccarellis, we make the best of a bad situation, yes?"

Sonny smiled.

Just then he heard the front door open. A moment later, his mother entered the kitchen, dressed in her nurse's uniform, a Superfresh bag slung over her wrist and a cake box in her hands. "Happy birthday, sport," she said, kissing her boy on the cheek and handing him the plastic bag. "Ice cream. Be a peach and put it in the fridge."

Karen Ciccarelli sat down at the dinette table, took off her shoes, and rubbed her feet. Antonia dropped cabbage leaves into the boiling water, walked over, and lifted the cake box lid. She wrinkled her nose. "Why not use the bakery I suggest?"

Karen lit a cigarette. "Cut me some slack."

"And why there no presents? Don't you know to spoil your son on his birthday?"

"Sonny's present is being doled out in installments."

Sonny slunk outside as the two women began to bicker. He sat on the back stoop and cradled his head in his hands, thinking of Richie and Dr. Rubenstein. He slipped his fingers down the back of his shirt to massage the skin between his shoulders. His body could be covered with tattoos or burned completely clean—it didn't matter. It wouldn't change how he felt inside. He wasn't sure how much he liked the person he was becoming.

Sonny buried his face in his palms. Beads of sweat trickled down his forehead. The city had grown hot and he wanted to get away from it. Until a few moments ago, he had thought there was a chance his parents would pardon his offense and take him to the shore, that he would again feel the sea washing over his body like a thousand cleansing hands. But he wasn't their perfect little boy anymore. He knew now there would be no more Wildwood trips for the Ciccarelli family, no more dizzying boardwalk rides, no more reassuring summertime romances.

Sonny's grandmother called him to dinner. He rubbed his eyes and went inside.

Antonia and Karen had set the table and Salvatore had pulled himself away from the boob-tube. Sonny's father poured a little red wine for everyone, and Grandmom Antonia toasted her grandson's health with a hearty *"Cent'anni."* Then they all sat down to the protracted agony of dinner. Sonny's mother critiqued his eating habits, then talked about patients and staffing shortages. His father complained about the construction work at the market, which the city still hadn't finished. His grandmother brought up embarrassing tales of Sonny's childhood, how for Halloween the year he was five she had spent hours sewing him a little Superman costume only to have him pee his pants at his first trick-or-treating stop. No one brought up Maria's name, which only made her absence more conspicuous.

Sonny started to clear the dishes, but his grandmother told him to sit back down. She rose and put fifteen candles in his birthday cake, then set it on the table, dimming the lights as she began to sing. Karen and Salvatore halfheartedly joined in.

Before Sonny could make a wish, there came the sound of the front door opening and bags being tossed onto the carpet. Everyone at the dinner table looked at one another, wondering who it could be. And then Maria appeared in the dining room archway, her bleach-blond curls redyed jet black. Mascara ran down her cheeks. She slumped against the wall and began to cry while Sonny's birthday candles melted into wax puddles atop his cake.

Undaunted by the small crowd of protesters, Karen Ciccarelli told the taxi driver to circle the block and let her and her children out down the street from Planned Parenthood. After a week of crying, arguing, and strategizing, mother and daughter had finally agreed to abort the unwanted pregnancy that had brought Maria home, and Sonny, scheduled for an appointment with Dr. Rubenstein that morning, had tagged along in the cab ride uptown.

Both mother and daughter secured headscarves and dark glasses as they climbed out of the taxi. Sonny followed them up the street. A Planned Parenthood escort approached and asked if they had an appointment. Maria nodded.

A patrol car pulled up. Two cops got out and forced the protesters onto the sidewalk across the street. The crowd held lit candles and held signs that read "Abort the Abortionists!" Some blew whistles or sang hymns as the escort led the Ciccarellis to the clinic's gated entrance. Beyond the protesters and across the street, the gay café was opening, and Sonny paused as a well-built, dark-haired man set chairs and tables on the sidewalk.

Sonny's mother poked her boy in the ribs so he'd move out of her way. Had she caught him looking? "You hightail it to Dr. Rubenstein's," she told him. "Watch yourself around here. And I'm not just talking about the Christian Coalition."

Sonny blushed and looked at his sister, who had removed her sunglasses to brush away a tear. He felt bad that her life with Richie hadn't worked out as planned. He wanted to tell her something, but didn't know how. Were there Hallmark cards for times like this?

Maria looked at him, as if she could read in Sonny's mind what he couldn't form into words. "You got off easy," she said.

Sonny wasn't so sure. Richie had screwed them both.

He waited until his mother and sister were safely inside, then cut across 12th Street past the crowd. A few people hissed at him, but the presence of the cops kept most of them in line. Sonny had an hour to kill, so he idled in front of the café. The dark-haired man carried two more chairs onto the sidewalk. He smiled at Sonny before going back in. Sonny moved closer to the large casement window and watched the man as he began to arrange croissants on a tray. The sun broke through the morning's haze, reflecting the abortion protesters in the window glass. Sonny's own image appeared as well, a double exposure that almost obscured the man inside.

Sonny cupped his hands around his eyes and leaned in close. He didn't care if the young man noticed him staring or if the police and protesters thought he was a freak. He hoped his mother would walk outside the clinic for a smoke and catch him. He wanted to ask her how she could talk about people the way she did, how she could be so gung-ho about Maria getting an abortion. He was beginning to understand that her words, and his father's too, were nothing more than air pushed from lungs, shaped by mouth and tongue into sound. Artificial constructions, something he could see past, something he didn't have to believe anymore. There were whole worlds beyond South Philly his parents didn't know a damn thing about.

The smiling man approached to open the window. Sonny stepped back. With a turn of a handle, the glass shifted, and Sonny watched his reflection disappear.

Up in Dr. Rubenstein's office, Sonny waited anxiously for the nurse to call his name. He thumbed through the magazines on the coffee table, but none interested him. His mind kept drifting back to the guy in the café. He tried picturing Maria, strapped in a set of stirrups. Did the doctors at the clinic use lasers, too?

Finally the nurse called him to the examination room, where Sonny took off his shirt and stretched out on the table. Dr. Rubenstein came in and pulled on a pair of gloves, the same kind the police had worn at the clinic. As the doctor bent over him, Sonny felt tantalized, eager for the medical laser to be rolled out, for Rubenstein to raise his magic wand and erase all evidenced that Richie had ever touched him.

But the medical equipment remained in place. Rubenstein clucked his tongue and said, "We're done. There's nothing left."

Sonny raised his head and stared at the doctor. He ached to feel the sting of the laser as it purified his body.

Dr. Rubenstein explained. "The last treatment worked better than I thought. Your tattoo is almost unnoticeable. I think in another month it will have faded altogether."

"That can't be true," Sonny said.

"The ink must have been very close to the surface. Be happy you're saving your mother some money." Dr. Rubenstein smiled, showing his even teeth. "You got off easy."

Sonny thought of Maria again, and what Richie had done to her. What Richie had done to them both. He watched the doctor remove his gloves, then drop them in the wastebasket. The handsome doctor said a polite goodbye and left. The room was silent, and the boy glanced down to find his shirt wrung tight in his hands. Sonny looked at the door, wanting to follow Dr. Rubenstein and tell him there was more work to do—much, much more.

GOLD

Alexander Chee

Jack woke to the sounds of the contemporary jazz radio station his mother played in the mornings. With his eyes closed, he could see her as she put on her eye makeup, chose her jewelry, held up a blouse and skirt across the tops of her shoes, and then held them up against her chest as she faced into the mirror. His mother worked as a loan officer in the Security Pacific Bank at the corners of 18th Street and Castro in San Francisco, and every day she dressed carefully.

He rolled over in bed and felt, like wetness against his legs, cold coins, reminding him it was Chinese New Year's Day. The coins were a game he and his mother had played since he was old enough to remember: "Money from your father for good luck," she told him when he was very young. "Your father was here last night, very quickly, and he left this for you. I am sorry I didn't wake you." Then later, when he was older, she would say, "He sent this for me to give you." Tradition was on New Year's that you went and bowed before your elders, and by showing your respect again for another year, your father rewarded you with money to go and celebrate. Koreans took Chinese New Year as the world's birthday all at once: Everyone counted their age by that day. Jack felt the coins warm up against his legs, and he reached down to pick them up. Seven quarters, and a gold dollar. He palmed the quarters and held the gold coin up to the morning light of his room.

He climbed from his bed and pulled on a pair of jeans. He opened his door, looking for some sign of her. "Mother," he said.

"Yes," she said, from her room down the hall.

She sat in front of her mirror, smiling at him in its reflection as he walked into the room. Her hair was in a sleek braid, her face powder smooth. She reddened the rest of her mouth with her lipstick as she watched him approach. He went down to his knees and bent until his forehead pressed into the salmon-colored carpet. "Thank you, Mother," he said.

"Your father is very generous this year," she said, her hand coming down from the chair to rest against his neck. "He knows you are his good son, and he sends money for you to save for college. He wishes you well in your fourteenth year."

Jack opened his eyes at this and looked into the cords of the carpeting. He paused. "Thank you, Father," he said.

Jack left for school that morning as he always did, walking so he could pass by the corner of Eureka and 23rd Street. There at the end of the rows of snowflake Victorians stood a sturdy and ramshackle Edwardian, rain-colored, two stories and held up, it seemed, by Swedish ivy. A fence ran around the yard, snaggle-toothed black iron, and inside it the grass and flowers grew wild. Raspberry bushes bristled against the sides of the house, and a magnolia tree reached branches down to the sidewalk. When the tree bloomed, Jack picked the branch bare. Jack would pick a blossom every day and keep walking, twirling it as he walked and daring himself to wear it over his ear.

The curtains hung ragged in the window, as if the sheers had been pulled apart by the weight of the daily sunlight, and the old glass warped the light like heat rising. There was always a light on in the front room, and for a very long time Jack thought it was a ruse to scare away prowlers. Then one night, he had climbed up onto the fence to peek inside and saw the old man who lived there by himself, seated in an overstuffed chair.

He was looking out the window, into the distance above Jack's head. In that view, Jack thought, was Noe Valley, the Mission, the tip of the China Basin. There was Twin Peaks, lit up by the radio tower and the headlights of lovers in cars ascending and descending the roads to the lookout, where they would look down to the city and this dim spot where Jack and the old man were. The chair seemed the only place he could ever be, in that enormous dark house with its eaves full of pigeons and bats, and it seemed he would never leave it. As if to leave might be to miss whoever the light was left on for. He did seem to be waiting. Jack recognized the expression as one he had seen on his mother. It belonged to people who had once been many places and were now here, waiting for something coming up from behind.

Jack wondered who he was, this old man with his white hair rising up off his smooth white face, a face smooth from a life indoors. His eyebrows rose out from his head, nearly streamers in the air, and his blue eyes slanted catlike. He asked his mother about him and she had shrugged. No one knows who lives in their neighborhood here, she said. It's not that kind of neighborhood. And so he made sure to pass it now every time he could, each time trying to see and remember something new: how the windows in the back of the second floor were boarded over, how the teeth on the fence were all different from one another, or how the Resurrection lilies lining the front of the house stank like rotting meat when they bloomed.

Now and then, he would see the old man out in the yard with garden shears or a hoe, cutting back at the raspberry vines where they pushed out onto the sidewalk. At these times Jack would pass quickly, not looking up. Every time he had the urge to say, Hey, how's your garden, or something else, innocent and plain. He wanted to get the man to speak. He felt that if he could hear his voice, he might even learn one thing about him. But instead, he would walk past, and the words he wanted to say fluttered in his ears. Nothing to say or reply to, just the old man thrusting with his hoe at a vine, or weaving the shears in the air above his hedges, squinting into the thin city sunlight and impervious to his understanding.

At school Jack's teachers and guidance counselors were having a career day. The students were urged to consider the future: internships, part-time jobs, summer programs, college, vocational schools, graduate work. He took tests: Do you enjoy working with other people? Are you comfortable in front of a camera or holding it? He was told to do his best at moving abstract shapes around a page, to make them match up with each other, and his results would tell him about his suitability to a variety of careers. What do you want to be? the test asked, and gave room for four answers, to be ranked by priority. Jack considered putting down "chanteuse," but aware of the implications, he restrained himself, though he was uncertain his guidance counselor knew what this word meant.

Jack wanted to be beautiful. He wanted to be loved by handsome men who drove Silver Ghost Rolls-Royces and smoked thick, short cigarettes with no filters. He wanted men who would always have to leave for some tragic reason or another, and then there would be the fade to black on Jack, in a long satin sheath dress, his face lit up from under his chin by the reflections off his diamante choker. He wanted to drive men to do great and terrible things just for the favor of his smile. This seemed like a calling, but hardly a vocation. He looked at the four blank spaces, and in each one, he wrote "Actor."

Later in the day, in his study hall, he sat at his desk and tried to imagine what it would be like inside the old man's house, how it would be decorated, the color of the light inside, whether there would be dusty red velvets, cobwebbed chandeliers, reproductions of Greek statuary, perhaps a sword or two on the wall. Perhaps a Japanese sword. There might be secret passages as well, bookcases that turned, paintings on hinges. Hollow books.

Jack thought again about the time he had peeked in the window and had tried to draw what he had seen, except this time from the old man's eyes. He sketched the small table covered over in magazines, feet at the bottom of the page crossed right over left, the arms of the chair. When he got to the window, he began to fill in the view, until it occurred to him: Windows at night are mirrors when the lights are on. They admitted no view. If the old man was looking at anyone he had been looking at himself.

At times, in the evenings, Jack's mother had told him stories about the men she had known, the stories coming slowly and in pieces, over time. She told the story of meeting Olivier as if it had come exactly after the story of his departure, when in fact three weeks fled in between. She told him of Andrew, the Marine poster boy, Edgar, the playboy whose yacht was always moored, then Ted, Marco, Jimmy, Ira. Also Gordon. From each one, there was some gift: a ring, a pendant, earrings, so it seemed to Jack that when a man loved a woman, it added up around her hands, neck, and ears in stones and soft metals.

In the hours of the afternoon when he was alone, Jack would put on his mother's jewelry. With topaz hanging from his ears, his hands shining with rings, he sang along to the songs on the radio sung by women about love, revenge, and loss, looking at himself as he did so in every mirror in the apartment. The weight of the jewelry changed even the way he walked or moved his hands. The women on the radio sang about the men they knew, and as he sang with them, he imagined himself with the men he knew and loved, in secret: Eusebio, the postal carrier with his mustache and goatee; Paul, the boy across the street who wore only cutoff jeans when he worked outdoors on his Camaro; Arden, the soccer player, who never failed to humiliate him at least once a week in algebra class. In the afternoons before his mother got home from work, Jack had a few hours to his own, and during these hours he dreamed up great love affairs: Eusebio, sweeping him into his arms and spilling envelopes and sales flyers as they spread out across the foyer; Paul, seducing him into his Camero and then driving him, quickly, north on 101, out of San Francisco and up the coast, to live together in a house by the sea; Arden, coming by with flowers and poems to declare his secret love, kissing the ground Jack had just walked on for forgiveness.

Jack's mother had a story she told for herself, and it was this: Her father had been an American Methodist missionary; her mother a Korean Sunday-school teacher. They were never married, as it was illegal then. But finally her father sent for her to come from Korea when she was sixteen to San Francisco, where she kept house for him while he sponsored her citizenship. Her mother had been increasingly unable to keep her daughter, and no one was willing to marry her, fatherless as she was, and half-American. When she was eighteen, she left and moved into a Chinatown residence hotel for

women. Her father gave her some money, enough for her to live
on, attend secretarial school and buy herself a few nice dresses, a
good pair of shoes. The girls she lived with had taught her how to
put on makeup to highlight her Western features best, and as they
combed out one another's hair at night, they reassured her this was
best: You will be able to work in white offices, they murmured in
her ear, as they counted off one hundred strokes. You will be able
to marry a white man. Her father would die before Jack was born.

"We practiced English with fashion magazines," she told Jack
one night, and she laughed. "We would sit around in the visitors'
lounge at night, in our dress slips and robes, our toenail polish drying. One evening, for fun, we all chose new American names for
ourselves. One girl, she would pick a name out of the new issue of
Vogue, and then another girl, she would stand up for it and walk
around the room in that name, shaking the other girls hands firmly,
saying, 'Hello, nice to meet you, I love your dress.' " His mother
stood then, and moved to show him: a bright, Doris Day smile cap-
ping an upright posture, a broad, firm stride. She was transported.
"And the names . . . Sarah, Natalie, Kara, Katie." She paused in front
of him and bit her thumb. "That was really it, though. I realized, I
needed a name, an American name to walk an American walk. We
all felt that way. We had never seen so many teeth all at once. And
so we have our names: Catherine and Jack O'Neill."

"How did you pick your name?" he said.

"I went to my father. I told him I wanted him to give me a
name. So he did. O'Neill is his last name, Catherine was his great-
grandmother's name. And so we have our very American name."
She knelt in front of him. He was ten at the time and was beginning to understand exactly how much power his mother had.
"Learn every word you don't know," she told him. "You can only
get those things you know how to ask for."

Jack's birth certificate was framed beside his mother's bed. On
the certificate his father's name was entered as Romelio Herez-
Sylva, nationality Argentinean. Two years ago, on New Year's, he
had asked her where this father was, as he had often asked, and this
time she didn't name a far-off place. Instead, she had raised her eye-

brows at this, walking briskly into the kitchen to set down her bag of groceries, and then came back to where he waited, near the door. She looked at him as she slowly removed one glove, and then the other. "All these other men I tell you about," she said, "they gave me many things, but your father, all he gave me was you." And here she smiled at him. "Which was plenty."

"Where is he?" Jack asked.

"He left," she replied, and headed off to her room. "This is something that men do," she said. "They leave. But they send money." Her heels clicked down the hall, and then were muffled by the carpet of her room.

Jack stayed there by the door, his mouth moving silently. Romelio. The way his mother said it sounded different from any other words she said. There had been different sounds, like a different alphabet, just to say his name. Romelio. Romelio. Ending in *O,* as in *Oh.* As in surprise, the mouth open and round.

After school, Jack got off the bus and walked to the corner where the old man's house was. He stood first at the front of the house. The light was not on. Jack considered that it was the middle of the day and that the old man must conserve energy, like anyone did. He tried to remember if he had ever seen the light off, and then stopped trying, convinced he would only end up imagining it and would confuse that for a memory.

He walked to the side of the house, and then to the back. He noticed now a door there, ajar, that he had not seen before. He chilled slightly and wondered if he was found out, if the force of his earlier imaginings that day had transmitted themselves to the old man and warned him of spies. He stood there on the sidewalk, as the door flickered under the weight of his stare.

It wouldn't, he thought, be an intrusion. The door was open. He could say he had been concerned for the old man living all alone.

He crossed the yard. The raspberry roots under his feet felt like fingers. He paused in the doorway, and the afternoon air shook around him in a draft. He breathed deep and stepped in.

There were no chandeliers. There were no swords, no old paintings, no velvet. There were rotting curtains in every window, and by the front window where the old man took his view, a brocade loveseat, colorless from the sun. Jack hadn't been able to see it when he peeked inside. He reached into the empty, overstuffed chair to touch the seat and felt the fabric there worn to the threads.

He went up the stairs into the second floor. There he found a bathroom, newly renovated and modern. A door in the hall was padlocked shut, and then farther down, there was a bedroom, empty, the single bed unmade against the far wall. Jack went and sat down at the edge of the bed. There was a groove there, pressed out by many nights of sleep. Jack lay down into it, where he stayed for some time, looking at the ceiling. His mouth moved quietly in the faint light, now and then, shaping soundlessly. Ro-me-li-o. Romelio. Where are you, Romelio, he thought. What could the world be made of, he thought, that people could ever leave each other? He wanted his father to return, rich, carrying flowers, happy to see his mother. Happy to see him.

Eventually, it became dark, and Jack was still alone, in the bed.

When he left, he went out the way he came in. He closed the door behind him.

His mother was still awake when he opened the door. He did not know what time it was. She had a scotch in her left hand and rubbed at her feet, crossed on her lap, with her right. A lit cigarette burned lazily on the table beside her, the smoke curling up through the lampshade. If left there, it would leave a stain she would complain of later. She was watching television. Her face was bare of makeup, something he was not used to seeing, and it occurred to him that he might be very late, that he might have missed the dinner they had every New Year's. She looked up at him as he came in, and then went back to watching the set.

"I give you the money every year," she said. "Did you know that?"

"Yes," he replied.

"Your father, he was a good man. He wanted to work. But he had to go where there was work. Times were very bad then, and there was no work here for him. He had no green card." She let go of her feet, and they dropped over the edge of the chair. "I didn't even know I was pregnant with you until he was gone."

They were quiet a moment.

She said, "He doesn't know he has a son." She looked at him to say this. "I really think he would have married me. I really do. But I was proud then, I wanted to live well. I am not so very proud in that way now." She took a hard drag from the cigarette, squinting as she did. "I can be proud of other things now."

She stood, went to the sink, and threw the contents of her glass in the drain. She rinsed her glass. "I am not a smart person," she said. "If I ever was, no one told me about it." She ran the water until it was warm and then bent over to splash her face. She blotted herself with a towel. "I know how to type. I can speak English with almost no mistakes. I know how to raise a child. Not that I will ever do it again."

She came back into the room and walked over to where he was. She put her hand in his hair.

"I thought you'd left," she said. She kissed his forehead. "Your crazy mother. Good night." She withdrew her hand, went into her room, and closed the door.

Jack went over to where she had left her cigarette burning and put it out. He went into his room and lay down on his bed. The wallpaper on his walls was the same as it had been since he was eight years old, and on the wall beside the door was a portrait photo of his mother. In it she was young, wearing an elegant dress, her hair cut jaw-length and curled outward. She was smiling. Jack looked at the photo. He pulled the gold dollar from his pocket. In the dark it could be almost any color, any metal, and no one would know, except perhaps for the weight of it, which was surprising for its size. He recalled then this was a quality of gold, it weighed more than it seemed to weigh. He thought of the door ajar, the house, and wondered if somewhere lived a woman and her son whom the man had thought would follow. Had he finally left, unable to continue waiting? He turned the coin in his hand. There was comfort in such an extra and surprising weight, a secret comfort. Was this why gold was precious? His heart in his chest grew heavy as he turned the coin in his hand. He could not remember this feeling from before, it was new to him, his heart heavier and heavier, like an ore under the weight of the earth pressed out and burning purely into itself, to be cherished in a future it cannot yet imagine, heavier and heavier. Heavier, still.

THE HOLY SPIRIT BANK

Brian Bouldrey

Of course, Grainger was going to die anyway. He thought this melodramatic thing as he lowered himself into a massive marble tub full of spa water, reportedly the most healthful water to be found in any spa in the world.

"All these essential vitamins and minerals," he said to his attendant, "I feel like presweetened cereal." He said it just to be polite, since this guy probably didn't speak a word of English.

The attendant was at least seventy and had a shock of perfectly white wavy hair, all combed neatly upward—like the symbol for the heater on a car dashboard, or like smoke pouring out of a barbecue vent. His eyebrows, however, were two dark patches, the hair that grew in birthmarks: carpet samples. He was lame and Grainger could tell he had been for life.

Probably, Grainger thought further, the old guy hadn't ventured far beyond the walls of this sanitarium, sent here in sickly childhood by a doctor and staying, depending so much on the healing waters that he just started working there one day and then, poof!, he was seventy.

Grainger had composed a whole history for the attendant while waiting with Rodney in one of the long line of sleek, cushioned reclining chairs fixed into the tile floor (the waiting hall was almost empty except for a snoozing Germanic-looking man with—good God!—a *goiter*). He heard the limping old guy approach and recede into the room he prepared for Grainger, the left leg half the size of his normal leg that echo-squeaked in the sanitarium like gym shoes on a basketball court.

"Or brandy," the old attendant said, without a smidgen of accent, folding a fat, thirsty towel over the chair. Grainger was going to say a surprised thing like "Wow, you speak English" or "Wow, you made a joke," but something further distracted him.

"I'm green!" he said, looking at his body submerged in the healthy steamy soup of whatever ran down five different copper pipes into the tub.

"Sulfur," agreed the attendant, "and iron. Now I have to go prepare the other room for your friend," he said, seeing Grainger settled.

"Come back if you get bored." Grainger splashed. The attendant smiled. Oh God, would he want a tip? What were the gratuity policies in the Azores?

When the door clicked shut Grainger assessed the room—a cube tile white from floor to ceiling, trimmed bright yellow. The single wooden chair with his towel, a small pointless changing stall where all his clothes hung on a single hook, a big glazed window, a toilet with a roll of strikingly pink toilet paper.

He had flushed the toilet before disrobing, as a part of an ongoing experiment he and Rodney were conducting, for they feared that Portuguese toilets were designed only to rinse the doodies, not get rid of them. In the hotels he'd stayed in on the emerald islands of Terceira, Flores, and now Sao Miguel, he'd been given bathrooms with that party-guest-nightmare toilet problem. Here at the health-minded *termas* Terra Nostra, however, where cleanliness was paramount and state-run, the toilet did not rinse nor flush, but eradicated waste into another dimension and made way too much noise in the process.

From the tub across the too-big room, the toilet seemed to be shrinking and lonely, but the paper was still fifi-pink.

He leaned his head against the stone. By now, Rodney was settled into his own tub. Rodney was a perfect traveler, but it was good to get away from him now and then. Easygoing and yet a leader, Rodney kept Grainger moving along when he might have stayed in the garden all day rather than walk into town or take a look at a local bar.

Oh, but Rodney was what the *San Francisco Chronicle* back home called, in a business section story about the success of the Weather Channel on cable, a target market known as "The Weather Involved."

Speaking of the weather involved, rain beat on the roof of the Furnas sanitarium, and had the violence of invading armies, or that toilet over there. The day after this long soak, Grainger would be just as transfixed as Rodney as the television news showed image after image of flood damage: overflowing rivers, chocolate waterfalls into the Atlantic, a little dog floating cutely around a deluged living room on a sofa cushion. Touring around for the rest of this trip, Grainger would feel like an insurance adjuster rather than a tourist. But he'd also feel a secret, dark privilege to have seen this disaster.

He posed for himself like he'd just discovered specific gravity, one finger in the air. The rain drummed so loudly he didn't hear the smoke-headed attendant return. Grainger was caught in that pose. He scrambled for an excuse. "I was doing my imitation of Archimedes. Eureka! You know."

The attendant smiled. "When my son comes here to visit, he likes to do the great bathtub tragedies. It's a routine he does. First he wraps his head in a towel and does Jean-Paul Marat. Then he lays back with a little wad of toilet paper like posies, and he's Ophelia. Then he sits with pots of coffee and paper and scratches himself like Balzac with his galleys and skin conditions."

Grainger furrowed his brow.

"You thought I was a stupid Azorean peasant, didn't you?" said the man.

Grainger would not have said stupid. He sank lower in the water. He had a pain in his neck from the too-flat posture-beneficial pillows at the hotel.

"You know that if you're sick, there are special treatments and a free doctor consultation," he said, thump-squeaking over to the chair and taking a load off.

"I'm not sick, though," said Grainger, trying to keep defensiveness out of his voice. "I came for the spa. I came to a health resort to keep healthy. Tonight we're going to lower a chicken into one of your boiling hot craters and cook it and eat it with a bottle of fizzy green wine. And then tomorrow morning we're going to hike along the edge of a volcano."

"So you're liking the Azores."

Was he? He'd been blowing all his travel on the great spas of Europe in the last few years: sunflowered Montepulciano, geriatric Orion in the Catalan hinterland, spas *en* Spa, Baden *am* Baden-Baden, baths in Bath. The vague boredom of taking the waters in those towns was mitigated by history, architecture, big-assed churches, and cafés. The Azores were Rodney's idea. Here in Furnas, what was there? A wide ferriginous orange-brown pool, hydrangeas up the wazoo, comical arts and crafts like flowers made out of fish scales, uninteresting ceramics, and, ugh, scrimshaw peace signs and Playboy bunny heads.

He loved coasting along in the slipstream of the strange corners of the globe. Grainger frequented a local bar in this town called O Gremio with a menu in eager-to-please but fractured English (mushles and other foods were served in doses), but yes, yes, he was liking the Azores, for now here—*here!*—he was talking up a lame old local.

Rain beat down even harder. Grainger, distracted by the torrent, had to ask loudly, "Do you always get rain like this?"

The man shook his head. "Never so early. December once or twice, but by then they're ready. The birds' nests are cleaned out of the roof tiles so they can drain. But never in September. This will be some trouble."

Grainger saw this man as a boy, cleaning tiles on his house with a stick. "You've lived here all your life?"

"Hell no. Moved to New Bedford when I was nine and lived there until I was sixty-five. The wife wanted peace and quiet." That explained his excellent English. He'd been speaking it almost twice as long as Grainger had been alive. "I wanted the water. Got to be close to the water."

"It's good for your leg." Grainger pointed at the shrunken limb, draped with his white sanitary smock.

The man seemed offended. It wasn't supposed to be obvious, obviously. "For the soul!"

"Oh, for the soul, the soul. How come everybody but I knows so much about the soul? What's good for it, what's bad for it."

"You're a gay, aren't you?" said the man. It was retaliation; Grainger revealed his lameness, he reveals Grainger's sexuality.

"Yes, a gay." He liked the "a." It made him feel like an item.

"My son is one in Boston." He leaned forward. Grainger said nothing, so the man said, "I'm hoping he doesn't die."

What was the bathroom graffiti joke? "What does 'gay' stand for? 'Got AIDS Yet?' Not quite. No. Working on it, but no. "He's a big boy. He can figure it out."

"He's older than you," the man said, and got up to do a squeaky circle around the chair like a dog on a tether. "He has the virus, but he hasn't been sick. Now he's got the new medicines."

"That's nice." Grainger sank into the enriched water until only his head stuck out.

"And I pray for him every day to the *Espiritu Santu.*"

Espiritu Santu. The Holy Spirit. The Azores found their greatest strength, a patron in that most oblique of all religious entities, invisible, characterless. Spacey. It was supposed to be the mysterious, most imaginative part of the Trinity—Father, Son, Blankety-Blank—and therefore without physical attributes. But ever since they came up with the concept way back when, everybody tried to give the spirit a body anyway, form, substance. The most common renditions were of a dove, or a crown.

It was three days after this visit to the spa that, on the steps of one of the little bright chapels dedicated to the Holy Spirit, Rodney and Grainger tried to get a picture of a little girl, in enough crinoline for a wedding dress, idly sucking on the tip of a silver crown, the kind that magically appeared on people's heads in commercials for Imperial margarine.

Rodney circled the girl, wanting to get some kind of candid shot. He was a good photographer, but meticulous and never ready for the spontaneous moment. He was also slow to snap picturesque peasants. "I don't want to treat them like specimens," he told Grainger.

"Oh, Rodney, we put them under the microscope the day we bought the plane tickets." And weren't they the real specimens?

Walking around in different clothes, different hair styles. Every local watched them, delighting in the difference. Even Grainger did, when inspecting Rodney. He looked very good in his soccer T-shirt and baggy nylon shorts. If Grainger squinted his eyes, he could pretend that Rodney was a handsome stranger.

Rodney never got that picture of the girl with the Holy Spirit crown in her mouth.

That was the same day, three days after the baths, that Rodney and Grainger would be in the city of Ponta Delgada unsuccessfully trying to use a credit card to get escudoes out of an ATM administered by the Banco Espiritu Santu. Even the money was invested in the Holy Spirit.

When the machine did not give, Grainger turned around and had an immediate view of the ocean. A strange light eeked through the clouds onto the surface that somehow miniaturized that vast body of water, and it looked to him like the Red Sea in Cecil B. DeMille's *The Ten Commandments,* which he had heard was done with gelatin. Just then, the church bells of Sao Pedro rang.

"It's Sunday," Rodney said. "Maybe the bank won't give us money on Sunday."

Grainger checked his watch. It was an odd hour to ring bells, 11:37 A.M. The song of the bells sounded urgent and complex and Chinese, with point and counterpoint. Grainger decided that the tune was set on a mechanical roll many years ago for a certain set of tuned bells, and as one or two at a time over time were replaced because of wear and tear or earthquakes or whatever, the tones of the bells no longer matched one another. Who would ever know the lost tune made foreign? He wanted to use the words "harsh" and "sour" to describe it, but that was unfair, for it pleased him.

"Why now?" he said, pointing at his watch.

"They're consecrating the host." Rodney knew more about being Catholic than Grainger did. Rodney was a Unitarian.

But here, long before that bell song, Grainger listened to this attendant talk about praying to the Holy Spirit. "It can't hurt, can it?" he shrugged. "You're a Catholic."

Grainger wondered whether the guy read tea leaves, too. "Now, how would you know that?"

"Because it bothers you when I talk about praying to the Holy Spirit. If you were Protestant or Jewish, you'd be amused."

"I don't even know what the Holy Spirit is." Grainger sat up again. He'd get too warm in the water and need to stick a leg out like a chimney to release the heat.

As a boy, he was told that a certain candle suspended over the altar in an orange censer indicated God's presence in the church. Grainger had worried his seven-year-old head, maybe even lost sleep: What if the candle went out? "Everybody is telling me about invisible things happening to me. Why should I believe it? I have the virus, just like your son, yes, but I've never been sick. Why should I believe I have it? And those new medicines that are helping your son? The doctor says they aren't helping me at all. But why should I believe it?"

Two years before, Grainger had been sitting in the murky steam of the YMCA sauna, nearly empty except for a beautiful Korean guy, who began to caress Grainger's thigh and then slipped his other hand between Grainger's legs. Grainger had nothing to do but reciprocate, he had not planned it, Rodney was the planner; this was something to take advantage of. He ran a hand down the guy's shocking smoothness, and just then a familiar hulking man stormed in through the steam. He'd been fast enough to catch Grainger red-handed and sat scowling across from him, the boiling sauna machine between them like a magic cauldron. The Korean guy had fled to the locker room, but Grainger's hard-on kept him rooted to the spot. The scowling man, heavily muscled with long brown hair, said to Grainger, "You shouldn't do that. It's bad for your soul."

That reproach chafed over the years, more than any antigay slur. He'd seen this guy many times before—he was a frequent punching-bag user, a boxer. He cultivated some kind of ascetic aura by being unchatty, solitary. Was boxing better for the soul? Punching somebody in the head—was it more purifying than running a searching hand over a body in mutual pleasure?

"It's a mystery," said the lame man. "Fate, my wife calls it."

"I'm just supposed to accept it, like you must accept being lame from birth and your son born gay."

The attendant laughed. He seemed to rally now and then from a tired decrepitness; certain things Grainger said wound him up like a toy soldier. "I wasn't lame from birth! I was a longshoreman for forty years, hauling heavy things until one day a block and tackle swang by and crushed my leg." He rolled up his pant leg for Grainger to see: It was a big piece of plastic.

They could hear Rodney down the hall, singing Gilbert and Sullivan at the top of his lungs. "What never? No never! What never? Well, hardly ever! He's hardly-yever sick! At! Sea!"

"Will that be bothering the other guests?" Grainger asked.

"There are no other guests, you're it. It's the off-season." The Azores had seemed curiously abandoned to Grainger, well-paved roads and empty grand hotels and big fat airports to handle just two or three flights a day. Empty shops with hopeful signs of non-existent tourists: "We Perform the Lay Away." Towns without restaurants, nor cafés, listless cabbies at the taxi stands. Cows on the roadway.

"Well, good, because I'd be embarrassed."

"Why? You're not responsible."

"I suppose you can tell he's not my boyfriend, too, Mr. Clair-voyant? Well, that's an easy one to figure out. He's much more good-looking than I am."

Grainger was not ugly, but he was very very tall, with a lantern jaw. But he had good skin and at one time a perfectly white shock of hair on the right side of his head, a raccoon patch, a lunar. These assets were of interest to certain men, they were attracted the way some deep-sea fish were lured to bigger predators that grew from their heads long bioluminescent bits of fancy bait. These days, though, Grainger was losing hair, and the raccoon patch could be mistaken for a massing of gray hair in what was left of it.

A week before, in a tiny, merry fishing village, where everybody seemed to break out in song, and the Sacred Heart over the front of the church had not only a crucifix piercing it, but an anchor as well, six little boys, absorbed in molesting a puppy, dropped what they were doing and began dancing around Grainger chanting *"O Monstro!"*—The Monster. Rodney loved it and took a picture. They posed, then scattered, following a peddler with a truck blaring inscrutable music, bearing a sign that read "Disco Boss," and stuffed full of junk for sale.

Rodney watched them scamper off and said, "Being tall must be what it's like to be pregnant. You're public property." That's why Rodney liked to travel with Grainger, he said, that and other things, although he sometimes grumbled, "I'm only here for scale."

"For scale?"

"I'm the dime they place in a photo to show how small the world's tiniest Bible is. I'm just here to make sure everybody knows how tall you really are."

Being tall meant hitting cobwebs nobody else's head cleared. It meant most doors were too low, that the change dispenser on BART was ergonomically impossible. That footboards on beds were cause for despair, and most bathtubs were too small. But not in the Furnas *termas!* This bathtub was just right.

The old attendant shrugged. "I know you find it hard to believe, but I was handsome once and my wife was considered very plain."

"What was the attraction?"

"She played hard to get. She could dance and swear and cook. Do you know our fish in the Azores, the one called espada? It's black and ugly with a grimace full of teeth and pop-eyes, big ones so they can see in the dark at the bottom of the ocean. It's the most delicious fish you ever ate, grilled, baked, boiled with a banana in a caldera."

"And you fell in love with your wife because she cooks great espada."

"No, my wife *looks* like an espada. But I love her. She's always been mysterious, like she's still got a few secrets from me."

"Like the Holy Spirit."

This man liked puzzles just as much as Rodney. Every mystery had its solution. Even though most solutions were silly and not worth the effort. How does the weather work? What language are those people speaking and what are they saying? On the plane, Rodney did crossword puzzles, nonstop, and at night, in bed, read Ellery Queen mysteries.

In that time after this conversation at the *termas,* when they had unsuccessfully attempted to get money from the Holy Spirit Bank or the photo of the girl gnawing the crown, Grainger and Rodney returned to their luxurious old-money Hotel de Sao Pedro and found the turn-down service had left them not chocolates on the bedside table, but a little card instead. The Azores, colonized by fishermen and navigators and farmers, were, like Rodney, Weather Involved. The card read, "Dear Guest, we wish you a very good night. Here is the weather forecast for tomorrow. May it help you to enjoy another day in S. Miguel." And below that, four symbols: a sun, clouds, an umbrella, and a thermometer. The clouds were checked, and the thermometer was filled up to the twenty-five-degree Centigrade mark.

"How will this help us enjoy Sao Miguel?" Grainger asked Rodney, who loved this little four-star touch.

"If it rains, we'll know. We can plan around it."

But it did rain the next day. "They can't forecast weather here, it's too changeable," Grainger told a glum Rodney.

For instance, who would have known that this monstrous deluge would come, drowning out even Rodney's Pinafore songs and bringing this one-legged harbinger of the Holy Spirit? Who could have predicted that the news would show pictures of ruined houses and dead cattle and bawling peasant ladies?

"What if you discover your wife's little secret, and it turns out to be something lame, like a birthmark on the top of her head, or a Madeiran in her lineage?"

"My wife is Jewish. I met her in the restaurant where she cooked in New Bedford."

"Jewish? And she doesn't mind being here with all these Catholics, she doesn't mind you praying to the Holy Spirit for the life of your sick gay son?"

"She doesn't know he's a gay, or sick."

This might have been irritating, all these false appraisals Grainger (who considered himself a quick study of a character) had made. If there had been a third person in the room, like Rodney, who would call Grainger a bad riddle solver, or the boxing man who knew so much about the soul, Grainger might have been furious. But alone with the mercurial attendant, the proposing and disposing had a merry nasty quality to it, Bugs Bunny and Daffy

Duck ripping a notice from the tree: "Duck Season! Wabbit Season! Duck Season! Wabbit Season!" until it came down to some as yet unknown punch line: Elmer Season?

"And why is the man in the other room not your boyfriend?"

Grainger frowned. "I think Rodney travels with me because he thinks it's good for his soul. That if he does enough good deeds, it will make up for something."

"I can also tell he doesn't have the virus."

A-ha! "That's not true," said Grainger. "You can't know that. Rodney's afraid to get tested. He doesn't want to know."

The attendant frowned. "That doesn't make any sense. It only helps to know."

On this point, Grainger was the Riddlemaster.

"Why are you staring at me," said the man.

"You're furious with me." Grainger sat up, for the truth of it came to him as it came out of his mouth. "And you're furious at your son. You can't believe we did what we did to endanger our lives and that we weren't good enough to ourselves—to our souls— to save us from doom."

"That's crazy," he said, kneading a place on his thigh where, perhaps, his artificial limb connected with his flesh.

"Can I tell you something? All that 'ruining my health'?—it was fun. Every minute of it was a blast. I'll bet your son agrees, even if he doesn't tell you. When you smoke cigarettes, when you toss back a drink, it's great. The rest of the time, you just sit around paying the consequences and you think, how is it that the most terrible thing in my life is also the most wonderful thing in my life?"

The man crossed his arms. Grainger could easily imagine him as a powerful foreman in the glory days of the unions on the docks, ordering stevedores around, cussing up a storm. To be so powerful in the body once, and then to have a leg shattered. To think you knew it all, how life worked, and then your kid is queer and sick. Wherein resides the soul? In the body or in the brain? What does it look like, and what does it any good? Good acts? Good thoughts?

"Let me ask you something," said Grainger. The water had completely relaxed him. After this visit, he would never see this man again. Grainger flourished under anonymous encounters. Strange men in parks, priests behind confessionals. "Do you think that if you sit here with me, it's good for you? For your soul?"

The attendant was agitated. He said, "Your friend is calling," and abruptly got up. Funny, Grainger hadn't heard Rodney call. Suddenly, he was alone. Alone, the room suddenly felt like a gas chamber, the pointlessly wide space had a killing-room floor feel to it, easy to hose down afterward.

All through these islands, he felt this same ghostly sense, that the whole place was abandoned. Certainly there were more buildings than needed and all the population was heading away from these places. The ones who stayed had an edge of island fever, exhibited in the mad way they drove cars down narrow alleys, like furious hornets mudded into their own nests. Grainger hated the traffic situation.

"It's like a chess game," Rodney would say when one almost hit Grainger. "They've already assessed the situation here and they're looking six moves ahead."

"Chess," snorted Grainger. "In chess, there's usually a loser."

Rodney commiserated. Easygoing, he never minded Grainger's shortcomings. In their room, the furniture, some Portuguese version of Beidermeier, managed to be both ponderous and fussy. Grainger said so. "I like it," Rodney countered. "It reminds me of you." He slapped Grainger in the shoulder affectionately.

Why weren't they together? Was the old attendant asking the right questions? Grainger had thought he could only be the boyfriend of somebody he'd initially had anonymous sex with, then enjoyed it so much to dare to have a conversation.

Rodney was a friend of a friend who had died. They had hit it off a few years back while taking turns caretaking. Caretaking was not a usual place for amorous overtures. And Grainger respected Rodney. Rodney was, on many subjects, more educated. He thought differently. Sometimes, Grainger conceded, puzzles needed to be solved. "All these cabinets and wardrobes," he sighed at that furniture. "It's a shame hotels are full of them. I wish I had this much storage at home."

The turn-down weather report card arrived on the second night with the same clouds checked off, the thermometer once again filled in to the twenty-five degree mark. "You see," said Grainger, "nobody knows what's going to happen."

When the old attendant returned with the squeak-slide, squeak-slide, he seemed even more shrunken than before. When he sat back down wearily, the smock had fallen away and now Grainger could see deep into the front pocket of the man's pants. It was like the pocket of a schoolboy: He could see a pack of cigarettes, a ball of string, surrendered *termas* tickets, change, a penknife, keys, a tiny ball of aluminum. Maybe Grainger just imagined some of it.

"Your friend is something of a ninny," he sighed. "He asked me to run more water for him because he's got a small leak in his tub, and when I turned the water for him"—he chuckled—"the heat from it made him make the funniest noise."

Grainger knew the noise; he'd heard him when the hotel showers shifted heat abruptly. "He squeals like a guinea pig handled by too many kindergartners."

The man slapped his fake leg and laughed.

Then it was quiet again, except for a drop of water echoing against the tile.

The fish market in Ponta Delgada would remind Grainger of this room when they encountered it the morning just before they couldn't get money at the Holy Spirit Bank. It was a vast room tiled and viewable from a gallery above. Long stainless steel tables where squids were sorted by size and the hideous eel-like espada that the attendant spoke of hung off the edge like slick black belts waiting to be cut into steaks. A customer would select one and the tail of the beast would be stuck into its own spike-toothed mouth, the way a fox stole's head bit demurely on a paw. They waited on row after row of tables like the theatre of an operating room, best for the lidless unblinking eyes of fish.

Grainger had watched the way the friends of fishermen would come up to the tables and greet these men, their hands completely gunked up by fish guts and blood. To shake, the clean friend would grab the fisherman by the forearm and shake it, to avoid getting gunked up, too.

Grainger looked at Rodney. This was the way it was between the two of them. Rodney shook him at the forearm, to avoid getting gunked up.

"I am tired so quickly," sighed the man. All the fight was gone from him, his mind had wandered. He probably didn't remember what the two of them had talked about. The momentum of their discussion was lost. Did old age afford forgetfulness now and then? Were there times when he did not remember that his own son was a time bomb ready to go off?

"Why don't you take a bath?" Grainger suggested.

The man grinned, like the fish at the lakeside where St. Anthony of Padua preached to them. "Because the attendant needs an attendant."

Grainger stood up, dripping. "Undress."

"What?"

"Undress, I'm going to help you." Grainger undid the man's smock by pulling the ties on the back, easy as shoestrings. He unbuckled the belt, removed the pants and shirt, not unlike a lover. "I don't know how to take off the leg."

The man had been silent until then. "Nobody knows how to take my leg off except me."

Grainger watched him unstrap the apparatus. It suggested stays and snaps on underwear, a secret, a symbol. "You should show your wife how to unhook your leg." Grainger grinned.

The man laughed. "Yes, I should."

The leg off, Grainger couldn't believe how far up it had been removed. Clairvoyant again, the attendant said, "And my hip was smithereens, too."

"Do you miss the shipyards?"

The man was almost ready to cry. "I'd be there now if it weren't for this. Do you know how good hard work feels?"

Grainger knew it was no reproach. He lifted the man to place him in the water. They were both naked.

"Don't you slip," said the man.

Grainger lowered him. He'd cared for sick friends long enough to know how to lift in the legs, not in the back.

The old man had his eyes shut and to Grainger, his eyelids looked like the very center end of a roll of yellow crepe paper, where the crimps were more thickly compressed.

Down the hall, they heard Rodney start up again: "He's hardly ever sick at sea! Then give three cheers and one cheer more for the hardy captain of the *Pinafore!*"

The man was submerged to the head. Grainger sat satisfied on the wooden chair. It was quiet except for the singing down the hall and the perfect roil of rain above.

"The ugly espada lives in waters so deep," said the man quietly, "scientists don't know anything about them. The fishermen drop lines down maybe a kilometer, and when they pull them up, the change in the pressure from coming up so far has already killed them, they die of the bends. And their eyes pop out. The fishermen put them back in so that they're more beautiful—ha, ha—to the buyers. Who knows how they live down there?"

"Maybe down there, they're beautiful," said Grainger. He looked down at him. His wavy white hair had gone flat against his head and looked marcelled, giving Grainger the all-around feeling that the attendant was getting smaller, dissolving in the bath.

And this was the beginning of a long, fierce time, about three days, in which it looked as if Grainger were vanquishing the world, melted in rain, putting it on his terms for a change, and it hurt only a little, the way a bloody nose does when you've been marveling at something in the sky and have walked into a post, or overeating at Thanksgiving.

"And as for the soul," said the man, who now ran his hands back and forth in front of himself, just below the surface of the green water, "whatever it is, it's more durable than anything around here, legs, hearts, heads. It's not your sickness that I am furious at. It's lack of love. What in the hell are you waiting for? And give me some more water."

Grainger found the keys to the spigots in the pocket of boys' things, and he filled the big tub until it almost overflowed. He thought, I am not going to marry your son.

Outside, the rain was just as powerful, dissolving the whole world. There was no safe place, no way to protect the soul. But it was tough, tough enough to survive the deepest ocean depths. Its eyes were huge, to see in the dark.

It was not until three days later, in front of the Holy Spirit Bank, their credit cards not working, the church bells bonging off-key, the Ten Commandments lights on the ocean, that Rodney suddenly leaned forward and in front of all the Azores, kissed Grainger.

He even slipped him a little tongue. And Grainger took the kiss like somebody had awakened him with it on a sunny weekend morning, and to the marvelous question in his eyes, Rodney said, "I felt I had something coming to me," and Grainger thought, No, I had it coming.

And after a delicious dinner of the ugly espadas smothered in a sauce of shrimps, he and Rodney came upon two bored German nine-year-olds lamenting the unseasonable rains in the Art Deco salon, idly shuffling a deck of cards, and the four of them played War (because it was a game everybody in the world seemed to know—*"Krieg!"* the boys shouted merrily every time two of the same card came up) and Grainger beat the pants off everybody because there's no real way to let somebody win at War, even kids know it's a game of chance, and maybe to somebody who was just looking in on this situation, he might have appeared a little cruel, him being such a big guy bullying kids, but who can tell what somebody looks like when they are having a moment of grace, for grace is unearned like a well-drawn ear of a poorly executed beginning artist's life study; and to top it all off, he had sex with Rodney, who was, as they say, "good in bed," and made that sound of an overhandled guinea pig when he came, and that made Grainger laugh, which might also have seemed cruel, but it was not.

HOME

Bill Gordon

Jay is on the couch and his eyes are rolling. "Oh," he says, "oh," and he tries to sit up.

"You were sleeping," I tell him.

"No, no, I . . . wait," he says, and he points to his cigarettes on the coffee table—the one between me and him. He just points, finger in the air, and then yawns.

I wish I wasn't this kind of person: someone who responds to a finger; someone who other people know will respond to a finger. But I do. I get up—no, pull up. I'm deep in this chair, a mass of old cushions. Stains upon stains. And I'm drunk, too, maybe twice as drunk as Jay is. He should know this.

I'm not sure Jay knows anything right now. I'm not even sure he can see. I want him to stay up, keep talking. I pull a Marlboro from the pack and try to hand it to him. He just opens his mouth.

"Oh," I say, and I press the filter against his bottom lip. His top lip closes down, and he waits for me to light it. I do. Then he takes a drag, blows out the smoke, and tells me to "Get down."

"Down?"

"Off the table," he says. "You should come sit here."

My knee is on the coffee table—so I realize—and I can see that it's made a mark: in the dust. Jay thinks this room is clean. It's the cleanest room in the house, so why shouldn't he?

He pats his hand on the couch, just once, right next to him.

"Come on," he says. "Sit."

I put all my body weight on my knee, the one that's on the coffee table—which seems like a pretty good trick at this point—and I spin. Only a foot or so, really. I stop when I get to his side. I flop onto the couch.

"You sure you never lived in a bigger house?" I ask him.

"Why, you think this one is small?"

"No," I say, "but the furniture is huge."

Jay's looking at the china cabinet when I say this—a giant dark mahogany thing in the middle of the room. Five, maybe six dishes in it, tops.

"That's the one," he says, changing the subject—or sort of. "She pushed it over. Right on my head." He raised his eyebrows; pretends to be shocked; makes sure I'm watching. "My own mother. Can you believe it?" Then he starts to laugh. "That's why it's so fucking empty."

I notice that next to the cabinet is a garbage bag. It's black and plastic and, in this dim light, it almost blends in with the mahogany.

He says, "The rest of the dishes are in there."

I look down at the bag, then up at the china cabinet. The doors have wood designs that swivel and cross. I move my head a little to the left, then the right, so I can see through them to shelves, the plates. Each plate has a red rose on it, just one, and each rose is in a different spot: top, bottom, middle. One of the roses is only half on the plate. All the plates are propped up, side by side, to try and fill the shelf—that one shelf, anyway. The other three shelves are empty, except for a dustpan on the lowest one, bottom right.

"Did the doors used to have glass?"

"Yeah," he says, "that's in the bag, too." Then he tells me that, if I want, we can break the rest. "She'll never know the difference," he says. He tells me that she ran out right after she pushed it; that she was screaming, yelling, crying—"the works."

"Maybe later," I say. I'm glad he's awake. Completely awake. I decide to tell him about the cat. It's the quiet one—gray and white. The cat Jay said was the oldest. Her name begins with an *M*. He thinks he locked them all out—all seven of them—with the dogs. Ten animals in all. They scare the shit out of me. He says they're friendly, but it doesn't seem that way. This *M* cat stayed behind, somehow.

While Jay was dozing off, I put a pillow under his head. I thought he was saying something, and I leaned over toward his face. "What?" I whispered, and I must have misjudged the distance, because my mouth landed on his ear. All of sudden, this *M* cat sprung out from nowhere—from behind the curtain, I think—and she jumped on top of the dining table.

The dining table is crammed into the corner—the right corner, the one next to the couch. It's got six chairs tucked underneath it. If you wanted to pull them all out—at the same time—you'd have to move the couch and close the door. This *M* cat, she just stayed there, arched and hissing, until I sat back in my chair—standing guard, like she knows Jay doesn't like to be kissed, like I was trying to kiss him in the first place. Then she disappeared again. I wasn't going to say anything; didn't want him to know that I was scared of her—a little cat. But I am. So fuck it.

"There's one left," I say.

"Don't worry," he tells me. "Just Marty; she never leaves."

"Marty?" I say. "For a *she*?"

"It's my mother's name."

"Right," I tell him, and I point to my head like I forgot, like I'm someone who always forgets these kinds of things. Which I'm not. Which he knows. "Sorry," I say. "Now I remember."

"She likes you," he says. He means his mother, I think. I only met the woman twice. Only once that Jay knows of. She's gray and white, too, now that I think of it: gray hair; pale, pale face. Like a very old ghost. She scared me, too, when I first saw her. She was in the kitchen—where Jay made me wait. The whole house is crooked, but the kitchen is even more so. She was making hamburgers and taking off her shoes.

"Veal burgers," she corrected me. "Would you like one?"

Her shoes were lace-ups with stubby little heels—an inch or two, maybe—and after she pried one off, she had to turn and check the frying pan. She stood there like that—one foot bare, one foot with a one- or two-inch heel, her back to me, for almost a minute, and she looked perfectly level. Two inches, I thought, left to right—a two-inch difference between two human feet. The house could fall down any minute. By rights, it should fall down. Can't stand much longer—how could it? I was stoned that day and my mouth was dry. I kept raising my voice and swallowing hard, trying not to sound high. I kept wishing Jay would hurry back downstairs. I'd never had a burger made of veal. I wound up screaming.

"No, thank you," I said.

"No, thank you," she repeated, and she pressed down on the spatula so the grease from the burger went *tssss*. "So polite you prep boys are."

Next to the frying pan, on the stove, was a teapot—porcelain, I think, and covered with spots. I noticed that the spots on the teapot matched the spots on the ceiling.

"Jay-tells-me-that-you-work-in-the-ci-ty," I said, lowering my voice, pronouncing each syllable—"that-you're-a-sec-re-tary."

"A le-gal secretary," she said, and again, she pressed down, *tssss*.

"She won't be back tonight," Jay tells me.

"I know," I say. "You told me."

"So you're staying?"

"Yes."

"Your last night . . ." he says.

I don't answer.

"Your last night for a while, I mean."

I look over at my school blazer; it's hanging on the back of a chair—a dining chair, the one closest to the door. It's blue with silver buttons, and it's already got little gray hairs on it. Never even touched an animal; just went from my body to the chair. The hairs must be flying. Flying through the air. I'm probably covered right now. Next to my jacket, on a different chair, is my shirt. I buttoned the top button, the one at the neck, to keep it from falling. It looks like a tiny person.

Jay follows my eyes and he looks over—at the chairs, the shirt, the jacket, the hairs.

"So neat," he says.

Now that I think of it, both chairs look like people. Two little people who came here to watch. I wish I'd just thrown them, dropped them on the table—maybe on the floor.

"You want me to get rid of Marty?" Jay asked me.

"Yes," I say—much too fast.

Jay gets up and bangs his shin on the coffee table. He starts to say something—"Ouch," maybe—then he realizes he can't feel it and keeps walking. Rubbing his eyes, laughing a little. He wipes the back of his hand across his mouth, then scratches his ear—the one I almost kissed. His hand is big and you can see all the bones in it. He scratches his chin with his knuckle. We just smoked another joint. A little one—a roach, really—but strong. When Jay's like this, he looks proud. Like it's taken him years to get to this point, instead of a half hour. He gets to the dining table, steps behind it, and bends over. His hip rubs against my blazer, and it falls. Then he bumps into the chair with my shirt on it, and that falls, too. My eyesight's getting blurry. I try to focus on something, and I realize that there's not a thing—not one thing—in this room that I want to look at. Not even the plates. Which is pretty funny—to me, anyway—and, as usual, I wind up staring at Jay. Staring and laughing a little. Not with him, but at the same time. I decide this is a highlight. He's still bent over. Just legs, now. Half a person. The tag on the back of his underwear is sticking out of the top of his jeans. I can almost make out the little cluster of grapes, apples, oranges—whatever. But I already know they're there, so that doesn't really count. The curtains rustle, then Jay stands up. He's got Marty by the scruff of her neck.

"She's smiling," he says, as he walked by me, toward the door. "She likes you, too."

Marty has her mouth open. Her legs are extended. Her claws are all out.

Jay likes Foster's Ale. It comes in a big can—a million ounces. By the fifth can, his spine disappears. He's had three already. One more and he'll look like a comma. Two more and his face will just about touch his knees. Unless he stands up. Then he'll just look like someone who's falling—which he usually does.

But right now he's still beautiful.

Jay is seventeen. Two years older than I am. But he was only one year ahead of me at school; he started late. He looks about twenty-five. My sister said that once, as a joke. But it wasn't a joke. She just wishes he was twenty-five because that's how old she is. He worked as a lifeguard this summer. After two weeks, he turned blonder and tanner than anyone I've ever known.

"It's from the sun," he said one day when I was staring at his head.

We went to Asbury Park that day. Or some day just like it—a day off. It was August, near my birthday—and his. We took a bus. I didn't tell my parents. Just said I'd be at Jay's. When we got there, we went swimming in the ocean, which was filthy. More like coffee than seawater. Still, it was better than that grimy Boulevard Pool—the place where Jay was working. I asked why he didn't lifeguard at the beach, instead. He said he wasn't a strong enough swimmer, and that he didn't have the bus fare, either. We went inside a fun house. A sad house, really. It was almost empty, and it needed a paint job. Even the mirrors—the ones that twist and dwarf your body—had those brown-red-orange spots that mirrors get when they're old. Actually, all of Asbury Park needed a paint job. You could tell it used to *be someplace,* and that a lot of the hotels used to be nice. And I know that Bruce Springsteen started out there. But still—it gave me the creeps.

The cat crawls up on Jay's shoulder. Jay puts his cigarette in his mouth. Smoking with no hands: Look, Ma. His cheekbones suck in and out; the smoke streams out his nose. It's almost October. He's still blond, still tan. In the winter, his looks disappear. He turns gray, like his mother—like his old, angry cat. Like the walls in this room if we ever turned up the lights. Which we won't. Not for a while.

All those hours at the camera store—alone in the dark room. No sun, no threat of sun. A man he works with is a photographer. Not his boss, but almost. The man wants to take pictures of Jay—naked. He told Jay they'll have to hurry, before the weather changes. Jay says they must be outdoor pictures, then—"Right?"

But the man's worked at the store for two years. I know he's seen Jay in the winter.

★   ★   ★

When Jay opens the door, the dogs try to rush in. They've been waiting right outside. They know his every move. Mine, too, maybe.

Jay throws Marty off his shoulder, out the door, and she doesn't make a sound. Like she's used to being thrown. I hear her claws as she hits the linoleum, or Formica, or—a *click,* then a fast and crazy scraping—the sound comes sooner than I expect; she must have landed on something high: the kitchen table, a countertop.

Jay kicks one of the dogs in the neck. It's Rose. She's managed to get her nose in the room. Rose is a collie. She's the oldest of the dogs—of them all. Even older than Marty. She's thirteen. The rest of the dogs are behind her, and they're barking. I jump up to see if Rose is hurt. But Jay's kick is like a soccer player's—a catch really. No impact. It just cradles, moves, redirects. Rose's beige and white hair blends in with Jay's Frye boot as she vanishes into the kitchen. I stand up for a minute and wave.

Jay presses the door closed and turns around. He starts walking toward me. As he gets closer, I see that his shirt's been ripped on the bottom. It's an undershirt, but it's light blue. He must be doing his own laundry.

"Did Marty do that?" I ask him. I point to the rip, but I'm staring at his stomach. It used to be flatter. I counted four little squares a year ago. Now he's down to two. I like it better this way—less shaped, slightly bulging.

"It was like that when I put it on," he says, as he tugs on his shirt. "But I had it tucked in."

"Yeah, but who ripped it?"

"Who says it's a who?" he says, and I wait for him to continue, but he doesn't. Just keeps walking my way. When he gets to the couch, he doesn't sit down, just stands right in front of me.

"Besides," he says, "what do you care?"

Cute? Yes, he's trying to be cute. He's never done this before; I hope he never does it again.

He stands still, right over me, in front of me. I put my hand on his stomach, and my fingers sort of sink in.

"Let's wait," I say, and I guide him with my other hand toward his side of the couch.

"Whatever," he says, and he reaches under the coffee table. He pulls out another can of Foster's for himself. Then he opens a bottle of Budweiser for me.

"Thanks," I say. "Should we smoke some more?"

"No," he says, "then we'll just pass out."

He tells me I should put my head on his lap.

"Okay," I say, but I don't move.

"Okay!" he says, and he slaps his thigh. I lean over, like a reflex, and put my head down where he slapped.

Jay's legs are like his chest: you see them from across the room, and think, Yes. Up close, though, they're all muscles and bone. No give. Like the hood of a car. No place you want to rub your face against—not for more than a minute, anyway.

His stomach's a different story. I slept on Jay's stomach once for a whole night. Outside. In a playground. The one near his grammar school—No. 17. Pat Bowling was there, too—a kid from my homeroom class. Jay's, too, before he left school. This was months ago, when Pat still followed us around. My parents threw me out that night, figured I'd come scraping at the door before morning. Jay's mother thought he was at my house. Pat's parents threw him out that night also. Little Pat—always at the library, the Irish club— this practice and that. He's probably never even been out past ten before. Past nine, maybe. And he gets thrown out, same as me.

"So now you're in another club," I told Pat, and I figured Jay would laugh. But he didn't.

"It's just for the night," Pat said. He wouldn't say why. He was already there when we hopped the fence. A half hour later, he was spread out on one of those mini merry-go-rounds, the kind you have to push yourself. He was on his back, sound asleep. I'd forgotten he was even there—the way I do at school. But then he started to mumble. No words, just a *gurgle, blah, blah, blah*. Pretty loud, though, because I could hear it from the basketball court— where Jay and I were sitting. I walked over and tried to make out what Pat was saying, which I couldn't. He was asleep—out, at least—but his eyes weren't closed. Not all the way. They were half open and they had this shiny, general stare like he was confused or happy or crying or all three.

"He's fine," Jay yelled over to me. Then he walked over and lowered his voice, almost to a whisper: "I saw what he took."

Jay leaned over and rolled Pat onto his stomach—"in case he throws up." Then he walked away and figured I'd follow.

"When?" I said, not moving.

"What?" Jay turned around—louder, exasperated. He threw his arms in the air: "What?"

"When did you see what he took?"

"Before," Jay said, and he came back, starting pulling me by the hand. "Come on," he said, and when I wouldn't walk, he pulled harder—dragging me, practically, toward the metal sliding pond, ten, maybe fifteen feet away, just outside the shine of the street light.

"Before . . . when?" I asked him, when we stopped.

"He's fine, I told you."

"When?"

Jay shook his head, stuck his hands in his pockets, and crouched down under the sliding pond—into the little spot of dark beneath it.

"Did you give it to him?" I asked.

He still didn't answer.

"Did you?" I said, this time leaning over.

"I don't give my stuff to everybody," he told me.

"Did you sell it?"

"Just get down here," he said.

I thought for a few seconds—about what I should do, where else I could go—and then, finally, I crouched down and crawled in next to Jay.

"Now keep quiet," Jay said.

"Maybe we should move Pat into the dark, too," I asked him.

"Maybe I should just go home," Jay said. "Maybe I should just go home and leave you here."

I shouldn't say I slept that night; I didn't. Jay did. I just laid my head down on his stomach and kept staring at Pat. I thought, for a while, that I should go and get some help. But I didn't want to. I just wanted to lay there, stay with Jay, see what happened.

★   ★   ★

Jay's house is a back house. The front house—the one that faces the street—is much bigger. And it has aluminum siding. Jay's mother grew up in that front house. The back house is covered with shingles—asphalt shingles painted red to look like brick. Up close, the shingles sparkle, and, when you touch them, they feel like the street. Most of the shingles are cracked, and the tack boards underneath are showing. It looks like a shed. A skinny, two-story, crooked old shed.

There used to be a chicken coop on the roof.

"A lot of Jersey City houses had coops," Jay told me when I asked him about it. But that was years ago—1910, '20, '30. You can still see stray wires on Jay's roof.

You have to walk through an alley to get to Jay's house. The alley is squeezed between two front houses. At the end of the alley, there's a metal gate with a lock on it. Behind the gate is a little yard. Jay's yard. It separates the front house from the back one. The weeds are out of control. They're growing through the cyclone fences on either side, and you can see that both neighbors have clipped off the weeds right at their sides of the fences. The neighbors' yards have back houses, too. You can see a whole row of back houses if you look up and down at the yards. But most of them are boarded up.

My aunt Beta had a back house. It was built into a hill—right into its side—and on top of the hill, there was a railroad track. She lived downtown. Downtown from Jay. Down a hill—literally. A different hill—the one in the middle of the city. Down past the statue of Peter Stuyvesant; down past Dickinson High School, where Aunt Beta used to wash blackboards.

Jay signed up for Dickinson, right after he failed out of St. Peter's. But he never went.

There was no grass in Aunt Beta's yard—just cement. When she boarded up the door to her back house, I asked why.

"Because he died," she said.

"Who died?"

"My tenant."

I'd never even known somebody lived there.

"Mr. Russo," she said. "His daughter lived there, too—for a

while. Divorced, the two of them," she said, "both father and daughter," and she shook her head. "Then the daughter moved to California, got remarried," and she shook her head, again. My aunt Beta never even moved out Mr. Russo's furniture. "So old," she said. "Just scraps of things. If his own daughter didn't want them, who else would?"

Aunt Beta wasn't really my aunt. She was my great aunt. I only called her "Aunt Beta" because it made her feel young. And the back house was built for her. My great grandfather had it built when she got married. "Because her husband was so poor," my mother told me. "He was poor and we knew he'd stay poor." But then he died—young, my mother said—and Aunt Beta moved back into the front house, back with the family. "Don't ask her about it," my mother told me, and I never did.

After they boarded up the house, somebody broke in anyway. "Who knows," Aunt Beta said. So she had more boards put up and tore down the stairs that led to the second story. After that, when you looked out her window you'd see a door—just there—up on the second floor, in midair, and no way to get to it. She didn't have it boarded because—because that was the point: there was no way to get there.

She never even locked it. When the train went by, sometimes, the second-story door would swing open.

I slept in Jay's yard once. I took the bus to his house one night— four, five weeks ago, maybe, about a month after that night in the playground. I rang his bell and his mother answered. That was the second time I saw her—and the last time, too. She had all three dogs by their collars—two in her left hand, one in her right, each barking and tugging to get loose. She said she thought Jay was with me.

"Oh," I said.

"Oh, what?" she said.

"He was . . . but we ran into some people. I lost them at the store."

"What store?" she asked me.

"The candy store . . ."

"Oh, for Christ's sake," she said, and she flopped back against the door frame. She was leaning on her right arm, and the dog in her right hand must have felt a limpness: He lunged forward—toward me—and almost got free. But Jay's mother tightened her grip, pulled him back down. "That's the best you can do?" she asked me. By now, she was almost laughing: "A candy store?"

"We stopped to get cigarettes."

"Okay, fine," she said. "Fine: you were at the candy store, the one on the corner—fine. But who? You and Jay and who?"

I made up some names. She kept staring. Finally, I said, "Look, never mind. I was supposed to meet him at Pat's house. I'm sorry." I knew that she liked Pat, that everybody's mother liked Pat.

"You all right?" she said, out of nowhere.

"I'm fine," I told her.

"Good," she said. "You're fine and I'm fine, too." Then she backed away, pulling the dogs in with her. "Tell Jay I'm locking the door. He knows where the key is."

I walked out to the front and waited for him to come down the block. After an hour or so, I walked back down the alley. I saw that Rose was in there and waited for the other dogs to run up to the gate. But they didn't. She was the only one out there. Jay's mother probably let them out for a while—to pee, walk, do whatever—then called them all in. Rose probably didn't make it in fast enough. Or she stayed back on purpose.

Rose didn't bark, not now that she was alone. She just came up to the gate and stuck her nose through one of the holes. I jumped over and we both waited for Jay to come home. He didn't.

In the morning, I stopped off at a diner: a little diner named D.K.'s, it's near Jay's house, under the overpass for the highway. Jay'd taken me there once, and the owner, D.K., recognized me; he let me wash up in the men's room. Then I went to school.

At lunchtime, I called Jay from a pay phone. He was at work, where I figured he'd be. I asked what he'd done last night.

"Nothing. Stayed home. Watched TV."

"Oh," I said. "Me, too."

I decided that Jay and his mother must go days without speaking. I got a detention that day for not wearing a tie.

★   ★   ★

Tonight, when I got here, I used the bathroom. Hanging on the back of the door were a pair of jeans. His jeans. They still had the shape of Jay's body. I reached up to touch them. Jay yelled through the door that he was going out to get more beer. I pulled the jeans down so I could try them on. The left pocket was full of pills but I didn't want any, so I left them there. Under the pants was one of Jay's work shirts. I pulled it down, and I put that on, too. In the front pocket were a stack of envelopes, all addressed to Jay—handwritten, self-addressed. It was Jay's handwriting. He did it. He wants me to keep in touch. There were six envelopes in all, one for each month I'll be away—away at my grandmother's . . . away from this city, from Jay, my parents, my school. . . .

I stashed the envelopes back in Jay's shirt pocket and I threw his shirt in the hamper. Then I moved his mother's robe from behind his pants to the tip of the door hook. That way, if he sees the shirt is missing, he'll think *she* moved it.

But chances are, he won't notice. He won't even look, won't remember. Not tonight anyway. And not in the morning. Not before I leave.

Jay's handwriting is neater than you'd think. It's all print—never any script—but the letters are all the same width, all the same size, like he pressed them through a stencil. Once, at school, he was writing something on a locker. Something about Brother Moramarco—a Jesuit, but not a full-fledged priest. Something about how Brother Moramarco has buck teeth and when he sucks your dick it hurts, but he pays a lot, so it's worth it. I asked Jay if that was true, if he let Brother Moramarco suck his dick, and Jay said that sometimes I was just plain stupid, and he wonders what other stupid things I think about him.

Underneath, Jay'd drawn a picture of Brother Moramarco, and it looked just like him.

I said, "Wow," or "That's impressive," and Jay said, "I know, you should see my mother." Then Jay told me about the plates; about how she'd drawn all these beautiful flowers—all in one day—and then she'd had them "pressed onto plates."

"That's her job?" I asked him.

"No," he said. "She doesn't sell them."

"Oh," I said. "So it's a hobby."

"Whatever," he said. "She drew the flowers on our curtains, too. They match the plates—but not exactly; that would be tacky. Do your curtains match your plates?"

"I don't know," I said, and then he started grinning—gloating, really—so I said, "It's hard to say; we have drapes."

The house in front of Jay's has a back door. Jay's grandparents live there.

"My grandmother still cooks for me," he says, as he walks me past a picture of her. She looks like a man, an old, old man—just a giant jaw and wrinkles. But she's wearing pink lipstick. Her photo is next to the china cabinet, but I couldn't see it from the couch. I don't even remember getting up. Jay must have picked me up. Yes. I finished my beer, lit a cigarette, leaned back for a minute—and now I'm walking.

"Almost every night," Jay continues. He's holding me by the arm, but his hand slips. Now he has me by my underarm. The picture won't stay still.

"You go over there for dinner?" I say. It's only my body that can't keep up. My mouth is going strong. My head falls against Jay's shoulder. I try to keep talking, but my lip sticks to his sleeve.

"No, she brings it back here. My grandfather eats alone."

I know that Jay is adopted. I decide that his grandfather doesn't like him, won't take him into the family. I try to put my hand on his head—to comfort him. But I miss, lose my balance, fall into the china cabinet. Another plate falls over and breaks. I say, "Sorry." Jays says, "Good." Now he has me by both arms. Both underarms. I decide that his parents were never married. There's a wedding picture on the wall, next to the grandmother, but I decide it's a fake. They lived together "common law," I decide, like the tenants in my parents' apartment building.

"She was pretty, my mother—right?"

She wasn't pretty at all. Just less gray.

And she had a nice body. "Look," he says, and he pulls the wedding picture off the wall. He pulls it out of its frame and, behind it, there are three other photos. They're all of Jay's parents, all taken at the beach. Jay's father has a tattoo on his right forearm.

"Does that say Marty?" I ask.

"No," he tells me. "It says 'Mac.' His nickname. Short for MacVee." His forearm is big, almost bigger than his upper arm. Like Jay's.

His mother is wearing a one-piece bathing suit. She's muscular, like a gymnast.

"She used to be a fit model," Jay tells me. "They'd sew the clothes right on her, all around her ass, her thighs, her chest—and then that was the perfect size."

"Your father looks like you," I say.

"Looked," he says.

"Looked," I repeat, mostly to myself, and I remember that Jay's father—who was never even his real father—left five years ago. He didn't die; I thought he did, when I first met Jay, and Jay let me think he did—for a while. But that wasn't the truth.

Jay pauses for a few seconds and stares at the photo. "That's impossible," he says.

"I know," I say, "but still . . ."

Jay drops the picture on the dining table. "Shut up."

There's nothing else downstairs. The dirty, crooked kitchen, the closed-off living room with the giant furniture, and the bathroom—which has no shower.

"We take baths," Jay told me when I got here tonight.

Jay's hair is always a mess—which I like—and I decided, for whatever reason, that *that* is why.

The stairs to the bedroom are covered with a rust-colored carpet. The rust-colored carpet is covered with cat hair. The cat hair is covered with dog hair. The dog hair is what we're walking on. The steps are less crooked than I expect them to be—but when I try to walk up them, I almost fall anyway. Jay pushes me from behind. Our feet make footprints.

Upstairs are the two bedrooms—his and hers. He opens her door and points my head inside, so I can look in. So I *have* to look in. Her bed has tons and tons of pillows on it. They're each a different color. Some have patterns—triangles, circles, little houses and horses and urns. Mostly blood red and purple. Some black and beige, too. The bed is meant to be a canopy, but there's nothing hanging from the rods.

"She went to India once. Or she planned a trip—and she was gonna do it over in that style."

"What style?"

"Like India. Indian, I guess."

"Did she go there or not?"

"Who cares," he says. "I was a little kid. Anyway, she never finished the job."

In Jay's room there's a bed, unmade, and then there's a separate room—almost like an office. It has a couch.

There's a fish tank in the corner and, though the whole room smells like cat litter, there's hardly anything out of place.

Jay walks me inside and drops me on his bed.

"Close the door," I say. "Before they all run in."

Jay used to smell like this at school. Damp and stale, like the cat litter. But that's just his clothes. His skin has no smell at all. Never did. Just cigarettes and soap. Sometimes a little sweat. But mostly just nothing—air. Hot, clean air.

"I have to go to the bathroom," he says.

"Okay," I say. "Shut the door."

I lie down on the bed and close my eyes. I'll be gone tomorrow. I won't come back. I don't have to. No reason at all. Jay can come see *me*. I didn't think of that. But it's a good idea. My grandmother will like him. *His* grandmother does. I'll make him wear a tie. Maybe I'll send him one in the mail. In the envelopes. I'll pull the envelopes out of the hamper in the morning.

My grandmother's house has shiny wood floors. She has area rugs: something Jay's probably never heard of—beautiful, hand-knit fabrics from other countries. She never says which countries—doesn't have to—just says, "They're from Europe" or "the East." Jay's house could never have an area rug; Jay's house has no area.

She has big hair, my grandmother. It's red and dyed and she gets it teased twice a week. Her chin disappears when she laughs. She doesn't laugh much, but it's always there waiting—just waiting to disappear. When my parents asked her to take me, they had to beg. I heard them on the phone. They took turns: "We'll pay," my father told her. Magic words. "For anything," my mother said. More magic. That was one week ago tonight, a Friday night happy night: they thought I was out, sleeping—who knows? I was on the downstairs extension. After they hung up, I ripped the phone out of the wall.

When I open my eyes, Jay is back. So quick. I didn't even hear him climb the stairs. I fell asleep, but something woke me. It was the door. Yes. The door slammed and I rolled over so I could see it. Now I remember. I rolled and the room rolled with me.

Jay has his work shirt in his hand. His right hand. It's blue. All his work shirts are blue; he has three in all. One of them is too tight and it pulls at the buttons, at the seams; the one he wears on Fridays. I wonder if it's that one. I wonder why he's holding it up, way up, over my head. I wonder if he'll put it on for me—this tight, tight shirt—and walk around the room.

"Get up," he says.

I look at his left hand and I see the envelopes.

"You didn't forget," I tell him, and I try to smile. But there's this *swish*—I have to keep my mouth closed. It's all through my body. A flood, really. I shouldn't have moved; shouldn't have rolled. I have to stay still now. I have to keep my mouth shut. Keep it inside. I put my hand on my forehead—it's streaming. A different flood. I'm all liquid, now, inside and out.

He's brought them to me. He didn't forget. I try to breathe through my nose, but that's streaming, too—a leak: I use my hand to plug it.

He must have found them in the—yes—but why were they in the—yes—that's what he's asking me—Why?

I put them there. I remember that I put them there, but I can't remember why.

I try to reach out to him, take his hand, and he backs away. I fall off the bed, onto the floor. The swishing is worse, now; I should have stayed still.

He still has the envelopes in his hand and he's yelling. I can't make out what he's saying, but he keeps getting louder.

"What?" I say. Then he throws them at me—the whole handful of envelopes. They fly in different directions, then fall, each one floating to the floor. One falls next to me and I shouldn't move— I know I shouldn't move—but I crawl to it.

"Get up," Jay says, again, and he steps toward me. His foot is near my face. "Get up and pick them up." My body is heavy and the room keeps getting lighter. It's spinning and spinning and soon it will be gone. Gone. There's no stopping it now. The whole little house will just lift off the ground, fly through the air. Like in that movie. I'll be left here on this bed. On the bed, in the yard. Just me and Rose. Jay will be gone, too.

"Get up," he says. He bends down, grabs me by my face. He has the skin, just the skin. I never knew I had so much skin. A whole other face.

"What's wrong with you?" he says. "What the fuck's wrong with you?"

I try to stand, but my legs won't hold me. They wobble and I fall. The rooms keeps going—faster and faster.

Jay tells me that he's glad.

"What?" I say. It's hard to hear, now. I close my mouth—fast. Then I look up, squint my eyes, and his voice gets clearer.

"Glad," he says. "I'm glad you're leaving." He tells me that it will be "easy, no problem at all."

"Easy?" I say. Then I shut my mouth, again—just in time.

"Anybody," Jay's saying. He's saying that he can find anybody to do what I do. He says that it's no wonder about my parents—"No wonder they don't . . ."

I can't hear him anymore. And I can't answer. I can't answer because I can't talk—not even if he let go of my face—not even then.

"Get out," he says. But he doesn't let go. He just stares down at me. His eyes fill up and his grip gets tighter. He's about to cry. Or hit me. I can't tell which. Neither can he. He grabs me with his other hand, this time by the back of my neck, and drags me to the couch. He throws me down. He stands in front of me and doesn't move. His mouth opens, like he's about to say something, but then it just shuts. I try to sit up and he pushes down on my shoulders.

He just stares at me, keeps quiet, holds me in place.

But wait, the room isn't spinning so fast. It's slowed down. It's nearly stopped. My face hurts, though. And my stomach, too. But there's no swishing. My nose is still leaking, and I touch it, but this time my hand comes back red. I look behind Jay. I look at the floor, at the mess on the carpet. Oh yes, I can open my mouth, now; I can breathe. But the smell. And the blood—I was wrong to think Jay might cry. He took the other option. Of course.

And he's still there—still standing in front of me, no plans to move. I notice that, under his left foot, is an envelope. I try to sit up—this time slowly—so I can kiss him.

"Don't," he says, when my face reaches his, and I sit back down.

Jay takes his hands off my shoulders. He leans forward—slightly—but his feet stay in place.

"Oh," I say. I wait for a minute—for him to unbutton his pants, at least. But he doesn't. He makes me do that, too.

Jay's jeans are still hanging on the bathroom door. I pull them down so I can wipe my face. He's asleep now, upstairs; I left the door open and the animals took back the house. But this bathroom is mine.

He asked me to stay here once. That's the truth. It was that night in the playground, that night Pat almost died. He asked me to come here and live with him—right here in this horrible little house that could fall down any minute. He said his mother wouldn't mind, that she's hardly ever home. He said he'd be eighteen next year and he'd get a real job, find his own place, take me with him. He was whispering, but I heard him just fine. My face was still on his stomach and, when he spoke, I could hear the echo fly down through his rib cage, feel the quiet rumble against my cheek.

"Don't go back," he said, like it were just that simple, like that was something I simply never thought of. "Come home with me." And he put his hand on my head, pressed my face in closer to the rumbling. "Come on," he said, and I didn't answer.

"All right," he said after a minute or so, "go to sleep, then . . . As soon as we wake up, though: my mother leaves early; she'll be gone by then."

Again I didn't answer.

"Come on," he said, finally: he was almost pleading. "Don't you want to?"

The next morning was a different story, though. The next morning the sun was out, and Jay wasn't stoned. Not half as stoned, anyway. And Pat wasn't half sleeping; he was wide awake and staring at us. So were two old Polish ladies who were walking by.

"What?" he said when I asked him about it—"What?"—and he sat up, shrugged his shoulders, started dusting off his sleeves. "In my house?" he said, "with my mother?" He made sure to laugh. It was a fake, nervous laugh, but a laugh nonetheless. "You smoke too much," he said. Then he put his hand over his pocket, his jacket pocket, the one where he keeps his joints, and said something—a joke—about cutting me off.

"Come," he said, "I'll walk you to the bus stop."

I'm resting my head against the side of Jay's tub right now—Jay's giant, water-stained, chipped-porcelain tub, the kind most people don't use anymore, except to grow flowers, the kind that stands high on four legs . . . four curved, hand-carved legs with feet that look like claws—which is where I'll be sleeping tonight, and it's cool, cool against my face, which is hurting. I'm sorry that he hit me tonight; he's never done that before. And I'm sorrier still that I wanted him to. I swallow, and my mouth has such a strong taste, though—so much blood and Jay and vomit and beer: I feel almost productive. So much smoke in there, too . . .

And I don't smoke too much. Jay was wrong about that. He was kidding, sure, but still, he was wrong. I think it's Jay who smokes too much. Way too much. So much that, if I asked him—which I wouldn't, not again—he'd probably tell me that he meant what he said that night in the playground; he'd probably say that he wants—really wants—me to stay here, right here, with him, in this horrible house that could fall down any minute—if only this house were his to offer. And he probably thinks he could be happy like that, or that I could . . . if only.

And he'd probably believe it. He probably thinks I meant it when I answered him that night, too. When I closed my eyes, turned my head, pressed my lips against his stomach so that no one could possibly hear me but him. When I finally said "Yes."

I'm glad that he thinks that—that he gave me something beautiful and then took it away . . . took it away because he had to. I'm happy he thinks he had it, this beautiful, perfect, simple thing to be giving. Or that I did, really. And that's the difference between him and me.

I'll leave in the morning, and I won't come back, but I'm happy for Jay. I wish I believed it, too. I wish I were that kind of person. But I'm not.

Quality Time

Jim Provenzano

Green Day Dookie CD
Pearl Jam concert T-shirt
Asics International Light wrestling shoes, size 8, black
  (or just Gel style if it's too $$)
2 Champion MED sweatpants, blue and red
Prentice Alvin **part II and III (seen at Waldenbooks)**
Gray's Anatomy **CD-ROM**

I stuff Donnie's wish list in the glove compartment under the cell phone. He faxed it to my office. He would have e-mailed it, but he knows I don't always answer in a timely manner.

Donnie makes me feel old and young at the same time. Young, because I like most of his music, even though I'm thirty-four. We went to a Green Day concert together. People brought their babies.

He thinks I'm posing, pretending to like what he likes, but I do. He's me half a life ago, only better.

I tape all his matches. I'd go to them if they were on the other side of the world, which they might be someday, if he really works hard, but I don't push. I know what pushing does. That's when I feel old, hearing myself impersonating my dad, when I call him, ask about school, and he says, "That's Mom's department."

Sports is mine, which is funny, considering I only remember football players by the caliber of their butts. But Donnie's wrestling, that's different. That, I adore.

Yesterday, when the pot thing happened, She Who Will Not Be Discussed handed him over to me like she used to hand over broken vacuums: "Fix it." I left work early, went to her place. He was scowling on the couch while she held half a joint, in a Ziploc like sealed evidence.

I was supposed to be very upset. I was supposed to lecture. I took Donnie for a drive, all the time hoping, Does this mean I get him for an extra day?

So maybe I messed up, maybe I shouldn't have held it up to his face like evidence, like a cop, then burst out laughing with him. Maybe I should have smoked it in front of him. Maybe I should have listened to him more when he later accused me of being "two-faced." Maybe I should just let him be when it comes to some problems. Maybe I should have smacked him like She Who suggested. Maybe I should get another self-help book. Maybe I can't afford it, because I had to buy Green Day CDs and wrestling shoes and Duraflames just to please him, and make this weekend the best ever.

No, just good. No pressure. Can't pressure him into being some kind of good son. Last night he listened more when I told him the effects of pot, what it did to me. What got him most was his vanity, and he is vain. Told him how it messes up his complexion. That got him. Charged right to the mirror.

See, I don't need to hit him. I remember getting hit, which does not make you behave. Getting hit makes you want to steal cars.

The pot discussion did grant me another day. I bite my tongue thinking he misbehaves just to make an excuse to be with me more often. I took him to the match. I waited around, back in the empty bleachers, watched his team warm up, happy to simply observe him.

I'm supposed to be thankful for the extra quality time, and I am, really. For another moment to catch the sun shining through his peach fuzz, see him slouch in faux-cynical poses, I'd do anything.

Of course, he's beautiful. He makes me think thoughts we are told not to think about our children. But he is gorgeous, besides looking like I wish I looked then. When I was fifteen, my body was my only lover; the tension of muscle, the trajectory of fluids. He doesn't know how perfect he is right now.

Having a gay dad was brought up at one of those conferences with the referee, not the one with the whistle, but in court, the one who said how Donnie needs a "normal" home. And how is a recovering alcoholic real estate divorcee, excuse me, divorceé, who still Suzanne Somers–tints her hair, any more normal than me, with my steady job, my dog, a home I rent, yes, but hey. At least I don't bleach my hair. I don't even have an earring. Anymore.

My house is spotless. I don't have porno or chaps or dildoes, anything a "normal" gay man might own for an evening's entertainment. I have sacrificed to make my home palatable to those Kourt Kounselor Kreeps who swoop down on their flying clipboards.

I have not warped this boy. Anybody could have a Herb Ritts poster over their bed. And the "Fuck Me . . . and the Horse I Rode In On" T-shirt was a gift from Steve, which I only wore at home once while Donnie was visiting.

But this is not about that, or them, but about Donnie, who thinks he lost when he was struggling, fighting under the arms of that beast from Falmouth who nearly broke his neck, and no, the ref was not looking, and yes, that was an illegal hold. Donnie was bridging out of an attempted pin, upside down, the top of his head pressed into the mat, the other boy chokeholding him, Donnie's face ready to burst blood. Wouldn't any father get a little upset? I am not some nut job who thinks he can save him from disaster, but boys have died playing high school sports, okay? Yes, I stepped on the mat, for just a moment, and for that I will apologize to Donnie. I already apologized to the ref, and his coach, whose handshake and smile spoke volumes. People can be so polite when you wear the badge of dishonor.

Volatility is not my usual state. My job could have something to do with it. I read that someone did a study comparing the stock exchange rate with investors' emotional states. I don't think that applies to me. Donnie is my investment. My job is just playing with other people's money.

But sometimes this things happens at work, mid–phone call. Or

I'm at the Y. Halfway through another scoop into the pool water, during my umpteenth lap, I'll just stop, short out. At work, I freeze, and the cloud of office noise surrounds me like pool water. I float, motionless, begin to sink.

Then I reengage. What stirs me is not hunger, or work, or a lover, or God. Donnie is my only spark plug. I don't want to wear him out.

We don't ask each other about the romance department these days. Steve, the closest candidate to Boyfriend I ever had, hit it off with Donnie. We all liked Steve, but this is not about Steve, or any of the other men I've met who veered away when family entered the conversation, or the others, whose eyes lit up at the mention of Donnie, as if he were an extra helping of me.

Not that I'm shocked.

I think things, too, while I'm sitting in the car, waiting for him to finish up his little locker room rituals with his buddies, all of them naked, or shucking off tight singlets, shiny as candy wrappers. Imagining sex with his friends bears a lighter burden of guilt.

I've looked at the video in the viewfinder. I'm embarrassed by the tape, the part where I blew up and left it on.

The view is pretty funny, Donnie wrestling, rolling, then getting caught in that hold, then my shaky camera work, then just the floor, the mat out of focus, while I yell at the ref. I can't hear the sound, but I remember it. It reminds me of everything I did wrong, like thinking I was straight for ten years.

But look, look what I got for my mistake.

This little man, fifteen years old and so arrogant and shy, with a life all his own of plans and problems and pouting, the button eyes of She Who, and my chin, and my hair, but it's cut so short. Some days he catches me staring at the back of his head. His buzz cut swirls out like a tiny universe whose only limits are two stubby ears.

I could get lost in missing him, but he's back with me, ambling down the sidewalk. His friend Joey is with him, their gym bags so big it looks like they've been to Europe. They're mumbling, smiling, bumping shoulders, framed in my car window like a wedding picture. Down the aisle.

The boys get in, their hair wet, the smell of shrugged-off victory and soap filling my car. And then, as if it's nothing, as if this was just any other day, not one of six days a month I get to see him and hear his crackly voice, listen to him chew shredded wheat in the morning, ask me about the purpose of geometry, if any, as if this is just any other day, he says, "So, can Joey come to dinner with us?"

There's a moment where my throat catches, I know they heard it, in the soft warmth of the car, but I look back at the boy, my son's friend, who looks like a Steiff toy from FAO Schwarz. He's got a hand half-fastening the seat belt, caught, like, *Should I even strap in?*, *Don't hate me, Mister Khors, sir,* and of course I'm shanghaied. His friend is his friend, who maybe loves him, too. I can't cut into that. Besides, this is just another day. This is the point. This is what we are attempting here.

"Sure," I say. "Ya call your parents?"

"Oh, it's okay," Joey the Toy says.

"Call." I don't need two more parents on my case: *You took my son where?*

Donnie takes the cell phone from the glove compartment, not to be showy, but to be sure. The list falls out. He sees my check marks. His smile, his eyebrows darting up in mock surprise; these are my gifts.

Donnie lets Joey play with the camera. I should have rewound it, let him eliminate the evidence, but I don't. I tell him to fast forward, since after I calmed down I taped all the other boys' matches, like Donnie asked. I want to hear the play by play, store details about the boys my son calls friends.

We'll watch it tonight, whether Joey stays over or not. It'll be funny. I know they'll like it. We'll laugh like hounds.

QUIET GAME

William Lane Clark

Anderson no longer hated the situation. He had hated the situation for so long that it no longer seemed like a situation at all. It was now normal. A given. Sonny was gone and would not come back. He would call to talk to the boys, acting like everything was normal. Like he was just midway in a long planned vacation. Like they should all be happy for him. Happy to hear from him. Happy to know that Hawaii was just beautiful. That his new life, that's what he would call the situation, the situation that now seemed normal, that his new life with Felipe was *putting his head back together*. He would call again later to check in. No permanent number yet. He'd keep in touch.

"What did your dad say?"

"Nothing. Just said he was checking in."

Anderson had felt like screaming. But not at Runyon, who climbed from the stool where he had been talking to Sonny on the kitchen wall phone.

He felt then that if he didn't scream, he'd somehow disappear. Disappear into this unbelievable mess that Sonny had left him. No longer a parent. No longer able to control or at least guide the craziness of the situation. Just another one of Sonny's boys, untethered, loosed, set free, abandoned.

"Can I have another Twix?"

Runyon was pointing to the last candy bar on the kitchen counter. He had seen it while standing on the stool, talking to his father on the phone. He had eaten all the other Twix bars in the family pack. Anderson was about to reach for the candy. Give it to Runyon. That was when the situation began to change, he thought later. Before the phone call he would have just handed the bar to the boy. Now he wondered why.

He analyzed his behavior with a new sense of awareness. Payment, he supposed. Bartering for a little connection, a little bit of a normal relationship, a little time. *You have been idle for a while. Do you wish to remain on-line?* That's what his Internet provider would ask when he had been too long at other sites. When he was no longer a potential customer. When he had found other interests than those the provider thought were "Hot Now!" He could never anticipate the sudden interruption. His absorption in whatever pornographic picture gallery he had been scanning, or whatever correspondence was under way, would suddenly evaporate, and he would be wrenched back to that previous reality, the Anderson who had clicked the icon acknowledging he understood this site was devoted to explicit gay sex and homosexual images, had clicked "yes" that he was over eighteen years of age, that he was an adult.

An adult would not have let a five-year-old eat nearly a dozen candy bars. One after the other. Watching him violate the normal rules and regulations of being a kid, of not getting your way, of waiting till after dinner for one Twix bar, of not having too much sugar, of not asking again, of understanding "When I say no I mean no." Watching the boy eat the candy. Anderson, leaning against the refrigerator with his arms crossed over his belly, like he was hugging himself. Watching Sonny's boy break the rules. Breaking the rules with him. For him.

But then the situation changed. He suddenly felt different. Not like his old self, he thought. Not like before Sonny left. But different. Awake, like he had been dreaming or sleepwalking for a long time. Like he just realized that now. Like he had snapped out of it, had been slapped in the face for being hysterical like some girl in a movie, had jerked his head away from the smelling salts and come to, had suddenly recognized Auntie Em and the farm hands peering at him from bedside. *There's no place like home.* He didn't care that Sonny wouldn't talk to him. He cared, he concluded, whether or not Runyon ate that last candy bar.

"We've had enough, Runyon."

That had been nearly four weeks ago. He had thrown the remaining candy bar in the trash and enlisted Runyon in cleaning up his little brother, whose whimpers from the playpen in the bedroom announced that his nap was over. They had made a game of it, changing Benjamin's diaper, acting like they were competing with another pair of diaper changers, *Team Runyon*. Benjamin shifting from sleepy whine to leg-kicking giggles in the process. Just like when Sonny was still home, he realized. Sonny never cleaned up Benjamin. Or Runyon for that matter. It had always been Anderson's job. He really didn't mind.

Since that phone call that day, the family situation had become normal, and he had established a new sense of routine out of the old. Anderson took the boys to day care each day and picked them up after work. He played games with them. Read to them. Took them to their mother's house every other weekend. Those visit days were hard. He realized, on those days, that he lived alone. He was the Anderson whom Sonny had met at the gym so many years ago. The Anderson who had been waiting since adolescence for a man like Sonny. He was really more boy than man when Sonny ended their weeks of smiling across the Nautilus circuit and asked if he needed a free weight spotter. That was the feeling he had when the boys went to Marion's for weekends. He once again became unattached. Single. But unlike his days before Sonny, he wasn't available. He was just lonely. He would be lonely this weekend. Thinking about the two days without them, he realized Runyon was asking a question, maybe for the second or third time. Why shouldn't they tell Mommy that Daddy's not home.

"Yeah, why?" Benjamin repeated the question, imitating his brother.

"Because your mommy doesn't really care if Daddy's still gone." Not a good answer, Anderson knew, but was saved from trying to think of a better one by Runyon, who was happy to have the dialogue resume.

"It's a secret, isn't it?" Runyon cocked an eyebrow from behind Benjamin, who looked up into Anderson's face while getting his hair brushed. *Smarty. Conspirator.* You and I understand, Dad. Benjamin's still a kid.

"Well, sort of a secret," Anderson mumbled, wishing to make less of his instructions not to let Marion know that Sonny was still in Hawaii. "It's sort of like a secret, but"—and he winked in league with Runyon—"it's more like a game."

"Like the quiet game." Runyon winked back.

"Exactly."

Anderson pulled the loose thread that dangled from Runyon's new shirt at its untucked hem. Oversized. A Nike swoosh across the chest. Athletic. Sonny had purchased it before he left, but this was the first time Runyon had worn it. Ball player like his dad. Looked like him already. Looked like a miniature adult. A miniature adult jock. Baggy shorts, baggy shirt, sneakers so high-tech they looked like sci-fi footwear. Anderson realized that Runyon hadn't touched a basketball for almost a year now. Sonny's one area of interest in Runyon coincided with his principal area of self-interest: sports. He wondered if Runyon missed playing ball with his dad. He certainly didn't seem to miss his dad.

"Can you stay for a bit?"

Marion pushed the hair from her forehead that had plopped forward when she bent to pick Benjamin up from the porch. She looked, as usual, frazzled. Perhaps a little more so today in army fatigue pants and a paint splattered man's button-down with the sleeves missing. She was refurbishing the guest room with Mel. They were painting.

"I hate to ask you, but I was hoping you could watch the boys here for a few minutes till Mel and I get the ceiling done. Twenty-five minutes, Anderson, tops. Swear to God."

"I can take them back home till you're ready, if you want to just give me a call." Anderson laughed good-naturedly. He had always liked Marion, even when she was Sonny's wife and they were having troubles in their marriage. Anderson was one of those troubles back then. He had felt guilty about falling for Sonny when he found out about Marion and Runyon. Then Benjamin came after Sonny moved in with him. *There's no perfect scenario for everyone. We can't all live happily ever after.* That's the way Sonny explained it. Something was going to give. Marion or Anderson. Sonny never entered that equation. It was just understood by everyone involved that Sonny would have his way. If Marion gave in. If Anderson could take it. In the end they would both sacrifice for Sonny. In the end they both liked each other enormously. Sonny had predicted they would. Sonny just naturally got his way. Got custody, for example.

"No, no, no." Marion held the screen door open. "Come in and have a smart cocktail while the missus and I power roll that ceiling. We can talk while we work if you watch the boys. We haven't talked for ages." She walked Benjamin toward the sofa on the tops of her workboots. "So how's Sonny? I haven't even *seen* the bastard for ages. Out of town?" She looked over at Runyon as she goose-stepped with his brother. "Mother's just kidding, Runyon. Your daddy's a lovely man." She hoisted Benjamin nearly to her shoulders and dropped him squealing on the couch. "Not as lovely as your other daddy"—she kissed Anderson on the cheek as she pulled him toward the kitchen—"but lovely in his manly way."

Runyon ignored the patter, intent on the video game he began playing as soon as he entered the house.

Anderson watched Marion prepare his drink. A negroni, without asking. Marion always presumed Anderson wanted the best. No asking if he wanted a beer. She had Bombay blue gin, thank God. Not that Anderson would say anything if the bottle weren't blue. Marion actually felt better giving Anderson the best. She always wanted to please him. Partly because he was so readily pleased. She could hold no match to his cooking skills, but she took him to the best restaurants when it was her turn to treat, when Sonny was on one of his trips and they could get together. The boys at Sonny's mom's. She kept quality snacks in the cupboard for Anderson. Those little Niçoise olives and cornichons and tins of goose liver. Stuff she only ate when he was over. Marion liked chips, salsa, light beer. Regular food. But she enjoyed going out with Anderson, he knew. She thought him handsome, sweet, accomplished. It was always like prom night. She dressed. Not to please him necessarily. It pleased her to look as good as her escort. Time with Anderson was make-believe for her, she said, but more real to her than the three years spent married to Sonny. Sonny wasn't real in the end. She never really knew him. Not the way Anderson probably does, she would say. No, Sonny wasn't real. Not make-believe at all. Just unbelievable. Unbelievably beautiful in that lug-nut-jaw, square-chested, piercing-eyes sort of way. Sonny turned heads. But mostly unbelievable. She realized after the divorce, she once told Anderson one boozy night together, that she had never really trusted a word that came out of Sonny's perfect mouth. He wasn't a bad man, she had come to accept. He was just a better boy than he was a man. Fun. Energetic. Ready to play games at any time. His car trunk filled with every imaginable ball and the sports equipment to play any game. Anderson knew what she meant.

"Got another beer?"

Mel stood in the kitchen doorway, paint roller raised in one hand, scratching herself perfunctorily at the crotch of her painter's paints. She smiled goofily when she saw Anderson perched next to the sink on the countertop. Embarrassed.

"Anderson." She nodded as she took the beer from Marion, who returned to the cabinet and grabbed the Campari bottle and shot glass to finish the drink.

"Mel." Anderson smiled at her. He'd known her for years. Not as long as Marion had. She'd been Marion's maid of honor. First college roommate, or something like that. Marion's best friend. He didn't like her lover, Ron. Cold. Lipstick type who said little but seemed to be making judgments constantly. He often thought Mel and Marion would make a great couple, if Marion were gay. So did Ron, Mel's lover, he'd bet.

A few hours later Anderson sipped another negroni, this time at home. Nobody in the house. Sonny surfing or biking or fucking somewhere in Hawaii with Felipe, the trainer Anderson never got to know. The boys at the movies with Marion. Anderson alone on the deck Sonny had built himself three summers ago to support his

Jacuzzi. An amenity Anderson never used. He looked at the covered tub and the patio furniture. He'd have to winterize the deck before too long. Drain the Jacuzzi. Store the furniture in the basement. He sat on the steps that dropped to the sideyard garden. His garden. Lush. Perfect. Eden in the city. Short flight of stairs from here to paradise. He looked at his nearly finished drink and thought about making another. He got up, but then decided to sit back down on a step halfway between deck and garden. Suspended. Indecisive.

He thought about what Marion had said. No need for the quiet game. Sonny had been in touch with her. When he brought the boys over that morning, she said, she wasn't sure Anderson knew about Felipe, that Sonny wasn't coming back. She told him Sonny called to ask her permission to take the boys to Hawaii. She could stay with Felipe and him any time she visited, he said. The boys could spend summertime with her. She asked him what about Anderson? Sonny played the quiet game. She hung up. She told Anderson all this after the room had been painted, the mess cleaned up. Mel gone. The boys both napping on the carpet beneath their feet. Anderson cried. Marion sat next to him. Jaws clenched. Red-faced. Not looking at him.

The next morning he woke up without raising his head or opening his eyes. He wasn't hiding, but he wanted time to think without distractions. It was Sunday. The boys at Marion's. He would go to the farmers' market early. But first, he needed to think. Eyes tight. Curled in upon himself. He felt sick to his stomach. Nausea rolling in waves. Was he actually sick? Sick from worry, he guessed, opening his eyes, the early morning sun brightening the room, calming him. The nightmares of Runyon and Benjamin being lost, the repeating storyline of his sleep, were still fresh as the sweat on his forehead. In a forest? On the ocean? No. The worst part of the city at night. Frightened boys alone, looking for their father among the hustlers, the homeless, the urban predators. Anderson was there but not there. Observer status only. The nightmares fading to recognizable dreams. Bad dreams. Bad night. Anderson felt like crying again. The alarm went off.

The morning wasn't going much better for Anderson than the

night. The time since Sonny let him know he wasn't coming back, the new routine he'd gotten comfortable with, he knew, leaning down with one arm over the refrigerator door, looking for the oranges to squeeze for juice, forgetting why he was peering into the refrigerator after a while, the new routine he knew was only a temporary respite. The calm before the storm. Worse was coming. The plastic bags of fruit in the plastic keeper began swimming around in the refrigerator bin. Still leaning on the door. His other hand on top of his head now. Grimacing. Hot tears. Christ. If he had anything in his stomach, he would throw up.

He set about grinding coffee beans, busying himself with filters, water, coffeepot. Mind off everything but the morning ritual. Hands still shaking, but head clearing. Thank God the kids were with Marion. The headlines on the Sunday paper made no sense. Nothing sank in. He stared at the paper as though it were some exotically folded and decorated paper piece on display in a gallery. Something meant to be a newspaper, but with the meaning of the thing somehow attached to the context in which the object sat, not the paper itself. If one looked closely, the print would reveal one of those Latinesque pseudo-languages used in computer mock-ups. You had to be sophisticated, a connoisseur, knowledgeable, to distinguish this piece of art from the thing it represented. You'd have to be the kind who liked Warhol to understand this newspaper. You'd have to know something more, bring something to the piece to get it. That's what they would say. You had to be in on it to get it, to pick up on the irony, the kitsch, the camp that came from the aesthetic detachment once you understood the context. Anderson was having trouble with context.

Coffee worked. Caffeine snaking through him like a thrown lifeline. He showered, shaved, dressed, set the house alarm, and turned the dead bolt from the front steps when he realized he had left the garage door remote inside. He suddenly hadn't the energy to reverse his trajectory, that well laid out path from his morning coffee to the farmers' market that had consumed him in his single-minded concentration. He didn't want to go back through the vestibule, through the house to the kitchen, to the drawer with the remote. He didn't want to start over. The alarm beeped behind the bolted door. It was arming itself, but it was not too late to open the door and go back inside. One hand on the doorknob. One hand with the key. He couldn't. Maybe he'd just walk to the market. He sat on the front stoop to consider the possibility. If he didn't buy all that much, he could lug it back on foot. Getting a cab would be impossible. Musing, he noticed someone in the car parked at the curb in front of his house. Waiting. Marion.

"Want to go to the market?" she hollered to him through the open passenger window. She was alone. The car was running. How long had she been there?

"Where are the boys," Anderson asked her as he looked around and pulled the seatbelt across his chest. Marion's car always smelled new. He looked for a "new car smell" air freshener. It wouldn't be unusual for Marion to have something like that. The kind of thing he liked about her.

"Sonny's folks." She hadn't dropped them off this morning. The grandparents had called before they went to the movies last night, asked to tag along. Took the kids home with them for a sleepover.

Not much to say on the way to the market. The discomfort of yesterday sat between them, daring them to open their mouths. Marion patted Anderson's leg as she pulled into the parking area. It was comforting. He squeezed her hand and smiled at her. She blushed as she took the keys from the ignition.

Last of the tomatoes. End of the season. It seemed to Anderson that everything was winding down. Pumpkins and gourds were already showing up in small numbers next to the squashes. Potted mums had replaced wildflowers at the flower stands. The market would go on nearly to Christmas, but it lost its personality, its true self, around this time of year. Anderson noted it each season. The thrill of buying the first asparagus of the season, the delight of that first peck of home-grown heirloom tomatoes, the succeeding wonders of cherries and peaches, of each fruit that came into its season, could hardly be matched by the arrival of dull fall produce, buttressed though it was by holiday wreaths and non-food items to fill the stands later in the year.

They were talking about the lackluster root vegetables when Marion's face fell. Anderson touched her arm as if to question. She looked at him and then back across the stalls toward the pit beef stand, where Anderson saw them. Sonny's parents in line for pit beef. Sonny's parents without the boys.

When the phone rang at Marion's house, she and Anderson were sitting together on the couch, their jackets still on. Marion had just said he can't do this. He won't get away with this. Anderson said nothing. When she said that Sonny's mom wanted to talk to him, he put his finger to his lips as if to say *sssssssssh* and walked out the door.

Anderson headed home on foot.

He didn't think he wanted to see Marion again. He knew he'd never hear from Sonny. What was there to say? The wind blew his breath ahead of him as he walked. It was definitely colder. It felt like fall. He knew that whatever happened would happen between the parents and the grandparents, the father, the mother and their children, their family.

A REALLY WEIRD THING HAPPENED RECENTLY

Len Ingenito-DeSio

A really weird thing happened recently. It's about Martin. My noisy blond friend who can't keep still. You got to a party with him and he keeps jumping up and down, screaming to people across the room. So it's about him, Martin, and also about his boyfriend, Bob. Tall, lanky, and very WASP-y. Nice, regular features, but average, who hasn't seen a million of him . . . ? I wouldn't describe Martin as exactly gorgeous, but at least he's interesting. And smart, don't forget *that*. He's a professional, a *dentist*. Doing *very* well . . . He's got an office uptown and he's thinking about opening another down in SoHo or NoHo or Homo, one of those fancy new neighborhoods. . . . And Bob, well, he's just Bob. He does something on Wall Street. You never think anything about him, except he's tall and skinny, big grin, cute-looking. Ordinary, but in the top ten percent of ordinary . . .

As it happens, Martin didn't meet Bob at the Anvil, only because the Anvil is long gone. Otherwise, he would have met him at the Anvil. He met him at the infamous Bat Club, that club on 20th and Tenth Avenue, where you pay seven dollars to get in. Friday nights, it opens at midnight and stays open until nine in the morning. They check your wallet for free, a free wallet-check, which is *very . . . highly . . . recommended*. They've got a bar and torture equipment, and there's a stage where you can see live sex shows while they play this sleazy music, and a big back room, a little too dark, but these days they've got a guy going around with a flashlight to make sure you're practicing "safe sex." It's great, a *fun* place, the Bat, and once Martin found it, you couldn't get him out of there.

So that's where he was this one Friday night and he meets Bob. Tall, lanky, very WASP-y looking. He's got a ruddy complexion that makes you think maybe he drinks too much, and you should, because he does. Like, in spurts. Last I heard, though, he's been 12-high-stepping it from one AA meeting to another.

Anyway, Martin and Bob meet in that back room and they have sex. But first let me tell you what Martin does whenever he goes out to these places. Right away, he heads straight for the back room, he hates to waste time. Then he basically feels around for the largest penis. On this Friday, apparently, Bob met his standards, so Martin took him home. They stayed together that night, or what remained of that night, and they stayed together the whole next day, too. By Sunday evening, when Martin's finally coming up for air, he phones me, very emotional. "I have to tell you," he says, his voice quavering, "it was love at first grope."

Now I hear this at the end of every weekend, so I don't get too excited. I say, "Good, that's nice," and Martin sighs, he's carried away, and he tells me they made a date for the following weekend. (I'm thinking, If Bob shows . . .)

"Where does Bob live?" I ask Martin. I have to know these things, I can't say why. I like to be able to locate a stranger on the map in my head.

"In Washington Heights."

"In *Washington Heights*?"

"Yeah, you see, Bob comes from Connecticut and he works on Wall Street, and he figured Washington Heights was halfway between Connecticut and Wall Street, so he looked for an apartment there."

"How clever," I go. Really, isn't that a perfect example of WASP thinking? They use reason and they use logic and nothing they come up with makes any sense. Like what people used to call "a queen's arithmetic."

So that's how it began. Martin and Bob see each other the next weekend, and again after that, and Martin becomes *somewhat* monogamous, which, let me tell you, is *rare*. Martin's the most promiscuous human being I know.

And he's also HIV negative because he's promiscuous only in certain activities. He's a total whore, but, as luck would have it, on the most infantile level. Good for him, he's got "safe sex" built in. . . . Did I already mention that Martin comes from one of those Jewish intellectual families? Both his parents are businesspeople? Who own things? Businesses or parts of businesses, like shares in this and that? So Martin grew up in the kind of apartment on Riverside Drive folks like this generally seem to have, you know, eight rooms, two maids, one kid. His mother never changed a diaper in her life. And of course they gave their only child everything they could, a wonderful education, private tutors, summers in the Hamptons, and they sent him to dental school.

He's a good dentist, too. He's got that *touch*. Kids love him. In fact, years ago, when I first met him, he was working in elementary school as the visiting dentist. When he was getting started, while he was setting up his first office. Back then, Martin would come home from work, eat a big meal, and go to bed, although most of the time it was still light outside, and set his alarm for four a.m., and then he'd get up and shower and shave and tweeze and spray on cologne and go to the Blue Ballroom and spend the night getting involved in wild circle jerks with mostly Third World men. . . . In fact, that's where Martin and I met, at the Blue Ballroom. During one of those nights . . . I've almost forgotten. That . . . *event,* if you could call it that, and I frankly cannot . . . happened so long ago, it's completely unimportant now. Maybe I saw Martin—*saw,* you know?—once or twice afterward, way before I started going with Vinnie, and that was it. Then we became friends, and after, good friends.

Too good. Martin's like herpes, he won't go away. It doesn't help, either, that by some coincidence he lives right across the street from me, another high-rise, same floor. *He won't go away.*

I'll give you an example. One night a few months ago, about three in the morning, I get up to have some ice cream. I'm sitting there in my living room with only a sheet around me and suddenly my phone rings. Remember, it's three a.m. and Vinnie's fast asleep. I pick it up, it's Martin. What are you eating, he wants to know. He sees me through his window.

Oh, forget it, let me get back to the story. Where was I? The Blue

Ballroom, circle jerks. Oh, yes. Then Martin would dash home by seven in the morning, shower and shave all over again, spray more cologne, and put on his dentist outfit, all white and starched, and rush to the inner-city school on his schedule for that day, Martin, the children's dentist. He'd run in with this giant-size red toothbrush, bigger than himself, and sing songs to it and then to the kiddies while he drilled away at their teeth. I suppose you could say he led sort of a double life.

Still, he excelled at everything he did. He's a great dentist and he wasn't bad, either, in *his* fashion, in those after-hours clubs.

Anyway, the night after they met, Martin took Bob home and then Bob came back again, and again, and pretty soon things were getting serious. We even went out to dinner with them, Vinnie and I, a *first*! I couldn't believe *Martin* was doing *that*. As two *couples*. Sometime during dinner, he and I go to the can together and Martin says, "You know, this number is getting so hot and heavy that I'd better talk to Bob about his HIV status."

"You mean you haven't yet?"

"I saw no reason to."

"You're counting swapping spit?"

"Don't be silly, tongue kissing's no reason."

I myself wouldn't do it, not with a total stranger, not even with my best friend, for that matter, if I didn't know for sure he was negative. And I mean *sure*. "Well, you're into science," I say, "I'm not. I don't believe in taking chances."

See, I know Martin very well, he's pretty neurotic, but he's also smart. And practical. He's a realist. He did go to dental school, after all, he *does* know science. Before he learned it, though, he was already a realist, long before that, it's his nature. He can be crazy, but he's no dope. Also, Martin's always had a clear, precise picture of what he wanted, and that includes what he wanted in a lover. "I would never get involved with a person who's HIV positive," he's told me again and again, way before Bob. "Because I know my own limits. It's not what I *do*"—and he gives me this meaningful look, like when you meet a stranger at the meat rack and first thing he says is "What do you do?"—"it's who I *am*. . . ." Well, that's Martin. A prince among men who are queers.

The next day he calls me at work. "So?" I go. "What happened?"

"I'm not sure," he tells me. "We get home from the restaurant, we sit down, and I start to talk. 'Listen, Bob,' I say, 'I see how this is going. We're starting to get serious. And before we get serious, I want to talk about HIV.'

"Bob goes, 'Why, are you positive?'

"I say, 'No, are you?' and Bob goes, 'I don't know.'

" 'Well,' I say, 'I think we should both get tested. Quite frankly, I don't have the stamina to pursue a relationship with someone who's positive. I don't have the strength. I'm not right for that kind of person.'

" 'I understand,' Bob tells me. 'I'll get tested right away.'

"So now I'm waiting," Martin says.

But Bob procrastinates. And procrastinates and procrastinates. Days go by and he comes up with all these stories about why he didn't get tested yet. One time he has an appointment but he gets too busy at work to keep it, another time he goes but he has the wrong hours and the lab's closed. . . . It was always something.

So one night Martin makes this terrific dinner, lobster *and* steak. He serves it on the good tablecloth and then he pours Bob a stiff drink, Absolut on the rocks. "What are you doing?" Bob goes. "You know I can't drink."

Martin goes, "Oh, don't be such a fairy, you can have one single drink. Look at this fabulous dinner I cooked! Some nights I just need to be grand! Relax, girl, let your hair down! *I'm* having a drink!"

But the glass Martin shows him is only full of tonic. So Bob, he's such an agreeable guy, picks up his drink and sips a little and shakes around the ice cubes and before he's half done, Martin's pouring him another. And serving more fantastic food. And they're clinking glasses by the candlelight.

Then Martin pours a little more vodka into Bob's glass and he sips his own tonic, then a little more vodka for Bob, and pretty soon Bob's getting a little *stu-NAD*. So Martin pours him another, filling the glass, and then another, and by this time Bob is throwing the vodka right down his throat, until Martin starts to complain. "Look at you," he says. "Now you're getting drunk. You're going to have some hangover tomorrow. How will you get to work? Here, you'd better take these aspirins," and he gives Bob two 10mg Valiums.

"Oh, wow!" I interrupt him. "Weren't you scared? What if you had another Karen Ann Quinlan on your hands?"

"No, I knew what I was doing. That dosage is okay for a big guy like Bob."

Anyway, now Bob's unconscious, Martin is telling me, so he undresses him and puts him to bed. Then, once he's got Bob settled in there, Martin pulls out his medical equipment—he's all prepared. He takes out a syringe and a needle and gets a blood sample out of Bob's arm. Then he puts the vial, full of blood, in a bag with the lunch he's packed for himself for the next day, and throws a rubber band around the whole thing and sticks it in the fridge.

The next morning, they get up and Bob hasn't a clue what's gone down. Martin's a whiz with needles. After all, he's always taking blood from children. You know how kids are, how they screech and carry on at the sight of a needle, so Martin was quick to get really expert at it, he's fast and smooth. Before a kid can get red in the face, wham, it's all over. So, as I said, Bob felt nothing when Martin took the blood . . . How could he? He was out cold. Next day, there wasn't even a mark on his arm.

So now it's morning and they're in the breakfast nook with the flocked wallpaper, ready for coffee. Meanwhile, remember, Martin's got the vial in the fridge, in the bag with his lunch. Bob goes to the fridge to get milk for the coffee and sees the bag. "What's this?"

"It's my lunch," Martin tells him.

"Since when do you pack a lunch?"

"I just started. I'm on this new diet. I've got to watch my sodium and fat intake. Who knows what they put in the cafeteria sandwiches?"

Bob smiles, he's pleased to hear that. He likes when Martin takes care of himself.

So Martin, as usual, leaves the house first, the rubber band around his lunch, and with Bob's blood sample inside. Before work, he stops off at the lab that does confidential AIDS testing and a few days later, guess what. Bob's positive.

Right away, Martin calls me up. He doesn't know what to do. "Martin," I tell him, "confront him."

"How can I? I would never do something so rotten, get somebody drunk and take a blood sample. How can I say I did?"

"You can say you did because you did."

"Don't be stupid. Why would I want to humiliate myself? To admit I acted like a shit?"

"You acted like a shit because you had to. Bob drove you to it. He's not moral. He lied. Maybe you behaved like a shit, but still, you're not going to be a patsy shit, waiting hand and foot on a dying faggot who's set you up. Or worse, a dead shit yourself."

"You asshole!" Martin screams. "You're hysterical! You think you get AIDS from jerking off? Why don't you mind your own fucking business!" And the cocksucker, he should be so lucky, hangs up on me.

So what do you think happens next?

Don't ask *me*. I ran into the two of them the next night, just by accident, one of those special perks like the view into my window Martin gets, living right across the street. They had their arms around each other and neither of them would speak to me. They saw me, too. They looked straight into my face and then they both turned away. Now, what the fuck do you make of that?

I couldn't imagine what the devil was going on.

I decide to send Vinnie to give them a call, invite them over.

It was a short conversation. "They can't come," Vinnie says. "Bob answered. They're going on a vacation together, he told me. They're taking a month off, both of them. They have reservations for *tomorrow* on one of those gay cruise ships that go around the Caribbean, can you beat that? In the middle of March? A whole month? Boy, they must be loaded! They'll come back just in time for summer and a two-week rest in the Hamptons, then pretty soon they'll fly away again for Christmas. . . . What a life! Oh, wow!"

Oh, shit, I say to myself. I already know where this is going. Vinnie's already wearing that guinea pout. When he gets jealous, he blows up like a balloon full of olive oil.

"Vinnie honey." I try to reason with him. "I told you Bob was sick. That he's positive. Maybe he's running symptoms, maybe his numbers dropped, maybe he needs a rest, to get out of the city."

"What do I care? Because we test negative, we have to be workaholics?"

"No." I'm still patient. "Not because we're negative, because we have a future. Because we're saving up for a bigger place, because we want to buy a condo . . ."

"Stick it up your ass," Vinnie says. "Since I met you, I've gone nowhere, done nothing but work all week and maybe see a movie on the weekend." He flounces off into the bedroom, where I hear him throw himself on the bed and sob.

"Maybe I should give them a ring?" I call to him, making believe nothing's wrong. "Say good-bye, wish them a wonderful trip?"

"Lay off," Vinnie yells back through his tears. "Bob told me to say good-bye to you for them, they're too busy to talk on the phone, they're packing."

"Pack *this*," I mutter under my breath, and get busy loading the dishwasher and sweeping the floor, listening all the while to the noises from the bedroom until I hear them fade out and the TV in there go on. Soon I hear Vinnie softly snoring.

The next morning, Vinnie's still all blown up. He says two words to me and goes off to work, slamming the door. At night, he's the same. Finally, just to pacify him, I get us reservations on one of those weekend cruises to nowhere, and he cheers right up. He's such a big baby. You give him anything, a piece of candy, and he's happy, he gets all excited. Then he goes wild shopping for clothes for the weekend, and Friday night comes and off we go. Of course it's a dreadful flop. The boat is tacky and cold, and it's full, a straight crowd, and lots of single girls with big hair looking to make out keep hitting on both of us until we finally have to dance with a few of them so we don't look gay. By nightfall, Vinnie's furious with me. So I take him to our cabin and we make love all night long and I promise him a real fairy cruise when we have our summer vacations, we'll sail to the same Caribbean as Bob and Martin are riding around in, and at last he shuts up, satisfied.

After that, we get along just fine.

Vinnie calls the gay shipping lines for brochures, and life is quiet. We go to work, we come home, Vinnie reads the brochures aloud to me and time passes. On and off, though, all through the month, I keep thinking about Martin, about Martin and Bob, about Martin with Bob.

Strange thoughts.

For instance, I keep trying to figure out why the both of them are mad at me, at *me,* for no reason at all!

Except there has to be a reason, only I haven't found it yet. After all, what did *I* do? Absolutely nothing, nothing whatsoever.

Then I start thinking back further, much further back, I'm remembering some crazy stuff from long ago. Years and years ago, like when I was a kid and went to Catholic school. My mother started me in Catholic kindergarten and I stayed in that school, Our Lady of Mount Carmel, right through the eighth grade. One of the priests there, Father Joe, liked me and, although I never showed it, I liked him, too. He used to talk a lot about acts of grace, they were kind of his specialty. Who understood him? Not us kids, for sure. But we liked how his voice softened when he spoke of such things, how his face shone. In time, I think I did get the general idea. That for no reason at all, nothing to do with deserve or not deserve, God would sometimes toss down an act of grace on a person, out of the blue, just because God felt like it. Then, afterward, that person was different. He *had* something different. He didn't always do things you expected him to do, considering the way his personality was, his nature. An act of grace, it was something like a blessing. A person who received it was able, then, to do better, to do more, to act in kind of a higher way, to become unselfish. I'm not sure I'm remembering all this right, but as I recall, acts of grace, besides being like a blessing, were like love.

Like love. They transformed you. They made you more of a human being. So I began to wonder, maybe such a thing had happened to Martin? Maybe God threw him an act of grace, so that his feelings for Bob transcended—that's the word, *transcended*—his usual asshole instincts, beginning and ending with ME! ME! ME! That maybe out of that act of grace his love for Bob had grown. Maybe Martin was able for the first time in his life to care more about the person he loved than for himself.

Maybe it's like a miracle! Maybe, after Martin had those talks with me and told me how he tricked Bob and got the blood sample. When Martin explained to me how he was meant to be cared for, not to give care.

And then maybe it just changed his mind? I mean, like his feelings grew and grew and *they* changed his mind?

Maybe, when he stopped being the same Martin I'd always known, he had to throw me away with the old Martin because I knew too much? Because he'd told me too much? People do shit like that, I've seen it before. It's one of the risks you take, being the kind of guy people confide in. They change their minds suddenly, and then, wham, *you're* the enemy!

Remember, I'm not a little girl like Vinnie. I never cry. I shut up and do what I have to do, no matter how I feel. And I'm far from a sentimental theatrical type like my mother, say, or my sister Connie. . . . The both of them all at once will *feel* something, hear a song, smell a smell, see a sight, and *whoosh,* they turn into Niagara Falls, which has on occasion frightened the life out of me. I would run over to them and yell, "What's wrong, what's wrong?" and they would say, looking way over my head, into the sky, "Oh, I'm so happy!" I would stare at them as if they were crazy.

But I have to admit that, imagining now maybe that's what happened to Martin, and figuring, what else could it be, nothing else made sense, started me, *me,* crying one night! It's unbelievable! Sure, I was alone, Vinnie never knew, but *still* . . . it made me very nervous!

So, after that, I said no more. I put it away. I put the whole thing out of my head, Martin, Bob, fuck it, who needed it. In fact, as soon as that happened, the tears, I practically forgot about the two of them. Out of sight, out of mind, and good-bye, Charlie.

Then, a week or so later, I wake up in the middle of the night, the way I do, and wrap the bedsheet around me and go to the fridge for some ice cream and sit down on the couch in the living room with a carton of Ben & Jerry's, and wham, the phone rings. Again, the middle of the night. Again, Vinnie's in the bedroom, sound asleep.

My mouth is full of Cherry Garcia. Even so, I grab the phone

and garble something. Guess who's there. Who else. Martin. "I saw
your light on—what are you eating?" he wants to know.

I gulp down the ice cream. "When did you get back?"

"Yesterday. How've you been?" He sounds easy, friendly, as
though he'd never stopped talking to me. As though nothing had
happened.

"How was the cruise?" I ask him. "Did you have a good time?"

"What could be bad?" he says. "Eight ports, all that swell food
and hot sunshine . . . A giant pool on the ship, hundreds of dressed-
up fairies ballroom dancing every night, a twelve-piece band. I
came in third in the Limbo contest. . . ."

"While Vinnie and I are running to catch the subway, freezing
our asses . . ." I put in.

He's not listening, he goes right on. "All the lobster you can eat,
jumbo shrimp every night, a fancy faggot cocktail hour, with
everybody singing show tunes. Even the captain was gay . . . I won't
even mention the humpy lifeguards. . . . Wait till you see my *tan*! I
look marvelous! They're going to drop dead at the sight of me in
the Bat. *If* there's a ray of light so people can see my face."

"I never knew it was your face that particular clientele was interested in . . ." I point out.

Martin giggled, a long, breathy giggle.

Then there was a pause. An uneasy silence. He waited for me to
break it. I waited for him to break it.

I broke it. "How's Bob?"

"All right, I guess."

"You guess? He's not there?"

"No, sweetie, he's home where he belongs. In Washington
Heights. Where I dropped him off, after we docked. It cost me a
fortune, first taking a cab all the way uptown there, then coming
back all the way downtown here."

"How come you did it that way?"

"Seemed easier. You tell somebody good-bye in a taxi and drop
them off at their place, there's not time for scenes. You know there's
no way I could tolerate that situation. It was bad enough on the
ship, the pills eight times a day in twelve different combinations,
everything gets written down, God!"

"Oh, Martin," I blurt out, not that I meant to. "I thought you'd changed your mind. That you were really in love, taking the time out for romance at sea . . ."

"Are you crazy? Where did you get that idea? You thought I was going to drop dentistry and become a full-time *nurse* . . . ? Say, want to go out with me late tonight? I mean, tomorrow night, but it's really tonight? Tell Vinnie your boss put you on the night shift again?"

We'd done that before. Not often. Once in a while. It's always fun.

"No," I say, "I can't. I'm too tired. In fact, I'm falling asleep right now. I gotta go back to bed . . . Bob okay? How'd he take it?"

"You know, at first, he was pretty upset. Don't worry, he'll get over it. People do. I told him when we got to about Forty-second Street. He blew a fit, he was furious. He actually accused me of setting him up, of arranging the cruise so I could secretly do one of those long Jewish operatic good-byes. . . . Plus come back looking sunburned and fit, for future cruising. On *land*." Martin laughs. "We're sailing along, I'm at a funeral, he's on a honeymoon. . . . That's how Bob described it. Sometimes those quiet ones have quite a way with words."

"I'm tired, Martin," I tell him. " 'Bye. I'll call you."

I hang up, kill the light, and go back to bed.

That's it, that's all. That was two nights ago, I haven't called him back yet.

REGULAR FLATTOP

J. G. Hayes

I can't deal with being in this stinking cemetery—

So I close my eyes and see a field of green, the greenest field you've ever seen. There's a boy moving across the field, running in slow motion. . . .

There. That's better. I feel The Crazies subside. Audrey Hepburn called them The Mean Reds in *Breakfast at Tiffany's,* and oh I know what she meant. But we always call them The Crazies, and our names for whatdya whatdya are as good as anybody's.

Now you might be asking what's a Projects kid doing knowing Audrey Hepburn movies. See, Ms. Loomis in sophomore year social studies made us watch movies once a week, it was pretty cool, and once we watched *Breakfast at Tiffany's,* though you couldn't really concentrate—Wacko Gibbons had taken a leak in a squirt gun, and every now and then was shooting kiss-ass, straight-A Francis McKay with it two seats in front of him. Francis kept whining that the ceiling was leaking, which was funny, but the best part was when finally Ms. Loomis said, "Francis, just *shut up!*"

'Course, we took the squirt gun away from Wacko at lunchtime, me and some of the other D Street Boys, we're kinda The Law at school, and you can't really have that kinda shit going on. Especially when we hadn't . . . sanctioned Wacko's actions. You know?

So like I was saying, I close my eyes and see a field of green— the greenest field you've ever seen. The grass is perfect, mowed to a regulation three-eighths of an inch. Flawless. There's a boy moving across this field, moving in slow motion like it's time for the broadcasters to be thanking the sponsors and they're replaying highlights from the game to swelling music, he's moving in slow motion, muscles working beneath the smooth uniform, he's flowing like slow electricity, his face is full of quiet intent, the eyes steady, full of purpose, meaning, the chin square, and he's reaching, running, and soon we see for what, a spiraling ball enters the sphere of blue above him, it's to catch this ball that he's yearning, toward which the muscles are swirling beneath the clean uniform.

And I feel The Crazies subside as I see all this, as I occupy my mind with trying to see if this is a day game or a night game I'm playing in.

Listen, I do this all the time. Some of us boys drink and some of us do a little drugging ("Scooby Snacks") and some of us do a little of both. But the only thing that helps me any lately is my field of green.

Calmer now, I open my eyes. Maybe I can handle this now . . .

Before me is a field of green. But it's not my field of green. This field's bumpy, and the early summer sun's already desecrated the grass with these browned-out splotches like oil spills, only dry, because this ain't the ocean, see, it's Gate of Heaven Cemetery. A hungry hole gapes at my feet, even the June sun won't go down there, though Dad's flowered, flagged (of course he's a veteran— who do you think fights all these wars, we do) coffin does go down there, four fat guys from Ryans' Funeral Parlor are huffing puffing getting red-faced as they struggle with the screeching pulleys. And the coffin descends before my eyes.

Ma goes into a flop and The Girls more or less catch her. The Girls are Dad's two unmarried sisters, about fiftyish, they own the Hair Say Salon down on West Broadway. They're twins, they got identical jet-black beehives and matching black mustaches and huge jiggly triceps the size of Cincinnati. And moles, that's the only way you can tell them apart, Claire's is on the right side of her lip and Shirley's is on the left, and sometimes when I'm weird in the head I think of them in Grandma Donovan's womb, like they started out not as an egg but as a mole, and as they grew they were face to face, mole to mole, floating in fluidy inner space, they were like Siamese twins joined at the mole until the mole split and they were born.

"Don't say mole, you retard, say beauty mark," Ma corrected me one time in her very own nurturing way when The Girls were over our house for Friday Night cards.

"Whatdya whatdya," I said back to her, I always say that we always say that, The Boys and me. I mean really, what the hell else you gonna say sometimes, I'd like to know.

The Girls kind of prop Ma up. A wave of satisfied sympathy wiggles through the crowd. "God help us" and "the poor thing" run through the gathered mourners like the first flu bug of the school year, quick like that. People like Ma's display of grief, it's what they came here for.

But I remain unmoved.

I know she's just drunk again.

I remind myself not to look east, in the direction of the ocean three blocks away, Bib's buried down that end of the cemetery somewheres, I try to find his grave once in a while but I get all fucked up, that's Crazies Turf big time down there, all those dead people, too many, who would've thought there was so many dead people in the world, and I start sweating and running crazy like in a dream.

Fuckin' Bib, man. People always say We Don't Know Why, We Don't Know Why—

But I know why.

Tommy puts his arm around my shoulder and squeezes my right delt. This relaxes me a bit. I'd maybe be flopping too if Tommy wasn't here with me, all six feet of muscle and bone and blue eyes of him. He's my best friend, Tommy Flaherty, always has been, one of my best friends, him and me and Bib, and also Sean and Kevin and Brian. We're part of The Boys, The Project Boys, The D Street Boys, you can tell who we are, we got the shamrock tattoo on the right delt and the DSBF (D Street Boys Forever) on the left, and we got the certain way of dressing and the certain way of walking—like, like—and we got smooth skin I wish mine was hairier and we tan it down at Castle Island playing ball or just hanging out. Though me and Bib and Tommy decided at the last minute to get a heart around the DSBF. The other Boys were a little pissed but didn't say nothing.

"You need a haircut," Tommy whispers in my ear. I've let my flattop grow out a little since I promised Dad I'd get the hell out of here, this is the first sign and Tommy knows it.

"You still thinkin' o' leavin'?" he mumbles.

I squeeze my eyes bite my lip I didn't even know I was crying The Boys don't really ever cry but I feel a embarrassing tear squirming down my cheek. Tommy takes one long finger from his hand on my delt and wipes it away.

"Fuck," he says. "You can't leave."

We're back at the house now for the Back to the House, there's a million people in the kitchen but not Tommy, he had to go back to work, his brother gets him this job every summer roofin'. You wouldn't think Tommy, this big strong kid, would have stuffed animals, but he does, there's five or six of them on his bed, Teddy, Fuzzy, what's up with that? But when he was twelve (I'll tell you all about it) his father ran off with his own second cousin Rita Flaherty (remember her?) and Tommy was playing in the Babe Ruth Championship the next day, and before they started they had like this father-son game for the players and their dads and they had these pregame introductions with a real microphone and they kept calling and calling Tommy's father. But no. And everyone knew why. On the biggest day of his kid's life. Tommy was standing out there on the third base line all alone, wind blowing his uniform with everyone else, except everyone else had a father beside him or at least an uncle or something. Tommy didn't talk for weeks after that, no not a word, even the nuns at school couldn't get him to talk ("Defiant! March yourself down to the principal, Mr. Defiant!") Then one day we were up to Woolworth's and Tommy pulled this teddy bear out of a bin, it was buried beneath the others and all mushed and dusty, he stole it and brought it home. And every year close to the anniversary of that Babe Ruth game he goes out and does the same, gets this really sad-looking Teddy Bear and adds him to his collection.

I asked him about it one night we were fifteen, "What's up with those bears?" and he looked at me but wouldn't answer then, about a week later we were playing in a game and right in the middle of the third inning he called time and walked over to me and said, "They don't go back on you, that's why."

Whatdya whatdya. We all got our thing and it ain't for me to say. I got my Field of Green, Tommy's got his bears, and Bib—

I don't know, maybe Bib figured he had me.

Those losers from Dot High one time after a game jumped Tommy and insulted his bears, I don't know how they heard, and Tommy kicked the shit out of them all, but at the last second one of them pulled a knife and sliced Tommy's face open. He's got this scar that runs from his eyebrow all the way down to his chin, like the Master Hand that carved his chiseled face oopsed at the last second.

I wish he was back to the house with me now but he's not, I think of him up on a roof a couple of blocks away banging nails with his shirt off, dangling a tool belt, and something goes click inside me. Me, I still got my paper route even though I'm going into senior year, what the hell, I'm free by six every morning and then I can go back to bed and whatdya whatdya, then go play ball.

Baseball's really the only game worth playing. There's this beauty about it, the flow of the game's like Life, it can be as nice and easy as a summer sky or as crazy and intense as a Fellini movie on Scooby Snacks (Ms. Loomis made us watch one of them too) and there's no such thing as a regulation-size outfield (that's where I play), it goes on and on forever; even if you jumped over the left-field fence and caught a ball a mile from the stadium it would still be an out. It goes on is what I'm saying. Man, nothing like a neon green ballpark on a summer's night, Excitement, Stretching, Sweat, The Crowds, Sweet Summer Smell, Boys in Clean Uniforms, Anything Can Happen (but within reason, you know?) Your Best Nine Against Ours. *You* try hitting a ball coming at you ninety miles an hour with a piece of wood three inches in diameter. It's Art, man.

Bib always dreamed of going to art school.

Bib played left field next to me, Tommy still plays right, I'm in the middle, the center fielder, always been. I'm sitting at the kitchen table at Back to the House, my father was buried today, but I'm thinking about something Bib said about a month ago, right before he died. We were playing rich kids from some prep school way the fuck out in the suburbs somewhere. There was trouble of course, two of the rich kids were talking before the game and one of them said to the other "Is your pater coming today, I just e-mailed mine with directions," and Tommy behind them thought they were talking over his head on purpose so he said, "Who the fuck's pater," and gave one of them a wedgie. Coach benched Tommy, told us all You Embarrassed Yourselves, but hey, they're gonna have everything and us the shit end of the stick so for once, plus they won the game that day you wonder why does God let shit like that happen you'd think just once, but I wouldn't trade places, they're geeks and we're cool and it must really suck being a geek even if you do have everything.

Bib of course didn't get involved, he never would in that kind of thing unless someone was about to hurt me.

He'd been quiet that day, more than usual I mean, then he yelled over to me from left field when there was a lull in the game and said, "Timmy. You can't go nowhere no more."

I turned to look at him. Someone hit a ball toward Bib just then and I guided him like we always did for each other, Back Back Left Now Stay, and he caught it, carefully like he always did, both hands clutched softly like he was catching a bird you wouldn't want to hurt. Then he'd take the ball—always—out of his glove and look at it, like he was surprised that such a thing as a baseball was in his glove, his head would like jump back a little. Then he'd throw the ball in.

"You can't go nowhere," he repeated, his eyes like open wounds. Bib was the redhead in our group but he had the same Regular Boys Flattop we all did, that's another way you can tell we're The Boys. Except I'm letting mine grow out a little, I promised Dad I'd get the fuck outta here.

Someone made the last out and we trotted in together.

Bib put his arm around me, you could get away with that in a game. Bib was always careful about when he touched me, looking scared even when we were alone. Just funny things you notice.

"In the olden days you could go off to the woods, the frontier or something," he said lowly, holding me back as we got near the bench, "you could start a new life. Say we lived a hunnert years ago, if you and me wanted to—I mean, as an example, I mean—we could just get the fuck outta here and be smelling pines by the end of the day and just ... just squat on some land and start a farm."

I got that sizzle again, the one I got whenever he talked about me and him. But these talks about our future only went so far with Bib. Maybe, I think now, that's as far as he could go without me meeting him halfway, which I was always afraid to do. But that sizzle, it started in my mouth like you just had novocaine, then shot down to your stomach and settled where your protective cup goes, right there and behind.

Tommy was sitting on the bench, he didn't like not to be included when it was just me and Bib, and when Bib got up to bat he slid over to me and said, "What were you and Bib talking about?"

"Just Bib shit," I answered, sometimes Bib said weird stuff.

"Whatdya whatdya," Tommy said, kicking his left cleat forward, raising a mini–dust storm. That meant, Okay Don't Tell Me I Don't Give a Shit.

I had to wait for us to get back to the outfield for Bib to finish what he was driving at.

"You can't do that no more, go somewheres," he called over from left. "The ... see, the whole world's been snatched and deeded and clicked off and turned into ... into Windermere, An Exclusive Executive Community By The Sea. Architect Designed, and Gated for Your Protection."

He didn't say nothing more, went right home after the bus trip back to town.

I think of Bib's words today at my father's funeral party. But then I'm always thinking of Bib's words lately. Trying not to really.

I'm sitting at the kitchen table, and Uncle Joe's latest girlfriend, I think her name's Sally, she's sitting next to me and she's listening to Ma harangue across the table from us and I want to tell this Sally lady, Look, You Don't Have to Try and Impress Ma, She's Going to Forget Everything Later Anyway, and the one thing I like about Ma, the thing I hate about her the most is, She Just Don't Give a Fuck.

About anything. Or anyone.

And you can't go nowhere no more.

Whatdya whatdya.

"He wahs a saint," Ma's blurring now, her plastic cup has a butt floating in it but she has her red hand in a vise grip around it like she's going to drink from it and I sit here hoping she will, wondering if she will. "And let me tell you something, Missy!" she rasps, changing tack, and now her finger is in this Sally's face and I know trouble's about to start and Uncle Joe sails over from the getting-moldy cold cuts on the counter where he's been having a race I think with some yellow-toothed fat guy to see who can cram the most sandwiches down his gullet. He pulls Sally up from the table and leads her to less troubled waters, Hey Cousin Pat, Have You Met Sally?, and I look up and notice one of The Girls is eyeing me rather ill-humoredly, I think it's Shirley but I'm confused today, they just buried my father.

My mistake is—see, you want to hate us, The Boys, 'cuz we're cocky and maybe beautiful some of us, but we always make mistakes and we crash and burn just as you others are getting ready for Grad School, Thanks Pater—my mistake is I make eye contact with Shirley (I think) and she springs to life like she's a Disney animatron programmed to come alive once someone makes eye contact with her. She dumps her hairy forearms onto the table, leans toward me and rasps, "Your mother's gonna need a lot more help around the house, mister, now that your father's . . . *g-g-gone!*" This last word comes out like a hippopotamus pre-charge warning bellow I saw once on one of those nature shows on cable, and now all eyes are on me, which I hate except on the ballfield. Ma and The Girls light up fresh cigarettes of grief at this latest display, adding to the pall that's stuck just below the ceiling, like incense that Heaven doesn't want. Oh, I forgot to say that Ma and The Girls are still wearing their sunglasses from the graveside service an hour ago, which makes them look like the Furies we read about in Greek mythology, only like postmodern, burned-out versions, all fucked up at what they've done but compelled nevertheless to Do It Again Do It Again Harder, Harder.

Ma jerks to life at Shirley's words.

"What, him?" she snorts, jerking her rat's nest hair in my general direction. "Oh, forget it, brother! Goddamn paperboy! Thinks he'sh gonna be another Ted Williams—the stupid dreamer!"

The Girls shake their beehives in collective sympathy. Relations I haven't seen in years and strangers I've never met before stare at me as if Ma's appraisal is the definitive one.

"Whatdya whatdya," I mumble back, downing the last of my beer in one gulp, but I close my eyes and see a field of green, the greenest field you've ever seen, and there's order here, there's, yes, symmetry, beauty, as a boy with my smooth face, my eyes, black smudges beneath the too-long-for-a-boy lashes moves in slow motion across this field. Above, a sky of blue arches over me like a gymnast stretching before a meet at a track, or maybe out in woods still undeeded, where you could go start a farm with a friend.

But Bib died a month ago.

I lift myself up from the table, excuse myself through the crowd that seems to part for me and climb the stairs knees shaking to my attic bedroom. The walls are covered with my heroes, baseball players all. I like the full-length posters best, that way I can compare my body alone at night with my heroes', I'm catching up to them here in the biceps, there in the shoulders, but beneath my belt down there you know my pants aren't quite as full, but when I think about that The Crazies come so I try to come quick and not tell myself what I'm thinking about. I have Thoughts. But I have to be careful of these Thoughts or Mr. Cozy will get me again and then they'll be no stopping anything.

Like before.

I told the priest once. I talked about It. I had to or I would have imploded with The Crazies. It was two years ago I was sixteen, I went to confession and picked the priest visiting from Ireland, he's blind so you could see, his eyes open all the time, that he was kind and not looking at you like some of the others sniffing out Thoughts. The New Curriculum brought these Thoughts to a head. Let me explain.

They'd given certain ones of us a special curriculum at school, *Urban Youth at Risk,* they called it, new teachers, skinny angry guys with long hair, sour-faced women pickled in patchouli, How Do

You Feel, Tell Us How Does That Make You Feel?, they'd constantly ask us, but we could tell they looked down on us Projects Kids, Aggressive White Males they said, but they couldn't see how scared living in The Projects made us: dirty needles, wife beating, husband beating, kid beating, dick beating, to try and forget broken glass grass won't grow it tries but it's dead by May that's when my birthday is Ma forgot this year so we'd just say Whatdya Whatdya, That's How I Fuckin' Feel, and then they'd send you to the principal like any other teacher. One of these new courses was Processing Feelings, and one time the teacher wanted us to talk about our dreams and Tommy said deadpan that he had one recurring that he couldn't figure none, a hotdog was chasing a doughnut down Broadway. We all laughed but the teacher turned red instead, Go to the Principal You, yeah funny but the important thing was, that night wet I dreamt of a hotdog chasing another hotdog down Broadway then catching up rubbing against each other sweating and then Tommy was there with a hotdog dangling from his mouth it was mine.

I thought I'd go crazy every night these dreams came back but different so I went to see the blind priest from Ireland. Bless Me Father For I Have Sinned.

"I have Thoughts," I whispered through the screen, Mrs. McGillicuddy was right outside the confessional booth and she's a gossip with Mother Ears you gotta be careful.

"And what are these thoughts, my son?"

My thoughts are Bib in the locker room drying off one foot up on the bench open up like that and I could see standing behind it was hanging there and I want to catch it soft like a bird you wouldn't want to hurt and Tommy the way his neck looks after a regular boy's flattop there's a ribbon of white flesh where the sun hasn't tanned it yet and I want to take his teddy bears' places at night and hold him and tell him everything will be okay and that I'll always go to his games, all of them, and I want to climb on top of him I'm a hard drill there's never been nothing in the universe half so hard and drill into him till I strike oil but I don't know how and this is the worst thing a nightmare of desire and you can't ever tell anyone—

"And what are those thoughts?" the priest asks again.

"Whatdya whatdya," I whisper. I start to get up.

"Don't go," he says. "Don't be afraid."

I kneel back down. I think I'm going to puke.

"Is it . . . is it other boys?" he asks.

I panic, it must show. "How the—how did you—"

"I can feel your despair," he says. "I can tell. Everyone thinks it's the worst. It isn't. It's what you've been given."

I feel sweat running down my sides. The Crazies have entered the church and are getting closer, they know I'm here though they don't know exactly where yet.

"I can't go on," I say. It's odd—the words come out casually, like I'm saying Bismarck is the capital of North Dakota, instead of relating suicidal thoughts.

"You're not alone," he says. "Try . . . try thinking of this as a blessing, instead of a curse. A blessing. That's a good beginning. Can you do that?"

"Thank you," I say. I have to leave. I think I might faint or scream, so I lurch to the front of the church and kneel before the altar. I like the smell of churches when there's hardly anyone here beeswax candles furniture polish oak benches wet wool brought in from the rain altar flowers incense.

A Blessing. I've been given a Blessing. Actually I was hoping for a Longines. Then I think of something. I raise my eyes up to the statue of Jesus before me, he's pointing to his open heart like he's down at the Free Clinic describing his symptoms.

"God," I pray, "bless Bib and Tommy."

Up in my room I hear the voices from Back to the House downstairs the laughing the crying the shrieking the yelling the singing the arguing the tale telling, they don't hear me but The Crazies do, they bound up the stairs merciless motherfuckers two at a time after me. The Crazies: They are a jumbo-size anxiety attack a baker's dozen of anxiety attacks a battalion of anxiety attacks and finally they catch up to me in my room, I'm sitting on the floor in a corner of my bedroom with my fingers jammed into my ears and they find me and finally at last I must think of Bib. My father was buried today but thoughts of Bib finally get me. They lay me low. I lay down flat and let them wash over me like acid rain or the terrible coming of God I have no choice I start dry heaving I haven't eaten yet today.

My whole body begins to shake. My mind hits the turbo-charge button and I hear those engines hum. Weird thoughts come at me like obstacles in a road to me the speeding car and I crash into them again and again. I think: Somewhere in this city at this moment there is a woman, and she is trying to decide whether to do her afternoon shopping at Neiman Marcus or The Talbots. Somewhere downtown, there is a man moving vast amounts of imaginary money from Singapore to Sydney for his banking firm, identifying all the while with the corporate careerist ads scrolling away at the top of his computer screen while two feet away from him, separated by a wall, lurks the Upper Management Rest Room and its porcelain heart, where today's power lunch will eventually make its way. Closeby, I think also, there's someone else working for an ad agency, and he or she is airbrushing a platinum-toothed model so that this model will look even more perfect. But perhaps, I think, this airbrusher has a child with Down's syndrome. Who will never be in an ad. Meanwhile, while they are doing all that, I'm lying here on the floor wondering if I can stand up. I try but I can't. But maybe I can crawl. I do crawl. I crawl to the opposite corner of my bedroom. There's a shrine here. There's a shrine to Bib here. Dusty baseball trophies I pulled from his mother's trash a week after he died how could she the sweatshirt that Oh God still smells of him I borrowed and never got to return soft against my face like a bird you wouldn't want to hurt ever some photos: First Holy Communion Day, some times at Fenway Park, flexing down at the beach when no one was looking I bring these things to my chest I think I might be dying or giving birth something inside like *Aliens* I'm wracked by sobs like knives I double over Oh Bib I'm So Sorry, So So Sorry, Can You Come Back I'll Tell You, I Swear Bib I'll Tell You Everything, I Should Have Told You That Night Bib But I Couldn't, I couldn't. . . .

And more. Private though.

I have to get to Tommy's. Or die.

This thought hits me quick. I have to get to Tommy. I wonder if he's home from work yet and I wonder if he's . . . okay. He'd never do what Bib did would he?

Would he?

There's this game at the arcade we used to play, Save the Princess, a video game (they got rid of it), you could push either button once you put your quarters in, Save the Princess or Save the Prince. If you were a boy, you were supposed to push the Save the Princess button and your character was a Big Stud who kicked ass for ten screens, then finally rescued The Princess in this temple or something on the very last screen, she was lying there on this fancy couch with this look on her face like she wanted to do something she'd have to go to Confession for later. If you were a girl you were supposed to push the Save the Prince button and your character was this very pissed-off Amazon who kicked ass for ten screens and then finally rescued the Prince in his castle but just standing there like he was waiting for the Broadway bus not like he wanted to do something. But this one time it must have been broken 'cuz I was the Big Stud, but when I got to the final screen I was pretty good at this there was The Prince there by accident not The Princess, I guess the machine was broken once, it never happened again. But for once I was the Big Stud and I rescued The Prince and hotdogs chased each other around the castle all afternoon.

It was broken.

That's not why they got rid of it. It had an ending that's why, you could win this game, see, now all the games have no ending but the screens just get harder and harder and they used psychology I guess they know how to drive you crazy and I sit here in my bedroom and think I have to get to Tommy's but on this day it's like that video game there'll be all these badasses to overcome, My Anxiety The Crazies The People Downstairs My Grief My Guilt My Shame, but I must get to him. I wonder, is there an end to this game called Life or does it go on and on driving you crazy, is God a kindly programmer who lets you win once in a while or a greedy consultant with a marketing degree who knows just how to drive you shithouse putting in quarters all the time hoping, when you can't really ever.

The sun is coming into my bedroom like a stab. Perhaps God or whatever is like the sun, dumping goofy goodness across half the world at a time. You're not in its path, you're shit out of luck.

Tommy—

I change: cutoff navy blue sweat pants, black Cons, no socks, a Tommy H. tank top, Nike hat backward, it's black, I'll wear something black for a year in honor of Dad and Bib, I decide. No undies. But I won't think about that right now, I'll allow myself to feel this fact as I go to save The Prince but I won't think too much about it that might be disrespectful, Dad was buried today.

Dad. Ma's a mean drunk but Dad was different. Giddy after one drink.

> *Now why didn't I marry Old Mary Tunney;*
> *She's as ugly as sin but has boo-tee-ful money!*

Morose for old Ireland after two,

> *Do you remember in Black '54,*
> *The Dead buried the dead,*
> *And still there were more. . . .*

and if he wasn't home by midnight I'd go look for him up to Casey's, or the Banshee, or any other of a dozen piss-smelling dumps between home and the hospital he washed floors at, second shift. Sometimes you know I'd find him on the edge of Broadway, never the sidewalk ("I bumped into a woman with a stroller once and I'll never forgive myself"), weaving in and out of the honking cars, singing that same old *Heart of My Heart*. Other times he'd be sitting in some dark door stoop, staring out at nothing and everything with eyes like a homeless dog, finding comfort nowhere.

But his face would light up when he saw me, each time was like the first time I'd done this, Oh, 'Tis Timmy, Oh Look Timmy Now, Oh, 'Tis Glad I Am to See You, Boy, My Boy, My Beautiful Beautiful Boy, like we hadn't seen each other in years, and I don't know why but we'd both cry, yeah all right sometimes I'd be high on Scooby Snacks but most times not, he'd hug me and say If I've

Done Nothing Else I've Brought Someone as Beautiful as You, Boy, into the World, and then he'd say what a dismal father he was, what a rotten example he'd set, he'd wanted to be an artist but got the dengue fever in the war and it'd given him the shakes so bad he couldn't hope to Hit a Bull's Ass With a Handful of Rice, he'd say, let alone take a brush to canvas, and that Ma loved me even though she had a Tongue Could Clip a Hedge, Remember Now Timmy She Lost Three in the Womb Before You Come to Bless Us and She Don't Dare Love You for Fear You'll Be Taken Too, and he drank, he said, because his dreams had died, so Don't Ever Let Your Dreams Die, Timothy Donovan, and Remember All This When I'm Gone.

Which he is now.

Bib, too, buried about a hundred yards from my father, though I can never find his grave, it's Crazies Turf down there big time, that's their East Coast Headquarters.

"Fly," Dad said the last time I visited him in the hospital, where once he washed floors at but then came to die in. "Get out, as far as you can go, Timothy. Promise me now, there's a good boy. Go somewhere you've never been before. Somewhere . . . somewhere beautiful."

I promised. Which is why my hair's a little longer now.

I begin The Game, making my way to Tommy's.

The thing about The Projects is, you can shinny down a drainpipe, hop a few fences and you're everywhere you need to be, with the lit-up-like-Oz towers of the City in the background. That makes me sizzle, too, that view, that sizzle I told you about earlier that I'd get whenever me and Bib talked about our future, or, well, when Bib talked about it and I'd sit there and tingle staring back into his green eyes, green like a perfect ballfield, like my field of green, the greenest field you've ever seen. I'd sit there and stare back at him and tingle. But he never knew. I guess I was always hoping that The Tingles were somehow telepathic.

They're not, you know.

I'm over three fences already. Little kids with runny noses from the sea breeze are playing ball in a dirty alley. I stop, stare, put my hands on my hips, spread my legs. Their mouths drop and their game comes to a halt, bounce bounce bounce goes their ball down the alley and no one even notices it 'cuz I'm one of the D Street Boys and they don't know if I'm going to shake them down for cigarette and beer money or give them a beating just for shits though I never would or whatdya whatdya.

I'm on my way to Tommy's and this is another screen I have to get through first.

"Get this when you're fourteen," I say, pointing to the shamrock tattoo. "This means . . . you survive. Think of everything we been through. Starvation, war, oppression . . . we're still here." They're blinking, drinking this all in. One of them nods.

"Get this when you're sixteen," I say, showing the DSBF. "This means you stick together. This means . . . you don't let no one you love die."

I squat down. I put on my Bolle shades as my eyes are beginning to fill up. This would never do, they would dis me and everything I've just said if they saw me crying.

"What about the heart?" the tallest of them choir boy voice asks, pointing. "The heart around the DSBF?"

I pause. What about the heart.

"You get that if you're blessed," I say. "You'll know when you're older."

I want to open my arms to them like the statue of Jesus at the entrance to Gate of Heaven Cemetery, because some of them are already sniffing paint thinner at the age of ten. But I don't. I want to gather them into my arms. But I don't. I wanted to tell Bib that from the top of the Edison Plant you could see this island way out in the harbor, way out, you could tell it was deserted, I watched it all the time when we'd be up there drinking. I wanted to tell Bib we could go there, just me and him, we could go there and start a farm, they were talking about making a national park out of the whole fucking harbor but not yet, we could go there, we could float out one night with all our stuff and start a farm.

But I never told him. That's what I want to say when I try and find his grave, I want to lift his grave up to the top of the Edison Plant and show him our island, but I can't find his goddamn grave, it's the center of The Crazies' Black Hole down there did I already mention that?

"Stay in school," I tell the kids. I don't gather them in, though I want to. I open one arm, but scratch my head with it instead.

Then I resume my journey to Tommy's, I need him and maybe vice versa, and besides, Tommy's got Mr. Cozy and I think I might need him too.

Mr. Cozy, he's a stuffed animal, a Teddy Bear, but we were running back from the East Side one night a month ago, the cops were chasing us because we walked on the hoods of these Range Rovers, BMWs, Volvo wagons with cages in the back for trophy dogs named Josh and Sam, there's new people moving in and they're driving lots of other people out. The New People want to live in an urban neighborhood so their lives can resemble what they see in their fat smelly magazines, what they watch on TV in their media rooms. The cops were chasing us because Cop Theorem Number One: When Rich People Call the Cops About Projects Kids Walking on the Hoods of Their Expensive Cars, The Cops Respond. Up this alley, over that fence—wait, there's the lights— Fuck, run! And we melt back into the West Side like the coming of the night, and we flew up this alley, seven of us, it was trash night and there was Mr. Cozy sitting in a smelly barrel that someone threw out. I saw Tommy in front of me do a double take when we ran by, because Mr. Cozy had all the sadness of this world in his eyes.

We stopped breathless, panting at the end of the alley, and the glare of the streetlight behind him made Tommy's scar vanish for a minute and my breath left me more, like a punch in the belly from Hambone Kelly.

Tommy said, "I gotta go back."

"What the *fuck*!" one of the other guys said. The sirens got closer and everyone screwed over the alley wall thump thump of sneakers but Tommy just stood there didn't move so of course me and Bib stuck with him. I watched Tommy burst back down the alley just as the cops were shining their flashlights from the other end of the alley Hey You Fuckin' Kids Stop, and a flash of lightning coiled through the steamy night. A groan of thunder rumbled overhead like grownups fighting upstairs and you don't know why.

Tommy came back to us in three bounds we flew over the wall I could see under his arm he had that teddy bear we were running fast man Tommy was in front he's fastest like a greyhound with those long legs working like pistons churning and under his arm facing me I could see this liberated Teddy Bear. He had extended arms as if to hug, a little hole on his side where some of his innards had leaked out, and the words "Mr. Cozy" stenciled across his chest in floppy red felt.

We came to another alley halfway down. There was this two-story chain-link fence. Cop Theorem Number Two: Cops Will Sometimes Climb a One-Story Fence but Never a Two-Story One, so we sprang up the fence the three of us Mr. Cozy made four and I could see our shadows on the ground below us, we looked like bugs caught in a web, then plop we're in some kind of indoor/outdoor garage neither the one nor the other with big mother concrete pillars. We stood behind one huddled close so they wouldn't see, listening, straining for the sound of fat feet flat feet running in the service of the rich because these are just the types of young urbans The Mayor wants to attract to our neighborhood and he'll be damned if any trashy kids make it uncomfortable for them by walking on the hoods of their fine automobiles.

We were a circle facing each other a triangle I could feel their breath Tommy pulled Mr. Cozy from under his arm and stuck him in the middle of us, all three of us holding him up with our chests. Then cop voices harsh like dogs chasing us beams of light farther down Quiet Here They Come and I guess part of me was sticking out behind the pillar because Bib then put his hand there where no one else ever had except this drunk girl down the beach one night Nice Bum Where You From she said but Bib didn't say anything just put his hand there and pushed in but didn't take his hand away and it's like I'm turning into liquid fire from the inside out. Our bodies were in this circle facing each other wicked close pressed together Mr. Cozy was in the middle looking scared and sad and Tommy was stroking him lightly you wouldn't think such big hands, then the flashlight beams like stabs probing for an organ like a blind surgeon or a blind priest feeling for where it hurt the most and I found I was stroking Mr. Cozy, Bib was, too, you couldn't help it 'cuz Mr. Cozy was scared he wasn't used to this cop stuff you could tell he was trembling but I don't know if it was me or Tommy or Bib or all three of us and *not* because the cops were chasing us, that shit happened all the time, man.

Then the lights were gone.

Still we kept stroking Mr. Cozy—very quietly—you gotta be careful those cops are sneaky sometimes, our hands brushed each others a little bit.

Stroking Mr. Cozy and now I think maybe he was like a genie's lamp in that alley just waiting to be rubbed and make Something happen 'cuz after all these years DSBF with a heart around it but no way to talk about it no way to think about it no way to do anything about it and now this 'cuz Tommy then put his long arms around me and Bib and pulled us in closer still our faces together like origami we did once in art class Tommy's cheek against mine soft with tickly little bristles. Lightning flashed or maybe it was inside me. Then Bib's lips against my forehead he was shaking, a mouth I'd seen all my life tight with swears or ejecting puked-up beer or receiving Holy Communion was now soft tender electricity against my skin. And his hand was still Down There but rubbing now across back and forth and then Tommy's hand too and then both their hands went down the back of my baggy nylon gym shorts against my skin white and never before.

The rain started then, Hollywood rain that was nowhere then everywhere we pulled closer still and breathing fast again now Tommy was shaking hard and his blue eye like white in the night I watched it as it watched Bib undo his shorts and they fell with a *whoosh* sound to his knees and then it was like in my dreams there was a hotdog hard looking for its fellow hotdogs lurching sniffing.

Tommy reached for it slow like he wasn't sure if it was heaven, or hell, but then his hand stopped midway. He backed up. He screamed, or maybe it was thunder. His fists clenched by his sides— I knew so well without seeing. Mr. Cozy fell to the concrete floor wet already. Tommy snatched him up quick like that.

"We . . . better . . . stop or . . . Mr. Cozy's gonna get us all," he panted. He kind of snorted like a laugh but not funny.

"Fuck," he said.

"Whatdya whatdya," I said, attempting normal voice but no.

Bib had his head down and his face was scarlet like he was waiting to see what next. Man, the courage of him that night.

Tommy looked at us both, then flew back up the fence and was gone.

I kept watching the rain plop on the garage floor between my sneakers but eventually I had to look. You see I had to.

I didn't see Tommy again till after Bib's funeral, which was three days after that night. I couldn't go to Bib's funeral, I couldn't say nothing to him after we did what we did in the garage that night after Tommy left, couldn't even look him in the eye, couldn't even walk home with him Guilt of course more

Guilt now sure but lately my guilt is being joined by rage as I wonder WHO MADE THIS THING SO FUCKING BAD THAT YOU CAN'T EVEN LOOK SOMEONE IN THE EYE, CAN'T EVEN WALK SOMEONE HOME, 'cuz I couldn't. Couldn't even walk home with him 'cuz I was shaking and puking after all these years and then finally.

Just like how now, I can't gather these kids into my arms, though I want to. All my life I've heard from everyone priests cops nuns judges parents We Must Have Laws, What Kind of Crazy World Would It Be if Everyone Just Did What They Wanted to All the Time, and You've Broken the Law and Therefore You Must Be Punished, but I want to tell you this world is plenty crazy for me and I think it would be better the other way, if we all only did what we wanted to. But are too afraid to.

I'm almost at Tommy's. I begin to slow down as I get closer. It's getting harder the closer I get.

Now, what exactly was I going to say to him?

My D Street whistle brings him out to his back porch. It's Tommy and he's very much alive. He's okay and alive and standing on his back porch. That's where they found Bib, too, on his back porch.

Tommy's big hands grip the deck railing as he leans over, one story above me. He's only wearing plaid boxers and his tattooed delts, blue on white skin, look like epaulets from a war.

We stare at each other.

"How was Back to the House?" he finally asks.

"Nahhh . . . it sucked," I mumble.

We keep staring at each other.

"Sorry," he says.

I nod. Then I take a deep breath, no idea what I'm going to say—

"I was ahhhh . . . thinking . . . I . . . I was like wondering if maybe I might borrow Mr. Cozy tonight," I blurt.

Tommy freezes. Our eyes lock and I think he's holding his breath. We haven't ever talked about it but I think he feels like me it's now or never, the neighborhood's full up with bars where you can go and happily drown the words you can't say until you're dead and can't say them then even if you wanted to.

And I promised Dad.

"The n-nights are hardest," I say, kind of mumbly. I look up. I see Tommy gulp, the large Adam's apple riding up, then down, his smooth thick throat.

"I know," he says, nodding. "I . . . Aw fuck, Timmy. If . . . if I didn't freak out that night . . . I keep thinking if only I stayed. . . ." His hand makes a futile gesture, then drops slowly back to the railing again.

He looks at me. I think he's crying.

I see now that Tommy has Mr. Cozy's eyes, all that sadness. It hits me that we have more than one thing in common, more than two things in common.

We stare at each other.

"Tommy," I say.

"Yeah?" he murmurs, cocking his head toward me.

"I . . . I don't . . . I don't think I'm going to leave," I say. "I think."

I know he knows what I mean.

He's still staring at me. I see his jaw tighten. He turns away for a minute, blinks hard. He takes a deep breath, cracks his knuckles. He turns back and looks down at me again, searching for something. By now I have my arms wide open, like the statue of Jesus.

This time for once I finally do.

I see a look on Tommy's face I've never seen in its entirety, only its beginnings.

He bolts from the porch. A minute or two later I hear him bounding down his back stairs. He comes through the fence door into his backyard. He stops ten feet away from me. He's put on green striped sweat pants and a white T-shirt.

We stare at each other.

Somewhere in this city, someone's raising his finger for another drink. Somewhere down the street, a very busy realtor with bright red lipstick, a little on her teeth, is rearranging her face into a smile to ask a young couple in consuming mode what their budget might be, deciding by their answer whether or not she could be bothered with them. Right out front there's an abandoned dog purposefully walking, intent on dog business.

But here in Tommy's backyard, I think a miracle is happening, right in between the rusted clothes line and the pealing-painted bulkhead door. There's no angel choirs or nothing, I mean, you'd probably just walk by. It's a miracle of a long stare, a smile.

"C'mon," Tommy says finally.

"Where we goin'?" I walk over to him.

"You need a haircut," he says, running his hand lightly through my hair.

I nod my head slowly, keeping my eyes on his as his hands linger in my hair. The smiles fades from his face and he gulps again.

We slide up Broadway without saying anything. We get to Dom's Barbershop. Dom's sitting inside reading the newspaper in the slanting sunlight. The place smells of geraniums and talcum powder.

"Both o' yous today?" Dom asks, rising slowly. He shakes out a nylon protective cloth with black and white daisies on it.

"Naw, just him," Tommy answers, jerking his head. I sit down on the squishy red seat and swallow hard. Dom folds a white protective collar around my neck. His fingers are cold, I notice, not like Tommy's were that night—

Tommy doesn't sit down. He folds his smooth arms across his chest. He stands right beside my chair, towering over Dom. Dom puts on little half-glasses, then pins the protective cloth tight around my neck.

"Too tight for you?" Tommy asks me. I half laugh and shake my head. Dom gives Tommy a funny look, I see this in the mirror but Tommy doesn't, he's looking down at me.

"Eh . . . how 'bout dem Red Sox?" Dom asks.

"Yeah, how 'bout 'em," Tommy says. "Regular flattop for the young man here."

I'm looking at the pictures of pouty men on the wall and the haircuts they illustrate, The Sheraton, The Continental, The Bristol—which is way dumb—if you came in here and asked for The Bristol they'd just look at you. But to tell the truth I'm only aware of Tommy. Tommy, Tommy, and nothing but Tommy, standing so close I can feel his breath on my neck.

"Good and close now, Dom," Tommy instructs, half-pointing a finger.

"Mebbe you wanna do it yo'se'f, eh?" Dom asks, laughing.

Tommy snaps to his full height. He clenches his fists. I know this is the moment. Either we will take a lifetime of knee-jerk shit, or never take shit.

A smile breaks across Tommy's face like the sun pouring through Dom's windows.

"Yeah," he says, nodding, "yeah, as a matter of fact I do. Here." He reaches into his pocket, pulls out a twenty. "Go take a break, old man. Take your keys. We'll lock up when we're through."

"What, are you crazy?" Dom asks, but he's already shoving the twenty into the pocket of his baby blue barber's shirt. He shakes his head, shuffles over to the register, empties it, then grabs his sweater and limps out the door. He turns as he's almost through it.

"I know yo' uncle if someting's broken," he warns Tommy.

"Yeah, whatever," Tommy laughs back.

"Crazy Irish kids," Dom mutters. The door shuts behind him with a tinkling of bells. Me and Tommy's eyes meet in the mirror. I see him swallow hard again. He walks over to the door, locks it, then turns the Open sign around so that it says Closed facing the street, the world.

He's breathing faster when he comes back to me. I watch him in the mirror. Very gently, he loosens up my collar. He brings the buzzer to my head. He turns it on, jumps a little when it whirs to life, then slowly brings it to my head. He presses it against scalp. A spurt of something jags through me. His breath is in my ear. He starts slow at first, then seems to get more confident. I watch his arms in the mirror, up down back forth. I notice the skin of his forearms looks like a sweater too tight to contain the muscles beneath.

"Bib," I say above the whir. "Tommy listen, me and Bib—"

"Later," Tommy says, he's all business cutting my hair. He continues buzzing along, blowing the hair off every now and then with his breath, which smells like strawberry ice cream, my favorite. He puts his other hand on my shoulder, lightly at first, then harder. I don't mind.

When he's done he runs his hands along the back of my head where the hair's all bristly and sharp. My eyes close and a sound comes out of my mouth.

"I know," he says, laughing nervously. He tightens. "Me too . . . baby." His last word ricochets around the barbershop like a bullet in a Saturday morning cartoon, smashing things. Our eyes lock in the mirror again.

"Everybody's out at my house for the night," he says. His words sound like they were barbecued before they came out of his mouth.

"Ahhh . . . okay," I say. I gulp, audibly. We continue to stare at each other via the mirror. But quick now, like birds' wings.

"Well," Tommy says after a bit, clearing his throat. "What do you think?"

"About what?"

"The haircut, duh."

I make an appraising face in the mirror.

"Where's my hat?" I ask.

Tommy laughs, punches me in the shoulder. Really, it's not that bad, maybe the best I ever had.

★   ★   ★

We lock up. We step outside into the early evening sun.

"Tommy," I say, "there's this island out in the harbor. Way out? Nobody ever goes there. You can see it from the top of the Edison Plant."

"Tim," he says. We stop. We turn and face each other. I see myself reflected in his sunglasses, and beyond me, the sky, flawless and blue, the bluest blue—

"We got everything right here," he says. "Everything."

"Tommy," I say.

He smiles and pulls out a lollipop he must've swiped from Dom's when I wasn't looking. He unwraps it and holds it like a dart, but before he can do anything I snatch it from him and shove it into his shocked mouth.

"You bashtarhd!" he chortles, laughing with his mouth full, and I take off down Broadway, him chasing me close behind. I'm laughing too 'cuz I know I'm about to keep my promise to Dad, to go somewhere I've never been before—

Somewhere beautiful.

SCARECROW

Tom House

That Saturday was different, and at times Alan's dour mood yielded
to an unexpected lightness, and even a kind of giddiness—particularly in the evening, as he watched snatches of the six o'clock news,
and the clips of Anita Bryant and the Save Our Children Crusade:
a protester had rushed up to a convertible Anita had been rolling
along in with her husband, Bob, and socked in her face with a banana cream pie. "Oh, how terrible," his mother said, and "See" to
Alan, and yet, as he looked from the downcast and pie-smeared
face of the woman on the screen to his mother's own grimacing
profile, he couldn't completely suppress the smirk that wanted to
creep across his lips: the tail of it surfaced, finally, at the left, slightly
upturned corner of his mouth.

Then later that evening, after all the good nights had been said,
and little Theresa was asleep, and he was sitting at his desk reread-
ing passages from *Romeo and Juliet* for Sister Wenzler's test on Monday, he looked up for a moment, remembering the clownish image,
and chuckled aloud. And it was all he could do to quell the con-
vulsions, and tell himself that it was childish and disrespectful to
laugh at such a thing—wasn't it childish and disrespectful? Of
course it was. And so he swallowed, and cleared his throat, and tried
to return, with a more mature and sober attitude, to the beautiful
words the lovers spoke.

The attitude didn't last long: soon he was off on another tack,
substituting the name of Chris Deal, the blond boy who sat across

from him in homeroom, for Romeo, and tinkering around with the lines.

Who's that which doth enrich the hand of yonder knight? Chris would say, peeking around a pillar in a Zorro-like mask; then Jimmy Martin, his Benvolio, would lean in close to the boy's ear and whisper Alan's name.

O, he doth teach the torches to burn bright! / It seems he hangs upon the cheek of night / As a rich jewel in an Ethiop's ear— / Beauty too rich for use, for earth too dear! / So shows a snowy dove trooping with crows, / As yonder Alan o'er his fellows shows. / The measure done, I'll watch his place of stand, / And touching his, make blessed my rude hand—

Alan dropped the dog-eared paperback to the desktop and leaned back in his chair, leaping ahead to Act III, and to the wedding night, when Chris would climb up to the window. In the real play there was no climbing-up scene, just a waking-up-in-the-morning scene, but his play would have it, and it would be a window very much like his own, small and square, with wood-framed sashes, navy blue curtains, and the boy would drop softly down from the sill, onto the carpet, and rush over to the bed, where his wife lay, waiting.

At that, Alan whisked across the room, and flopped down onto the mattress, blinking up, as it were, at his new husband's face, better than any boy's.

And now, Chris would say, dropping a kind of cloak to the floor, *now, my rich jewel of love; now, my winsome wench of nightly pleasures . . .*

But suddenly Alan paused, and stared at the ceiling, stunned by a new and wilder idea taking shape in his mind. Then he leapt up again, waving aside the image of Chris that stood before him— velvet-shirted, threatening to yank the tights from his hips—and ran quietly and swiftly down to the kitchen, where, out of sight of his mother and father in the TV room, he snapped a particularly fat banana from the bunch on top of the refrigerator; next he swooped upon the laundry room in search of his old brown corduroys, and, finding them at the bottom of the hamper, rushed back upstairs, and locked his door, and jimmied the back of his desk chair up under the knob, and pulled down the window shade. That accomplished, he rummaged through his dresser drawers for thick sweaters, and rolled them up, and stuffed them into the legs of the pants, until they were full and solid as a boy's. Second, he grabbed his pillow out from under his spread, and, managing a pair of his Fruit of the Looms around one of the shorter ends, positioned the secret part lengthwise and curve down beneath the crotch, and stuffed the whole works waist-deep into the pants. But the pillow, he found, made for insubstantial, squashy hips, compared to the well-packed legs, and so he filled up the behind-area with a bunched-up sweatshirt jacket, which served to press the pillow and stashed-away secret up nicely to the front, and then, over the chest portion of the pillow, he put his tan corduroy shirt, stuffing the arms with T-shirts before buttoning it, and tucking the tail in; and lastly, he slipped his belt through the loops of the waistband and buckled it.

The whirl of activity ended, he straightened up beside the bed, trembling slightly as he looked down at the strange thing he had assembled. Like a scarecrow of himself, he thought, or like the ones children made at Halloween, packing dead oak leaves into their fathers' old clothes. But those would be rigged with jack-o'-lanterns, and the jack-o'-lanterns lit from the inside with candles; Alan's scarecrow was headless, and his body looked more real, and when he lay down next to it—he did, eventually, lie down next to it—and brought his leg over its leg, there was the palpable impression of a limb beneath; and when he rolled over onto his back, and pulled the thing on top of him, and positioned its legs between his, it had weight and dimension and hips for him to place his hands on.

And now, my luscious gush of love and hope . . .

But no, he wasn't ready yet, because he saw there was further he could go, a way of feeling it even more against him, and so he slipped off his pajama shirt and undershirt and pajama pants, and threw them all down on the floor; he peeled off his underwear and both his socks, and lay back again, completely, thrillingly bare, and pulled the thing up over him a second time, and oh, then he could really feel it, the substantialness of it, and the smoothness of the corduroy, right up against his stomach and his nipples and the insides of his legs.

Now, my little frolicking floozy, I will take the length and stunning girth of my manhood and pierce the very core of thee with wild pleasure.

Oh, core me, Sir Chris, pierce me with thy wild pleasure. Cleave me in twain with the hot rod of ecstasy, my lord, my life and all.

At once Alan's hand plunged beneath the waistbands, his palm slipping over the thick ridged skin, disappointingly cool, his fingers grazing the rough and un-skinlike tip; but then as his fist closed around the firm, meaty middle, he was more impressed and believed the sensation quite close to that of actually holding one, a fat one.

But first there is something you must for me doeth.

Doeth?

Sir Chris whispered it in his ear, and Alan paused to blush demurely, then pushed the boy onto his back, and slid right down, unfastening the belt, and the pants button; he watched the slow, systematic unlocking of the zipper's copper-colored teeth, the unfurling of the fly, the exposure of the long, fat, cotton-stretching lump, and this, too, seemed real, and just the way it would be, and then he yanked down the waistband, and snatched it up, garishly yellow; he snapped the stem and peeled the first section of skin, imagining once more the parting zipper, the white lump, and then he peeled the second section, the third, and finally, the slightly curved column of fruit stood before him.

O happy dagger. He licked at the tip, imagining it a slotted, tannish-pink, and Chris moaned and moved his hips from side to side. He wanted him to take it all the way in his mouth.

"All right, if you want me to I will."

Gently, Alan curled his wetted lips over the edges of his teeth and slipped his mouth down over it, as far as it would go, until he felt the tip nearing the back of his throat. *This is thy sheath.* Then gently, too, he pulled his head back, and let it slip down again to the very end of his tongue, before he took it back in, not quite as far, and it wasn't hard to do; in fact, he said he could easily do it faster, and set at once to the task, gradually increasing the speed of his lips and mouth over the warming, softening fruit—imagining, as he did, Chris's moans growing louder and wilder, and soon, when Alan couldn't bear it anymore, he stopped, and pushed Chris aside again, and rolled onto his back:

On the beach now, beneath the boy and his blanket; Alan kissing up at his neck and shoulder and placing his hands on the sides
of his behind, rubbing the beautiful, golden-downed loaves, and all
the while he can feel it, hard and feverish, sliding up and down his
stomach, jabbing at the hinge of his leg; he feels it pressing and
pushing and knocking for a door that will open, and let it inside,
and Alan spreads his legs wider, and wishes the space between them
to part, as if it could, as if he could lift the sac of skin and there it
would be, the red, petaled edges of an opening, unfurled, ready.

This is my body, which will be given up for you, Alan says, an image
now in the air, hovering over the bed, one hand held to his heart,
the other pointing toward heaven; white robes are slipping from his
shoulders, his skin is smooth and bright, a smooth bare-bright temple that Chris can climb the steps of, enter to the heart of, and live
right in. The boy on the bed knows this; his hands are clasped behind his head, his tongue licking his lips in anticipation of the sacrifice; at last he nods, willing him to waft down again, and no
sooner do the blades of Alan's back touch the mattress than Chris
is bearing down on him, and stabbing into him, roughly and accu-
rately, and Alan lets him, every last inch of him he lets—fill him up,
stretch him up, all fat, all f— Wet. Right up the center of him, rip
right up the middle, split right up the two of 'im. Fuck 'im.

Fuck me, you goddam fucken fucker, you fuck you bitch—slam it, slam
that—bash that munchin', gummed-up, blood-mouthed—ram that hard
fucken knife edge—rust, you fuck, you shitrippin'—rust in me and let me
die you goddam son of a fucken—

And this time, as the stuff rushed out, he didn't place his tissues
down to catch it, but let it rain warm and white upon his stomach;
and as it did, he imagined he could feel Chris's, also, shooting up
into his dark, slippery inside, that it was raining both in him and
over him, and finally, once the contractions passed, and he was
breathing deeply and regularly, bits of his outburst came back to
him, and he was shocked at the force and harsh sound of the
words, some he had never thought before, or heard—*shitrippin'* he
had never heard, and *blood-mouthed*—shocked, above all, that he was
the one who had thought them up.

But at once he shook the troublesome string of curses from his mind, and his thoughts turned to Chris, and to the scarecrow, and, "Poor thing," he said, because it looked so cast off, its shoulders cater-cornered between the bed and wall. "I'm sorry," he told it, and, sliding his arm out sideways, so as not to tilt his stomach, pulled it in closer by the belt. "That was so nice."

Yes, Chris says, no longer Sir Chris—that was silly, really, and Alan wanted them to just be lying now, in a regular, costumeless way on the bed. *You did it the best anyone ever did it.*

Again Alan blushes, and Chris kisses his proud, reddening cheek. *Better than Didi?* he asks.

You know about her?

He nods; he's heard the stories since September, of how she went from boy to boy under a blanket at the beach, taking them all in her mouth.

Much better than her. Didi was nothing.

Better than Shelley? His current girlfriend, a cheerleader, with beautiful, feathered hair and monogrammed sweaters.

Shelley doesn't do those things. She's never even seen it.

Has Janice? His girlfriend before Shelley, in the eighth grade; it was said they lay on a lounge in her screened-in patio, tongue-kissing and slipping their hands down each other's pants.

No, she only had her hand on it. Once. But that was all before. You're the only one I want to do anything to me now. He wants to say more. *What?*

The boy smiles bashfully. *Nothing,* he says, but he's thinking: My heart has never loved till now; *Forswear it, sight!/For I ne'er saw true beauty till this night.*

Still it was ruined, and Alan tried to imagine a time before the girls, and a place they wouldn't have come into, and then, it was only a desert island he could think of, he and Chris having survived a *Minnow*-like shipwreck at an early age, and living off the land like Gilligan and Skipper; or he imagined himself, instead, the only girl Chris had ever wanted, and that he could trade in his sex that way, and go back—plaid-skirted, bloused, longer hair barretted—to his desk at the front of the room in the sixth grade, and then the minute Chris walked in, and Miss Valencia introduced "the new boy" to the class, their eyes would meet, fatefully and for

life, and how gladly Alan would go through all those days again—
three years of learning all the same things, and doing all the same
homework, and still it would be worth it, still he would relish every
repeated second, because it would all be essentially different, shared
with Chris; and oh, if even that was too impossible, if a lifetime together was too much, too greedy, then couldn't it just happen for
a day, couldn't he wake up just one day—the week before Janice
had touched it, for instance, and months before he had stumbled
onto Didi at the beach, and a whole year before he had started
going out with Shelley—as a girl Chris would like more than anyone he had ever seen or ever would, and then Alan could magically
appear somehow, on Chris's block, when Chris was walking down
it, alone, with time to spare—a Saturday afternoon, perhaps, a Sunday afternoon—and Alan would wave, *Hi, Chris,* and the boy
would say, *Do I know you?* but then the power of their attraction
and automatic love would throw all questions aside, and before either of them knew it they would be in a beautifully appointed
room, kissing, and Alan would become the first person ever to
touch it, and the first person ever to take it in his mouth, and the
first person Chris would ever enter, and they would do it all over
and over and over again, trying to store up enough love and passion to last them the rest of their lives, but finally the clock would
approach midnight, and Alan would have to say, with tears, *I'm
sorry, my love. I must go now. You will never see me again,* and, running
from the room, and down the street, he would turn back into a
boy, and when Chris caught up with him and asked, *Did you see a
beautiful girl run by?* he would have to answer, *No, I haven't,* and
watch him run on then, uselessly, through Janice and Didi and
Shelley, and all the way through to the woman he finally, reluc-
tantly married he would still be running after the girl who had appeared one day on his block. *Only Alan understood the sadness and
searching behind Chris's eyes after that; morning after morning, month after
month, he looked across the aisle to the side of a face perpetually turned
away from him and thought, I'm right here, Chris. Right here.*

Alan sighed, and said what a sad story that was, and what a sad,
sweet feeling of emptiness it left inside him. But the very next instant, he grew restless with himself, and argued how silly it was, and

stupid, to be feeling emotions that came from the made-up facts of a story, when the truth was different, and much worse: Chris had never even wanted to be his *friend,* and it was just a crazy scarecrow Alan was lying next to, and that was the closest he would ever get.

He gasped softly, and shook his head again; "Tsh," he said, and "See," and looked to the headless pillow with a mixture of pain and scorn—because it was terrible, terrible and unfair, that the boy should go on that way, laughing and happy without him, that he should always have gone on that way, and that Alan should never have been a part of it, when he had wanted so to be, and when there was so much he felt for him, and if only there was a way to make him see, a way to capture him—yes, if he could only just capture Chris for a short while.

Again he gasped, because that seemed such a sudden, criminal thought, and yet his mind ran off with it, imagining himself a kind of stalker, soundlessly following the boy down some out-of-the-way street, at some out-of-the-way hour; he imagined sneaking up behind him with an ether-soaked rag, and, in just the same way he had once seen it done on *Charlie's Angels,* smothering his face with it. Chris would struggle slightly before collapsing into his arms, the way the woman had struggled before falling to the leather-jacketed man, and then Alan could drag him off somehow, to a basement, say, where no one ever came, and he could gag him, and chain him there, in a standing-up position, between two metal pillars, so that when he took the boy's pants down, he could look at him all he wanted, from the front and from the back, and when he regained consciousness, he could show him pictures from *Playboy* magazine until it rose up, red and puffy, and then Alan could quickly toss the pictures aside, and drop to his knees, and take it in his mouth; again and again he could take it in, all he wanted to, and eventually—not too soon, but before an overlong amount of time had passed—he could tap the boy on the side of the head with a special hammer, and in just the right place, so that he would forget everything that had happened since the ether, but nothing else, and then when he woke up again—on the corner of his block, beside some woods—it would be with just a slight headache, and a paradoxical sense of well-being, and he would rub his temples curiously, wondering

why he was sitting on the side of the road, and where all the time
had gone, and, "Oh," Alan said, his mind reeling back to the images
of the boy's naked behind and naked front, and the way it would
flap, to and fro, when he woke and shook himself within the
chains, like Samson, or Charlton Heston from *The Ten Commandments,* and then suddenly it happened again, more warm rain sprin-
kling down over the cooled, liquefied puddles, and finally, when
the last of it had dribbled out, and Alan had shuddered, and taken
several deep, measured breaths, sleep, of all things, came pressing
down on him, as if he might just close his eyes that minute and run
along with it; but of course he couldn't, not with his stomach spat-
tered this way, and with the scarecrow still lying beside him, and,
summoning what seemed his last reserve of energy, he reached for
his tissues and wiped himself; and then he got up, and began the
disassembly, and refolded all the clothes, and returned them to his
drawers; he took the peeled and uneaten banana, and tossed it out
his window, down to the hedge by the fence—for the night animals, he said—and then he slipped on his corduroys, and removed
the chair from under the door, and walked, briefless and shirtless,
across the dark hall to the bathroom. There he flushed away the tissues, and washed his stomach and his hands, and brushed his teeth;
then he crossed the hall again, and locked his door, and flicked off
the light; he let his pants drop to the floor and walked for his bed,
naked again, and lay down, and there was much more room now,
without the scarecrow, room to stretch out in, and to arrange the
pillows just so, and assume a comfortable position, and once he did,
and stared up into the dark, spacious quiet, he found that all his
giddiness and excitement had vanished, too, that it was just the
heaviness again, just himself, drifting, on a long, empty raft, toward
sleep.

SECOND ISLAND

Patrick Ryan

I'd have my walk without distractions. No tourist sights. No museums. My lover, Max, would want to see them with me. Tickets. Only tickets. And a quick stop at the Arsenal des Galéres because Max wasn't impressed by military paraphernalia. But I did it nonetheless. I followed the boy for seven blocks on the Canebière. It began at rue des Capucins within sight of the Palais de la Bourse. *You are an apocalypse. I could ask for nothing better,* I wanted to tell him. The visit to the Roman ruins was left for later, the tickets at La Criée as well. *I will follow you to the Marché aux Poissons or the train station bathrooms. Believe me!*

He had a backpack over his left shoulder. He walked as if he had jazz in his head, and his hair was blond and unkempt—dreggy. I didn't think he was dangerous. No, that didn't cross my mind. He might be a university student. Or work in a café just up here. He was not an American. He had none of the chagrin for it.

I didn't know then whether he was aware of me.

He kept on without a cue. No winks or finger pointing. No quick tocsin to give me a burst of nerve. But I had my hunch. I had hunch enough to follow him onto rue de Rome. Off the Canebière.

He bought cigarettes from a street vendor. I believe they were Gitanes.

I considered offering him a light, but he was quick enough to do it himself.

He smoked and leaned against a newspaper machine.

"Paul! Salut!" he shouted into an open window.

"Yes! Okay, Sebie! Wait!" a man's voice replied.

"I forgot my keys!" His voice cracked here and there. "Open up!"

A small Arab man answered the door. He wore a stringy mustache below his nose. Two of his fingers tickled its ends forever and ever as if it were his pet, and Sebie, but I wasn't really sure of his name yet, disappeared into the bowels of the place.

I waited for a few minutes.

I bought cigarettes as well. The same brand as his own.

I smoked and whistled. It was cold.

Then just before I would've become grumpy and chicken-hearted (I was about to take the bus back to the Quai des Belges) he came out—or no, he gushed out of the door with his arms full of bags and bags of garbage—like a circus contortionist.

He'd left his backpack behind. The garbage he deposited on the street.

We made no eye contact. He had no use for it.

We walked toward Rue de Toulone, on to Rue Saint Ferréol and to the left Le Préfecture. I thought to myself: *I'm a daredevil. A horny cockamamie Yank. Fuck it all.*

I kept a good space between us. Two or three times I thought he'd discovered me, so I stopped at a window full of Banol and Cassis. Six varieties of melon jams. Or another window with porno tapes and vacuum pumps. I said a few words out loud, like "Ah, oui" or "Mon dieu, c'est cher!"—*no, of course I'm not following you*—and continued on.

I could see one or two things about him then. He was skinny, fair-skinned, and had unusually big ears. He wore a gauged ring through his nose. He'd written all over his tennis shoes: Solaar and Cam and Le Tone. He had dirt under his nails and had no love for shoe laces. When he passed by the electronics stores or music shops, he danced there on the sidewalk—like a gypsy.

Past Rue Paradis it was two o'clock. Then Rue Beauvais and finally the Quai des Belges. We waited next to each other at the stoplight—two great and dark racehorses blowing out brumes of

hot air. *What a beautiful sea!* I thought. I pulled out my tourist guide
and tried to look lost.

I turned and asked him "Do you live here in Marseilles?"

The fishermen were coming in for the day. Next to me, a small
woman with braided hair was trying to find a Métro ticket in her
purse. The boy replied "You're speaking to me?" and I replied to
that—"Yes. You. Juste toi."

Then him: "Why do you keep following me?"

The light wouldn't change. People rushed down to the Métro.
I'd make a mistake.

"What do you want?" He let his tongue hang out in between
phrases—just over his bottom teeth. Like he was chewing on a
toothpick. Or had just killed a small insect.

I held open my book. I looked for a map.

Was that curiosity there? A quick look he gave me from nose to
belly. He'd summed me up. I waited until he did it again. Yes, that
was it. The light changed. And absolutely rushed and insane, without a thought of Max, I said:

"You. I want you. Do you have a few minutes?"

I had no thought of consequence. Nothing. I'd done it all. More
than I thought I'd do. Each moment lived, had its joy, and then died
without hesitation. What did the next moment matter?

We walked together (I don't remember how we chose where or
which direction) and between the Quai des Belges and the boat he
asked me "Are you one of those rich American men who come to
Marseilles to be bad?" He was being easy with me. He agreed to a
boat ride and said: "I tend to like people who make history. Do you
make history?" and he never let it slip once that money was to be
exchanged. For all I know he was a kid who liked an older man's
company. He just questioned me with things like: "They only take
one or two credit cards on the boat. Which do you have?"

On the Quai there were people here and there. Busy and distracted. They minded their own business. School had not let out.
So he adopted a licentious groove in his demeanor. He slid his
hands into his pockets pulling and scratching jeans that seemed to
fall lower and lower.

I will not look at him. I'm being completely paranoid, but I won't look at him right now. Not so close to the hotel.

Instead I concerned myself with finding the boat company, but he was intent on distracting me. He pulled up his shirt and made for an itch but showed skin for a second too long to be accidental. He rubbed his hands over the butt of his jeans so if I hadn't yet I'd see it now: *Yeah, kid—you have a perfect ass.*

I knew what he was doing. He was barbarous about it. I explained to him: *You've no reason to turn me on any more than you already have. I'm done. I'm at your command. Stop playing with yourself.* No, I didn't say this exactly. I remarked on La Criée and mentioned the tickets I'd planned to buy earlier. I mentioned Max and the hotel. I gave him my reasons for pussyfooting.

Then we were on the boat—we abandoned Marseilles.

The most ancient city in France. How many other men had done this?

We crossed between the two forts: St. Nicholas and St. Jean. I was nauseated. I've always gotten sick in new cars, airplanes, boats. Why a ferry? Next, the Bassin de Carénage and finally, the Jardin du Pharo. Where has the sound mind gone? Lequesne's Bonne Mère—she withdrew into the miasma. The engines slowed and we proceeded at a moderate pace.

My companion kept quiet. He balanced himself on one foot and struck at the air with his fists. Made popping noises with his cheeks. He had an interest in martial arts maybe or Bruce Lee films? I continued to think: *Come on—I'm a disgusting middle-aged fag. He has no use for me. I can't undress in front of him. The moment will come and I'll fail horribly.* He was steadfast against the Mistral wind. How famous it is here. If Max had been with me, I would have narrated our arrival at Ratonneau: That there—it's D'If. There are three towers in the castle. That one, yes, the middle one, was the backdrop for Dumas and his José Faria. And Edmond Dantés dug his hole in there—that one. Look. Amazing view, isn't it? A prison as beautiful as that. Tiboulen was out there. I could see her stuck; struggling in the ink. I was in love with the sea. All except the nausea. I could do without that.

We docked next. A large Russian family boarded our boat to return to the mainland, and we made for the beach. I was exhausted.

I lost my footing on the rocks. We felt each other up behind a big square sign announcing the natural reserve ahead. We hiked up to the wreckage of a military base—German I had no doubt. No one was there. We took off our pants and fucked each other until our shirts stuck like barnacles to our underarms and we were sufficiently exhausted. I fucked him while he squeezed and hung onto the painted metal cranks jutting out of the shed beside a roofless subterranean room, a cylindrical inconsolable remnant of the war. The sunken room, the old mess hall, was a full twenty, thirty feet down. He stripped off his pullover. I finished him off with my mouth and lapped at his wet balls like a puppy dog. We sat on our pants, which we'd laid out like beach towels near the crag of the man-made gorge, and watched a little gash in the sky—full of bloodshot sun—repair itself near a few clouds. I didn't think about the time. About what was happening in Marseilles and what I should've been doing. I thought of us as lovers in some other, it would be temporary, reality—our verisimilitude. Enjoying a picnic. Celebrating our first anniversary. He had a scar on the top of his left ear.

"I think I could stay here until tomorrow morning," I told him. I said something not so clever about the beach and the yellowish rocks and the barbed precipice over the sea like: the geometry of the geography. It was all very mannish—cold white pricks prodding out of Mother Earth. The military base made us feel like soldiers. He was pulling weeds out of the old sod on either side of him and throwing the skinny stalks off to the sunken room ten or twelve feet to his left.

"But I have to admit I'm getting a little cold," I said. We had both worked up a sweat and the wintertime was hardly noticeable when we first arrived. But that didn't last—not for me. I was used to the frowning, sweltering heat of New Orleans. My fingers were dead in no time—the cold came up out of the ground and bit me. I made a move for my pants, ready to pull them on, and he tackled me. I was alarmed first (was he going to rob me or murder me?) but that was all I needed—the warmth came back. We wrestled playfully. I chased him around our pants—my body waggishly jumping to and fro. Then before I could catch him, take his socks off, and lick his toes clean, something I'd wanted to do the first time around, he slipped. He lost his footing in a molehill-ish pile of sand. I was about to laugh at his little screwup. It could've been me. I had two left feet really. His bare-skinned leg jerked and twisted outward and he fell off the rock face. Down into the mess hall: head first. Gone from me.

Can I describe this? He's made of ghost skin—already a devil to me. Smudged into limestone. So what I mean is: I don't know where rock begins and where he ends.

Could I be imagining this? He might be the carcass of a soldier five decades old. Who came back from Marseilles, got drunk, didn't hear the planes overhead, and watched his whole battalion jump from the cliffs, felt nothing but a gust of air against his neck and—who actually feels the blast? But the shaved sides of his head, the tennis shoes. No, I can be sure, he's my hustler. Dead.

If he were to look down from wherever he is now (not in his body for sure), he would see this ragged version of himself. The long body resembling a milky eel. A beached water-creature. Twenty feet down or so at the bottom of this pit. Not dark enough to conceal the white tangle of his body, not even dark enough to conceal the features of his face: a rough twenty-two-year-old with uncombed, bleached hair and deep gray eyes that turned heads, I'm sure, at a sex shop on the Canebiere.

My French boy. With his French nose—very much like mine. A q-shaped rock is lodged under his head. Is it blood on his—? Yes, it's blood. His cock is still half-hard jutting up in his briefs. We were ready to go at it a second time. Where had he thrown his pants? My shirt? I have to find them. I remember: his legs, two things like a bonne bouche, that I had just held between clenched fists—spider legs. *Look at them now.* Pushed into crazy angles, all but pulled apart from the rest of him. He is half-nude and that is unexplainable to any of the authorities, aside from what I've already said: the underwear, his tennis shoes.

I'm insane to think that he's still beautiful. Death can be very beautiful, but the manner of his death is disgusting. Disgusting because of who I am: his last john. And he is beautiful. I am over the pit, hands on top of my head, looking down, cigarette burning forever in my lips now, staring at the bewildered body of Sebie. Still with the fifty francs in my pocket.

It is time almost. I look at my watch. I didn't think of looking at my watch until now. Very soon the boat will leave to take me back to Marseilles. Here I am still on Ratonneau, the second island off Marseilles. Max is waiting at the Hotel Nice. Dressed for an evening at the opera. Or perhaps waiting to dress until I return. He will be looking at the clock beside the hotel bed. Will be worried perhaps. A star out of the window will remind him of the first night we met because it is our anniversary and stars had so much to do with the way we met.

It is a story I've told quite a few times, how Max and I met: As is the case most summers, a hurricane had dragged itself over New Orleans and disturbed the last days of vacation. Its name escapes me. I created havoc for no more than a week, then we returned to the revels and forgot it except in a newscast here and there and because of a few streetlights that had blown out. Trees had fallen the day before, windows were boarded up with plywood sheets or blue tarps.

I found Max on the doorsteps to my building (the old two-story at the end of Saint Andrew Street). He was spending the hurricane with a friend in the bottom flat and staying at a hotel in the Quarter. I cannot remember my neighbor's name, either. But Max was in from Boston—on his way to Mexico and then Honduras. "Kinda scary down here," he said.

"Oh this?" I said. "This is nothing." We didn't worry about hurricanes. I sat on the stoop and stuck my tongue out into the rain. I'd been to New York, Oklahoma, Montana. Taxicabs scared me. Mountains made me asthmatic. I thought: I can understand being scared. "But you should've seen Betsy."

We found two beers in my neighbor's fridge. He told me about Liza Minnelli's apartment in New York. The top floor of St. Mark's Baths. Tripping over Ed White's foot in Balducci's. I told him about the politics of Andrew Jackson, who really won the Civil War, and where the Creoles came from. I was finishing my doctorate in nineteenth-century history. My books were always on my back. He was Italian-blooded. An interior decorator who had no native taste for the South. That we could walk down the street drinking our beers shocked him. He'll grow to love it, I thought.

Everything was dog-tired. All the roofs. Stop signs. Electric men. I explained the ways of a storm over the racket of a grocery basket passing on its own accord—eyes, categories, names: boy, girl, boy, girl, boy. I managed to move us up to the roof through a big round window in the attic and we watched the stars.

I asked him if he thought himself lucky: visiting during the first hurricane of the year.

"Yes, in a weird kinda way."

I asked if he had a boyfriend back in Bean Town (I regretted my cuteness the second it was out of my mouth).

"No. No, not now."

Then I asked about his hotel. Was it a decent place? How expensive?

"The bed is too short," he complained. He couldn't hide a little wanton grin. "And the blankets have lice."

"And why aren't you staying—?" I indicated the front door to his friend's house.

He said, "We hardly know each other. Hardly at all. So I'd just as soon spend the night with you."

And it had happened like that. Twelve years ago. Max's first trip to New Orleans. He'd been to Greece, where since I was in tenth grade I'd wanted to go. Had been to Germany and everywhere but France. And now he'd decided to remain at the hotel while I explored the city alone for the second time.

It's nearly eight o'clock when I arrive at Vieux Port and our hotel. The desk clerk is showing an American couple to the dining room and doesn't notice I'm short-winded and choking. The husband is tall as a little tree and wears one of those hats that tourists wear to look French. He walks with a funny wobble, like a pigeon. I avoid their eyes. I've seen the wife before. In a magazine or on BBC. She's speaking to a little old woman dressed entirely in red; her blouse could pass for a cardinal's dress. It's she who is holding their conversation, moving her hands up and down as if she were painting a wall. I excuse myself past them, try not to be too discourteous, and go up to our room. I still haven't gotten my breath back. Max isn't there. I learn, from the desk clerk when I go back down, that he's already gone to the opera.

"Take the bus. It's quick. You'll get there ten minutes into the opera. Plenty of time," he says. He offers to call a cab if I feel rushed. "No, no," I say. A bit too loud maybe. Money is a thing I save nowadays. I'll need to rehearse my excuses. I'll take Rue Glandeves by foot.

I scoot down a row of Frenchmen in blue Italian suits to Max only to find him out like a light. His medications put him to sleep. They cloy the soul, he says. He's tired of them. I run through my lines again. I cannot lose my anxious state. It's chasing me.

This is all very depressing. I cannot watch the opera.

My heart is racing and I know I could wake him up but I don't.

I become paranoid that I've forgotten a piece of evidence. A stain somewhere. A piece of my clothing. But it's impossible. I didn't touch the body. Not after it fell. Max won't notice anything. I'll say: I was held up at Maison Diamantée. They blocked off the streets for a funeral.

"You're sweaty," he says. Has he been awake since I arrived? I might have said something out loud. "Did you get lost?" he asks.

"The bus was late," I tell him. "There was a funeral—Arabs."

He lets it go. A breath of relief. I've missed nothing. It's Britten's *Death in Venice*. An old tenor who cannot pronounce the ends of words. A charlatan Tadzio cast for his brawniness but devoid of any tender beauty. Tadzio, have you ever been older than this?

And we are suddenly at intermission.

I daydream without getting up. I could have walked further. To Rue Sainte Gotharde. Past the Opera House. Max would have slept through it all like a baby.

I need to think. I haven't thought enough.

The night goes on like this. The second act begins: *I am full of disease. I don't want to hear any dark words.*

Max (he's always the little devil about gifts) hands me a little box wrapped in gold tissue. This year it's a book of pictures. The epic of our twelve years. He says, "I still love you, kiddo. Even if you're a lying old fart. And you still love me don't you? You still love me too?"

"Of course I do," I say.

Professor Locks asks me: Did you know that Edmond Dantés fished every day of his life? Not for trout. Or the little white ones. For squid. Did he use a line or a net? I ask him. And no, I say. I have no recollection of Dantés sporting habits.

I cannot understand my dreams. I don't think I need to understand them.

In all the years I've taught history, I've never come across a dream that mattered.

But the holes—they interest me. Last night, I dreamt of Professor Locks. I know he was only a fraction of what I really dreamt. I know I must've dreamt about Sebie, too. It makes perfect sense that I wouldn't remember it. And the moments before I go to sleep or before I wake up—these affect me as much or more. They're like death or a good drug. The crosscut of body-life and spirit-life.

Just two or three minutes ago I was dreaming of the telephone. René Char was on the other end. He was complaining about migraines. I realized I was awake maybe a minute later. Max was answering the door. Our breakfast had arrived. He was talking to the boy who delivers meals and makes the beds.

"He doesn't understand," Max says. "Baby, how do you say hard-boiled?"

I do not open my eyes. Funny how these things mix up.

"Dur," I say. "Oeuf dur."

I cannot open my eyes.

Am I dead?

Each of my eyes are trapped like an insect in a box. I am a science experiment. My eyelids are stuck together. I remind myself: I drool. I ejaculate. I perspire. I piss. I've simply secreted too much mucilage. I've had a hell of a night. I'm paranoid. My eyes have been sewn shut and I'm in the Marseilles morgue. Yes? But then I recognize the smell of coffee, strong coffee; and I remember living along with the crisis that was yesterday. I rub out the glue. I get up.

I grab a cup of coffee. I disassemble the morning paper with a ferocious appetite. Trying to find a word, a tiny headline or news-flash.

Nothing. Nothing. Nothing.

Nothing but scandals and insignificant news. I close the paper and Max and I spend the day shopping at the Turkish markets.

Max has had cancer for three years now—so we take it slow. One day he coughed up blood. The doctors found a tumor on his small intestine. He couldn't keep solid food down for seven weeks, stopped chemo after twenty-two weeks, and searched out the alternatives in Western medicine. Acupuncture and herbs followed. We took a class together at the community college. I did the best I could in the kitchen: fresh juice, mashed potatoes, peas, and carrots, shredded beef and chicken, and soup—always soup.

Today Max watches me shop. He is all worry. He says to me, "Tell me sooner or later. I won't be mad."

"Tell you what?" I ask him.

He says nothing. Does nothing.

Don't lose your head. Don't lose it.

We have three or four bags each. I complain of a sore throat. That's enough to volte-face. Then there's a boy in the crowd up ahead who interrupts my thoughts. When I say this I mean: I forget about my throat. Feel a sudden surge of juice in my veins. I focus like a hawk on nothing but his shoes. The graffiti. His shoes—they're Sebie's. No doubt of it. Animals, I think. I walk faster. Ready to chase the boy. I want to cry out. "Thief!" but then decide suddenly: No, they're not his. They can't be his. It's impossible. *Look closer, idiot. They were white. These are gray.*

I am a wreck. I am tempted to go back to the body and drag it out to the sea. Or call the police and report the body anonymously. But I do neither. The boy goes into a music store. We continue into a large, fashionable clothing store and then to the bus stop outside—we've decided to visit Notre Dame before the day is over—to reach the top of La Garde hill.

We cannot get into the higher church of La Basilique—it's too late when we arrive. The lower church and crypt have longer hours and we interrupt a tour to join it. I feel a bit odd. Sluggish. The young French tour guide recites his verse: "Le Monseigneur de Mazenod a initiaté le constructionne de la Basilique—"There are seven other people in the tour group. We are the only Americans from what I can tell, although my presumptions aren't always correct and a younger couple with money bags around their waist may prove me wrong. I am not in the best condition.

"L'architecte Espérandieu—" he continues, but I've read this all in the tourist guide. I'll describe it as the guide describes: on a 154-meter hill in Romano-Byzantine style with a higher church dedicated to the Virgin and a lower church and crypt for public mass. Napoleon III had the basilica built between 1853 and 1854. Etc. Etc.

The basilica, although quite lovely here by the sea, is similar to cathedrals I've visited in Rome. Some in Istanbul. The crucifix has long, limber legs that resemble the vines of a tomato bush. The light from the sea colors it in moody shades, a dozen greens. The stained windows depict the saints' lives: John, Matthew, Luke; the blind Virgin in the middle. She is hauntingly blue here—birthed of the sea. What is it at her feet? I strain to see clearly, then suddenly I am light-headed. I begin to sway back and forth. Max peers lovingly at the tenth station of the cross and my head swoops down toward the floor. There is a blur of cardinal's red and I am out.

The hustler is burned into me. Into the essential nature of everyday thought. My eating, drinking, small talk—these circumduct him. I am disgusting. I could be thinking of how he tugged me around my gut with his skinny legs, or how his fingers found the canyons of a spine along my back and gripped until I heard little cracking—his weight was suspended from me. But no, I don't. I think of him inanimate, the ten minutes I spent watching him after the fact. Even looking up at this ceiling painted with colors as old and as soft as me. He is the dead spider hung over the dull sandstone sky waiting for a breeze to let it go.

I remember instead: slight motions, maybe a lift of the arm, a twinge in the foot after it first happened. It was only rocks breaking under his weight. Eyes were still open. Did he see where he was falling to? No, I'd guess. Instead he saw me, his john, pulled up like a puppet until there was a hard whack and—

★   ★   ★

I regain consciousness and Max deposits us on a bus back to the Canebiere. We're both starved and want to eat before we go back to the Hotel Nice. We take our time up the boulevard. I walk with a cool rag on my neck, which Max relates I received from the young tour guide. We walk past the Office de Tourisme and past quite a few modern restaurants that serve pigeon and fleur de courgettes farcie but don't tempt us as much as some of the more traditional establishments and their bouillabaisse and fresh oysters. I'm still light-headed and not very sure of what's happening. I know from Max that: A woman caught me by my shirt collar in the basilica and my head never reached the floor.

He says that I'm still white as a ghost. "So should we leave Marseilles early?"

"No," I answer with my teeth clenched. It's always cold.

"Listen here, buddy," he continues. "There's a morning TGV back to Paris. And Lyon might get snowed up if we don't leave soon. I think—" He loses his balance on a curb, but that doesn't interrupt him. He has his solution. "Eddie and Bernard can take care of you so much better than Monsieur Hard-Face."

"Really, dear, it's probably just bad cheese or unpasteurized orange juice. We haven't seen the prison yet. And—" I stop in mid-sentence. It's the boy again—although I know the shoes aren't the same. He's galloping in front of us like a Guido. He's no more than nineteen. Barefoot with fiery red hair. There's no need to follow him but I think: he knows something, he's from that same house on Rue de Rome. He's as white as picked cotton. He turns into a butchery.

I tell Max, "Let's buy something here. Meat pies or seafood, okay? I don't want to sit in a restaurant."

We walk in and the barefoot boy isn't anywhere I can see. Did he go into a different store? He might work in the kitchen. Or live upstairs. I look for a staircase or a door. Max tries to change my mind and wants to find a cozy Indian place.

I take in my surroundings: the boucherie is boarded with pine wood from floor to ceiling and gives the faint impression of a great big box, or a cheap coffin. From three large steel hooks three wild boars are hanging by their hooves. Beside them—laid across a marble counter—are a dozen rabbit and roast kid. Then, in a refrigerated glass case: eel and cod, as well as a platter of boeuf en daube and a few meat pies. The boars and the rabbit are skinned. The meat pies are labeled with colored flags: red, yellow and green.

"I don't like the smell in here," Max says. His hand over his stomach. "Please—can we leave?"

I don't want to deny him fresh air. We don't want to see death on our plates or in our grocery stores (we Americans). Meat dissembles as art although to me the difference is slight, isn't it? I've seen things like this in Chinatowns or Chicano groceries maybe but not in New Orleans. The meat would spoil in the heat, or else cockroaches would infest the store. "If you want to wait outside," I tell Max, "You can. I won't be long. I'll just get dinner."

He leaves me alone and I count how many laths of wood there are between me and the register. My number is called: 32. I approach the counter and the racks. I'm not so light-headed now but my body—I notice a tingling in my groin. My legs are weak. There's a chance that I won't be able to stand up in a few minutes. I'll need a chair.

I cannot remember the French for meat pie. I begin to point to them, but I want to touch the cadavers and I point to the wild boars instead. She is getting impatient with me. I don't speak. She moves on to another customer and I reach out and touch one—I don't use the little gloves that are beside the rabbits.

"Don't touch!" she hollers at me. "Don't touch! Don't touch!"

But I keep at it. I push a finger into the fat—and it gives. She slaps my hand away and a big Moroccan man, her husband I'd guess, comes around the counter waving his hands and pushing other customers out of his way as he makes for me. I withdraw my finger.

"I'm sorry. Je suis désolé. I'm sorry," I say. No danger here.

They are not amused. So I leave without getting dinner. Room service will do tonight. Or else stopping somewhere else further up—one of the modern groceries, a bakery. But I'm not satisfied with anything. At the hotel, we eat veal and potatoes fried in butter. Max only finishes half of his dinner. An hour later, I bend a pil-

low under my back listening to Max snore. Next I wrap it around
my head. Nothing helps.

Another morning—something is happening today. The hotel has
no morning papers. They've run out of pasteurized orange juice
too. I buy both from the café beside the hotel. Nothing. Not a word
again. I begin to think: the secret to murder is not how deep the
knife or how hard the push but how we compose ourselves after-
wards. *I cannot freak out. I'm not a murderer.* Not by a long-shot. But
the police—these French police—would they view it as so artless a
matter? If he had any sort of record or if he was just a rent-boy. Was
it a house full of street urchins he lived in—all for sale?

No. He was clean. I was his first.

No. I'm kidding myself.

Thinking these things, while Max is still snoring and drooling on
his pillow, I decide to return to the island.

The Hôpital Caroline is deserted. I rest on a bench near the gates
and marvel at the sharp emptiness here before I continue up the
hill. I fill the silence by humming: the quiet and the antiseptic beige
buildings, empty and treeless. The people have all run away. I can
see Marseilles. They've all gone there. Off to the living. I hear the
dead. Is that crazy to say?

I've brought water and an apple. The Tramontane is freezing my
bones. I climb up the sandy hummock toward the naval base re-
counting to myself the death rituals of the Romani. I will plug his
nose with pearls. I will let his muló follow me and do its business.
They want revenge. He'll want revenge. On me? No—on the other
men. The worst men. The ones who smelled. Or the ones who hit
too hard. I kick through the little yellow stones and cut my ankles
on abstruse thorns, thorns that other hikers will have missed because they are more observant. I'm leaving a trail of my blood that
leads to Sebie and the base. I eat the apple quickly.

One thousand sparrows reside on the island. I find them perched
on top of white cantilevers where the roof is now gone. What's left
is three dozen rows of long-trunked crosses as if it were a memo-
rial for giants. Not the mess hall or a section of battalion housing
that's underneath—I can't see it. Umpteen of these great skinny

monoliths for umpteen dead soldiers, for Sebie too, where the sparrows squat. They caw and flap their greasy wings. They have no intention of leaving me to mourn my boy in peace. They're like the pigeons around Andrew Jackson. Stubborn birds.

I can only see the sea now—not Marseilles, not the boat dock. One bird has stationed itself on the crag over the pit. I creep toward the site of our accident and wag my arms back and forth: "Scat! Go away!" I tell it. Little lavender flowers have grown out of the cracks in the rocks. I don't remember them—no, not at all. The bird hops off. I look down: Sebie is still there. The police haven't come. No tourists visit here in the winter: maybe to D'If or maybe to the boat docks but not up the hill, not to the base. I look for a route to the bottom. I see three doors in the pit that might or might not lead to stairs that might or might not still exist. I need access. I want to see up close.

I drink water and circle the pit. Then the next pit. I'm thirsty still. There's a scant stairwell decussated with reddish iron bars. Once I'm down it, I see a rusted three-wheel bicycle and a dozen or so pipes, perfectly new, rolled together like giant telephone wires. Should I have called Max?

I haven't thought of Max enough. How can I when there's Sebie? Max is doing fine. He's probably sleeping late. Rejuvenating cells. Keeping the cancer at arm's length. He is resilient enough. Sebie on the other hand— Yes, what about Sebie? What's got me over here?

I walk into a room and I can't see its walls. Only a little light gets in, a boy-with-jaundice yellow, and brightens a rectangle of perilous, icy floor. I'll have to be careful. Smashed plates and a few Coca-Cola bottles. I am sure there's a mirror, fractured or not, off to my left. Every fourth step I make provokes a short coruscation from somewhere near it. I spot my reflection finally. Just a black evil thing in the room's grisaille. Yes, a mirror. I walk toward another door on the opposite side to the pit. I keep on until I am at the entry. To his tomb or his—yes, the old pantheon no one's ever found. No one here to worship. Go in, I tell myself.

No, no one else is here.

No, you don't believe in ghosts.

No, Max hasn't followed you.
No, Sebie isn't still alive.
And then I see him. I am alive. I am in the light. Outside.

He's beautiful after two days. No creatures. A force field's around him. Can I say this? I've read this somewhere: I am aching for the boy's ass and touch and lips and tongue and tits and legs and salty toes and involuntary spurting cock. I want to read it again. Think of Sebie this time through. What book was it? I pull him into the room. He'll be safer. He's not very heavy. Only slightly more than an old Zenith television. But his muscles have gone tight and wooden. He's mechanical—like a piece of farm equipment. Instead of slithering over the various shapes of rocks under him, he rolls them over and drags them.

I position him up against the darkest wall. Near the busted mirror. An empty cereal box under his head and he looks as if he's only sleeping: a vagrant who's passed out. Or he'll be mistaken for carpet. A sleeping bag. Garbage. The light's no good. Another visitor trekking down here is a slim bet. The sites are all up there. But I'd be invidious if another man—a lonely bum—found him, and so I take one of the plywood boards, a good sturdy piece of wood, eight feet by two feet, and block him into a little rectangle of his own. A few rocks here and there keep it upright. It's good.

I don't want to stay any longer. Max is waking up. I drink more water and head out. Maybe I'm coming down with a sore throat after all.

I've acquired a certain feeling of inadequacy in the past two days. The empty hotel room is full of my stink—Max's too of course—and I have a hard time breathing properly. The air is laced with fractions. I cannot make my thoughts fuse. I've left something on the island, of course nothing tangible, but more important than a piece of concrete me. I've left a few of my thoughts. The blue walls of the room might take the edge off my troubles. It's a nice room and I haven't taken the time to find that out. Max has gone for a walk and will stop at the train station to buy tickets to Carcassonne: a castle city in the southwest of France, the Languedec-Rousillon region. There's a medieval festival there at the end of next week. We'll stop in Perpignon, where the boys are darker and some speak Catalan as well, and we'll take a few photos. For now, to rest my legs and recover from my recent fainting spell, I begin writing letters to America (or postcards depending on the person). I start each with: "My dear American, how little you know about life until you've" and end each with "I miss you terribly, you've not fallen far from my thoughts."

The window is stuck in our room. I've tried to open it but the paint has soldered the two panels of wood together. Five days in Marseilles and I haven't noticed we are shut up in the room like a pair of punished children. I risk damaging our room if I use a screwdriver—although I haven't got one anyway. I stop writing and push the ballpoint of my pen into the crack. Two boats are coming into the port side by side. I pick off a few flakes of dry paint and drop them on the carpet. It's no use.

I remember I have an appointment with Mrs. Kartopoulas in half an hour. I've thought of Sebie night and day and turned my back on work. I haven't written down any questions to ask her. I'll speak off the cuff—fake it. I'm happy that I can get out of the room and talk to another person. I have a fluid thought of explaining my preoccupation with Sebie to her, my imbroglio of telling or not telling, leaving him or not leaving him. She would understand. She is a gem. From the letters I've read and the interviews with Professor Locks I have no doubt she'll be full of exquisite information. She's a living myth, a walking fable. She's mourned her husband for a year, burned his appurtenances including an automobile (out of accordance to Romani law), swallowed poverty complaisantly, and will host a pomana, a sumptuous feast where she'll end her grieving officially, on this coming Thursday. But the thought of telling her about Sebie disappears and I obsess on him again. I'm possessive. I cannot share him. I leave a note and I follow directions to the Cassien, where I'm to meet the woman.

The sidewalks are smeared with ice and salt. I wonder about him and what I didn't have a chance to know about him. I've been strafed by his dead features: the hole in his nose where the ring fits, warped upper lip, arms, legs, whiskerless Cadinot ass, little brown nipples. Now—I'm thinking who was he? Which part of him died first? If it was the brain then it was quick. That's what I've heard. If it was a less substantial organ like the lungs then his mind was dunked in assorted panic while he lapped his tongue out for air. Or perhaps his neck snapped into two beautiful parts. Then, arriving at the restaurant, I sew him back up with the deficient threads of my memories. I lose my breath suddenly. This is Rue de Rome—across the boulevard is the house and the cigarette vendor. He was alive, wasn't he? He was here two days ago.

Mrs. Kartopoulas is already at a table. She doesn't know what I look like—but I've seen her photo. I walk straight past her. The veins in her head are white as earthworms. I'm very frightened to see them swim over her temples of fuschia skin when she speaks to the waiter. "I'll take the liberty of ordering for my guest," she says.

Funny how I don't remember the front door being blue—very blue like the tops of houses on Mykonos or the very first meter of water off the coasts here. I turn back to Mrs. Kartopoulas, I must do the interview, and in a very sumptuous way she rolls her eyes to the back of her bulldoggish head and toots like she has spinach in her teeth. "No, no dear. More napkins is what I asked for." The building is four stories, not three stories. I can enter through the window on the right—the ledge is a few feet from the stairway. She puts two sugars into her hot tea and stirs it into a miniature tsunami. The pleasant and plump waiter walks past me and smiles courteously.

I cannot help ignoring her, looking past her at the weak little building across the street. I begin to number the steps of breaking in, burping a bit and grinning as if I were a little boy. I'll find an open window (or the door will be unlocked, yes, even easier). I'll wear gloves. I'll be in and out so quickly as not to disturb a goose. His backpack—I have to have his backpack and everything else he has left in his room or corner or closet or whatever it was that he had there.

I leave the restaurant. I'll only be a few minutes. The Arab man is standing in the window straightening a greenish hat on his head. It's gone past nippy to downright Siberian cold—and Marseilles has the best of it. I'm an abominable creature masked with a plain black scarf, bundled in the wrinkles of my coat, beside a telephone where I am attempting to look uninvolved or better, unperceivable. I breathe. It congeals into ice and falls. It crashes to the ground in front of me. My eyes lop from left to right while tiny cars pass and honk their horns. The man is waiting for something or someone. He puts on his coat. I wait for one and a half hours. Mrs. Kartopoulas has left and I didn't speak to her. He makes a telephone call. His mouth contorts and relaxes. Then he's not at the window anymore. He comes outside and shuts the door behind him. He's wrapped a scarf around his jaw too and sloshes down the street through a small amount of snow.

Should I do it? Should I follow him?

I start toward the intersection. I cross and walk behind him a step or two. I'll trip on his foot or bump him a little and strike up a conversation. Unreachable dollops of shaving cream are still behind his ears—he's a wreck without his Sebie, isn't he? He's headed for the Métro station. "Excuse me," I say but he doesn't hear me. "Excuse me, sir?" and then I don't try again.

Instead I return to Rue de Rome and the house with the orphaned backpack. It's an insignificant building that might have been luxurious and even imposing two centuries ago but now is weighted with kinked clotheslines and carpets hung over the sills like baby's bibs. Which was Sebie's? Which window? Here and there, going up the front of the building, an empty red flowerpot sits and looks vulnerable or a cat pirouettes its tail up on the next floor. I could've saved him from it—the pinch of this house. Instead I can see blue, the building was blue before it was this oatmeal-color like the very tip of a white mushroom. The top layer of paint—the cold's shaved it off (or the sun) into long rubbery shards. I sit on the steps and wait for the Arab man to come back.

He does. He's got a bag full of canned food now. Cat food, dog food and some food for himself, too. I think I see water chestnuts or lima beans. He walks with his head down. With his feet pointed outward. He sees me and swabs his black mustache with two fingertips (I think it's an annoying habit) then mumbles something or other. He must think I'm a vagrant—how funny. Or that I'm resting and waiting for the city bus. "Hello," I offer.

"Can I help you find something?" he says to me. He doesn't have such a crass accent—it's not so bad. It must have been the yelling at his son—lover—nephew—trick. Should I throw out the question? "You want to rent a room?" he asks.

"Yes, a room," I go along with him. I nod my head as if I'm pleased and I am really. I tell him I'm a writer from Chicago and I'm finishing a novel. I need a room for a few days—yes, three days. Can I see one of your rooms?

"We're all full," he says. "Nothing left, monsieur." Then he continues up to the door. He stops. A taxi pulls up in front of the house. Honks its horn. Should I take it as a warning? No one comes out. The Arab man is waiting. Maybe he sees that I'm wearing an expensive coat or expensive shoes because he stops and says with a smile that he must manage infrequently, it looks dreadful, that "I might have something though—if you don't mind a little mess—a few odds and ends from a bad tenant who hasn't moved his things out. But if he comes back you'll have to go."

The inside stairs—they're straight up and slender and lead to Purgatory. They'd give way under four people. He travels in front of me. Hoisting his legs up like fragile cubist sculptures. Providing momentum. It must only be these stairs that are hard for him. I hadn't noticed his handicap until now. "You saw an ad in the paper?" he asks.

"Yes," I smile. I hope it's the right answer.

The room is on the third floor. I travel toward it—here we are, two chimerical creatures, and the rug is lifting under my feet, so I try to nudge it back down. We drivel past the other doors. He has nothing interesting to say. The carpet is loose and nicotine-stained. The walls are mostly wooden, dark grained. I've erupted with sweat. The U of my hairline, behind my ears, above my lip—all wet.

I have a sudden burst in my heart—the kind when you run into a beautiful man you'd never thought you'd see again. I'm wildly impatient now. It makes my stomach cramp. I want to move the man out of my way. He fumbles with his keys, and they chinkle against the door. *Get on with it. Move out of the way.* A long squeak and he steps to the side. I'm introduced to the room. Sebie's room. It must be. It has to be.

A bed. A window. A yellow cup.

"Okay, please—" the Arab man says. "Have a look around. It's just the one room and a bath through there. A sink, too. Two hundred francs." A telephone rings downstairs. He darts out of the room as if the call must be important and indicates that I'm to stay in the room: "Keep looking. Keep looking."

So I'm alone and I can do what I want.

A photograph of Brigitte Bardot. A reproduction of Rembrandt's *Dutch Boy* beside it. The latter being much smaller and of less quality. Cardboard maybe. A little alarm clock on a nightstand. The room has a low ceiling, so low that Max would hit his head if he were here, and the walls are spinach green. What a tiny and pedestrian room. Is this what Sebie fell asleep to each night? On this bed?

The sheets haven't been changed. A layer of dust has collected in the dark.

I'm nauseated again. Sleepy, too.

His backpack is resting on a little wooden chair by the bathroom door. I hear the Arab man pick up the phone. "Hello! Hello! Bernard—you turn down that shit!" But I don't hear any music. No one else yells back. I hear a bus outside. A squeak from the ceiling—someone's feet. He'll be back up in a minute or two. He'll hoard it all. Steal it from me. Everything that's Sebie's. He'll shove it into a safe for a year and then sell it for a few francs. I am soulless. I've practiced being a thief. I act quick. I snatch up the bag. It's very light. I open drawers and find rolled-up socks. I turn the drawers upside down and ferret out a pair of underwear in the bathroom. A damp bathtowel, too. "Yes—yes. We have a delivery scheduled for the morning. Yes. The morning." The clank of the receiver. I cram them all into the backpack and stash it on the top shelf of the closet. I turn up another sock and a mathematics book from under the bed and make a go for them, but the man is at the top of the stairs already. He comes into the room grinning as if we were in the middle of an afternoon repartee. His teeth are chocolate-colored.

"Sorry for the interruption. Will you take it now? It won't be here tomorrow. I've just had a call—" He gives the room a once-over and scratches his priggish mustache. "I can have the sheets changed when my wife comes home."

"No, no. I'll take it. As it is. I'll have them washed up tomorrow."

"They've been used for—"

"I'm very tired," I say. "Really. It's no trouble."

I have the keys in my hand. I've paid him. I'm alone in the room now. I fall onto the bed and bundle myself up in the sheets repeating his name like a voluptuous mantra. One pillow possesses the gingery stink of dirty cotton spiked with his drool. The second one of soured come. The delivery of a night before he met me. I swept my hand over the sheets hoping for a blotch of it—dried up.

I go to the closet and pull down Sebie's backpack. Then onto the bed again.

Inside: chewable vitamin C, two lighters, twenty handwritten poems (he was a poet?) in a ledger notebook, some condoms, an unopened letter from a Mademoiselle N. DuPont, a transcript from Marseilles University, a bag of peanuts, three or four cassette tapes and a Walkman, a toothbrush and toothpaste. I dump it all onto the bed. The socks and the underwear and the wet bath towel too. I stretch out and imagine I'm waiting for him to strut in like Marlon Brando and catch me with his briefs in my mouth—humping the pile of his things and trying to gag myself.

Then I dream about Germany. I'm in a discotheque. I have a portable tape recorder and I'm dictating a letter to Professor Locks about Mrs. Kartopoulas. Techno music kicking my insides. A handful of boys wearing Xeroxed clothes. Two belly-dancers in the corner. One says to the other: "He's writing about us. For a big American magazine." Sebie is wearing, and wearing very well, tight black jeans and a silver T-shirt. Very eighties. He spots me and scuffs over. Maybe he's doing a samba. "You're having a good time?" he asks me. "Am I being a good host?" He kisses me on the cheek and after a few moments slips back to the dance floor. I see now, I didn't before, that he's dancing with a big black man who has both of his nipples pierced with safety pins. *Hey,* I want to say to him, *You're dead. I saw you fall. Go back to the island. How could you lie about this? Couldn't you have told me you weren't dead?* But he doesn't want to leave. He's jacking off the black guy. I try to see. "Bring your friend along," Sebie says to me. The gypsy women are throwing plates on the floor. I shut off the tape recorder. What are you saying? "Let's meet your friend—Max. Wake up."

I've blacked out for three hours. I wake to a familiar smell—like beer and my dog. I've drooled on his underwear and I'm wearing his socks. My pants are pulled down around my ankles. Max. I've forgotten Max. I'm very jealous of Max. He can buy his tickets and eat his dinners and sleep next to me and the most horrible thought that will cross his mind is "What if he's gotten lost?" My skin rumbles into gooseflesh so I get up and try to find the heater. Where is it? The slants of the curtains make me think someone is spying on me, and it's dark outside now. I reach for the phone. "Hello? Hello!" I talk like a crude little Frenchman because I have cottonmouth. There's something exciting about living like a criminal but—"Can you leave a message for Maxwell Pinter. Yes. Yes. This is his friend. I'll be running a lit—"

I must have set the alarm before I dozed off. The radio is playing. Not very loudly. It's French techno music and the clock-radio jiggles at the end of the night table. I sit and watch and listen and wait until I can make a logical decision. I take a shower. I do make some decisions: I wear his underwear and put on his socks again. I turn off the radio but I leave it on the same station. I call Mrs. Kartopoulas and leave a message on her machine. I put everything on the bed into the backpack and leave the room.

A light rain falls busily into the street and makes puddles in between the snow like mini-reservoirs. I have a note in my hand that reads: *Edward. We need to talk. You can't deny that. I feel abandoned on this trip. Love, Max.* I find it on our door at the Hotel Nice but Max isn't inside. The tall fellow who is always at the boat terminal greets me again with his pleasant but silent smile. His beard has grown out and his hands feel very warm when he hands me my ticket. "You must be fond of the island," he offers as small talk. I don't know quite what to say for a minute. He's never talked to me before. "Yes," I say. "I'm a historian, you see. It's a very historical place."

I ride inside the boat today—at first. It's too cold to ride on the

deck. The air tastes just like metal. As if I was running my tongue
across a giant sheet of stainless steel or chewing a ball of aluminum
foil. I sit beside a fisherman with a blue skimmer hat on his
head—little pieces of straw have twisted off and dug into his hair.
He reeks of fish and salt. His propitious features charm me: a
roundish and boyish jaw, thick lower lip, deep-set eyes that happen to run in my family as well. I snap the buttons of my coat
closed and smile at him good-heartedly but it's no use—he's too
smug. He makes rude comments to another shipmate about stupid tourists and foreign cars in French. *You haven't thought that
maybe I understand you, have you?*

The clouds are following our boat like fleets of black insects. I'd
feed him to them. I got outside for the rest of the trip, passing an
attractive Asian boy in the doorway. We're on the last boat out—
where is he going? Where are any of these people going? We smile
at each other and both smiles curl from the sides of our mouths
like we're at the bar or a sex club. I have the backpack over my left
shoulder. I wonder if I look like a student. If it makes me look
younger. I sit on the little blue boards along the edges of the boat
and read Sebie's notebook. It's mediocre at best. The poetry of a
lonely adolescent. The stuff of rock songs but my curiosity is satisfied. I feel the blood squirting through my veins, the zip of electricity in my head. I feel the magnet at the top of that hill pulling
me in. I hear fish jumping out of the water. I hear the bump of
their return to the deep sea—a bump.

The Asian boy walks toward the dock restaurants while I wind
up through the four alleys that populate Ratonneau and grip the
backpack as if it were a parachute—holding it to my chest and
pushing into the predictable wind. The body won't be there. That's
the way it will have to be. Look at the weather. Even if he hasn't
been found the rain has slid him into some drain or another hole
that will slide him into the Mediterranean.

Bells jingle behind me from a pair of wood chimes dangling
from a hook on the porch of the last house. Or is someone following me? Have I won favor with the dead because I've recognized their beauty? Or I know: this is the muló. This is because
he's sleeping in someone else's grave and he had a better life (and

death) in mind and this isn't how it was supposed to work out. The little village diminishes into gray and black and blue outlines. It's already sundown and I have my view of the water for another fifteen minutes and the strange sensation that's behind me. A pair of women are exercising on the public beach. The last stragglers of a never-ending day. I wonder if they see him sneaking up on me. *Tell me.*

The room is studded with silverish water. I've walked into this silence in the middle of chaos and bombastic sound where no excuse is necessary. I have no one to talk to and no one to listen to. The board is still upright and the body still arranged behind it: in a classical pose. The beautiful scent of coffee. Turkish coffee perhaps and a day old like the kind in a tiny café off Banks Street back home. I touch his feet. I feel between his toes and he's wet. The last light is leaving the room in a shriveling yellow V beneath the doorway. I open the backpack and pile the items near his head. I pick up one of the lighters and flick it on. That same expression has remained on his bitter-colored face: *I have seen where I came from and now I see where I am going and maybe I'll be happier than in my little rented room.*

The paper burns easiest. The letter from N. DuPont, the school transcript and the poems go up in flames like insinuating letters of a French traitor, like scriptures of a God who's been outlawed. I squat and I read a few more words while they crumble and turn black. I wonder if I'll remember them tomorrow: *I have my own wings and I had no choice in the matter because my heart is crazy and my mind isn't. So I dream. I dream of good things.* The vitamins bulge and pop. The cassette tapes are reduced to one blob—the size of a serving dish. The lighters catch fire and explode in their two-foot radius. I have my little campfire of tangibles. I undress with my eyes on Sebie. I put his socks into the flames. I worm out of his underwear and throw them down to be incinerated, too. Then I scoot over to Sebie and warm my hands over the fire. I'm almost naked—I have my shirt on and a jacket. I've put my pants somewhere. It isn't as cold as when we were fucking out in the open but my skin remembers. The board between us falls and a loud boom echoes from each corner. I only want to watch the body now. Before I go back to the Hotel Nice. This is the proof that I'll have for myself. That I've had death. And for a moment Max enters my thoughts. I imagine him where Sebie is: thin and smooth and dead. I reach out and rub his forehead.

SILENT PROTEST

Craig T. McWhorter

On the nights when Jessica isn't with me, I go to a bench. It's in the park, across the street from the house I used to live in. The bench is old and painted a thick, flat green. I sit there at night and look up into the windows of the house, but the ceiling is all I can see from the street because the living quarters are all on the second and third floors.

The first floor is a book shop. I took my class there once to see a writer of children's books. She was an elderly black woman who wrote books about flowers that lived like humans—they held jobs, built cities, and lived in houses. Bart asked me later if the flowers planted people in their window boxes.

The writer had a great voice, deep with inflection and character, like a bassoon. I stood behind her and tried to convey the beauty of her voice and words with my hands and facial expressions. My students' eyes darted from the brightly colored pages of the book to my hands and back, working hard to hear the story. The other children laughed at the way the author read, her interpretation of the various voices, first high and squeaky, then low and slow. My kids laughed too, but at the faces I made, maybe at me.

Jessica sat in the back, on Bart's lap. Her eyes also darted from the pages to my flying hands, not because she can't hear, but because it was her dad up there. She leaned back against Bart's chest with a contented smile on her face.

Tonight, from my bench, I watch the shadows play on the ceilings of the second floor. The exposed beams glow orange, and there is a brighter spot where the antique mirror over the mantle reflects the light doubly. I know Jessica's shadow by now. It is small, and it dances and flirts across the beams in a haphazard way, like a bee in a flower patch. I look at my watch. Nine o'clock. A larger shadow merges with the bee, and then they both disappear. Bart—putting Jessica to bed.

Soon, his shadow returns, and then the light of the TV flickers across the beams like a blue flame. I watch until my breath begins to freeze on my mustache and form little icicles hanging down over my mouth, and then I walk back to my apartment, my legs stiff at first from sitting on the bench so long.

Biological is a big word. It makes all the difference. I hear it in my ears as I walk home from the bench. I see it in Jessica's face, in those enormous dimples when she smiles, and I think of Bart and how, when we first met, I used to say or do anything that I thought might make him smile and reveal those same dimples.

The courts were puzzled by our family. They didn't know what to do with two men who made a decision on parenthood by flipping a coin and then sent a vial of sperm and an enormous check off to a surrogacy agency in another state.

"Heads," I'd said.

I still see the glint of silver as the quarter spins and catches the light before falling to earth between Bart's and my feet, the eagle looking up at us, wings spread as though ready to take flight again.

Sometimes at night, in my mind, he does fly again, and I shout out, "Tails," and herald the eagle's arrival and my impending fatherhood.

Had that happened, I would have a different child, one who maybe looked like me, one who lived with me. But there would be no Jessica. And I picture her sitting in the bathtub laughing at the shampoo horns on her head, or eating her Froot Loops, all the pink ones first. I'll keep Jessica, even if it's only for the every-other weekend that the judge gave me, granting primary custody to Bart, the biological father.

The next day, I'm reading *Clifford, the Big Red Dog* to my first-graders, but it's Friday, and I get to pick up Jessica after school, so

I'm racing through the words, dropping signs and confusing the kids. I flip quickly through the pages as if moving my hands faster will make the hands on the clock move faster.

I look up, and Wilson is standing before me. His steady gaze leaves my startled one and looks down upon his classmates. They are still seated in front of me, but none are listening. Instead, they have turned to face one another in twos and threes and are busy talking, their hands in the air, their mouths silent. One twosome begins to laugh, and the low gurgle fills the room.

Wilson looks back at me.

"Recess?" he asks.

Wilson knows that on every other Friday, extra recess is always an option. He shrugs and tilts his head to the side.

Rebecca stands up next to Wilson. "Please, Roger," she asks.

Finally I nod and Rebecca runs and flips the lights on and off to get everyone's attention.

"Recess," I say, "until your parents come."

It's easier this way, I think, as I watch them scattering throughout the school yard, claiming the swings and the monkey bars. I don't have to pretend to teach, and they don't have to pretend to pay attention. I'm free to think of the things I'll do with Jessica.

Today, Wilson hangs back and stands with me near the door to the classroom.

"What's up?" I ask. Usually he is the first one out the door, the one to go farthest into the field and the last one to come back in.

He shrugs.

Doesn't want to talk about it, I guess. But it's companionable to have him around, helping me watch the others.

Soon enough their parents begin to arrive. Some are single and have partial custody like me. I know who they are, that they only pick up their children on Fridays. Every other Friday. The occasional weekday if it's cleared with the principal's office first.

I hear Wilson's parents before I see them.

I hear, "Don't start this, Karen," and "Why? Because you know it's true? Can't you handle it?" They're walking toward Wilson and me, shouting at each other and dodging the children in their way.

I look down at Wilson, and his eyes are fixed on his parents. He looks up at me and shrugs. Don't they know that he's deaf, not blind?

When his parents reach us, his mother kneels and asks Wilson if he's ready. He runs inside to get his book bag.

"He notices, you know, the way you're talking to each other." I am out of line. It's none of my business, but I say it before I have a chance to think.

His mother looks at me like I've slapped her. When she speaks, her tone is like acid. "Is he having problems in school?"

"No. Wilson's an excellent student."

"Then what exactly is your problem, Roger?" I've encouraged both parents and students to use my first name, but now it feels as if it's being hurled back at me as a gesture of disrespect.

I don't dare answer, and silence ensues until Wilson returns. He stands before me with his fist held out. I curl my fingers in and tap my fist, first on top of his, then underneath, then straight on so that our knuckles push into each other.

He turns and runs to catch up with his parents, who are already on their way to the parking lot, their voices louder than before.

My problem is that you don't deserve him. You don't respect him. Wilson trails his parents, his book sack dragging on the asphalt.

I kept my unhappiness with Bart quiet for a long time. There was Jessica, and at first she filled every minute of my day. I stayed home for four years after she was born. Jessica and I alone all day. At night, I spent my time catching Bart up. She walked today. She asked to go pee today. She spit up on my favorite shirt today. When she went to preschool, I started back to work, but Bart wasn't so interested in my students' exploits. It seemed like if we weren't talking about Jessica, we weren't talking.

Bart started to wear his boxers to bed, and I started going out at night, after Jessica was asleep, and walking the streets, preferring the sounds of the city to the silence of my relationship. I always stopped at the bench and looked up into the windows, much like I do now, before going back in. Bart's shadow would move about, shutting off the TV, picking up clothes. I knew what he was doing. I'd seen him do it all often enough. Everything in its place, in

order. "It's a natural progression," he told me, "that after becoming parents our sex life fizzles."

It wasn't natural for me. I wanted to be throwing off my clothes in the rush to have sex, not picking them up and sorting them for the next day's laundry.

Then I got offered a job in Ecuador, teaching English at a university. It took me a long time to tell Bart. I spent that time planning how things would be different. In Ecuador, Bart could relax, let me earn the money. In Ecuador, the tropical heat would invade our souls and reignite our sex life. In Ecuador, our lives would once again be exciting, and Bart and I would have things to talk about.

But Bart wouldn't go. He said it was too dangerous for Jessica, but he meant it was too dangerous for him. He couldn't leave his job or the house. He couldn't stand to make less money than I did. He didn't see the problems in our relationship. He wouldn't listen to me.

I made arrangements to go anyway. I thought he would cave in. I thought, I'd have Jessica regardless and that to grow up being exposed to different peoples and cultures and to learn so early to adapt to change would be an excellent way to raise her.

Bart didn't agree, and he called his lawyer. Now, I can't even take Jessica out of the house without a judge's permission.

So I never went to Ecuador. Instead, I went to an apartment as close to Bart's house as I could get where I float like a satellite in orbit around my old life.

I have been standing outside too long. All the children are gone, and the empty swings rock and turn gently with the wind. I shiver and go back inside to get my things. In a half an hour, I will pick up Jessica, and then we will go out to eat. It's sort of a routine, but I change the restaurant every time, trying to get her to at least try new foods.

When I knock on Bart's door, I can hear Jessica on the other side. "Daddeeee, Daddeeee." Bart is "Dad," and I am "Daddy." She opens the door, and I lift her up into my arms, bounce her a couple of times and check her weight. Then I set her down and kneel in the hall so that I can look her over. I look at the length and color of her hair, her teeth when she smiles, her clothes.

"Have you grown?"

She looks back at Bart who has appeared behind her and says in a patient voice, "No, Daddy. I'm the same. I'm always the same."

"Those are new overalls," I say.

She spins for me. "Grandma gave them to me."

"You look beautiful."

She rolls her eyes and stomps. "Daddy."

I stand up. "Okay. I'm sorry. No compliments. Are you ready?"

She nods and runs off to her room to get her bag.

Bart smiles at me. Dimples. "How are you, Roger?" he asks.

"Good. You?"

He's good, too, and then Jessica returns. She kisses Bart on the way out the door, and he shouts, "Be good. Be careful," down the stairwell.

Jessica and I hold hands and swing our arms as we walk to my apartment. She tells me about school, that she's read a big book all by herself. Thirty pages and no pictures.

At my apartment, she goes to her room to make sure that I haven't changed anything. I hear her squeal when she sees the alligator that I bought yesterday and placed on her pillow. She comes back hugging it.

"It's an alligator," I tell her. I keep telling myself that she needs a set of toys at each house, but it's been five months, and she's gotten a new toy every time she comes over.

She strokes the green fake fur. "What's his name?"

"Maybe it's a her."

"Okay. What's her name?"

"You decide."

She puts her finger in her mouth, thinking. "Amanda."

I know that Amanda is the name of Bart's mother's horse, and that Jessica has probably just been to see her grandma. I want to ask about it. I want to know if she rode Amanda, what she ate, if she still gets car sick on the ride into the country. I want to know why she hasn't mentioned it. Instead, I ask, "Are you ready to go to dinner?"

"I have to unpack."

I'm impatient to leave. "You can do it later."

She shakes her head slowly. "No, Daddy. I have to do it now."

So I follow her into her room and watch as she puts two outfits into an empty drawer and then takes her toothbrush and toothpaste into the bathroom and puts them in the cup with the teddy bears on it next to the bathroom sink. Bart has taught her this: everything in its place.

She walks back into the bedroom, myself in tow, and puts Amanda on the pillow exactly where she'd found her earlier. "Okay. I'm ready."

We go to a Mexican restaurant where I eat often, but which Jessica has never been to. Her face is hidden behind the menu, and occasionally she drops the menu to the table, points to a word, and says, "What's this?" I guide her through, explaining the different kinds of foods. She orders a hamburger.

"Just try an enchilada," I say, but she makes a face and says, "Eww." She does eat the chips, but not the salsa.

The next morning after she's had her Froot Loops, and I've brushed her hair, I ask her what she'd like to do. She wants to go to the movies, but I resist. I only have forty-eight hours. I do not want to waste two of them in the dark with Jessica's attention focused on the screen. So I say, "Why don't we go to the park?"

She laughs at me. Apparently, my stupidity is obvious. "Daddy, it's too cold. We can't go to the park."

"Sure we can. Then we won't have to share the swings or the jungle gym."

Jessica rolls her eyes. "But you said I'm s'pose' to share."

"That's right, I did."

She's looking straight at me. We've become sidetracked from the subject of a movie and her mind is trying to find a way to get back to what she really wants. "Jimmy saw it. He said it was really funny."

"Saw what?"

"The movie!"

I give in. "Okay. We'll go to the movie."

She doesn't jump for joy, or leap up and kiss me or any of the rewards an overindulgent father should receive as advance payment on the later consequences of his behavior. She runs and gets the paper and brings it to me so that I can look up the time of the film.

When we get there, she joins the throngs of children at the candy counter. I have told her she may have one item, and she takes her time, looking at each of the boxes and wrappers. Her mouth opens and closes as though she's practicing eating, weighing the various attributes of the different types of candy. She chooses Hot Tamales. I suspect it's because they're red but pretend that it's an attempt to prove to me that she likes Mexican food after all.

We find seats, and I help her pull off her coat and tuck it around behind her. She sits with a Coke that looks half her size between her legs and slowly chews on the candy.

"Everything okay?" I ask.

She nods, but her eyes don't leave the curtain where soon the movie will appear. When it does, she leans back into her seat, her legs sticking straight out into the aisle, and sighs deeply. Contentment.

I watch her, not the movie, keeping track of what makes her laugh or her eyes go wide with excitement.

When it's over, she stays through the credits while I fidget to be gone. The lights come back on, and she rolls her head to the side and looks at me for the first time. "Thank you," she says. She sleeps in the car on the way home.

The time to take her back to Bart comes long before I'm ready. I'm afraid that sometime in the coming two weeks, I'll forget how she looks or how her hair feels in my fingers. I won't know her voice when she says, "Daddy."

I spent Sunday afternoon watching her do her homework. The next time I see her, she'll be studying completely new things. We have no continuity.

Bart invites me in for a drink. I end up staying for dinner, making the salad while Bart makes a sauce and Jessica colors at the kitchen table. After, we watch TV—something about animals that all three of us enjoy—until it is time for her to go to bed. I tuck her in, observing her every ritual, reading a chapter of the nighttime book she and Bart have been reading together. He sits at the foot of the bed and listens.

When her eyes close, and I'm sure she's asleep, I mark the page where Bart will continue the next night, and he and I go back into the living room.

"It's been nice having you here," he says.

"Yeah."

He is standing in front of me, close, in my air space. "You could stay, you know."

I look down, but his hand comes up and cups my chin and pulls me into him, my mouth to his.

After we make love, he tells me, "There's been no one else." He strokes my hair. "Have you?"

I know what he is asking. "No one," I say.

I wake up in the middle of the night thinking I hear Jessica calling out. Bart's arms and legs are wrapped around me, and I'm hot. It's hard to breathe. I listen for Jessica, but there is nothing. I think that if she came in I'd have to hide under the bed or in the closet. I don't want to confuse her. I don't want her to think I'm coming back. Carefully, I slide away from Bart until I'm standing on the carpeting next to the bed. He is awake now. I can tell. But we both pretend he's still asleep as I get dressed in the dark and slip out of the apartment.

When I get to school the next morning, I wait outside my classroom door and hug myself against the morning chill. The students see me and begin to trickle indoors where they struggle out of coats and hats and gloves. Most leave their garments heaped on the floor below empty hooks with their names printed above. Later I'll have to ask them to go and hang their belongings correctly.

I start to wave in an exaggerated way so that the girls on the swings can no longer pretend not to notice me. They kick and drag their feet through the sand underneath the swing set, slowly coming to a halt. They move so slowly, I think they must be frozen to the seats of the swings, like tongues on icicles.

I keep spinning my arms, trying to hurry them, trying to stay warm.

Then, I see movement in the parking lot and watch as Wilson drops to the ground from the backseat of his dad's Suburban. In the front seats, I can see his parents fighting. His mother's mouth is contorted as she screams out words I cannot hear. His father's fists slam against the steering wheel.

Wilson's struggle to push the heavy car door shut goes unnoticed by them, and I move toward the parking lot to help him. Finally he gets it shut on his own, but he nearly falls over backward in the process.

He begins walking toward me, head down, arms swinging at his sides. When he looks up, his face is pinched and red. He wipes his nose on the sleeve of his coat and keeps walking.

Meeting him halfway, I take his hand in mine. His fingers are only large enough to hold three of mine, but those he squeezes like a vise. I hurry to get him inside and unbundled.

When he comes to join the rest of the class, I start to sign, telling him all the things we'll do today, that we get to start a new book. But his eyes drift away. Then his face crumples, and he starts to cry.

So I grab a chair and sit down. It's a chair made for six- and seven-year-olds, and it pushes my knees high into the air. When I try to pull Wilson onto my lap, he slides down until he's flat against my chest where he starts to cry full bore. His fingers pull at the fabric of my shirt and the chest hair underneath.

I wrap my arms around him, and his body shakes rhythmically against me. His crying is loud and has a raw and frightening element, the sound of someone who's never heard another cry.

Though they cannot hear, the other children gradually notice Wilson and me, and they stop their conversation and games and books. One by one, they gather around us, and their fingers fly with questions. What's wrong? Why is Wilson crying? What's the matter?

I hold Wilson tighter and bend my head so that my nose sits on the silk strands of his blond hair. Children all smell the same, I think, even Jessica.

The hands around us continue to question and in their light and erratic movements remind me of a flock of butterflies. I don't want to let Wilson go, not even long enough to answer their questions.

Then Rebecca places her hands on Wilson's shoulder and arm, and lets them rest there. They are joined by another classmate's hands on Wilson's other shoulder, and, one by one, the other children bring their hands to rest on Wilson. When there is no room left on his back, their hands begin to land on my arms and shoulders until all the little butterflies lie silent and warm against our bodies, comforting. Wilson's sobs reach out into the silence.

SPERM-AND-EGG TANGO

David Tuller

She glances up from her glass of carrot juice and notices Jimmy staring at her with that "I want your womb" look again. She can tell that is what he is thinking, even if he hasn't mentioned it yet today. She can tell because of his arched eyebrows and that funny way he's tilting his head forward.

"Stop it right now!" She tries to stiffen her voice with resolve.

"What?" His mouth forms a perfect O of surprise.

"You know what. Stop it. I can't take the pressure."

He takes a bite of his frozen yogurt and pouts. "All I want is a little favor. Just one egg, and nine months. What's one little egg between friends?"

A lot, she tells him. One little egg is an awful lot between friends.

Sara and Jimmy have known each other for more than ten years, since Psych 101—everyone called it "Nuts and Sluts"—during their sophomore year of college. They bonded the day she grabbed his notebook and drew lewd pictures of Oedipus and his sisters. Jimmy loved her take-no-prisoners swagger and the edge of excitement it promised; the air around her rippled with the sense that things were about to happen. She was drawn to his dark humor and his spectacular way with pasta. Then Jimmy discovered that he had crabs. He didn't know who he'd caught them from and he didn't care; he just wanted them gone. Like a postmodern Florence

Nightingale, Sara gritted her teeth and nursed the stricken. She shampooed the abundant hair on his back with Quell and, when necessary, plucked the vile creatures off one by one.

Jimmy pledged eternal faith. If there was a better definition of true friendship than plucking the crabs off someone's back, he told her over and over, then he didn't know it.

But now, as Sara watches Jimmy watching her, she knows that true friendship does not mean that she owes him her eggs.

Jimmy is still pouting. "Look, I told you, I'll take on all the responsibility once he or she is born. You don't even have to do anything if you're not interested." This has been his line of reasoning from the beginning, as if bearing an infant is an act no more significant or complicated than emptying the garbage or writing a check to UNICEF so that some nameless, starving kid in Sri Lanka or Sierra Leone can eat fresh buffalo cheese or sun-dried tomatoes for a year.

Sara attacks the red peppers in her salad. "Yeah, right."

"What?"

"Like I'll come over and it'll be running around screaming or peeing and I'll just ignore it . . . or her, or whatever."

Jimmy reaches over and strokes her arm. His fingers feel cool and powdery, like silk. He's a fag and she's a dyke, but they've always been a little bit in love with each other. She likes the feeling and especially loves that she'll never have to do anything about it.

"I know," he says, "I know, I'm being awful. I'm just disappointed, that's all. It would be so cool, you know?" He grins slyly. "But I guess I'll have to make another plan."

That catches Sara's attention, as he intends. "Wait a minute, I haven't said no. I said I didn't think so, but I'm still thinking about it. I mean, it's a shock, okay? I need time." She flicks her hand through her hair, annoyed at herself for letting him get to her.

He tilts his head again and narrows his eyes. She knows that look, too. He is trying to see through her, the way he can sometimes, trying to take the measure of her ambivalence. She is ambivalent about everything, about what flavor ice cream to order or which movie to see, so obviously she is ambivalent about this, too.

The thing she knows he is attempting to discern is this: Is she really seriously thinking about it? Or is she just playing at really seriously thinking about it, in order to keep her options open?

She knows he can't tell. But then neither can she.

Sara is the most generous person Jimmy knows. She has fine
long hair and a short, tough body. She looks great in torn jeans that
tug her butt, but sometimes she dolls up in tight black skirts slit
every which way. If she has a fault, it is that she loves her friends
extravagantly, excessively; and sometimes, if the object of love dis-
appoints her one time too many, the love curdles into something
seething and ugly.

Sara still hates Karen. She's the ex who dumped Sara a year ago,
after meeting a motorcycle dyke in gay traffic school. After the
breakup, Sara looked bigger somehow, round and puffy, as if inflated with rage. Twice she almost slashed the motorcycle dyke's
tires with a massive carving knife that Karen had once given her.
She wishes she could say that conscience or sanity stayed her hand,
but she knows that would be a lie; both times it was a random
passerby, nothing else, that pulled her back from the edge of craziness. She nursed and coddled the rage for months, but finally wea-
ried of it; and then, around the time that Karen broke up with the
motorcycle dyke and moved to Hawaii to work on a pot and or-
chid farm, she allowed the emotion to subside to a quieter, soft-
edged—almost soothing—hate.

Then, a week ago, Jimmy screwed up her life by announcing
that he wanted a child. Her child.

He called her that day from his office—he works as a dental
technician—and said he wanted to come by later. Sara lives in a
cozy one-bedroom apartment in the Mission District, tossed about
with throw rugs and big, plush pillows, most of them some shade
of red or burnt orange. The apartment is above La Fiesta, a Mexican restaurant with year-round Christmas lights. Jimmy brought up
two veggie burritos and they settled down on her bed to watch *The
Bad Seed*. Sara loved that movie, especially the part where little six-
year-old Rhoda, perfectly poised and heaving with evil, confesses
to her mother that she killed her horrid little classmate, Claude

Daigle, because he won the penmanship medal. That's when Jimmy
spilled the beans.

"Let's get pregnant," he said.

She looked at him. "What?"

"I want a child, and I think you should be the mother."

She snatched up the remote and pressed the pause button. The
movie kept playing.

"It's on television," he said.

Sara glared at the remote. "Oh, right." She rolled over to face
him. "Now, what the fuck are you talking about?"

"Oh, come on, you know I've thought about it."

She tried another tack. "But a couple of years ago you said you
were over the idea."

He looked down at his hands. "Well, that's when Rich was dying.
When I thought about babies back then, it made me feel crazy, like
I hated them for being born." He looked back at her. "But Rich is
gone, and I'm still here. And now just seems like a good time."

Sara remained silent. She missed Rich, who had lived with
Jimmy for six years. She had helped Jimmy administer Rich's IVs,
feed him pureed vegetables, change the diapers. She kept hoping
Jimmy would meet someone else he could love, but she hoped this
time it would be someone negative.

Jimmy continued talking about babies. She tried to listen, but
she floated in and out of attention, nodding on occasion to convey
the impression that she knew what he was talking about.

Sara waved her hand in the direction of the television. "Haven't
you been watching? Look at that little bitch. She's knocked off
everyone in her path." She paused. "You sure you want a child?"

". . . menstrual cycle . . . jerk off here every month . . ." he said.

". . . Syringe or turkey baster . . . my mother thinks . . . crib in
the corner . . ." he said.

". . . medical expenses . . . gay Tele Tubbies . . ." he said.

She just nodded and stared at the television. Rhoda's mother was
trying to get the little monster to swallow all the sleeping pills.

That night Sara lay in bed, shivering. She had to get up early for
a court appearance—she is a lawyer for a tenants' rights organiza-

tion, trying to force scum landlords to make repairs—but she couldn't sleep. It wasn't cold outside, but she climbed out of bed and pulled another comforter down from the top shelf in her closet. She snuggled under it and rubbed her hand over her stomach, which felt plump and round from the burrito. She imagined the burrito growing tiny paws and tucking them into its tiny chest. She imagined that the burrito twisted and twitched and twitched a little, and then a lot. And then it would be born, and it wouldn't be a burrito anymore, and it would constantly need to be scratched, washed, fed, burped, wiped.

Then it would turn fifteen and it would scream at Sara that it hated her forever, and it would run from the house into the night to ingest strange, exotic drugs and have sex with strange, exotic people or objects or whatever. Just like Sara had done when she was fifteen.

She knew she wouldn't be able to take it.

She woke up the next morning to a cotton-dry mouth, an itch in her throat, and the odd sensation that she'd misplaced her insides. She recognized what this was: a nicotine craving. She ached all over for a cigarette. Since breaking the habit two years before, she only had cravings when nerves struck; the last time was when she had to appear before an IRS auditor, who ended up disallowing the cost of getting her hair done before a court appearance. Then he asked her on a date.

On the way to work, her eye zeroed in on a semi-smoked Marlboro Light, seductively nestled in a sidewalk crack. Sara stopped, bent over, straightened up, started walking past, stopped, whistled a few bars of the theme from *Gilligan's Island,* glanced around, stepped back. She glanced around again and bent over; her arm swooped down and scooped it up. She caressed it in her palm, stroked it with her fingers.

She held it up a foot from her face. It was a lovely three inches long and retained its lovely, elegant, tubular shape; the previous owner, rushing to catch a cab or cross the street, must have forgotten to grind it flat with her heel or toe, or maybe left it just as it was, beautiful and intact, for Sara or someone else to find.

Sara brought it to her nose and sniffed in deeply; its acrid crispness made her thighs itch. She dipped into an alley and clawed through her knapsack for the matchbook at the bottom. She closed her eyes and savored the first taste, creamy and luscious—as rich and haunting as all the world's chocolate. She sighed as the smoke flowed down her throat and stung her lungs. She felt her heart pump three times, felt the drug *whoosh* through her veins to the most desolate outposts of her body. She didn't believe in heaven, but if she did, it would have been this, and the baby question, she was sure, would work itself out just fine.

The glorious rush abandoned her to a bout of self-loathing. She knew she was out of her mind to even begin to think about considering the remote possibility of having a baby.

In the two weeks since, she has avoided cigarettes and cigarette stubs, but she has noticed babies everywhere. She has noticed them especially on her way to work, because that's when she's most alert and focused. She can't believe how ugly they are. Those tight little mouths, ears like cauliflower, stumpy little legs that ripple over with fat, arms of destruction that mow down everything in their path. And all the while the thing screams or giggles for no discernible reason, drools, spittles up white goop onto newly pressed blouses and expensive Persian rugs, tosses cupfuls of apple juice all over the floor.

The truth is, Sara doesn't think she has a biological clock. Her friends hear theirs ticking; she hears nothing. It is possible, she supposes, that she has a biological wristwatch that operates below her auditory threshold, or a biodigital clock-radio that counts down years in electronic silence and will jangle her awake with "It's My Party" or "Born Free" only at the outer limits of her reproductive capabilities. But right now, she hears nothing, and so far she's liked it that way.

Not that the idea hasn't stumbled through her mind now and then, like a lost, disoriented hiker wandering across inhospitable terrain. She has always shoved the notion aside. She has watched as her friends, one by one, have abandoned themselves to these peculiar urges, and she finds their transformations—from outta-my-face dynamos to cooing, lactating matrons—profoundly troubling.

She also dislikes the child-acquisition options available to them. She doesn't want to adopt a Chinese girl, an approach currently in vogue. Who knows what horrible things might have happened to these babies before they arrive? Also, the logistics of organizing a bat mitzvah at the Great Wall seem daunting. And Sara isn't ready to cope with the inevitable cultural dislocations. Prospective parents stock up on children's books of the *Why Are My Eyes So Different From Mommy's?* variety, but Sara is sure nonetheless that in twenty years there will be huge numbers of recovery groups for the Chinese daughters of Jewish lesbians.

Flipping through donor profiles at a sperm bank strikes her as even less appealing. The idea reminds her of the times she has examined chips of paint colors with ridiculous names like "burnt mud" and "sesame sprinkle." Sara knows from experience that colors—like genes, undoubtedly—always look different when brought to life. One year she and Karen selected "rice cake" for their kitchen; on the one-square-inch sample it looked like white with just the tiniest—almost imperceptible, really—smidgen of yellow mixed in. When the painting was done, the walls screamed so loudly that guests refused to remove their sunglasses.

So when it comes to babies, the only way she would even consider doing this crazy thing—if she were going to do it, which she isn't—is to know whose genes she is getting. To see the genes embodied in the flesh, so to speak.

Sara decides to visit her mother, Lily, who lives in Walnut Creek. Sara and Lily do not get along. They meet and argue once every two months, always over dinner at a dingy Chinese diner in downtown Oakland. The noodles are greasy and the waiters are rude, but the women welcome the chance to complain about the food and the service, since it's one of the few things they agree on. They meet in Oakland because they both refuse to travel all the way to the other one's home. The practice, rooted in stubbornness and pride, has taken on the prickly glow of something shared, a tradition that they have been reluctant to breach.

Sara breaches it now. She's not sure exactly why. She just feels a twitch in her gut that tells her it is time. She has seen Lily's condominium only three times—once when her mother first moved there seven years ago shortly after Sara's father died, once on Lily's sixty-fifth birthday, and once to bring over antibiotics and make chicken soup when a bout of pneumonia confined Lily to her bed.

Lily opens the door. A smirk creases the corners of her mouth. She leans forward so Sara can peck her cheek. Lily's bouncy hair smothers her tiny face. The condo smells of Lysol and fried potatoes. She pours Sara a cup of coffee. "If you want milk or sugar, I don't have any." Her diction is flinty and hard. "You know I don't eat sugar."

"It's fine, this is fine." Sara takes a sip and wonders why she's come. The blue light of late afternoon scatters pointy shadows on the kitchen floor. "Things are okay?"

Her mother settles down across from her and cradles her cup between her hands. "Sure. Why shouldn't they be?"

"I don't know. I was just asking." Sara drums her fingers on the Formica tabletop. A ball of sweat slips down her neck. She remembers how, when she was a child, her mother used to feed her apples and peanut butter at night; then Sara would clamber into bed and Lily would tickle her before tucking her in. Those were the happy moments. Sara can't imagine her mother tickling anyone now.

"Your aunt's going walking again," mutters Lily. "Eastern Europe this time. I forget why." Lily's younger sister, Christine, has a habit of quitting jobs and going on months-long walk-a-thons for environmental causes. Down the western coast of South America to draw attention to the hole in the ozone layer. Across the U.S. in support of electric cars. "I don't know how she can live that way," says Lily. "Here, there, one day Chile, the next day Boise, then Budapest. Why doesn't she stay somewhere for a while?"

Sara has heard this before. "She likes it, Ma. She wants to do that."

"Well, I think it's crazy." Lily wipes her hands on her apron. Her fingertips are smudged from newsprint; she reads three newspapers a day. She clips articles on breast cancer and stock market fluctuations and stuffs them into thick manila folders. "What good does it do? Last time I checked, there weren't too many electric cars around."

Sara decides not to discuss her dilemma with Lily. Her mother would pretend to offer support but would just complain about it to Christine, if Christine wasn't off walking somewhere. Sara used to blame Lily for behaving like that, but she doesn't anymore—most of the time, anyway. She knows her mother's life hasn't turned out the way she wanted. She knows that for many years Lily regretted marrying Sara's father, Joe, a lawyer who specialized in bankruptcies. During their courtship he told her he wanted to move to Los Angeles, where he thought there would be more demand for his services. Sara's parents pressured her not to go. California was a wild place, they told her, too wild for a Jewish girl from Brooklyn. She was nineteen. She half-believed them, but yearned for excitement, so she left everything behind and linked her life with Joe's.

The marriage was thorny with fights and infidelities. Lily dodged her sorrow by shopping at flea markets. She collected antique thimbles and then African stamps. Then she had a pig phase—pig posters, pig pencils, pig dolls, porcelain pigs. Each month for several years she added a couple of pigs to her collection, till it filled several cardboard boxes.

When Sara was eleven, she gave her mother a plastic pig figurine she bought at a booth in a local amusement park. Lily nodded vaguely and said, "I'm not interested in pigs anymore." After that she gave up collecting. Sara asked why, but her mother just smiled sadly and touched her hand to the bridge of her nose.

Now Lily sighs and picks at the cuticle of her thumb with her middle finger. This is a habit that has always irritated Sara. She hates the red, ragged look of Lily's thumb. She puts her own hand on top of Lily's and presses down lightly. Lily's fingers protest, fluttering against the pressure. Then Lily turns her hand over and laces fingers with her daughter. She closes her eyes and turns her face toward the sun-streaked window. "If I just ran off all the time like Christine, how would I have raised you?" she says.

Lily's long fingers feel cool and elegant to Sara. "Who knows why anybody does anything, Ma," she says. She silently promises to visit her mother more often, but she knows she won't.

Sara's friend Lisa tells her about a monthly Sunday brunch at

which gay men and lesbians brood about their reproductive des-
tinies and evaluate each other as potential genetic partners over
quiche and bagels and fruit salad. It is officially called the Gay/
Lesbian/Bisexual/Transgender Parenting Discussion Group of San
Francisco, but everybody refers to it as "the sperm-and-egg mixer."
It sounds ridiculous to Sara, who giggles when she mentions it to
Jimmy. But his face shines like a floor that's just been waxed. "Let's
go, let's find out when the next meeting is. It'll be great, it will give
us some ideas."

Her eyes narrow to slits. "No way," she says. "No fucking way am
I going to sit there and have people stare at me trying to figure out
whether my kid will have a Pinocchio nose or a lumpy ass. You
hear me?"

Sara and Jimmy arrive at the meeting that Sunday a few minutes
early. The apartment where the gathering takes place is sleek and
gleaming with mirrors, wine goblets, and Mapplethorpe prints.
The host, Serge, is plump and wears his dark hair slicked back, with
an off-center part. He fusses over the food, ferrying platters and
glasses and utensils back and forth from the kitchen and nudging
everyone to take more. Sara glances about nervously; she knows no
one here, and she prefers it that way. She notices that men and
women arrive in various gender and number configurations, depending, she assumes, on their domestic arrangements and pro-
posed genetic couplings. The room hums lightly with the sounds
of greeting: kissing, whispering, laughing, back patting. Sara glances
at Jimmy, who is slowly eating a bagel with salmon spread; he sur-
veys the crowd and beams. For a few seconds, Sara hates him for
convincing her to come. Then she sighs and looks for somewhere
to sit.

The furniture is all corners and hard edges, better for effect than
comfort. She settles down gingerly on a black trapezoidal object
that she assumes is a chair, although it is devoid of arms and cushions.

"Glad to see you all," says a fortyish woman dressed in black
slacks and open-toed sandals. She introduces herself as Lynn ("the
mother of Bethany, who is six, and, I hope, another baby in the not
too distant future, if I can find the right donor"), and smiles crisply.

Lynn's teeth are very, very straight and unnaturally bright, and Sara wonders—a little maliciously, she knows—whether little Bethany has the same problems with her bite that Lynn clearly felt forced to correct.

The conversation, something of a free-for-all, touches upon lots of sperm-and-egg basics: custody, financial arrangements, conflicts between donors and nonbiological moms, playing daddy versus playing uncle. Some of those present already have children and want more. Others, like Sara and Jimmy, are just contemplating it. A cheerful, big-cheeked woman describes a lovely weekend visit that she and her two-year-old son paid to "the granddonors"—the parents of her sperm donor. Serge wipes his forehead and complains that a potential egg source has dumped him because he insisted on an equal share in decision making; this has already happened to him twice, and he is getting discouraged. He waves his hand vaguely around the group. "Aren't there women who want an equal partner in child raising?"

Lynn nods and smiles; light boomerangs off her white teeth. "Anyone? How about you, Elena? You've all been dealing with that, right?"

Heads swivel toward a slender blonde woman in a tie-dyed T-shirt and blue jeans. She is sitting across the circle from Sara, staring at her toes. She looks miserable. "Right," she says.

Elena explains that six months ago she met Sam—she jerks her thumb at a square-shouldered guy with huge biceps who is sitting on her right—at one of the group's meetings. They had hoped to start inseminating soon. But their negotiations have stalled over whether Sam will waive his paternal rights so Elena's girlfriend, June, can co-adopt the baby; at first he said he probably wouldn't mind, but now he's balking. As Elena talks, the tiny woman sitting on her other side—Sara assumes it is June—twists and untwists a piece of purple thread around the thumb and pinky. Her gaze skips back and forth between Sam and Elena.

When Elena finishes, attention turn expectantly to Sam, who squirms and runs his hand up and down his arm. "It just doesn't feel right, to create this thing and then sign some paper that says it's not yours," he tells the group. A few feet away, a woman rolls her eyes and whispers something to her neighbor, who glares at Sam and nods.

Elena shakes her head. "You knew we wanted an uncle-type person, not a daddy. It kind of throws a wrench into the plans. I just wish you'd said this before we spent six months talking about it all. It's not like my body can wait forever."

"Well, I didn't really know myself," says Sam defensively. "I mean, how could I have known? I haven't done this before." He hesitates. "Maybe we can still go ahead and just work it out as we go along."

"Yeah, right, that's just how we should do it," says June.

This is the first time she has spoken, and her voice is so soft that it takes Sam a couple of seconds to grasp the depth of her sarcasm. When he does, he flinches a little, then leans forward and holds out his hands, palms lifted toward the ceiling. "So what are you two saying? We should just call the whole thing off? I mean, I've put time into this, too." He sounds hurt and incredulous.

"You've got time," retorts the woman wearing the beret.

Two other people start to speak, but Lynn breaks in and calls a time-out. People stand up, stretch their legs, pour themselves another cup of coffee. Sara grabs a Fig Newton and some fruit salad. In a corner, Sam, Elena and June huddle beneath a framed poster of Joan Crawford in *Mildred Pierce*. Sam bounces on the balls of his feet and whispers something to Elena, gesturing toward the room. June touches Elena's arm and massages her girlfriend's neck a little. Elena rests her head on June's shoulder; her hair laces down June's back. The two women nod curtly to Sam and leave. Sam stares at the door as it thwacks shut. He turns around to see if anyone has noticed. His eye catches Sara's. He shrugs and smiles ruefully.

The discussion picks up again in a few minutes, but Sara isn't listening. She thinks these people are nuts; they treat baby making like a business deal, a question of rights and costs and negotiating positions, and it disturbs her. But the next day at work she experiences an epiphany of sorts. It arrives while she's on the toilet, pants around her ankles, which is convenient because no one will disturb her while she thinks it through. If seeking an unknown partner for this experiment seems bizarre to her, then doing it with Jimmy, a man whose back hair she knows intimately, suddenly seems comparatively sane. Or saner, anyway.

Jimmy's genes are not perfect, she realizes. He suffers from depression sometimes, and he's kind of bony. Also, he hates cats. But he's a good guy, with a good heart. She figures she could do a lot worse.

She pees with newfound purpose, and flushes the toilet hard. She glances at the mirror as she washes her hands, puffing up her cheeks with air and exhaling loudly. She dislikes her crooked chin but feels that her widow's peak and broad forehead convey an air of moral purpose. She asks herself, Is this a mother's face? Maybe it is, she thinks. Maybe it is.

Sara doesn't tell Jimmy, though. She wants to preserve her options. When he brings the subject up, she murmurs noncommittal phrases. She knows that he wants to say more; she can sense the edge of his irritation. But for now she's not ready to talk about it.

Sitting on her front porch one evening, she hears an ambulance siren whining in the distance. She wonders if it's for a child who is sick or dead, and then she remembers how, when she was seven, she fell while playing monkey-bar tag with Cookie Fernandez next door. She scraped her scalp on an exposed screw. The wound bled fiercely; Lily screamed when she saw it. She drove Sara to the hospital. She cradled her daughter's head in her lap and pressed a fresh white towel against the bright red gash. The doctors sewed it up with twenty-one stitches and gave her a grape-flavored lollipop when they finished. Sara still has a little moon-shaped scar near her temple. She touches her hand to the scar and rubs it. The vividness of the memory amazes and frightens her. The next morning, her eyes stop at a bus plunge item in *The New York Times*. The two-sentence item about a bus plunge off a mountain pass in Venezuela, is tucked neatly at the end of a story about Russian prostitutes. Number of dead: thirty-three.

She tears the article out, folds it in half, and shoves it in her pocket. Later that evening she wonders why she's saved it.

Over lunch one day, he presents the details of his plan. He would cover all the bills. She could chip in if she wanted to, but she wouldn't have to. The baby would live with him, but if she wanted it part-time or even half-time, that was cool, too. If not, she could come and see it whenever she wanted. She would be, after all—if she wanted to be—its mother.

She listens to his speech, but it's almost as if he's talking in Norwegian or Swahili. She hears a low crackling in her ears, like the sound of paper being crumpled. She hears that sound when she's confused or anxious. She picks up a spoon and runs her finger up and down the handle, then wraps her fist around it. She tries to focus on what he is saying, but she can't, and frustration simmers inside her chest. "I want you to shut up about it," she says. "All I can think about for weeks now is babies, all I see is babies, every other word is 'baby.' So just shut up."

He smacks his hand on the table. The glasses jiggle. His voice is dangerously low. "Look, you've been suspicious of this idea ever since I raised it. You don't like this, here's why it won't work, what about that, and on and on. You don't want to? Fine. Just fucking say so, finally, and let's move on." He pauses and opens his mouth again, not to speak, but in surprise, as if startled by his own vehemence.

They sit silently for several minutes.

"I don't know," she finally says.

"What don't you know?"

"About this. About any of it."

"Let's be specific. Can't you be specific?"

"What about morning sickness?"

"I'll clean up the vomit and bring the raw chicken hearts."

"Great, thanks." She points at his beer. "But I'm the one who has to give up grass and booze."

"What? You don't smoke and you almost never drink."

She frowns. "What does that have to do with it? It's the principle of the thing." She squints, as if capturing thoughts from the air. "And what about the universe?"

He stares at her. "What? What about the universe?"

"I mean, the universe is flying apart at the rate of zillions of miles a second. How can we talk about having a baby under conditions like that?" She has no idea why she has said this. The expansion of the universe has never terrified her before.

Jimmy raises his thin eyebrows. "I don't—"

"And what about the asteroids colliding into earth? What if she falls from a ferris wheel? What if there's no ozone layer next year and every child born dies a horrible death at age three from melanoma?" Sara feels dizzy and presses a palm to her forehead. She knows she's talking very loudly and she's not sure why, except that her voice feels like it's bubbling up through her from somewhere below her chair.

He pushes his chair away from the table, steps over to her side. Her shoulders heave, and she gasps. He circles her from behind with his arms and presses his torso against her back. She is crying a little now, silently. A thin ribbon of tears drips onto his hand. He brushes his mouth against her hair and massages her temple with his thumb. He wants to kiss the fear right out of her, or extract it with a needle. But he knows he can't.

"It's all right," he says.

She sniffles and runs a wet hand across her nose. "No. I don't think it is," she whispers.

THE THIRD PERSON

David Groff

"Dammit, dance, Peter, dance," Alec urged him. Peter would not dance. He would not allow his body to move in time. Though he let his lover's fingers slip from his neck to his armpit, he made the touch feel clinical. Idly, as if he were watching and not dancing at all, he looked beyond his partner's shoulder and saw how easily the men around him, some of them with the shiny red faces and inflated bodies of the sick but reprieved, abandoned themselves to the music. Alec himself was dancing as if he never would again. But Peter would not dance.

"Peter's sulking," Alec sang. He pulled Peter to him and ground his pelvis against Peter's pants. "Why is that, when everybody here wants Peterboy to have a good time?"

"I'm *not* sulking," Peter said. But he knew how he sounded.

Alec didn't let Peter pull away. The song quickened into its bridge and Alec licked the side of Peter's jaw. "It's Saturday night, we're young, sort of, Monday's a day away, we're alive. Reason to celebrate."

Peter looked past Alec's ear to the edge of the dance floor. Standing under a wide green banner reading "People with AIDS Alliance: Yeah, We're Still Here," the crowd looked like a multicultural drug company pitch for the promise of antivirals. All they needed was mountaineering equipment and a couple more women. Among the black and Puerto Rican regulars here at Hudson Boy, Peter caught the Anglican face of their friend Marc, diag-

nosed with AIDS a thousand years ago, and fresh from Assumption
Hospital. Pneumonia, even these days. "Now it's as if getting PCP
is a failure of character," Marc had murmured two weeks ago.
Tonight he looked as ostentatiously hale as the healthy ones, sleek
in his tuxedo, his hair shiny. Just as the lights strobed off, Marc
grinned at him and raised his glass. His face disappeared before
Peter could manage to smile back.

"It's a success, don't you think?" Alec shouted as the decibels as-
cended. "Tommy says they've raised ten thousand."

"Yeah," Peter grunted back.

"That's not how you danced at the Morning Party."

"I had drugs then."

"So this is you as a real person?" Alec shot back.

Alec was a doctor. Tonight was a benefit for one of his lesser-
known causes, and making money was especially important these
days when people with real, live, full-blown AIDS were as popular
as second-generation welfare recipients. In the seven years Peter
had known him, Alec had been Dr. AIDS, first to know of every
new treatment, his patients lined up to touch the hem of his gar-
ment. He even went to funerals. Now, with people healthier, he
managed to be back from the hospital by seven at night in time to
talk back to the *PBS News Hour.* He didn't seem to know what to
do with himself, and Peter didn't, either. In the last year Alec had
started to go gray—or dusty-looking, which was how blond men
aged. Parenthetical seams had appeared around his mouth that
made his lips seem like an afterthought. "I'm having fun," Alec had
announced to him earlier in the evening as they stood in an impossible line for the buffet dinner—chicken breasts clammy from
the steam table, vegetable sushi oxygenating in the open air, and
genuine, archaic iceberg lettuce. "I am actually having fun. Isn't that
strange?" Peter had just looked at him. He wasn't persuaded that
either of them would recognize real fun if it mounted them on the
street.

When the song changed, a very round man came up and stroked
Alec's back to get his attention. "The mayor made it," he said.

Alec separated himself from Peter. "I've got to go perform," he
said as he sidled his way across the floor. "He'll love to know how

much we raised. One more excuse for cutting support from the city. Go entertain yourself."

Now Peter was alone in the center of the dancers. He wriggled through them and stood still at the edge of the dance floor. He thought about getting another drink at the bar, but he couldn't stand Cosmopolitans, which was the only cocktail being served for free. He thought about disappearing to the Spike a block away, though in black tie he would stand out like an *Architectural Digest* critic. He thought about sitting in the car, childish and freezing, until Alec would let himself be taken back home to Brooklyn.

"Why is that ugly man running off with your lover?" Peter turned to find Marc, impeccable in his tuxedo but sweating around the forehead. "Oh, the mad mayor's here. I'd ask you to dance, but I don't exactly feel like Carmen."

Peter smiled uncertainly. He never quite knew how to react to Marc's humor, even when he basically got the references. When Marc had opened his own law practice, Peter had designed his stationery and business cards. Once last month he had been dragged to Marc's hospital bedside, hanging in the back of the room among the paralegals and secretaries who seemed to take shifts to keep him from being alone. Marc had seemed to concentrate more on breathing than speaking. Lying there, he had looked ancient, not just because AIDS had aged him—Peter had seen that before, how a thirty-year-old man could look older and sicker than his own father—but because he seemed like an anachronism, an alien come from the Boring Reality Planet to shake a fist and remind him that things for gay men still could be terrible. People were supposed to get better, to die of normal heterosexual things like heart attacks and colon cancer. Yet when Marc had collapsed coughing in Alec's office, after every miracle drug cocktail had been exhausted and the pneumonia virus gone rampant, Alec seemed nourished, renewed somehow; he knew the lyrics to this old song.

"How are you?" he asked Marc.

"This is my first night out since the dread event," Marc said. "You could really write some gay marriage prenuptial agreements here, couldn't you? Lots of assets and asses." He took a big swallow of his red cocktail. "They all look so goddamn healthy."

"It's hard to tell who's well," Peter said. "You look well."

Marc arched an eyebrow. "I'm not sure that came out right, Peter." The music began to get louder, and over the whoops of the dancers, Marc yelled, "I hear you guys are breaking up with Chuck tomorrow."

"How did you know?"

"Alec. He asked my advice. I'm good at breaking up."

"I'm worried about Chuck," Peter said.

"His health?"

"No. I don't want him to be hurt."

"Oh, he'll be fine." Marc pulled a Marlboro from its crumpled pack.

"Don't let Alec see you do that. He'll have a hissy fit."

"Chuck's been broken up before. I've broken up with him my-self. A menage has the same expiration date as Entenmann's."

Marc and Chuck. Alex and Peter and Chuck. Alec with others, Peter with others, with Marc, too. Everyone had slept with every-one else. It was like the conga line forming on the dance floor, a progression of the well, the infected well, and the ambulatory sick like Marc, all arm in arm, all laughing, their conditions indistin-guishable in light this red.

After Marc left, saying he had to get up early for church—"I'm trying to find God, but his Web site seems to be down"—Peter sat in the corner of the club where Alec would have the hardest time finding him. He *was* sulking, he knew it, and thought he wasn't proud of it and couldn't explain it to himself. He liked the picture he made when Alec came upon him: slumped on a barstool, in his hands a shredded styrofoam cup. He was sullen enough to be a fashion model, he thought, if he had the nose for it. Alec didn't seem to notice. He carried both their overcoats. His black tie was undone and his face was shining.

"Twelve thousand five hundred dollars! That covers three issues of the newsletter, a coffee machine, and a couple dozen Blue Cross premiums. How are you?"

"Weary."

"Did my Peterboy dance too much?"

"No, his Alecboy was off endorsing checks."

Alec placed himself in between Peter's knees, grinned, and pulled Peter's tie open.

"No, you'll mess it up."

"Oh, I forgot. Peterboy likes to go home looking just the way he did when he left. Did you have fun at all?"

"Kind of." Peter made an effort to look at Alec's eyes, but he stopped short at his jaw. "Good turnout," he said lamely.

"Too much AIDS for you."

"No."

"It's still around, baby, even when you can't see it. And they still dance like there's no tomorrow, 'cause who knows when the viral load goes up?"

"So."

"So Peter has descended to monosyllables. Time to get my Peterboy home."

"I hate it when you refer to me in the third person. And *no*, it's not the AIDS thing."

"Tell that to Marc."

"I was fine to Marc," Peter protested, alert now.

"You didn't kiss him. I saw you not kiss him."

"I forgot."

"You forgot."

"I don't kiss everybody."

"Turning over a new leaf?"

It wasn't like Alec to be bitchy. He seemed to be doing it because it was something you were supposed to do when you decide to have fun. Usually his bedside manner was a kind of bluntly genial efficiency. He gave honest diagnoses. Suddenly he looked exhausted. "We've got a big day tomorrow." He draped Peter's coat across his shoulders and with both hands on his forearms pulled Peter to his feet. "Bedtime for all good Peterboys."

It took a long time to get out of the club. Those well-to-do white gay men attending the benefit, who underwrote the efforts of AIDS and HIV organizations whose clientele was largely neither white, well-to-do, or even gay, had been engulfed by the regular Hudson Boy patrons when the doors had opened at midnight. The tuxedoed gentlemen stood out like czarists among Bolsheviks. Everyone had a parting word or joke for Dr. Alec DeWitt. Peter didn't know so many people knew his lover so well; as Alec grinned at them, trading jibes or thanks with that twitching, tired politeness Peter knew so well. It seemed as if Alec had an entire life secret from him, that all these men were men with whom he was having affairs, men who could give him something Peter couldn't. He successively pictured the better-looking ones in bed with Alec, their studs undone, poring over checks and exchanging mortality statistics the way straight men trade basketball scores. Peter had the same reaction when one of Alec's patients from the clinic called and Alec spoke to him fluently in Spanish. His lover seemed at once a man to be proud of, and yet more remote too, a public man, someone you knew from television. "You should run for office," Peter muttered, as they finally escaped into the cold February night.

Alec grinned. "Are you ready to be first lady?"

Peter pulled the car keys from his pocket. "That's an insensitive thing to say."

"Peter, I was sensitive all evening long."

You'd better be sensitive tomorrow with Chuck, Peter said to himself. He unlocked the passenger side, walked around the front of the car without saying a word, and got in.

Alec leaned his skull against the headrest and shut his eyes. "Turn on the heater. I am so tired." Peter started the car. "Take the tunnel. It's faster. I'll spring for the toll."

Peter gunned the car too fast in the cold, slipped into gear, and sped down West 18th Street, headed toward the Brooklyn Bridge. Alec opened his eyes. In his peripheral vision Peter saw him decide to say nothing.

They drove in silence down Seventh Avenue among the Chelsea boys hurriedly cruising the cold streets, and then into the brighter lights of the Village, which made the milling crowds look warmer. Traffic was heavy for a Saturday night, with the suburban straight kids out in force, the Village their exotic shopping mall. Peter had to steer through them slowly.

"What are you going to make for brunch?" Alec asked.

"Chuck steak. *Crow.*"

Peter slipped the car into third, too soon. Alec turned in his seat. "That's why you're sulking, isn't it? You're mad about Chuck. We have *discussed* this. I thought we agreed that our relationship with Chuck had become unproductive for our relationship."

"That is *such* therapy talk," Peter said, taking the left at Chambers Street too fast.

"Therapy or not, it's true. We can't live for Chuck. We've got to live for each other."

"Don't expect me to be more interested in you in bed just because Chuck's not around." Peter roared up onto the Brooklyn Bridge, darted around a newspaper truck, and swept into the right lane. From the corner of his eye he could see the solid modern mass of lower Manhattan, towering on its bedrock. Before them, straight ahead, nestled in the industrial edge of Brooklyn Heights, lay their apartment, the perfect top floor of an old carriage house. As soon as they passed the arc of the bridge they would glimpse its single lighted window. Alec would have left the bedside lamp on. Peter slowed the car to a crawl. Alec folded his arms over his coat.

They crept one after the other into their bed. Before Peter could consider whether or not to say good night Alec was asleep, breathing evenly, deliberately, his hands flattened on top of the blanket. Peter regarded him in the faint glow from the windows as his wide chest rose and fell. One night shortly after they had first met, Alec had announced he would no longer lie awake at night; doing AIDS required all his waking energy. Peter, lying next to him, had watched surreptitiously as Alec, with all the resolve of a Christian Scientist, willed himself asleep within one minute.

Part of Peter's initial attraction to Alec had been his capacity to deal with life as a sequence of rational problems—that, and Alec's leanness, how he moved like a blade through space. Peter himself always felt as if he were a pile of pens about to spill out of a coffee can. He still loved Alec's body, but now he felt as if his lover brought only one dogged equation to his life. He wasn't even sure the equation even worked for Alec anymore. His wit, once brave, goofy, and medicinal, had grown brittle; he had taken on the humorless irony of lawyers, political activists, and the student council presidents Peter had happily despised in high school. Alec's body always seemed tensed. It would not give way even in the midst of sex.

When Peter had been introduced to Alec at a Fourth of July party seven and a half years ago, Alec had just become a partner with an older, heterosexual dermatologist whose patients seldom had any complaint more serious than herpes. In his early months with Peter, he gossiped about his patients (never by name) but not about their illnesses. When the senior doctor died—of melanoma, perversely enough—Alec began to see his own friends, and their friends, as patients. Many of them had lost their own doctors to AIDS. Very gradually, Alec became more serious; his persona, once almost playboy-light, grew weightier. Alec spoke of his patients by name now at the dinner table, even when Peter tried to change the subject to something lighter, like fag-bashing.

Alec had known for a decade he was HIV negative. Peter, wary of getting tested, would wait AIDS out. He had swallowed his worry so much that after a few years it lost is bitter taste. He'd been fine this long. In bed when Peter would touch his lover with his fingers or his tongue in certain ways and places, the catch in Alec's breath would indicate that he had stopped to consider whether the risk in that particular intimacy—however slight, like deep kissing—was worth it. But Peter had decided it was the price he'd have to pay.

Which made it all the stranger when, six months ago, Alec had suggested they introduce Chuck into their bed. Over seven years, both of them had had their separate dalliances, occasional, hurried, safe, and unmentioned, but Peter had been astonished that Alec would want such a thing. Still, he had assented, curious, maybe even relieved. He had wondered not just about what the sex would be like but what new corners of Alec it might illuminate.

Chuck, thirty, built, black, prosperous but prickly about having grown up poor in Fort Greene—blocks and several income levels further down from Alec and Peter in Brooklyn—had leapt into their bed like a puppy. Peter had never slept with a black man before, and he decided he was pleased with himself when the novelty of Chuck's skin wore off and he could deal with Chuck just as a man. He was aware how much the three of them contrasted each other: light, dark, darker. It cheered him, as if they covered the range of possibilities. Alec had never commented on Chuck's race. With Peter and Chuck in bed, he had been modestly enthusiastic, a resolutely even-handed choreographer. To Peter and Alec's previous twice-weekly pas de deux they effortlessly added a weekly pas de trois, with the principal dancers changing from time to time. The two of them seldom discussed Chuck before he arrived or after he left. Except for a certain postcoital tenderness Alec applied to him, Peter saw no new light in his lover. Maybe it was just boredom that had made Alec beckon Chuck to their bed.

Peter settled into the chilly covers beside his lover. The heat from Alec's torso and thighs began to warm him. Peter did not know this man. He knew only his behavior, or some manifestations of it. Alec had opened them to Chuck. Alec could do something else, like leave, or stop breathing.

Peter had not fallen asleep until nearly six and woke three hours later to the rasp of Alec on the floor beside him, doing sit-ups. He half-buried his head in the pillow, muttering that if breakfast was to be made Alec had better shop for it. Alec had looked at him— irked or tender, Peter couldn't tell which—and then had disappeared into the living room and out the front door.

The phone rang almost at once. Peter grappled the blankets to reach it.

"Alec."

"No, it's Peter. Alec's out."

"Alec's not there?"

"Alec's *out*. Who is this?"

"Peter, honey, it's Marc. Did you have a good time last night?"

"Uh-huh."

"You looked terrific in evening clothes. You and Alec should wear them every night, even to bed."

Peter could barely hear him. Either the connection was bad or Marc's voice was weak with sleep. "Thanks, Marc. What do you want?"

"I needed to chat with Alec for a just a minute," he breathed. "Just to talk."

"He went to get breakfast. Chuck is coming."

"Oh my, Chuck," Marc murmured. "What a complicated life. Will Alec be back soon?"

"If he comes back he'll be back," Peter said. "You okay?"

"Oh, dandy," Marc breathed. "Will you tell him to call me? I just need to talk for a minute."

"Oh yes. Goodbye, Marc."

As soon as he hung up the phone Peter was asleep again.

Chuck arrived at one o'clock. Alec, who had in fact come back, went downstairs to the front door while Peter groggily pulled on a rugby shirt and rushed into the kitchen. He hadn't even started breakfast.

"Dr. DeWitt," Peter heard Chuck say, as he always did, as if the fact of Alec's M.D. was at once awesome and funny. He heard Alec's kiss and his hospitable murmur as the two of them treaded the stairs. Furiously, he began cracking eggs into a copper bowl.

"Look what I found," Alec said, giving Chuck a chiropractic knead to the back of his neck. Chuck seemed to duck his touch, the way an adolescent son wriggles away from his father's affections. He had taken on a more natural assurance in the last months. A manly dignity had seeped into him. He had become a licensed real estate broker who could terrify people fresh to the city, which might have been part of his new attitude. Peter thought he and Alec had something to do with the change, as if Chuck were the new frosh who had just made varsity, whatever varsity was exactly. Sometimes, Chuck acted like a silent student of their couplehood, taking mental notes about gay male domestic life, as if earnestly studying for some admission exam.

Peter held his eggy hands away from Chuck and let himself be kissed hello. Chuck's lips were moister than Alec's and his eyelids heavier. "We're slow on breakfast," Peter said. "Alec and I got a late start this morning."

Alec grimaced at him. "We missed you at the benefit last night. The music was all the hoary old favorites. It would have been fun to dance with you."

"Oh, it was a success?" he asked tentatively. For all his fascination with Peter and Alec, he was wary of hearing about any part of their lives that did not include him. He shed his leather jacket. He wore only a plain white T-shirt that stretched translucent over his pectorals. Peter felt slightly dizzy looking at him.

"Twelve thousand five hundred dollars' worth of success. We even got out a whole mess of closet cases, the queens who normally wouldn't be caught dead at Hudson Boy or anywhere else south of the East Side Club. Just because it's AIDS doesn't mean they don't care."

"Either that or they knew how great Alec would look in a tuxedo," Peter added amiably.

"I can imagine," Chuck said. "I have to admit," he added, "I had this fantasy last night about the three of us in tuxes? And *not* in tuxes?" He went into the hall and put his coat in the closet, then came back into the kitchen, unlatched the cabinet, took out a goblet, opened the refrigerator, found the orange juice, and poured himself a glass. Peter marveled at how easily he moved around their home. "So what's for breakfast?" Chuck asked.

"Humble pie," Peter said under his breath.

"The usual," Alec said quickly. "Today we'll be the cholesterol capital of the new world. I got sausage—"

"Alec, you got *sausage*? That'll stink up the apartment for a week."

"Peterboy doesn't like to smell breakfast the next day," Alec explained.

Peter opened the refrigerator and found a paper package already drooling grease. "*Peter* doesn't like to be called *Peterboy* in front of strangers," he said to the sausage.

Alec and Chuck fell silent at that. "I like sausage," Chuck finally said, apologetically.

"Sorry," said Alec. "Peter's a little strung out today. Too much dancing."

Peter leaned against the refrigerator door and shut it with a thump. *"Coffee?"* They nodded.

Chuck followed Alec into the living room. Peter could hear snatches of their conversation between the sound of the whisk and the growl of the coffee grinder. Chuck was laughing; Alec's voice alone seemed enough to delight him. Alec seemed to have launched into a point-by-point analysis of the mayor's dereliction on HIV needle exchange for intravenous drug users, and Chuck, who volunteered with God's Love We Deliver, was saying something about the families he delivered food to. The conversation left Peter unaccountably mad. It was all so impersonal; any fag could talk this talk. When the coffee was ready, he grabbed the three mugs and walked into the living room. Without quite meaning to, he said to Chuck, "Alec needs to tell you something."

Chuck, who was curled up on the sofa, his T-shirt riding up to reveal an inch of taut belly, sat up straight. Peter knew what he was thinking. But this announcement would not be a diagnosis. "Alec?" Peter prompted.

Alec looked at him, annoyed. "Peter, I thought we were going to wait until later."

"Why not now? Cream?"

"What is it you need to tell me?" asked Chuck in a small voice.

"I wanted to discuss this later," Alec began, "but maybe Peter is right." He shot Peter a look that said Peter wasn't right at all, and took a deep breath. "We and you have had a wonderful time this last six months. I know Peter agrees with me that you've given us new life, and we love you very much. But he and I have been doing a lot of talking."

Alec's been doing a lot of talking, Peter grumbled. As Alec's words marched out in precise little battalions of hurt, Peter watched Chuck's face move from disbelief to embarrassment to a mask for pain. He stared into his coffee. Each phrase of rational regret pulled Chuck's fresh young self further away. Peter felt as if he would never have sex again, that Alec was making him a leper of some kind, clicking a lock on a hope that others had and he could not have. Looking at Chuck's arms, the biceps taut, he wanted him more than he ever wanted anyone before, including Alec; he wanted to rip the T-shirt away and crawl against Chuck's big young rib cage.

"It just seems that these things run a natural course, and at a certain point become counterproductive, not just for us but for you.

It's time, we think, for you to find yourself what Peter and I have. There's only so much intimacy that we can provide. We can't let ourselves become your crutch. Now, I know we've got a bond between us, among us rather, and that bond is going to last. It's just not best manifested in sex any longer. It sounds cruel to say, but you need one man, one you can have completely, and one who's your own age, preferably. There's a whole life out there to lead, Chuck, and we're going to help you in any way we can." Alec chuckled, as if it had been written into the monologue he'd memorized. "You've got a whole generation to choose from."

Chuck's eyes were wet. He looked at Peter, who still stood above them, hugging his cooling coffee. "You feel this way, too? You agree with him?"

Peter looked at Alec. His face was sharp with command. "Yes," Peter said.

They were quiet for a moment. Peter sat down. Chuck looked carefully around the room, as if to memorize it. "This place, I don't know . . . I guess I'd better go."

"No," Peter heard himself saying. "There's no reason that just this once—"

"We invited you to breakfast and we want you to have breakfast," Alec broke in. The phone interrupted him.

Relieved, Peter shot up to answer. "Doctor DeWitt?" asked a female voice. He could hear a loudspeaker in the background and knew this was Assumption Hospital, where Alec worked.

"No, this is not Dr. DeWitt. Hold on one moment for Dr. DeWitt."

Alec took the phone. "Yes? Yes, this is Dr. DeWitt. Oh. Oh, shit. Put him on." He cupped the phone. "Marc is back in the hospital. Alan is with him."

Peter instantly remembered Marc's phone call. He hadn't told Alec. He looked away and his eyes fell on Chuck. He was sitting with his knees against his chest, his sneaker heels on the edge of the white linen sofa, listening hard.

"Alan, what's wrong? I just saw him last night. He looked pretty good, didn't he, Peter?"

Peter nodded, watching Chuck listen.

"He got out too soon. Who's the attending? Yeah, well, she'll know what to do. Yes, he could handle the pentamidine before. If he walked in, he'll be okay. We must have just not suppressed it all the first time around. Okay. Yes. Keep the coffee warm."

Alec hung up. "Marc woke up with fever and shortness of breath and called Alan. Alan said Marc tried to call me but got Peter. It seems Peter didn't remember to tell me." He walked to the closet. "I'm going in to see him. Chuck, do you want a ride back into Manhattan?"

"Yeah, I guess."

"Peter, do you want to come too?"

"I'll clean up from breakfast."

"I'm sure Marc would like to see you. He got himself a private room this time, so you won't be distracted by other sick people."

The idea of seeing Marc was more than Peter could face. "I'll see him later."

"Have it your way," said Alec, already shrugging on his coat and tossing Chuck's jacket to him. "Chuck and I are going."

Peter tried to nap and could not. He tried to work on designing a new logo for the People with AIDS Alliance, a job Alec had assigned him in an attempt to get Peter engaged with the cause. Idly he blocked out the initial caps and sketched in barbed wire, then a thermometer. He tore the sketch in tiny pieces. He took another shower. He selected some of Alec's suits, his own slacks, and their evening clothes, balling them all up for the dry cleaner. The tuxedos reeked of smoke. He stuffed the sausage deep in the trash and felt like a child.

The winter afternoon slid quickly into dusk. Peter wondered whether Marc truly was okay. Peter had often encountered him at the gym, "an AIDS cocktail waitress," as he called himself, blooming with steroids, his T-cells a three-figure overnight success for the first time in a decade. AIDS used to be a sniper for men like Marc; they would fall over dead in the street or else trudge the same sloping path, step by step into sickness, until the path gave into a steep, breath-killing drop. Those men had lived with a lengthening fear, a gentle decline in weight, stamina, and T-cells, no matter the acronym-dance of antivirals, until pneumonia, toxo, or lymphoma ambushed them, the opportunistic infections that would be suppressed to allow the sick man to appear in the gym again, thinned but optimistic, telling the unwilling Peter that yes, he loved himself, that AIDS wasn't a war but a journey—until crypto hit them, or CMV left them blind or cathetered, necessitating a permanent departure from gym floor or coffee bar, and more and longer times in the hospital, and more scared phone calls in the night to Alec when it seemed the body's cells were dropping and all would be lost. Then came transfusions, the crucifix by the bed, the visiting mother who needed consolation and needed to be put to use, the blustery father who demanded the best treatment and threatened to take his son home. Then the will. The planning of the service. More dismal hope. The triumph of a two-block walk. A numbness in the legs. A private healing service, crystals, subliminal healing tapes. PCP again. Dementia, the gift of teddy bears. The egg-crate mattress meant to prevent bedsores. Incontinence. Coma. The ex-lover sick now, too, on the same ward. Death. Wake. The service that summed up a life in one rattling hour. The necessary laughter. Peter had walked it all, overheard it as it happened. It was an awful story. He was reassured to know how the story ended.

Now they were teased with promise. Even if many men lived, some would not. Marc might not. "I used to be a dead man walking," Marc had told Alec. "Still am. The governor hasn't exactly commuted my sentence to life." Hope meant a new and somehow more embarrassing fear—that the drugs wouldn't work, that HIV would awake and the reinflated body pop, spraying betrayal. Sometimes the fear changed to terror when Alec's phone rang, the voice on the other end raspy with panic. Marc's voice.

A few days after Alec informed him his T-cells had finally edged into three digits, Marc had cornered Peter by the water fountain at the gym, Prescriptive Fitness, where they both worked out. Wiping his moist mouth, Marc had said, "You know, I used to want to be that hot young thing on the bench press. Now I'd settle for being that tired old fart on the bike. I happen to know he has five hundred and eleven bouncing baby T-cells."

Peter didn't have a cheerful answer to that. He didn't know

whether he was helpmate, nurse, bystander, or soldier. He had long since stopped probing his lymph nodes or examining his ankles for bruises that would not go white when he pressed them. It seemed such an eighties thing to do. He squirmed away from Alec when he would give Peter his flu shot and probe his stomachache. Sometimes in the night, especially if theirs had been a sex of surfaces, Peter would press his entire body against Alec's sleeping form, trying for every inch of contact, and imagine himself as immune as he knew Alec was.

By dark he had thought himself into a frenzy. He cleaned the kitchen, ate an egg, laid out his clothes for Monday and Tuesday, did sit-ups, and repeatedly considered calling Alec at the hospital. It was unlike Alec not to phone him. He monitored Peter as carefully as any of his patients. Clearly Alec was angry at him, but for which of his many transgressions Peter was unsure.

After eight he heard the crunch of Alec's tires on the snow. He sat in a chair in the living room and awaited the sound of feet on the stairs and a key in the lock.

Alec entered. In the half-light of the hallway his face was dark and baggy and the part in his hair was crooked. He dropped his keys on the table, pulled off first one glove and then the other, and began unwinding his scarf. Peter remained silent and seated, the prisoner in the docket.

"You didn't tell me Marc had called. That is a cardinal sin in the household of a doctor."

"I am *so* sorry, Alec. I mean it."

Alec took off his jacket and tossed it on a chair. "Marc had a recurrence of pneumocystis this morning. He was feverish and was calling his physician. He could have collapsed in his apartment, alone, the way David did, last year. He is, fortunately, now stabilized. He even entertained guests this afternoon. You were not among them."

Alec disappeared into the kitchen. Peter heard him pour coffee. "So what did you do with yourself today? Did you design the logo? Did you read a comic book? Did you go to the gym and build your body big? Did you call Chuck?"

"I didn't call Chuck," Peter said.

"Good, because Chuck was very upset. He loves Marc."

"He wasn't upset because of Marc," Peter said to the empty room. "He was upset because you took our relationship and fucking diagnosed it."

"I did not," Alec said, reappearing now. He sank into a chair far from Peter and held the warm cup against his throat. "I told him the truth."

"The truth is, you're in love with AIDS. You don't know what to do when AIDS isn't around. You're hooked on it."

Alec sat up, his neck tendons taut. For a moment Peter thought Alec would throw the coffee cup at him. In the darkish room Peter saw his jaw sharpen. "What a coward you are." He was speaking through his teeth. "Caught up in denial. A child afraid of the dark, desperate to be distracted. I can't believe I want you in my house."

Peter went cold.

"You treat Chuck like your lifeline to youth. And when I try to remove the placebo, you just sulk."

"Who wanted to screw Chuck in the first place?" Peter asked, his voice tight.

"I did. I wanted some life around me. I thought he would relieve your tension, make you lively again. I thought if you wanted him you'd want me, too."

"I always wanted you!"

"No, you don't want AIDS." Alec pulled himself up and crossed the room to Peter. He tousled Peter's hair. "Something's got to change." He drained the rest of his coffee. "You know what I liked best about him? I knew he was negative."

"I'm not going to get sick," Peter said.

"Probably not," Alec said. "But you never know. Do you?"

"Don't say it."

Alec sank to his haunches in front of Peter. "One thing *will* change, Peter, whether Peterboy likes it or not. I'm tired of hiding."

Peter went colder.

"When I examined you at the clinic last week I didn't just take blood for cholesterol. I took blood for an HIV-antibody test."

"You fucker!" Peter felt the room tilt. "You can't do that! Why didn't you tell me?"

"I wanted to know, even if you didn't. I wasn't going to tell you. I was going to keep it to myself. But I think you need to know."

"I could fucking sue you!"

"Yeah. You could."

The cold in Peter's veins turned to steam. He shot up from his chair, dodged Alec's body, and made for the door, grabbing Alec's coat along the way.

"Where are you going?" Alec stood and blinked at him. Even in his fury Peter could see him swaying, his hands clumsy, maybe gesturing at him, maybe not.

"Away. Home. I don't know." Peter slammed the door behind him.

In Alec's pocket were two crumpled dollars and change. With the coat zippered to the top and his hands balled into the pockets, Peter half-ran toward the subway. The mist of his breath clouded his vision. A gray-black night had long since fallen onto Brooklyn. The neighborhood was nearly deserted, with those few people on the streets hurrying to destinations.

Peter traded most of the money for a token and rushed into the elevator. The platform was deserted but the train came swiftly nonetheless, with a blast of hot wind that sucked Peter into its open doors.

When he climbed the stairs to Christopher Street the air was visibly warmer. Sheridan Square was sprinkled with people walking with purpose in the cold, into bars and restaurants, a few sharing cigarettes. Peter walked once around the triangle of the square and then began moving north, slipping past people, their heads bent with cold.

Chuck lived in a walk-up west of Seventh Avenue. Peter had been there only to honk the horn and drive him to Brooklyn. Chuck's apartment would remind him of his own early days in nasty walk-ups shared with near-strangers. The bathtub would be in the kitchen, the bedspread Indian, red and frayed, the pine shelves stacked with egg crates or cement blocks, pillows scattered on the floor among the clutter of two person's dissimilar possessions and unfinished tastes. Maybe Chuck would even have some African art. That, he thought, would be educational to see. The scene soothed him.

He crossed Seventh Avenue where it intersected with Assumption Hospital and walked down 12th Street to the crumbling portal that was Chuck's doorway. The vestibule was comparatively warm. In the ancient New York practice, Chuck's name was not on the buzzer. Peter had a moment of mild panic, trying to remember which of the old labels represented Chuck's. 4-B. He pressed the button and waited.

"Who is it?" Chuck's voice was reedy through the speaker.

"Chuck, it's Peter. Can you let me in?"

There was a long pause. "What do you want?"

"I need to talk to you."

"What about?"

"I just need to chat." Peter reconsidered. "I want to apologize for this morning."

No sound came from the speaker for a long time. The vestibule was windless but still cold. "I want to take you out to breakfast. I owe you breakfast," Peter said to the buzzer. Then he realized he had no money and that when Chuck let him in he'd have one more thing to apologize for.

"Fucking asshole white men," the speaker said.

"Chuck, honey, it's Peterboy. Come on, I'm cold!"

"Go away. Go home to your lover and your bourgeois Brooklyn apartment." With a flash of static the speaker sputtered off.

Peter leaned on the buzzer. No response. He started pounding one button after another. At last the door buzzer went off. Some stranger would let him in, without caring who was there.

Peter threw himself against the door. Just as it gave he caught his own face, close up, in the glass. He could make out his unshaven chin and his own cowed eyes, like the eyes of a dog about to be kicked. With those eyes he couldn't face a stranger.

"Who is it?" came a quavery voice over the speaker. "Who's there?"

Peter turned, opened the outer door, walked down the steps, and sat on the lowest one. He put his head in his hands. His skull seemed oddly light, as if it had been frozen and could just crackle into pieces.

After a moment he got up and, feeling weightless, drifted to the corner. At the public phone he inserted two dimes and a nickel. When the phone rang the machine clicked on to Alec's professional cheerful voice.

"Alec, pick up."

There was the sound of a phone being lifted from its cradle, and a wispy inhalation of breath.

"Where are you?" Alec said, without tone.

"In Manhattan," Peter said.

"Where in Manhattan?"

"Outside Chuck's."

"Oh. How is Chuck?"

"He wouldn't let me in," Peter said.

"Well, maybe you should sit on his doorstep all night. He'll have to come out in the morning. It's Groundhog Day. Spring will come."

"Alec."

"Yes."

"Will you come pick me up?"

Alec breathed. Peter could hear the electronic chatter of other voices, women's voices. He could almost make out their words.

"I'm just so tired," Alec said.

"It was a terrible thing you did. You had no right."

"I know. But I did it."

"Alec, I'm going to freeze to death out here."

"Take two aspirin."

"You want me to walk home?" Peter asked.

"Try." Alec hung up, his voice replaced by the nearly intelligible voices. Peter listened to them until they died. Then he hung up the phone.

On Sunday night Greenwich Village was always quiet, as if its tenants required a long, hot bath and a damp washcloth to recover from Saturday night and fortify themselves for the week's ambitions. The streets were almost empty except for taxicabs meandering through the steam that spiraled from the manholes. Peter put his cold hands in Alec's cold pockets and began to walk.

He walked east toward Seventh Avenue. There, before he had thought of it, was the white brick pile of Assumption Hospital, its windows irregularly gleaming. A half-dozen people sprawled in the glare of the emergency room, as inert as if they were waiting for a bus. Peter felt a rush of privilege, as if he carried his own warmth like the wallet he did not have.

Above him, on the top floor, was the AIDS ward. Peter knew it. Behind one of those windows, lighted or not, lay Marc, attached to tubes and retractors that all had names Peter didn't know. He could imagine Alec that afternoon, bending over the bed, full of antiseptic good cheer that might actually make Marc feel better, focusing on the details, the truths of pain. The unknowing that every body has to endure.

Peter crossed the street against the light and walked halfway up the block to the main entrance. He entered the hospital as if he belonged there. The woman drowsing at the front desk beside the elevator did not look up as he darted to the fire stairs and opened the door. Inside, balled up against a radiator, was a hospital gown. Had someone been well enough and restless enough to sneak out into the cold, leaving a human shape of pillows on his bed? Peter sniffled and hoped so. He climbed the ten flights to the ward. His lungs pleased him.

The hall hummed with machinery, discordant and indistinct, that mingled with Peter's breathlessness. Nearly all of the rooms were empty caves, their sheets pulled taut. In one of the darkened rooms a bearded man lay sprawled, arms stretched below his hips and palms open, his black hair tangled on the pillow. RUIZ, the name on the door said, and next to it, BRUBAKER. Larry Brubaker, Alec's good friend; Peter hadn't asked about him in two weeks. He looked into the bed beyond Ruiz and saw Larry's luminous blond head. Peter had heard that Larry's drug cocktail was working. Larry was even going to Africa, wasn't he? At the foot of the nearer bed was a narrow cot. A large woman was lying on it, a mother, her single earring glowing garish in the hallway light.

Peter went down the hall until he found GARDINER. Marc lay in bed, perfectly asleep, his hair combed back from his high forehead. The blanket had slipped to his waist. He wore a blue shirt with "ESSO" stitched in a little circle over the breast.

Peter sat and watched Marc's stomach rise and fall against the weight of the blanket. He had slept with Marc once, back when Bush was president. He didn't remember it very well. He did recall that five days later he had met Alec and, in a phone call, had to explain to Marc, who wanted to see him again, that he had found another man. Marc had been delighted. He had asked for every detail of Alec's anatomy and character, and then had realized he knew Alec already. "You are a very lucky boy," Marc had concluded. "You are going to live a long and happy life, says the Buddha, and come back as a golden retriever."

Marc's breathing seemed an achievement in steadiness. Peter watched him for a while and then, as he rose, pulled the blanket up over the IV in his arm to Marc's thin throat. It was at least a gesture.

Outside, the muffled buildings seemed to breathe straight into Peter's face. Numb, he walked block after block down Seventh Avenue until the buildings became shuttered, metallic and colder. His feet began to shriek in his sneakers as he laid one foot in front of the other. At Chambers Street he turned, passing the shuttered cheap stores that catered to the city's people of law. "Hey!" shouted a shadow. It was a man squatting in a doorway. He lifted his can of Colt .45. "Give me that coat! Hey!"

The Brooklyn Bridge walkway was empty, and he shivered in pedestrian fear as he mounted the steps and began to leave the dense borough behind him. The bridge trembled in the wind. The blast of traffic below the walkway merged with the creak of cable. Deserted, Peter turned around to see the city once more. The squat towers of Wall Street were empty and chilly, hardly lighted at all. Traffic swam at their bases. None of it seemed human. Peter felt as he did the day last summer when he had taken the seaplane from the 23rd Street Marina out to Fire Island. At first he had been overcome with euphoria, with the city beautifully sensible below him, but as the tiny plane circled this same East River to gain altitude, and the buzz of propellers cut into him, Peter had gotten scared, because among all the white-lined roadways and gridded buildings and tugboats with their symmetric plumes of wake, there was evident not one person.

He looked toward Brooklyn. There the buildings were smaller, comfortable, and on the Promenade a few grayish figures were hobbling along in the cold. He thought of the last time he and Alec had walked there, one late-summer Sunday afternoon—and immediately a procession of Alec's faces flew below him: Alec as a younger man, his face softer and unseamed; Alec toweling his head after a swim on the day they first would sleep together; Alec in candlelight, all lips and brow; Alec's face, streaked with passion and wordless, arching up toward's Peter's face as Peter penetrated him completely; and Alec as he would look right now, reading but restless, his right eye twitching.

Peter raised his head toward Brooklyn. At the end of this bridge, down those steps, through the dead ends, up five blocks on Hicks Street: the distance seemed immense, and it was very cold. Peter began walking faster toward the windows where his lover, a doctor, waited for him. He could go nowhere else.

THE UNIVERSE, CONCEALED

Richard McCann

for Ellen Geist, in memory of her son Jesse

My friend Helen and I are rowing a boat on Eagle Lake. It's almost dusk, but Helen is wearing her swimsuit because she's working on a tan. She has brought along her bottle of Hawaiian Tropical suntan oil and a Panasonic cassette player made of cheap white plastic, like a teenage girl's. As we row, we listen to *The Torah Tapes,* which Helen has secured from a Hasidic man who runs a shop on Eastern Parkway in Brooklyn. He also sells special *yahrzeit* candles, she tells me, although she prefers the ordinary kind that come in blue paper wrappers, available in regular grocery stores. She says they remind her of the Dixie cups of vanilla ice cream her father brought her when she was girl in Livingston, New Jersey.

"Be neither sad nor regretful," says Rabbi Ezekiel Stollman. Rabbi Stollman's our invisible passenger, the one whose voice we strain to hear when the Panasonic's batteries are running low. On *The Torah Tapes,* he speaks in a kind of up-and-down chanting. He says that sadness is arrogance and vanity. The things that sadden us are actually blessings, he says, coming to us from a universe that's concealed.

While Rabbi Stollman talks, I feel the rhythm of rowing—the bending forward, and then the long leaning back, pulling the oars through water—as a kind of secret davening. Helen sits across from me, adjusting her swimsuit's straps. "You think I'm getting too much sun?" she asks.

For several days now, since coming to the Eagle Lake Lodge and

Cottages, where we plan to spend a week, we've been making a list of the things we would see if the concealed universe were suddenly and astonishingly revealed to us. At the top of the list, we have written "UV rays."

Beneath that we have written "Joshua," the name of Helen's twelve-year-old son, who died a year ago, and then the names of my friends who have died—Jim, Edward, Marcellus, Larry, George, Darnell, Allen, Ricardo, Stanley, Paul, Jaime, my brother Davis, Billy, Matias, and, most recently, Francisco.

Helen says we should also make a list of the things we hope will remain concealed forever. At the top of that list, she says, she'll put the cotton prosthesis she was given after her mastectomy, not long before Josh was killed. On a third list, a list of things which are generally concealed, but which we believe might be revealed to us with a minimum of effort, if we put our minds to it, we plan to write "penises."

It's not surprising that we should take an interest in men's zippers, says Helen, since we're both descended from tailors who labored long hours in sweat shops. As for us: We labor in an editorial department, where our coworkers keep handing us grim, full-color brochures that advertise budget holidays that they believe Helen and I should take together. And who could blame them for wanting holidays from us? Even as spiritual projects, we must be tiresome, since we spend so much of our time discussing the lives of people who are dead.

"You'll have to admit one thing," the coworker who shares my cubicle said to me one day, while we were standing at a lunch counter, waiting for a clerk to bag our take-out orders. "When it comes to the dead, there are simply more of them than there are of us."

And although I saw at once the point that he was driving at, as sensible and tactless as it was, I thought, *Well, yes, that's it exactly, especially when you've lost the people you loved best—so many, in fact, that you couldn't possibly find a rental hall large enough in which to entertain them, other than the one inside your stunned but festooned head. . . .*

Then I thought of my mother, who outlived almost everyone she knew, and who solved this problem like a genius simply by allowing herself to become demented. Not long after my brother Davis died from an overdose she began calling the people in the nursing home by the names of people who were dead. Once, she introduced me to the nurse as her mother. Over and over, she kept saying to the nurse, "Have you met my mother yet?" Evidently this nurse had been around the block, because she didn't miss a trick. She took one of my hands within hers and said, "Tell me, has your daughter been a good girl today?" And I thought, *Well, yes, in fact, she has, and she was always more like a daughter than a mother anyway. . . .*

In this way my mother went on for years, descending from her seven heavens—from *Machon,* with its caverns of storm and noxious smoke, and from *Araboth,* which contains the dew that will one day revive the dead—only to accuse the nurses of stealing her brassieres.

But this isn't what Rabbi Stollman has in mind when he explains the Torah, even though he too must explain the nature and meaning of the concealed universe by telling stories. In one of his stories, the ancient Jews are praying the Creator's blessing, which they ask to come in the form of rain, since they are suffering from terrible drought and famine.

So it rains. It rains so much that their crops are destroyed. It rains so much that their beasts of burden are drowned in the fields. Then, says the rabbi, just as everything is almost lost, the Jews assemble again, with their heads bowed in submission, like beggars standing in a door. "Thank You, O Lord!" they start to pray again. "Thank You! You can stop! We've had enough blessings!"

"Make no mistake," says the rabbi. "The Creator takes an interest in prayers."

Even here at The Eagle Lake Lodge and Cottages—"AAA-AP-PROVED, SPECIAL SENIOR RATES, IN-ROOM PHONES AND TV LOUNGE"—there are many blessings. In the cluttered gift shop in the lobby, for instance, there are brightly painted iron trivets to bless the homes they'll one day decorate; and seated in the pine-paneled dining room, there are numerous old ladies, most of them widowed, who bow their Christian heads in silence to bless their dinners.

Rabbi Stollman would be impressed, we tell ourselves, if he were to see the old ladies as they congregate each night on the screened-in porch, in their Adirondack chairs, praising the things the revealed world has given them to gaze upon: hummingbirds, for instance, and fireflies rising from the honeysuckle bushes, and the deer that sometimes come along the shore at dusk to drink from Eagle Lake.

But tonight Helen and I are sitting in the dark, where the old ladies can't see us, down on the dock in folding chairs. We are staring at the deep blue line where the lake becomes sky.

"Tell me about the first time you met Francisco," Helen says.

I am remembering how as a child my brother Davis liked to hide at night in the shrubs by our front porch. When someone walked by, he would whisper, "Who goes there?"

Davis is my brother who died four years ago. I whisper into the water—*Davis? Who goes there?*

But Helen wants me to tell her about Francisco, every detail. How I still drank back then, when I was living in Germany, translating NATO manuals for the U.S. Army. And how what felt like an urge for the English language suddenly led me to the airport in Frankfurt, which led to a drunken weekend in Dublin, which led to an even longer bender in Galway, until one night I found myself propositioning a sailor who was pissing into the harbor from the edge of the quay. And how a penitential journey to the Aran Islands led to a terrified week of white-knuckled sobriety, which led to a boozy overnight ferry ride to Cherbourg, which led to a morning train to Paris, with the sun in my eyes the whole way. And how that whole journey returned me only to the sort of single room I had been trying to escape, and how that room then led me to a run-down porno theater on rue Vivienne, where a Filipino in a white shirt was sitting in silence beside me, solemnly stroking my cock through my pants.

That was Francisco, I tell her. Even before he had a chance to unfasten the buttons on my fly, I came.

This is the part of the story Helen likes best—the sweet, pre-AIDS mess I make in my drawers, a kind of "meeting cute," as she calls it, like on a sitcom. But these days, I suppose, the underwear would be marked BIOHAZARD.

She also likes the part where Francisco and I leave the dirty movie theater and go to the Cinema DeLuxe, a revival house, to see *West Side Story,* and the way we walk home later, along the Champs-Elysées, singing "I Feel Pretty." I never returned to Germany.

But as I talk I am thinking: *Helen, there are parts I have not told you, things I still conceal.* The drunken nights along the Boulevard Raspail, and the shame of my desire. The sullen fights and rages. The catacombs of tenderness, and the brittle apologies.

And the way I left him, in a drunken panic. And the way his letters kept following me back to America, saying, Save me. Each time I opened one, I felt as if the knife were slitting the envelope into a mouth.

"Well," he said after we slept together again, a few years later, when I was visiting Paris, "I guess we've said quite enough for ourselves already. In the old days."

Oh, I thought, *in the old days* . . . But now, if one wanted, how would one get back there? Ring the bell, monsieur—the green iron gate on rue de la Campagne Première. Then up five steep flights to the small room beneath the eaves where those two ghosts still live—*I love you, I love you.*

But I tell none of this to Helen. We didn't know each other's dead, so we are still able to invent them.

I tell her that I loved Francisco. I tell her it is terrible he died alone.

I tell her that it is terrible he died in that terrible apartment, in that terrible district near the airport, north of Paris, in that squalid suburb, that sort of *petite Afrique* to which the French consign their dark-skinned foreign workers. Terrible that his body went unclaimed for three days. Terrible—well, hardly *comme il faut.*

But I see Helen leaning forward in her folding chair. "It's my turn," she is saying. "I want to tell about Josh."

She leans back. "Josh told me he wanted to become a doctor when he grew up," she says. "The week before my mastectomy, he told me that he wanted to become a doctor so he could cure cancer. He even showed me that he'd gone to the public library to check out a chemistry book."

She says she can remember the book's exact title, which was *Organic Chemistry,* although it was out-of-date and totally useless. But of course she didn't tell this to Josh.

She liked to watch him while he read. She liked to watch him as he diligently studied *Organic Chemistry,* sitting in his straight chair at the dining room table, drinking glass after glass of iced water. He was drinking so much iced water, she says, because the first brutal heat wave of summer had just begun and the air conditioner in the living room window was broken.

All evening, Helen has been abstracted and unsettled, her voice taut with anxiety, and I can see that telling her own story isn't helping her, that it is taking Josh away from her again instead of restoring him. How could it be otherwise? Tomorrow is the first anniversary of the date of Josh's death.

According to the Hebrew calendar, Helen has told me, Josh died in the year 5754, on Tisha B'Av, which happens also to be the solemn fast day of mourning commemorating at least eight calamitous tragedies, including the destruction of the First and Second Temples, the expulsion of the Jews from Spain, the mass suicide of the Jews of York, and the initiation of the deportation of the Jews from the Warsaw Ghetto. These, says Helen, are precisely the sort of "ortho-facts" that make one realize that Hasidism is simply a brilliant cover for obsessive-compulsive disorder, given its passion for counting and numbers. For instance, according to the *Likutei-Amarim-Tanya,* the 613 organs of the soul are clothed in the 613 commandments of the Torah, which are further subdivided into 248 "organs," or positive precepts, and 365 "sinews," or prohibitions. The whole thing started with Adam, who contained 248 limbs (including parts of limbs) in his initially blameless human body.

This methodology suggests, says Helen, that all inquiries into the nature of the soul are essentially obsessive and autopsical.

But Helen herself believes in the revelatory power of numbers. For instance: Josh had an IQ of 158, which means that he was his school's brightest pupil.

He owned 323 baseball cards. Helen knows this because she counted and alphabetized them shortly after he died.

He lived—in this world, at least—for a total of 4,752 days, including three leap years.

And above all, this: The week of the third blistering heat wave— the week that her veins sclerosed from her second cycle of intravenous chemo, the week that Josh was killed—Helen yelled at him twice for not having fixed the air conditioner in the living room window. He had said he would fix the air conditioner in the living room window.

"Go ahead and yell at me if you want," Josh had answered her the first time. "You're just yelling at me because I'm the only one who's here with you now."

To prove this punishing point to her forever, the next time Helen yelled, God let Josh die.

As for that point, Helen says, it needs no proving. After all, we are sitting on this dock because he's dead.

She walks to the edge of the water. "Did I tell you what I told the Chassid in West Side Judaica the day I went to buy the *Tanya*?" she asks. "I told him I was thinking of becoming a Hasid, since I no longer trusted horoscope books. I told him I'd actually been quite a devoted reader of Linda Goodman's *Sun Signs*—at least until my son was hit by a car. I said, 'Now tell me, she was Jewish, wasn't she? You know, *Goodman*? Reformed, maybe? Reconstructionist?' "

She steps back from the water—*Who goes there, in the dark. . . .*

When she turns to me, her face is bloated with sorrow. "I think I want to go to the bar now," she says.

The bar is the one spot to which I won't follow her, not even tonight. But I follow her up the hill, through a stand of fir pines, and past the occasional wooden cottages whose porch lights dimly illuminate bags of garbage and beach towels draped on clotheslines to dry. When we come upon the lodge, I see the old ladies have retired for the night, their white chairs in straight rows glowing in the dark. In the taproom window a blue neon sign advertises "Genesee Beer."

"I can't believe you're really an alcoholic," Helen says as we cross the lawn toward the front door. "It's insane. Everyone knows that Jews can't be alcoholics."

"I'm not a Jew," I say. "I'm gay."

We separate in the lobby.

But I'm not ready to go upstairs to bed. For a while, I sit on an overstuffed sofa, its back cushions pinned with yellowing antimacassars, reading back issues of *People* and *Adirondack Life*. When I look up, I can see through the open door to the taproom; I can see Helen sitting on a barstool, her legs crossed, talking with one of the summer sportsmen who sometimes come here to drink, a man in an expensive fisherman's vest.

Because I know some things that Helen has told me, I imagine I can see what this man cannot. I can see the way she fiddles with her lavender blouse, for instance, nervously revealing and concealing a small part of her recently reconstructed breast; and I can see the way she adjusts its neckline, checking to see that it shields the small, puckered surgical scars which make her self-conscious. "Just a few dents in my flesh," she told me one day, as if her creator had accidentally marked her with his thumb—*as if we were clay, as if we were dust*.

In a few months her plastic surgeon will complete the reconstruction of the nipple, what she calls "frosting on the cake."

I watch as she leans back on her barstool and laughs. She hoists her cocktail glass into the air, as if making a toast.

Tomorrow at breakfast, I think, she will recount this whole thing for me. "Did you get a load of that guy?" she'll ask. "Right out of *Yankee Magazine*—or maybe L.L. Bean—what do I know from the goyim? Did you see me drinking a gimlet?"

"That must have been the Purple Lady in the bar last night!" she'll exclaim, speaking of herself in the third person, as if she were a victim of multiple personality disorder. She'll erase the night by working it up, by laughing at it, while we sit together at the breakfast table, spooning jam onto our English muffins.

And why should she say more? It's true: In the beginning was The Word. But sometimes, says Rabbi Stollman, an unhappy person can best work his way toward God by being silent, just as a hungry person can work his way toward God by delaying his meal. I know what Helen's doing.

But when I look up again, I see she is touching the man's hand.

She has grown serious, and I can tell from the way he studies her, with a convolution of sympathy and horror—a grim expression that I can recognize, having so often received it myself—that she is telling him how Josh was crossing Eighth Avenue, turning to wave to the friend who'd just called his name: "Josh!"

How the van was speeding and quickly bearing down. How the impact. How his glasses. How he was thrown.

How he rose and stood again for a moment.

How he fell. How blood. How his blue shirt. How the sirens and the stretcher.

How it happened. The whole story.

It is time for me to go upstairs.

I turn out the light. On the way up, I stop at the refrigerator the manager has placed in the stairwell and take out my medicine. On the door of the fridge, he has hung a sign: "Please Date Food." "Oh no," I think each time I see it, "God willing, I'd really rather date a man. . . ."

But I suppose the other guests have already guessed at that.

I know what I would guess, if I were one of them, and if I happened to open the small, brown paper bag that contains the clear glass vials: "New Drug. Limited by Federal Law to Investigational Use Only. For Subcutaneous Injection."

And what would I say if one of them were to ask me? "Oh no, dear sir or madam, certainly not *that*—not *that* disease at all, I assure you!"

Is it true, what I tell myself? That if I were pressed to say this, I'd rather stand with the dead?

I go upstairs to my room. I sit on the bed and mix the recombinant with sterile water, as the study nurse taught me, and draw the solution into the syringe. I swab my thigh with alcohol. When I'm done, I lie down.

Then it's quiet, except for an occasional loon calling from the lake. I lie still and try to masturbate. *Here is his body, silvery, like water . . . And here is what he felt like, the smooth warm chest . . . Francisco, the audible pulse at his wrist, restored . . . And he says . . .*

But it doesn't work. I turn on the bedside lamp.

I imagine Helen in the bar downstairs, feeding quarters to the jukebox, dancing with the man in the fisherman's vest. What does it matter if she prepares for Tisha B'Av not by fasting but by flirting and having a few drinks more? She's already reduced her level of happiness, as Rabbi Stollman says one must in the days preceding Tisha B'Av. Perhaps the management should post a sign by the gate to the Lodge to protect the innocent from straying up our driveway: "Caution. Mourners Ahead."

For a long time, I sit awake, thumbing through a magazine, until I hear Helen coming down the hallway, fumbling in her handbag, as if drunk, searching for the key to her room.

The next morning Helen doesn't come down to breakfast. I sit in the dining room, watching the old ladies as they congregate on the screened-in porch, where they'll spend their morning painting rocks to look like ladybugs and mice. Mrs. Chandra, a widow originally from Bombay, is standing among them, talking to her son Manil, who has come to visit her. Manil is slender and graceful, in a white linen shirt, not much more than twenty.

"Manil can stay only two days," his mother said, introducing him to Helen and me the previous morning, "because he's very busy in his business, as is proper." When he shook our hands—solemn, courteous—he looked at us directly, smiling, although as soon as I looked back at him, he quickly lowered his eyes.

"Do you think he might be gay?" I asked Helen.

"You're daydreaming," she said. She said she doubted the Diaspora was now leading Jews and queers to Eagle Lodge, ourselves excluded.

One of the widows, a straggler, stops at my table on her way from breakfast. "Where's your wife this morning?" she asks.

"Sleeping, I guess," I say.

I watch as she crosses the room toward the lobby, where she stops to check her mail at the desk. When I look back out to the porch, Mrs. Chandra and her son are gone.

I sit alone in silence, looking through a back issue of *Family Circle*. For a while, I close my eyes and attempt to imagine a white light traveling through my body, as a book on creative visualization has instructed me, through the complicated circuits of my arteries and veins, with healing warmth; and then I attempt to imagine that Francisco and I are once again sitting in the sunlight on a bench near the Orangerie. . . .

But what I recall is the day I learned that Francisco had died. I was at work when I received the phone call from Paris. Seven words, one for each day of the de-creation: *Oui, monsieur, je comprends, certainment, au revoir.*

I hung up. I rode the elevator down to the street and began to walk home from Hudson Street, one hundred blocks to the Upper West Side. The whole way, as I walked, I kept thinking one thought: I am walking the way a survivor walks, one foot in front of the other, deliberate, on his own two feet, alone. The farther I walked the more it seemed as if I'd walked so long that I had outlived almost everyone—even the people around me on the street seemed dead somehow, though still alive.

"It isn't just Francisco," I told Helen that night when I went to her apartment to talk. It wasn't just Francisco, though it seemed as if some memory of his body had been keeping me alive while the others died. It was Larry and the way he died, also, with PCP; and Henry, with KS lesions in his lungs; and Stanley, whose brain erupted with tumors; and Jaime, whose skin was so jaundiced it was almost the color of mahogany; and Paul, with dementia—Paul, whom I had known so long I could remember when he was still straight and married.

"Married," Helen murmured. "I was married. Twice."

Not even Helen could listen, it seemed.

That night I felt as if the whole world had died, or at least the world as I had known it, though I had no black armband to wear to show what I had lost or what that world had meant to me. But that was also the night Helen showed me the room that had been Josh's and said I could live there if I ever needed, that she'd help me if I got sick; there was no need for worry because I could stay with her if the time should come when . . .

I stood in the doorway, studying the small room, which looked stricken beneath the harsh brightness of the ceiling light—the unvarnished pine desk, the narrow bed covered with a thin blanket, the nightstand with its metal gooseneck lamp. *Well,* I thought, *it's a home, or a kind of home, at least,* and I felt happy to have it, as if I could breathe for the first time in years.

Afterward I went downtown to the Positive Immunity workshop I'd enrolled in to boost my immune system. I sat in a circle with the other men while the facilitator led us in chanting: "Living. Dying. Living. Dying. Two different words for just one thing."

I know what kind of ritual we'll get when we die, I thought each time I looked around the room at the bunch of us, the worried unwell, the last of our kind, *Homo urbanus.* It won't be Kaddish. It won't be a funeral pyre on the Ganges. It'll be a boombox playing "Je Ne Regrette Rien" in the rear of some Unitarian church hung with rainbow flags, like a gay Knights of Columbus hall.

One of the men in our circle started coughing. At first it was a small cough, but then it didn't stop, he just kept coughing and coughing, and we were all staring at him and thinking, *Oh shit, TB, maybe, or pneumonia . . .*

I don't need this, I was thinking, I don't need this. I just need to get out of here.

I walked out onto the street and started home. It was a cold night, and I could see all the way up Sixth Avenue. The sidewalk was crowded with people, some walking briskly and some pausing to look at things for sale in lighted store windows. *I'm an ordinary person,* I kept thinking, *I'm among the others, I'm one of them, that's who I am.* That's when it occurred to me that I'd never have to go back to that room where that man was coughing and coughing. I had a new fate now. I had Helen.

It's almost mid-afternoon when I spot Helen standing in the lobby, wearing her swimsuit covered with an old T-shirt that says "Poconos." She's looking through a rack of postcards.

"Where have you been?" I ask.

"Looking at postcards," she says.

"Since last night?"

Helen doesn't answer. We have a rule that neither of us is allowed to inquire into things about which nothing has been pre-volunteered. We also have a competing rule that we're not allowed to keep secrets.

She chooses a card from the rack and examines it. "What do you think of this one?" she asks.

She says she's been thinking she might send a card to Dr. Berlinski—"Thank Yahweh You're Not Here"—but I can't tell if she's kidding. Berlinski was her first oncologist, the one with whom she had an affair after she lost her hair from chemo. When he told her to take off her wig one night during sex, assuring her she'd still be beautiful, she believed that God had given her Berlinski as her reward for having cancer. That was the week before Josh was killed.

"Let's go," I tell her. We're supposed to be spending the day at the dock, preparing for Josh's *yahrzeit.*

"Just a minute," she says, retrieving the Panasonic cassette player from where's she left it on a sofa. She wants to bring it so we can listen to some tapes she's made of Josh's favorite music, like Lynyrd Skynyrd and Nirvana and Def Leppard doing "Pour Some Sugar on Me." Though music's forbidden on Tisha B'Av, Helen has decided these songs are special exceptions since they no longer constitute what Rabbi Stollman would call "a joyful noise." After all, they were Josh's songs and now Josh is dead.

Down at the dock, we spread out our beach towels. Helen starts unpacking a tote bag of things she's brought for the *yahrzeit,* which we plan to observe by rowing onto the lake at dusk and lighting a candle. We can't observe it earlier than dusk, Helen tells me, since the rabbi says people should mourn and lament only after they've concluded the important daytime obligations of the living, such as tending to business and making money. But we have no business to tend to, I want to tell her, other than mourning and listening to Rabbi Stollman.

"Look what I brought," she says, holding up a booklet Josh made her one Mother's Day, stapling together Xeroxes of his favorite poems—*real* poems, Helen points out, like by Muriel Rukeyser and Sharon Olds and people like that, not just the junk that most kids would choose. She shows me his Yankees baseball cap and his small collection of key chains, chronicling the history of each one—how he got this key chain on a school trip to Valley Forge and this one from a Hebrew school classmate who'd visited Tel

Aviv with her uncle's family. She shows me a key chain from which dangles a mini Magic 8-Ball.

As for me, I have even less than Helen, at least of Francisco's: a white cotton handkerchief; a Zippo lighter he once bought in a junk shop, engraved with a stranger's monogram.

"Let me tell you what I was planning for the bar mitzvah," Helen says. She'd hired a caterer, a real first-rate outfit, sort of a kosher Balducci's: buffet dinner for sixty, with salmon steaks and fish salads, five different kinds. Helen has told me all of this before. Josh didn't live to see his bar mitzvah.

I shift on my towel. I look over the edge of the dock, down into the water. Small fish dart in the shallows. For a moment, I want to tell Helen something I remembered a few nights ago—something Francisco once said, I think, though now I can't recall exactly what.

"You're not listening," she says.

"I'm listening," I tell her. But in truth I am staring into the water, trying to remember what Francisco looked like—how his hands looked, for instance, when he touched me, and what his body looked like when he stood before the mirror taking off his shirt. His chest was smooth and lightly muscular. I remember that.

"You want to listen to 'Pour Some Sugar on Me'?" Helen asks.

"No."

"I do," she says.

I watch her as she fiddles with the cassette player. The sun is harsh. In this light, she looks almost defeated, her arms covered with small patches of scaling skin, the residue of the psoriasis she got while undergoing chemo.

I don't want to be here, not right now, not on this sun-struck dock, listening to Helen. For a moment, it had almost seemed as if I were in Paris again, as if I'd been traveling there simply by gazing into the reflection of my own face on Eagle Lake. I want to tell Helen how Francisco looked the last time I saw him, standing on a concrete quay in the Gare du Nord—his dark face, the radiance of his white shirt.

"I can tell you aren't listening," Helen says. She can't get the cassette player to start working, though she keeps pushing the Play button. The tape is jammed.

I don't know what to say. I don't belong here, not with these widows, not even with Helen, though I can't imagine where I do belong, not any longer.

"What?" Helen asks.

"Nothing."

"You're acting like you're mad at me," she says.

"No," I tell her.

"I think you might be pissed about the guy I met in the bar last night," she says. "I think you're jealous."

I don't want to discuss this. "It's not like we're married," I tell her.

She puts down the cassette player. "That's right," she says. "That's exactly right. It's not like we're married."

She turns away, making a display of herself, arranging Josh's things into a circle around her. Stop it, I want to tell her. You're the one who gets to have a *yahrzeit*. You're the one who's in re-mission.

"Go ahead and be pissed if you want," she says as she works, "but don't take it out on Josh."

"I waited all morning," I answer. "I waited because of Josh." But that's not really true. I waited for Helen.

"Okay," she says. "Okay, forget it."

"It's not like I'm dead," I tell her, although as soon as I say it I realize it sounds like a non sequitur.

"No," she says. "It's not like you're dead."

Then we sit in silence, neither of us knowing what to say next. It's a draw, as it always is: Dead son trumps dead ex-lover, but AIDS trumps cancer. No matter how much the ante gets raised, no one ever wins the pot.

I stand up and start folding my towel. "I need to go," I tell her. I tell her I'm getting a headache.

"You can't," she says.

"I have to," I tell her, putting my T-shirt back on so that no one will see my unclothed torso when I get back to the lodge, now that I'm a member of the KS Club. *Helen, you'll live,* I'm thinking.

"It's Tisha B'Av," she says.

I look at her as she sits on her beach towel, holding the booklet that Josh made her, her shoulders streaked with sunburn. For a mo-

ment I want to tell her I'm sorry. I want to tell her it isn't important, it's just a feeling I had and I'll stay, but it seems too late to say
these things.

"I need to go my room to lie down," I say. I tell her I'll meet her
at dusk for the *yahrzeit*.

I start up the hill.

"Don't you want to listen to *The Torah Tapes?*" Helen shouts after
me. "Or don't you give a shit what happens to Jews?"

I don't answer. I keep going, past the tennis courts and through
the stand of fir pines. As soon as I'm alone, it occurs to me that
what I want is to drive somewhere, to drive and drive with no des-
tination, like in the old days, though it's not until I'm climbing the
front steps of the lodge that I realize what I'd like even more is a
drink. And why not?—I've got my own little *yahrzeit* coming up.
"You've got to give up drinking," the doctor said the day I was diagnosed almost fifteen months ago, though I'd told him I only
drank wine now and again. Alcohol, he said, causes the virus to
replicate at twice the speed.

Well, I thought, I knew it was good for something.

I know I'm on dangerous ground. I know the AA commandments—they're my version of the Torah—and I know how to keep
living after the world falls apart: Don't think. Don't drink. Go to
meetings.

I'm just thinking of a drink because of Francisco, I tell myself—
because Francisco died and then the friend who called to tell me
the news died too, a few months later, and then I no longer knew
anyone who could remember Francisco and me, at least not from
that time, not from back then.

I step onto the porch. The Adirondack chairs are empty, the
old ladies having gone in to take their naps before preparing for
dinner.

Then I see Manil standing in the corner.

"Hello," he says as if he's been watching me.

"What are you doing?" I ask.

"Looking at the water," he says. He steps toward me. He points
at Eagle Lake. It's late afternoon, almost evening. In this light, the
water is gray and still, almost as if it were something solid.

"Sometimes I row out there," I tell him.

He says he likes the lake, that it reminds him of the time he once spent in the north of India, almost near the border of China. In that region, he says, the whole world is made of water. The dry earth we live upon actually consists of floating islands.

He is beautiful, I'm thinking—his stillness; his calm, lean body; his serious, dark face. We're standing close to one another, our arms almost touching, though I don't know if what I'm feeling— shortness of breath, a kind of anticipatory paralysis—feels like loss or desire.

"I could take you with me," I tell him.

"I cannot put you to such a bother," he says. I can't tell if he's embarrassed by the suddenness of my invitation.

"It's no bother," I say. I don't khow to tell him he's saving me from something—from myself.

Soon we are walking the path to the boathouse. He's a few steps ahead of me, and I'm watching him as he touches a hand lightly to the honeysuckle bushes as he ambles by them. I can remember what it's like to be alive. It's simple, like pushing a button.

I ask him to choose a boat, and he picks the new one, the one painted blue, not the old one that Helen and I use. I kneel beside the boat to steady it as he steps in, seating himself in the bow. Then I untie the line and step in also, taking the middle seat, my hands on the oars. We're facing each other.

I row. I watch him. For a long time, he is silent, studying the shoreline, where late light is darkening the blue pines. Then he murmurs, "This is good."

When we reach the center of the lake, I lift the oars into the boat. I sit back. We drift in slow, loose circles.

I cannot stop watching him. He removes his shirt and holds it in his lap. He needs to keep it neat for dinner, he says.

I'm in no hurry to get back.

"There's an island on the lower lake we could row to," I tell him. I imagine us lying on its shore, side by side, naming the shapes we see in the dream-clouds above us. I imagine myself telling him what has happened that has brought me here: how my friends have died and how it sometimes feels as if I alone have somehow escaped to tell the tale, though there's no one left to whom I might tell it except Helen, who has her own story to share.

He shifts on his seat. "I wish I'd brought water," he says.

I close my eyes. This is what the revealed world has given me, I'm thinking, in exchange for my losses—this moment, this easeful drifting.

When I open my eyes, I see he is looking at me.

"What?" I ask.

"Nothing," he says.

"No, go ahead."

"I want to ask a question," he says.

I believe I know what he's thinking. It wasn't a daydream, my intuition about his being gay.

"It's personal," he says.

I nod. I want to encourage him.

He looks away, trailing his hand through the water. Then he looks back at me. "I am wondering about your sickness," he says.

I'm startled. "What?" I ask, my voice suddenly rising. "I don't know what you mean."

He can't know, or so I'm thinking. It's not like he's seen me shirtless on the dock; it's not like I've got what one friend used to call "the look"—drawn face and darkened eyes, the first vague traces of wasting.

"I'm wondering if you have it," he says. "You know. The virus. My mother showed me the medicine you keep in the fridge."

So there it is, in plain sight. I'd thought it was concealed within my blood, visible only if titered. What can I say?—*Please, kind sir, which virus would that be?*

"Yes," I tell him. "HIV. The virus."

He shakes his head. "I am very sorry. That is very bad." He asks if I have told my mother.

"She's dead," I tell him.

He leans forward as if to indicate that he wants to speak in confidence, as if there were some chance that another person might overhear. "I prefer men," he says, almost whispering. "But I have only one boyfriend because I do not wish to get this virus."

He looks at me as if he wants me to tell him something—that he'll be safe forever, perhaps.

"Please understand my mother does not know about me," he continues. "Please understand I am telling you a secret."

But I'm not listening, not really, not any longer. I'm staring into the water. Francisco's dead, I keep telling myself. Francisco died, but not for love of me.

Then I realize: It's dusk. It's Tisha B'Av.

I tap on her door: "Helen, Helen." I can hear that she's listening to the *The Torah Tapes,* though I can't make out what the rabbi is saying, only the strange but melodious singsong of his chanting.

"I want to come in," I say, but she doesn't answer.

When I open the door, I see that she's sitting cross-legged on the bed, cradling the Panasonic, rocking rapidly back and forth in what seems a kind of furious davening. The rabbi's chanting something, I'm not sure what, about seeing *chaluk,* the robes of brilliant light in which God wrapped Himself so He'd be visible to Moses.

Helen looks up and switches off the cassette, severing the rabbi in mid-passage. "What?" she asks. "What do you want?"

I don't know, I want to tell her.

"I'm busy," she says, "listening to the rabbi, learning all about God's faces." She starts to talk more quickly. "I bet you didn't know He's got lots of faces, different faces, I bet you thought He had no face or that He was invisible or something like that, but no, that's not what the rabbi says. . . ."

"Helen," I say.

"No," she says.

She leans back against the wall and shuts her eyes. She looks tired, her face mottled with grief. "You were supposed to be here," she says. "You were supposed to be here but you weren't."

I sit down on the bed beside her. For a moment I feel as if I'm her husband come home late from work; I've missed something important that I've promised I'd be back in time to see—a recital, perhaps, or a school play. We're discussing our son, whom I have disappointed.

I see the *yahrzeit* candle still sitting on her bureau. "You didn't light Josh's candle," I say.

"It got too late," she says.

I know the candle's supposed to be lit at sundown, as the rabbi has explained, just as soon as the day's extinguished, but I tell her that this doesn't really matter.

"It matters," she says. "It's a ritual."

There's nothing more to say, or so I imagine. I can hear a car engine idling roughly outside in the parking lot. I hear an occasional door opening and shutting in the hallway.

"I've got to take my medicine," I say.

Helen nods, "Go ahead."

I stand to go, though I don't want to leave like this. "We could meet in the boathouse," I tell her.

She doesn't answer.

I go down the back stairs to the refrigerator. It now seems public, the brown paper bag that holds the vials, though I carry it up to my room, where I give myself my injection, and then take two Tylenol, as I always do, to stave off side effects. When I'm done, I go downstairs, relieved to find no one sitting in the lobby.

It's dark inside the boathouse. There are only the muffled soft sounds of the rowboats striking against the rubber tires tied to the sides of the docks.

Then I see Helen, already seated in our boat, watching me.

"I didn't think you'd come," I say.

"I'm here," she says.

I step into the boat. Helen leans over to untie it, as she always does, and we push off.

There's almost no moon, though each time I row a long stroke, I can see the oars moving through the black water, as if they were pushing through darkness itself, then rising as pale emanations. I want to say a prayer. But I can't recall one.

"Look," Helen says, almost whispering. She points to the opposite shore. Someone's walking there, among the high weeds along the embankment, shining a flashlight into the water.

"Who is it?" Helen asks.

"I don't know. Maybe someone camping in the woods."

Whoever it is walks back into the trees. For a few moments, we watch as the flashlight's beam darts through the lower branches, briefly revealing them. Then it disappears.

"I want to light the *yahrzeit* candle," Helen says. She's brought it along, in her pocket. She sets it on the tip of the bow and strikes a wooden match. When she touches the match to the wick, a small flame sputters and then catches, though it makes too weak a light to guide us.

"I don't want to say Kaddish," Helen says.

"You don't have to," I tell her.

"I have to do something," she says.

"You can talk about him," I say. "You can tell me things you remember."

"No," she says, "I don't want to do that."

She says she thinks she'll sing a song; then she says she can't recall any songs to which she knows enough words. She hums "Greensleeves" instead.

I ask, "Did Josh like 'Greensleeves'?"

"I don't know," she says.

She looks out toward the shore. I can tell she's not sure what to do, that the *yahrzeit* isn't working.

Then she whispers, "Joshua."

She whispers it again, "Joshua, Joshua, Josh." Then says it aloud and then louder still, until she's calling it across the lake, one letter at a time: "J-O-S-H-U-A."

But there's no Joshua. The concealed world has not returned him. There's only Helen and me sitting in a boat, a space between us.

Helen lifts the candle. It flickers but doesn't blow out. Then she hold it out over the water as if she were trying to look down into darkness itself. Is it true what the rabbi says, that Heaven and earth were made of water? I know what Helen says about Genesis—that God didn't punish Adam by killing him but rather by letting him live.

I put down the oars. I lean over the side of the boat, but the water's too black to see through. "Who goes there, in the dark?" I whisper.

"We do," Helen answers.

A VENICE STORY

Edmund White

In August 1989, Austin rented an apartment in Venice. It was so many stories high that even though it was on the Grand Canal it was relatively quiet. Julien, Austin's young French lover, said he was sure he would find Venice "majestic" and was delighted to be going there, if only for a week.

Although Austin and Julien spent almost every night together in Paris, they hadn't said, "I love you," nor talked about their future. Austin had accepted a position teaching the history of European furniture at the Rhode Island School of Design, a job that was due to begin next January, just five months off, but he hadn't asked Julien yet to accompany him to the States. Julien's English was very approximate. Would he want to trade in his surefire job with a big Paris architectural firm for something vague in Boston or Providence? Would he need a work permit? A visa? And what about Julien's HIV status? What if he turned out to be positive? Weren't people who were known to be positive denied entry to the United States?

Austin had also invited Peter, his old lover, to fly from New York to Venice. Peter and Austin had been to Venice many times before in the previous decade and Austin hoped it would cheer him up. Venice suited Peter with its quiet strolls in back streets, its vegetable stalls under tents baking in the August sun like an African village hastily thrown up in a square bordered by settling, tilting palaces and the unseen but overheard lapping of out-of-sight canals.

Hordes of tourists shouted and shoved into one another around San Marco and the Rialto, but San Travaso and Santa Margherita and a dozen other backwater *piazzi* were so quiet and empty that sometimes the only sound was of two old woman lazily talking together as they strolled home for lunch with their shopping carts rattling along behind them, one wheel in need of oil.

Peter wasn't working, his health was deteriorating, and his mother told Austin that his prospects of living more than a year were dim. Though apparently he was rather frail he could still get about. He clung to his status as someone who had ARC, not AIDS, although that distinction was now dismissed by scientists as meaningless. He had only 103 T-cells and it was an anomaly that he hadn't already come down with a major opportunistic disease. Austin knew Peter was taking a risk by flying to Europe and back (long flights were supposed to be bad for the immune system) but he had to give Peter a treat. Peter wasn't a realistic, hard-headed sort of guy anyway. He lived for treats, surprises, parties, sprees, even miracles.

Austin loved him and wanted to be with him. Many of their friends, especially women, accused Austin of loving Peter like a son. That was a comprehensible relationship, father-son, and given their age difference it put a respectable gloss on a visual disparity that if it were simply sexual might have seemed indecent. But Austin wasn't clear and convinced enough about his own experience to assume the paternal role. Unlike a straight man of fifty-two, he had no children to ratchet him year after year another notch toward death or at least toward maturity.

Austin didn't like ordering anyone around, or teaching anyone, and without an appetite for authority where lay the interest in being a father? If he were a genetic father of a real son, at least he'd enjoy the benefits of being a recognizable player, but no one except a few indulgent friends were prepared to take their hats off to an aging queer and his thirty-something ex–toy boy. Real fathers must feel a steadying, nurturing pleasure in instructing, correcting, guiding their offspring, but such a pleasure started with being certain about what constitutes good and bad, about which values to inculcate, and Austin wasn't sure he could make such distinctions.

Anyway, when Peter and he were together they were both kids, not even adventuresome teens but timorous tots, little kids unconsciously holding hands as they stumbled toward the unknown. They assumed nursery voices with each other, reassured each other in the most unrealistic but pleasant way, baby-talked in an embarrassed parody of their very real affection. True, Austin was the one who had always worked and supported Peter—maybe that was the only kind of paternity that society could grasp: the economic.

Peter flew in to Milan from New York, then changed planes for Venice. He even took the boat all alone from the airport to San Marco, but perhaps because he was frail and tired and a bit less eagle-eyed, someone knocked into him as everyone was surging off the *vaporétto* onto the pontoon landing—and stole his wallet. He found the empty wallet twenty feet farther along with his passport and credit cards inside but plucked clean of his money.

Not that he had much. Through planning and sacrifice Peter had managed to accumulate three hundred dollars—"getting-around-town money," he called it.

He looked taller and older. As he stood in the repeating volleys of tourists who were following their flag-wielding leaders, his hair gleamed white in the bright midday sunlight. His eyes shone a paler blue as though the sea were now flowing faster and shallower over whiter sand. Even his hand felt bony and breakable when Austin clasped it.

"I can't believe the bastard—*all* my money—I *know* which one he was, too." Peter's eyes filled with tears, and a few vaguely curious passersby stared for a second at a rising drama, their sympathy almost stirred.

"Don't worry, Pete," Austin said. "I'm loaded."

"It's just so *damn* frustrating. If you only knew how for weeks and weeks I rationed myself to just one beer at the bar when I went out, saving, saving, or how I never had anyone over for dinner or went to a movie, just so I'd have a little getting-around-town money and not be a complete burden on you."

Austin hugged him and felt the delicate ribs and exposed backbone jutting their way through his clothes. "Poor Pete, don't worry." He grabbed his bag and scooped him onto the local *va-*

porétto that would deposit them in front of their *palazzo* on the other side of the Grand Canal. They stood on the central deck as the boat zigzagged up the canal from side to side (the Salute, the Giglio, the Accademia . . .) and passengers pressed around them at every stop, leaving or entering the *vaporétto.* Peter looked more and more frightened and angry, as if those these hostile foreigners might steal his suitcase next.

"You're just tired, Pete. That's a wicked flight." He'd put on his baby-talking voice.

"Actually, it wasn't bad," Peter said in a grown-up, matter-of-fact way. "I slept a little and the movie was some sentimental thing that made me cry, I don't understand why I cry all the time now."

Austin knew not to ask him the name of the film; Peter forgot so many things these days, which bothered him, since he'd always been proud of his grasp of pop culture, as though he'd been preparing himself for the ultimate trivia quiz. He wasn't like Austin, who'd sacrificed his knowledge of the twentieth century to his mastery of the seventeenth and eighteenth and who, by living cross-culturally, was never expected by his compatriots to know much about recent American crazes nor by the French to recognize the names of their pop singers or movie stars. The funny thing was that Austin knew the very name of the court ballet Louis XIV had danced in when he was twelve (the first time he'd dressed up as the Sun King), but he'd never knowingly heard any house music or techno or whatever they were calling it.

When Austin got Peter down the alleyway at the bottom of an architectural chasm six stories deep and just three feet wide, and through the surprisingly grandiose door of their palace (designed in another century when there must still have been an open space in which to stand back to admire the door) and into the elevator just big enough for two passengers, then down the windowless corridor upstairs and into the ultramodern apartment with its woven brown leather and chrome chairs, then and only then did Peter begin to relax. He opened the windows giving onto the Grand Canal and peered out with a fragile invalid's hesitant, carefully dosed curiosity at the plash and play of gondolas floating four abreast while an aging, wobbly-voiced tenor sang "O Sole Mio"

into a microphone for tourists who didn't know the difference between Naples and Venice.

From this high window he could see half a dozen churches and
the very top of the Campanile as well as a few of the lacy spikes
bristling along the domes of San Marco. The mysterious topogra-
phy of Venice, typified by street signs that pointed both to right *and*
to left for the path to the Rialto or to San Marco, suddenly looked
decipherable from this simplifying height.

Peter turned back from the window, a thin, very thin silhouette
pressed like a tall, unlit candle against the Venetian sky, Tiepolo blue
with fleecy Bellini clouds. "You look great, Pete," Austin said, hoping to sound casually convinced that nothing had changed, that he
didn't even notice the twenty pounds shed since the last time
they'd gotten together. His reassuring noises weren't a lie if taken
to mean that a new, birdlike nobility had descended on his features,
as though the victim, before he was sacrificed to the gods, had to
be encased in an avian mask.

"When is Jupien—" Peter asked.

"Julien. He's arriving two days from now. In the evening. He's
taking the train from Paris. It's his first time here, in Venice,"
Austin added, hoping to avoid the whole awkward, unhappy
business of his new lover by directing his old lover's attention to
some minor matter, the surprising fact that Julien had never been
to Venice before.

Peter perched on the chair beside Austin. His breathing was shal-
low and fast and his eyes were racing here and there. With the force
of a falling stone it came over Austin that they were occupying entirely different places. Austin, though positive, was still bloomingly
healthy, making enough money to travel and invite his friends
along, embarked on a new love affair, whereas Peter was markedly
ill, frightened and disoriented by the all-night flight and the pick-
pocket who'd welcomed him to Venice. Possibly Peter was alarmed
by Austin's busy life in Paris, crowded more and more with men
and women he didn't know. Austin had a present, even a future,
whereas Peter had only a past in which Austin bulked large.

While Peter slept Austin hurried out to the Rialto and bought
fruits, vegetables, and a white, flat fish with tiny, lusterless eyes, as

though they were just pale photosensory pores rather than proper image-isolating eyes. In the backed-up bilge of August, everyone moved slowly through the viscous heat. The greengrocers under the Rialto open-air market, which was held aloft by squat columns topped by dolphin capitals, misted their lettuce and basil with a garden hose, but even so everything looked parched. Someday August would be over, the aimless, milling three-day bargain tourists would be hauled away in their buses, the real Venetians would come back from the Dolomites, the rich international gay and social population (*i settembrini*) would alight once more for the season, and once again the shopkeepers would walk briskly, sliding wood crates of produce off barges, smiling and waving at their regular customers, calling out their marvels in their husky, mushy dialect, all hollow, resonant vowels deboned of every last shaping consonant, and the market would smell of shameless white truffles in rut and the poultry butcher would hold up soft brown feather puddles of tiny game birds, as though offering fistfuls of molding autumn leaves as a delicacy.

Now Austin contented himself with the albino fish, some fresh, pliant eggy tagliatelle, a bag of tomatoes and onions, and a bottle of olive oil for the sauce, an overblown lettuce the color and cut of a glam rock singer's hair *after* a three-hour concert (he smiled at his rare contemporary comparison). As he hurried home high-up shutters closed and a disembodied hand pulled a canary's cage into the cool, marble-lined fastness of a dim apartment before bolting shut curious cut louvers, jig-sawed to fit the flame-shaped window frame. Two cats hissed and growled, squabbling over a small bundle of garbage neatly tied in a transparent blue plastic bag and dumped, all by itself, in the middle of the pavement. Shop after shop, all selling *commedia dell'arte* masks and kitschy bits of Murano glass, filed past; metal grilles were rumbling down over the display windows. The long, sweaty reign of the afternoon siesta was beginning, a time for desultory family squabbling, suffocated sex, tiring, dreamless sleep.

By six in the evening Peter had awakened, showered and shaved, and was sitting up, lean and dressed up and sipping a chemically correct martini. He'd always looked like a New England patrician, but now his higher cheekbones, whiter hair, bonier shoulders, and the birdlike way he cocked his head from side to side made him resemble the patriarch of a ruling clan, someone outraged by fin-de-siècle depravity or the immorality of abroad.

But in fact he was none of these things. He only looked that way. He was still a kid—the ultimate boy with his sweet serious-ness and his steadily gazing concentration on the people around him, a boy who could be silly with his entranced enthusiasm for soap operas on TV, his long, overly detailed stories of personal mar-tyrdom, all the ways former friends or deranged relatives had done him in; it was hard to know where the hopped-up resentments manifested by the soaps stopped and his own real travails began.

Austin had cashed a few traveler's checks and stuffed Peter's wal-let with a sum that matched what had been stolen. Peter got tears in his eyes and said, "You're so nice, Austin, you've always been so nice to me. My life wouldn't have been half so fun without you, and you're steady and loyal, you don't forget your old friends." They sat side by side in the wide, matching leather and chrome chairs and held hands intermittently, though they each had a cer-tain fastidiousness about prolonged touching; Austin associated it with an unwanted display of affection even when, as now, he wanted it.

He knew Julien couldn't fathom this American puritanism, mixed in as it was with American licentiousness.

They went for a stroll down the echoing pedestrian walkways that contracted into a sordid little path smelling of cat urine, then dilated into a proper *calle* lined with elegant shops selling mar-bleized paper, men's silk pajamas, and, farther on, multihued sum-mer sweaters of silk and wool. A standing gondolier glided past, but neither the canal nor his barque were visible, and he looked as though he were a moving target in a shooting gallery. It was a city of unchecked fancy—the doors were large or tiny, grilled or painted, the knocker a bronze fist or a Moor's turbaned head or a sword-pierced heart. No two bridges were alike, not even any two street lamps. Austin wondered if Julien was the sort of architect who thought form should follow function; if so, he'd be sure to de-test Venice.

Now that the long siesta was ending the streets were reviving and even the shopkeepers' faces looked sponged clean by an oblivion that renewed all the necessary illusions. The evening tide would soon inundate the whole system of canals, even the narrowest and most remote, and the eccentrically shaped chimneys, widening as they rose, and oddly cut crenelations of the city roofline were casting their mysterious shadows across the treeless squares and sidewalks and the sealed round white marble wells, their polluted waters capped.

Austin bought Peter a beige silk sports jacket and a belted raincoat and three dress shirts on sale. When they emerged from the shop with its English look—the polished wood shelves, green library lamps, and brass-fitted counter—they were plunged back into the true Venice, the constant murmur of a thousand muted human voices ricocheting off stone pavements and walls, of stray sunbeams irradiating a window display of colored glass trinkets and projecting rainbows, of sweating tourists in shorts, their faces baked red and, darting quickly through them, elegant locals already in evening clothes as they rushed, bejeweled and coiffed and perfumed, toward an early dinner before an opera at La Fenice, a house that had burned down so often it had a stake in its name: the Phoenix.

Austin cut short their walk when he felt Peter losing strength. As they were threading their way through the narrow chasm leading to the door of their *palazzo,* Peter bent down stiffly to stroke a puppy muzzled with a little wicker cage. His master was trailing not far behind. Peter looked like a very old general tousling the hair of a child who'd brought him flowers.

Once upstairs Austin set to work making him his dinner while Peter perched on the roomy windowsill, sipping a wine so pale it resembled water. He was looking down at the canal, its noise and activity so far below they were generalized into a picturesque haze.

Peter went to his bedroom to hang up his new jacket and raincoat. He came into the kitchen, tears standing in his eyes, and said, "I'm sorry I'm being so teary, but you offered me new clothes and that suggests you think I'm going to go on living for a while. . . ."

★   ★   ★

When Julien arrived two days later it was in the evening. He'd boarded a *vaporétto* at the streamlined Mussolini-era train station and now, as he descended the boat at the Stae stop, he was exuberant, as though the brightness dancing in his eyes and his quick, excited movements were assembled out of the lights fractured by the myriad currents and crosscurrents of the flowing, sloshing Grand Canal.

He looks so young, Austin thought. Then he glanced over at Peter in a cruelly unconscious instant of comparison. Peter looks so—well, it wasn't old, exactly, but *dry,* as though Peter were the white-haired, stiff-jointed, desiccated version of this brunette young Frenchman with his full lips, rounded rump, his clear dark blue eyes focused on some distant point of pleasure, whereas Peter's washed-out blue eyes were blurred by the indistinctness of all his present woes.

Austin was so happy to be with Julien. For the first time since coming to Venice he was light-hearted.

Although Peter spoke some sort of pidgin French, he was too tired to summon it up, or maybe he'd forgotten it or found it embarrassing to test out. Julien scarcely registered this linguistic problem. He was so exuberant about being in Venice that he stormed the city, rushing across bridges and plunging into San Marco, which, if it was the drawing room of Europe, was at once more tattered and more solemnly majestic than any other salon one could imagine. Old-fashioned floor lamps with fringed silk shades had been dragged outdoors and lit above each of the three competing string orchestras, and the lights lent a slight credibility to the drawing room metaphor although the guests nibbling ices and the streams of shadowy passersby sauntering along under the dim arches were dwarfed and even mocked by the enameled church domes, the great brick upthrust of the campanile, the solemn entrances and exits of the huge Moorish figures of the corner clock, the soaring columns supporting saints and a crocodile, the illuminated stonework of the Doge's Palace like patterned fabric stretched above the tent pegs of the short, squat columns and the distant moonlike glow of the neoclassical church of San Giorgio on its own island, looking on but muted, really exactly like a moon on a foggy, unhappy night.

Austin and Peter were silent, sonambulistic tourists but Julien was the excitable kind who had to share his impressions, half of which Austin translated into English more or less at random and half of which he let skip like stones across the lagoon. Peter nodded encouragingly, smiling, his head lowered and his eyes rounded—maybe he was a bit attracted to Julien, since he was being ever so slightly seductive, or maybe coquetry, after all, was his only way of showing friendliness to a man.

They ate at the little restaurant Harry's Bar had opened over on the Giudecca, spaghetti vongole and grilled bronzino and silver cups of raspberries in sugared lemon juice. Peter drank too much and tried to interest Julien in his unhappy childhood and lonely if glamorous school years in Florence but Julien, though kindly and well-intentioned, didn't know what he was supposed to do with all the information, which wasn't exactly urgent or even recent. Besides, Austin was translating sketchily. Austin kept hoping that Julien would understand that Peter didn't have much to live for and that, after all, Austin would be sleeping with Julien later tonight and poor Peter would be alone.

Although they never really found a topic nevertheless Julien was a good sport and was even happy to go along for yet another drink to Haig's Bar, for if Venice was a crowded museum by day, at night it was nearly as deserted as a museum. English aristocrats and successful French decorators and rich Milanese businessmen—all the people who owned apartments here and were willing to endure the city's dullness for the sake of its chic—were laughing and talking loudly as they raced along, hoping to get to the Accademia for the midnight *vaporétto*. Most bars, the stand-up zinc counter kind, had closed long ago, but Haig's carried heroically on into the cool hours after midnight, perhaps exempt from the usual laws by virtue of its English name. Here Julien was happy to see the last remnants of an earlier Italian era consecrated to mindless pleasure. He watched with sympathy the bored, stylish young people in rumpled evening clothes, a black tie undone and dangling like an unfinished joke, a fragile chain mail evening bag slung carelessly from the back of a chair, thick black hair curling over a sickly forehead, the drinks—brought up on a salver in eccentric stemware—chosen for their colors: garnet, chartreuse, cloud.

Back in their rented apartment Peter was almost falling asleep standing up and crouched a bit, so Austin and Julien kissed him on the forehead, as though he were their son; then he toddled off and Julien rushed to the window for one last glimpse of a passing *vaporétto*, projecting its yellow lights in every direction as it zigzagged up the canal.

In the evening Julien would put lavender-scented brillantine in his hair and tie a complicated ascot for himself out of a blue silk scarf printed with gold hunting horns. Peter lifted an eyebrow fractionally at each of Julien's efforts to emulate the Haig's heroin-and-Campari crowd, but he also seemed amused by so much boyish posing.

Austin and Julien had become intensely romantic in their lovemaking (back in Paris sex had been rougher, even brutal). Austin's only worry when they embraced in the dim *salone* was that Peter might surprise them en route for the bathroom or kitchen; he was sure he was feeling what parents with young children must feel, and like a young parent his desire overcame his misgivings.

Because he was a Southerner, and a Southerner whose mother had been a Virginia lady, Austin always needed to know what his friends thought of one another and any reservation someone might express he considered an insult, any criticism a betrayal. Julien had figured out how much Peter meant to Austin and made vague but approving sounds. One night, when for professional reasons Austin had to dine with the Cinis and the Montebellos, Julien and Peter ate alone at the Grappa di Uva and came back laughing and stumbling drunkenly, arm in arm.

Austin was thrilled. He thought that now he could invite Julien to live with him in Providence. Of course Peter wouldn't want to leave New York for Providence, but he might have to spend longer and longer periods of convalescence with Austin—and with Julien, if they should stay together. Maybe because Austin was a product of the unpossessive 1970s, he'd always thought gay men shouldn't pair off in ugly little monogamous units. They should stay loyal to their old friends and lovers and take them in when necessary, not reject their former mates like heartless heterosexuals.

Anyway, Peter and Austin had promised that they'd take care of each other and now the time for honoring that pledge was speedily coming due. Austin had felt guilty about lingering on so long in Paris after Peter had gone back to live in New York, but Austin was comfortable with his cozy little life on the Ile St. Louis with his gang of fun young hellions. As long as Peter was still able to go out and meet the preppy black men he liked as they stood around the piano singing show tunes at the Town House, right after work, still dressed in coat and tie, then he wouldn't really like to share the East Village studio apartment again with Austin—he wouldn't want his style cramped. Peter was looking for a last lover as frantically as if he was searching for a cure.

And Austin, who paid for Peter's apartment, couldn't really afford to rent a second studio for himself. Besides, as long as he was based in Paris he could work regularly for several American shelter magazines as a journalist fluent in French, but if he lived in New York would the same editors think of flying him down to do a story about an Eaton Street renovation in Key West or sending him up to Litchfield to write about John Richardson's neoclassic *atelier*, where he and his researchers were preparing the successive volumes of the Picasso biography?

Now this teaching gig had come along and Austin would be at a useful but discreet distance from New York; he'd be teaching just three days a week and could devote the rest of his time to Peter, if Peter needed him.

In bed that night Julien whispered, "What do you and Peter have in common?"

"Nothing, really," Austin said, "but I've always loved him and wanted to take care of him. We lived together for so long—*that's* what we had in common, our life together."

"So being in love means you want to take care of someone? For you that's what it means?"

"Peter just wasn't made to work. He never had any ambition. When he first returned to New York after getting his degree in the history of furniture at the Louvre—I wrote his papers for him—I got him interviews with half a dozen decorators in New York, but nothing came of it. He doesn't make a good impression. He can't really follow a conversation. He dresses far too young—he thinks he's still a kid, but he's white-haired and in his mid-thirties. Certain gay men fall for his little boy act, but it makes straight women want to throw up, and they're the customers. They don't mind if a guy is gay so long as he's virile and smooth and intensely interested in them and even a little autocratic, but an aging sweet little boy who's self-centered and speaks in a high voice like a girl—well, that doesn't play."

Julien laughed and said, "You certainly have no illusions about him."

"But I love him. I feel bound to him. He's the witness to my life. I call him every day from Paris. If he's sad I think of treats to cheer him up. The last time he came to Paris, it was last summer, we had lunch at the Bagatelle. We looked at all the roses and we took photos of each other beside the ponds and the weeping willows and that greenhouse where they have Chopin concerts, then we sat in the shade and ate a long, complicated lunch that was so light it left us hungry and we drank a bottle of Chassigny-Montrachet, the best white wine in the world, and we were so happy that we held hands under the table, because even if AIDS wasn't going to kill us this year or even next, we knew it couldn't be far off and we were entirely happy. For a non-Christian time can't be, *mustn't* be linear and cumulative, it can only select out a few perfect moments, and this was one of them, perhaps the *most* perfect."

Austin went on thinking about that day in the Bagatelle even as he stood naked on the cold marble floor (for they had gotten out of bed one more time to look at the canal) and held Julien in his arms in a room lit only from the illuminated boats below and the unique street lamp with its three clear panes and its single pink one, for even the basic street furniture in Venice was irregular and strange. The water traffic had at last abated and most of the palaces were darkened, though soon enough low-riding barges powered with outboard motors would be bringing small dark-green melons to market, melons the size of children's heads.

WE'RE ALL CHICKEN HERE

Jeff Kuhr

Somehow, Duncan has convinced Jude to come to the funeral parlor to pick out a coffin.

"They're on sale," Duncan now explains in the car. "Twenty percent off. They have to make room for the 1999 models. Besides," he continues, "shopping is always more fun in twos."

Jude isn't sure how to respond, so he says nothing, and instead, stares out the window, watching cars pass, wondering where everyone is going. Then, for no other reason than he can, Jude holds his breath and imagines everything stopping.

"Damn it," Duncan cries. He is playing with the radio, trying to find a song he can sing along with. Earlier, as they were getting into the car, Duncan told Jude to think of this as a "merry adventure, something to write home about."

Jude is beginning to feel faint. He knows his face is changing color. When he was younger, he used to slip beneath the surface of the bath and count to sixty, then come up, gasping. Later, he made it all the way to one hundred eighty. Three minutes. He had hoped to be Aqua Boy, and go on tour with the circus, sharing beauty tips with the Bearded Lady. However, he settled for life on land. Became an architect. Grew the beard himself.

"You can't sing with any of these songs. It's all boom boom bitch and blah blah whine," Duncan mutters.

Jude puts his hand over his heart and is only slightly surprised to feel it still beating. He can't remember where, but he recently read that the heart is the strongest muscle in the human body. The article documented several cases in which, even after death, the heart kept beating. Like a reflex. Like a chicken running around with its head cut off. It was habit, Jude thought, and old habits die hard.

Jude exhales. His body goes limp. His heart continues to beat.

Duncan shakes his head, as if mourning. "All the good songs are used to sell hamburgers," he sighs.

They come to a red light, and Duncan steps too hard on the brake. Jude lurches forward, forehead nearly kissing dashboard.

"Why don't you have your seatbelt on?" Duncan asks. He seems angry, almost betrayed, as if for Jude to die first, even accidentally, would be unforgivable.

"I don't know," Jude says, reaching for the seatbelt and pulling it loosely around him.

"It's a twenty-percent-off sale," Duncan says lightly. "Not two-for-one." He laughs, and Jude knows he's supposed to, too. Instead, he coughs, and turns up the volume on the radio.

Death, Jude thinks as they pull into the parking lot of the funeral home, is no laughing matter. Yet Duncan believes it's the ultimate punchline. He once told Jude he wished to be the victim of a Lizzie Borden type of death, where nothing was left but his de-capitated head, an arm, two toes. This way, he said, his tombstone could read: "Duncan Lincoln: Rest in Pieces." He was also one of the first people Jude knew to have a "Life's a Bitch, Then You Die" bumper sticker on his car. Then, later, when Duncan was reading about Hinduism, he modified it to, "Life's a Bitch, Then You Die, Then You Die, Then You Die. . . ."

"I don't know about you," Duncan is saying now, getting out of the car, "but the word 'parlor' makes me think of ice cream. Thirty-one flavors of death. Today's specials are Pull the Plug Pecan and Stabbing Vanilla Swirl." He snickers and takes Jude's hand, kisses the knuckles gently. "Lighten up, baby. We're here for you. This is one less thing for you to think about when I meet Jimmy Dean."

Duncan's hand is hot and sweaty, probably from gripping the steering wheel too tightly. It makes Jude think of hours-old pasta.

He lets Duncan hold his hand for a moment, silently counts to ten, then lets go. Duncan stops in front of the door and looks at him. Jude coughs again, and takes out one of his contacts.

"I think I have something in my eye," Jude says, sticking the contact in his mouth.

"Mud probably," Duncan says, but not bitterly.

With one eye closed, Jude sees Duncan as someone who looks like he used to be famous. The kind of handsome guy you pass on the street and say, "Wasn't that . . ." and you follow him a block or so and then realize you were mistaken.

Jude removes the contact from his mouth and carefully sticks it back in his eye. Now, with both contacts in place, Jude takes in this man before him, examining him as if he were going to have to give a police report at a later time. His hair is graying on the sides, but has been dyed jet black several times. The face is clear, with one or two leftover scars from a childhood case of chicken pox. His eyes are really green, but he has colored contacts, and today they are blue. The cover-up makeup he wears is starting to flake; it makes him appear to be shedding.

"How do I look?" Duncan asks.

"Like a million bucks," Jude says. A million counterfeit bucks.

"Do I look like I'm dying?"

"What?"

"Do I look like Death is a block away, slowly making his way to my door, maybe pausing to kill a couple of kittens?"

"Not exactly," Jude says, but only halfway means it.

"Good," Duncan says, smiling. "I don't want to look too over-eager. I just want a good deal."

"Don't get me wrong," Duncan is saying to Myron, the funeral director. They are standing in front of a mahogany casket. "I like that one. It's just I was thinking of something a little more lasting." He looks over and winks at Jude, who has been lingering in the doorway.

Myron smiles, leans in toward Duncan, and whispers confidentially, but loud enough for Jude to hear. "I know what you mean. Maybe you'd like to see something in an oak."

"Oak," Duncan says, then pauses dramatically, pondering it. "I hadn't even considered oak."

Jude shrugs and looks away. The secretary, a woman of about forty with a gray bob, too much jewelry, and not enough makeup, is in the hall, sitting behind a desk. She's been talking on the phone since they came in.

"And then this guy says to Myron, and he's completely serious, he says, "I was wondering if maybe I could get one with a door on both sides."

Her laugh is loud and out of place. Jude wonders if she talks during movies.

The funeral parlor is chilly, and several times, after he exhales, Jude sees his breath float away. He notices there are two doors: one leading to the parking lot and another, at the end of the hall, leading downstairs. Even here, Jude thinks, there are only two choices.

"Is there another way out?" he asks, but the secretary doesn't hear him.

Jude sticks his head into the "showroom" again and watches as Duncan and Myron examine another coffin. Myron is gesturing for Duncan to touch the sides of it, but Duncan steps back, pointing to something Jude can't see. Myron shakes his head and smiles. Jude hears him say, "Oh yes. You have very good taste. It's very comfortable. Plush. Chicken feathers. Are you allergic?"

Jude turns to the secretary, who has hung up the phone and started to write something. "Mind if I smoke?" he asks her.

She nods and laughs. " 'Course not, honey. Just more business for us later."

Jude smiles meekly and lights a cigarette. He takes a long drag and exhales slowly. In the past two months, Jude has sent résumés to three different firms in San Francisco, two thousand miles away. Last week, one of the firms called and told him they would fly him out for an interview, that "things looked promising." Jude made arrangements. He has until midnight to call the airlines to confirm his ticket. Then, two days later, he will leave. His suitcase is already packed and ready to go, hidden beneath the spare tire in the trunk of his car. Jude has decided that once he leaves Duncan and moves west, he will stop smoking, cut his hair, and start wearing glasses again.

Everything will be different.

"That your brother in there?"

Jude looks up, remembers where he is. He stares at the woman behind the desk a moment, calculating all the different responses he could give, the variations of truth. How could he explain this relationship? How could he convey that where they are now is nowhere near where they began?

Everything was different.

Duncan and Jude met six years ago, their senior year in college, after they had both turned down the same girl for a date. In fact, it was she who introduced them to each other at the campus coffee house.

"Look," she said. "Obviously, both of you guys have no taste. Maybe you should be friends."

They stayed at the coffee house, drank four cups of coffee, smoked two packs of cigarettes, and by the time the place closed, had acknowledged they had only one thing in common.

"Isn't that a hoot?" Duncan cheered. "I didn't see you at any of the meetings."

"And you weren't in the directory."

They both laughed, and Duncan took Jude's hand. The touch, flesh meeting flesh for the first time, was hot, electric, but gave Jude goose pimples.

It was like that.

"Won't Tina be surprised?" Duncan whispered later, pulling him close.

They were in love. Jude's first time, Duncan's second.

"He was my past, baby," Duncan said one night after Jude found him looking at old letters. "You, my sweet, are my present and my future." And Jude believed him, his young heart wanted to, because that was what love was, one giant leap into the present moment, hoping you landed somewhere safe, somewhere familiar, the arms of someone you can't do without.

When they graduated, Jude declined a position at a firm in St. Louis, and followed Duncan to Japan, where he had a job teaching

English. It seemed like the right thing to do. To follow your lover to the ends of the earth, exploring new worlds that you could conquer together.

They stayed for one year, then, with their money nearly gone, decided to come back to the States. Jude quickly got a job in Kansas City, and this time Duncan followed, saying he would use his time to write the Great American Gay Novel.

Now, three years later, Jude is an associate partner, has his name on the door and his own secretary who calls him Mr. Goldman.

Duncan has a list of first sentences and a job at Book Depot.

Six years. Two thousand one hundred ninety days. Fifty-two thousand five hundred sixty hours. Jude has done the math, but it still doesn't add up. Duncan calls it serial monogamy. Jude has started to think of it as serious monotony.

"Yes," he says suddenly to the woman behind the desk. "My brother."

"Is he sick?"

Jude nods.

The woman shakes her head. "I'm sorry."

"Thank you, but it's okay. We've known for some time."

"It wasn't sudden?"

"No," Jude says, stepping closer to her desk to put out his cigarette. "Gradual. Over time. It's been better that way."

"I've often wondered whether or not I would want to go quickly, suddenly, without warning, or have things be drawn out, extended, even just a little while."

"Well," Jude says, taking out another cigarette, enjoying the conversation more than he probably should. "This way we've been able to make all the necessary preparations. Get things in order so we're ready when the time comes. I think it will be easier to say goodbye if we know we've done all we can."

They are quiet a moment.

"And besides," Jude abruptly continues. "All of this. This is the hardest part. Decisions like these. It will get easier. Maybe not right away, maybe not even after a month, but one day. One day it gets easier, and you'll be able to look back and see all was for the best." He pauses. "Right?"

The woman opens her mouth, about to answer, when the phone rings. She holds up a pudgy finger at Jude and winks.

Jude feels a hand on his back and turns around. Duncan is grinning. "Oh, love," he whispers. "I could just die now. These coffins are so much more comfortable than our bed."

Jude looks over at Duncan in the car and notices a black scab by the side of his ear. A shaving wound. Jude has the uncontrollable urge to pick it, to uncover it, and see what oozes out. He starts to reach over.

"What are you doing?" Duncan asks, turning slightly to face him.

"Nothing," Jude says softly, slowly retracting his outstretched finger.

Duncan puts his hand to his cheek and feels the scab. He picks it. A fine line of blood begins to slide down his cheek. It is red, real red, the color of life.

"Shit."

Jude reaches beneath the seat and grabs a box of tissues. He takes out several, probably too many, but maybe not enough, and holds it to Duncan's face.

"Thank you, Ms. Nightingale."

Jude removes the tissues carefully, balls them up tightly with the bloodstain deep in the center, like a prize, then rolls down the window and throws them outside. He wipes his hands repeatedly on his pants.

"I don't know what I'd do without you," Duncan says, only a hint of sarcasm.

Jude looks over at Duncan and wonders how much he suspects.

He says nothing, though, and Jude watches the balled-up tissues fade from view in the side mirror, more discarded trash on the side of the road. He suddenly wishes for darkness, a full moon, wings.

"You know what Myron told me?" Duncan asks as they enter the courtyard of their apartment building.

Jude shakes his head.

"He told me orgasm in French is 'le petit mort.'" He said, translated, it means 'the little death.' Isn't that precious? I think I'll title my book that."

His laughter bounces against the walls of the building, then falls short at their feet. They stop at their door, and Duncan takes out his keys, turning toward Jude.

"Are you ready for a little death?"

Jude puts his hand to his heart, tries to establish if there is a rhythm. He wonders if there are degrees of death.

Duncan opens the door, waves his hand forward. "Our kingdom."

It used to be, when Duncan would say "I want to hold you forever," that Jude felt a certain sense of relief knowing there would always be someone to hold him. Now, though, Jude sees the statement as being very selfish. He realizes it wasn't so much that Duncan wanted to hold Jude forever; rather, he wanted Jude to hold him forever. There is a difference. And this, as Jude understands it, is the gap that, over time, has widened between them.

Picking out a coffin together is a much stronger bond than a little gold ring. "This way things will be easier for you when I meet Jimmy Dean" is Duncan's exchange of vows, his own "till death do us part."

Duncan can't bear to live alone, and thus is terrified at the prospect of dying by himself.

Jude, on the other hand, takes his time driving home from work.

Inside, Jude looks at the clock above the stove. He has six more hours before he has to call the airlines to let them know he will be buying the ticket to San Francisco. He wonders if the line on his Visa statement will read: "New Life . . . $698."

Duncan has gone into the study under the pretense of resuming work on his novel. Jude knows, though, that what he does is sit in front of his computer, playing computer solitaire. If, later, when Duncan emerges and says, "Things are going well," it really means that he has won a couple of games. If he says, "Things are going poorly," it means that the computer has won.

Jude sits down on the couch and takes out the blueprint for his "outside-of-work-project." A dream home that changes year to year. He carefully spreads out the parchment on the table in front of him, running his hands over its surface to flatten the creases. He closes his eyes, slowly turns the key to the front door, steps inside.

In his mind, the house is a two-story Victorian, on a cliff, somewhere on the edge of the Pacific, north of San Francisco. The way he has designed it, there are windows everywhere, and you can see the ocean from all the rooms in the house. Already, he has imagined several sunsets, watching as the sky changes colors, how the shadows will move across the room like a parade. The room he is in now, the one he been working on lately, is his study, on the second floor. It is room of possessions, the objects of his future, the souvenirs of a new life. Pictures of people he has not yet met, but in which, in every one, he is smiling. A miniature Golden Gate Bridge paperweight. A work desk, made from refinished oak, by the window. Shelves of books, worn around the edges, the lines inside highlighted, passages of inspiration, of moving on. Hanging on the wall, a poster. It is the one thing in the room from before. Van Gogh's self-portrait. His bandaged head turned slightly, showing off his suffering. The things we discard to become whole.

He hears Duncan moving around in the study. Jude inhales deeply, opens his eyes, then takes out a pen and quickly makes a note that he needs to add a door to his study. He rolls up his house, places it carefully into its canister, then settles back on the couch, blows out breath, and again closes his eyes, letting the rings of light on his eyelids take form, willing himself to be somewhere different.

Relationships, he thinks, are a series of little deaths. You fall in love, then you die, then you die, then you die.

When Jude wakes up, Duncan is sitting beside him.

"Good night, baby," Duncan says, smiling.

Jude rubs his eyes, and looks at the clock on the VCR. It's after midnight. He's missed the time to call the airlines to confirm his seat. He feels his body go limp on the couch. No doubt he's been replaced. Someone has already purchased his ticket, become him and taken his seat, starting his life over in San Francisco.

"Do you know what today is?" Duncan asks.

Jude shakes his head. He knows everything today was supposed to be, but not what today is.

"I was working on my novel and things were going poorly, so I started looking through my old journals. Today is the day we met at the coffee house at school. Exactly six years ago today."

Jude can say nothing, but Duncan has started to cry.

"You know," he starts, but gets lost in his tears. Jude moves away, just slightly, and watches Duncan as if he were an actor on some made-for-TV movie.

Duncan takes a deep breath and tries to quiet himself.

"Why did the chicken cross the road?" he asks, between breaths. His mouth twitches. He is trying to smile.

This is how it began.

That night six years ago, Duncan took Jude home and asked him the same question. It was more than a joke, though, to Duncan. It was the meaning of life. He explained it was the premise of his senior thesis: the Existential Quandary of Poultry. In essence, Duncan had said, we are all just chickens trying to get to the other side without fear.

Jude looks around the room.

Everything is the same.

It was as if they had been picked out of the present and returned to the past, six years ago. The stereo was the same, the telephone was the same, the Van Gogh reproduction was the same. They even had the same television. And here they were again, on the same couch, the same small distance apart.

Jude shakes out a cigarette and lights it, inhaling deeply, letting the nicotine swim through his veins.

"It's just," Duncan begins, a leftover quaver in his voice. "I could, you know, die alone, but . . ."

Jude only nods his head and exhales. He reaches out and puts his hand on Duncan's cheek, wiping away the tears. They are quiet. Jude closes his eyes, takes in another lungful of smoke, and puts his hand over his heart. He is, he understands, no longer waiting for it to stop, but to start. For some reason, though, all Jude can think of is the one time he acted in a high school play and the drama coach yelled up at him from the darkness of the auditorium: "Once more, again. This time with feeling."

He opens his eyes. Duncan is waiting.

Jude slowly moves closer, and already, on the wall behind them, their shadows touch.

ABOUT THE AUTHORS

David Bergman is the author or editor of over a dozen books, including the last three volumes of *Men on Men*. His latest book is a collection of his poetry, *Heroic Measures*. With Joan Larkin he edits the book series OUT LIVES: Lesbian and Gay Autobiography. He is professor of English at Towson University and lives in Baltimore.

Brian Bouldrey is the author of the novel *The Genius of Desire* (Ballantine) and *Love, the Magician,* to be published in the spring of 2000 by Haworth Press. He is the editor of *Wrestling With the Angel* (Riverhead), the *Best American Gay Fiction* series (Little, Brown), *Traveling Souls* (Whereabouts Press), and *Writing Home* (Heyday Books). He is the associate editor of the *Lit* supplement of the *San Francisco Bay Guardian* and a frequent contributor to that paper. His fiction and essays have appeared most recently in *Zyzzva, Fourteen Hills, Harvard Review, TriQuarterly, Speak, Sewanee Review, Poets & Writers, Gay Travels, The James White Review, Flesh & the Word,* and *World Book Encyclopedia.*

Alexander Chee has published his stories and personal essays in the anthologies *His 3, The Literature of Tomorrow, Loss Within Loss, Boys Like Us,* and *Take Out,* and the magazines *Big, The James White Review, Hope,* and *Out.* He is the recipient of a 1999 Michener fellowship from the James Michener/Copernicus Society and lives in

Brooklyn, New York. He is at work on a novel and a collection of stories.

William Lane Clark was born in Seattle, Washington, received a doctorate in English literature from George Washington University, and currently resides in Baltimore, Maryland.

"A Really Weird Thing Happened Recently" is the first published story by (Len) **Rick Ingenito-DeSio,** a native New Yorker.

Bill Gordon is currently working on a novel set in Jersey City, New Jersey, where he grew up. He recently completed the graduate creative writing program at Columbia University. His stories and essays have appeared in *The New York Times Magazine, Mississippi Review, The James White Review, Fourteen Hills, Christopher Street,* and *New York Press.*

Jim Grimsley is a playwright and novelist who lives in Atlanta. His first novel, *Winter Birds,* was published by Algonquin Books in 1994 and won the 1995 Sue Kaufman Prize for First Fiction from the American Academy of Arts and Letters, and received a special citation from the Ernest Hemingway Foundation. His second novel, *Dream Boy,* won the American Library Association GLBT Award for Literature and was a Lambda finalist. His third novel, *My Drowning,* was released in January 1997 by Algonquin Books, and his fourth novel, *Comfort & Joy,* was published in October 1999. He is playwright in residence at 7Stages Theatre, and in 1987 received the George Oppenheimer/Newsday Award for Best New American Playwright for *Mr. Universe.* His collection of plays, *Mr. Universe and Other Plays,* was published by Algonquin Books in 1998, and was a Lambda finalist for drama. Mr. Grimsley received the Lila Wallace/Reader's Digest Writers Award in 1997, and teaches writing at Emory University in Atlanta, Georgia.

David Groff has published poetry and prose in *Out, Poz, Poetry,* and other magazines, and is co-author with the late Robin Hardy of *The Crisis of Desire: AIDS and the Fate of Gay Brotherhood,* published by Houghton Mifflin.

J. G. (Joe) Hayes is a writer and landscaper living in the Boston area.

Tom House's fiction has appeared in over a dozen publications, including *Harper's, The Gettysburg Review, The North American Review, Chicago Review,* and *Best American Gay Fiction,* Volumes. 2 and 3. "Scarecrow" is an adapted excerpt of his unpublished novel, *The Other Way Home.* Comments are welcome at Tomhouse1@aol.com.

Jeff Kuhr lives in Lawrence, Kansas, with his wife, writer Shelle Rosenfeld. He is currently working on his first collection of short stories.

Richard McCann is the author, most recently, of *Ghost Letters* and *Nights of 1990,* and the editor of *Things Shaped in Passing: More 'Poets for Life' Writing from the AIDS Pandemic.* His fiction and poetry have appeared in such magazines as *The Atlantic, Esquire,* and *Poz,* and in numerous anthologies, including *The Penguin Book of Gay Short Stories, Men on Men,* Volumes 2 and 5, *Survival Stories: Memoirs of Crisis,* and *Body.* For his work he has received a National Endowment for the Arts creative writing fellowship, as well as fellowships from the Rockefeller and Fulbright foundations, Yaddo, and the MacDowell Colony. He lives in Washington, D.C., where he co-directs the graduate program in creative writing at American University.

Kelly McQuain is a native of West Virginia now living in Philadelphia. His fiction has appeared in *The Philadelphia Inquirer Magazine, The Harrington Gay Men's Fiction Quarterly, Wilma Loves Betty, The James White Review, Kansas Quarterly / Arkansas Review, Best American Erotica 1997* and *1999.* His nonfiction has appeared in *Obsessed: A Flesh and the Word Collection, Art & Understanding, Generation Q, The Journal of Gay, Lesbian and Bisexual Studies, The Philadelphia Gay News,* and *The Philadelphia Inquirer.* He is a contributing editor to both *Art & Understanding* and *The Harrington Gay Men's Fiction Quarterly,* and is the first writer to win *The Philadelphia City Paper* Writing Award in both categories—Poetry in 1998 and Fiction in 1999.

Craig T. McWhorter grew up in Colorado, where he studied journalism before becoming a bum for several years. He now holds an MFA from the University of New Orleans and lives in Boston, Massachusetts. He teaches at Tufts University, paints houses, and is working on an as yet untitled novel.

Bruce Morrow is the co-editor of *SHADE: An Anthology of Fiction by Gay Men of African Descent* (Avon Books). His work has appeared in numerous publications, including *The New York Times, Callaloo: A Journal of African American and African Arts and Letters,* and the anthologies *Speak My Name: Black Men on Masculinity and the American Dream* (Beacon Press) and *Ancestral House: The Black Short Story in the Americas and Europe* (Westview Press). He has just completed his first novel.

Jim Provenzano's fiction has been included in a dozen anthologies. A recipient of fellowships from the National Endowment for the Arts, the Pennsylvania and New Jersey arts councils, and a BFA in dance from Ohio State, his plays include *Under the River* and *Bootless Cries.* He writes "Sports Complex" for the San Francisco *Bay Area Reporter.* "Quality Time" is based on characters from his novel, *PINS* (Myrmidude Press).

Patrick Ryan, a native of New Orleans, is assistant editor of *Harrington Gay Men's Fiction Quarterly* and editor-in-chief of *Fourteen Hills.* He has been published in *The James White Review, HGMFQ,* and *Crack,* among other journals.

David Tuller a former reporter at the *San Francisco Chronicle,* is the author of *Cracks in the Iron Closet: Travels in Gay and Lesbian Russia.*

David Vernon was born in New York and has lived in that city and Los Angeles his entire life. He received his BFA at New York University, where he studied film and television. His short fiction has appeared in *Men on Men,* Volumes 4 and 6, *His,* Volumes 1 and 2, *Indivisible, Blood Whispers,* Volumes 1 and 2, and *Frontiers* Magazine, and the upcoming *Writers for the Millennium*. He has taught fiction writing in New York at The Poets Theater and currently teaches in Los Angeles at Writers at Work. He is one of the founding members of the Los Angeles writing group, Precious and Few. "American Has Been," the sitcom pilot he co-wrote, is being developed at the Fox Television Network. He is currently at work on a play, "Nannies," a screenplay based on Eric Orner's popular comic strip, "The Mostly Unfabulous Social Life of Ethan Green," and a novel based on his experiences growing up as the son of a television comedian. "Arrival," in a condensed version, was a winner in *Story* magazine's 1999 short, short fiction competition.

Michael Villane is an actor/writer currently residing in New York City. He recently completed his first novel, *My Life as a Ciccone Youth,* and is currently working on a stage play based on "the color of rain."

Edmund White teaches writing at Princeton University. "A Venice Story" will appear as a chapter in his forthcoming novel, *The Married Man* (Knopf).

Karl Woelz is a contributing writer to *The Harvard Gay & Lesbian Review.* His short fiction, articles, and reviews have appeared in *Men on Men 6, Best American Gay Fiction 2, The James White Review, Cottonwood, Link, asspants, Lambda Book Report,* and *The Baltimore Alternative.* He holds degrees in English from Columbia University, the University of Texas at San Antonio, and the University of Kansas. He lives and works in Baltimore, Maryland.